NEW SUNS

ORIGINAL SPECULATIVE FICTION BY
PEOPLE OF COLOR

EDITED BY NISI SHAWL

"There's nothing new under the sun,
but there are new suns."

Octavia E. Butler

This book is dedicated to Sheree Renée Thomas,
writer and editor extraordinaire,
whose groundbreaking *Dark Matter* anthology series
inspired and empowered the careers of many
authors of color, including my own.

First published 2019 by Solaris
an imprint of Rebellion Publishing Ltd,
Riverside House, Osney Mead, Oxford, OX2 0ES, UK

www.solarisbooks.com

ISBN 978-1-78108-578-3

Designed & typeset by Rebellion Publishing

Printed in Denmark

CONTENTS

FOREWORD
LeVar Burton

I AM A huge fan of science fiction! Throughout my life I have marveled at the powerful, even transformative nature of speculative storytelling. The influence science fiction storytelling is having in popular culture right now is amazing to behold, and as a genuine fan of the medium, I truly believe we are in a New Age of speculative fiction. There is a pleasing phenomenon developing in the genre recently: the worthy inclusion of voices of color, which are being paid much overdue attention. Why this is important should be self-evident. However, for those sitting way in the back, consider this: we continually create the world we occupy—in our imaginations first, and only afterwards do we make those visions manifest in this world. So it stands to reason that a healthy society is one that respects and honors the voices of ALL of its components. For too long, the voices and visions for our future have been provided, for the most part, by and from a culturally European (if not Eurocentric) perspective. However, there is change afoot. The works of Octavia E. Butler are becoming mainstream, and names like Nnedi Okorafor and Lesley Nneka Arimah are bringing much needed flavor to the narratives that help shape our future.

I'm also a sucker for a good short story. In fact, reading short fiction is one of my favorite pastimes. I read a lot in this genre, and producing a podcast that celebrates the short story, LeVar Burton Reads, has not only deepened my love for the form, it has also provided me a platform to help audiences discover visionary voices.

Nothing less than mastery is required from the storyteller who must grab an audience, create compelling characters, build the requisite conflict/resolution, deliver a satisfying conclusion (often with a twist), and do it all in five to fifty pages. Whenever I am reading for the purest of pleasure, I am likely to have an anthology of science fiction short stories in my hand. Such as this one.

From the haunting, lyrical, "Give Me Your Black Wings Oh Sister," by Silvia Moreno- Garcia, to Anil Menon's "Robots of Eden," about a man's struggle to reconcile his feelings in an age where enhanced sensorial modification is commonplace, these stories are delivered by vibrant, authentic voices bursting to weigh in on the human condition and our journey of human evolution.

There are familiar voices, like that of Steven Barnes, an OG in the game, who delivers a wickedly satiric look at an advert targeted to a special demographic, interspersed with those with whom you may not be familiar: Jaymee Goh, Darcie Little Badger, Indrapramit Das. These are voices that are sorely needed if we are to chart a course for humanity that does not result in the destructive practices of our past.

The exploration of space and our eventual close encounters with other intelligent species will require us to leave our "colonizer" mentality behind and embrace an attitude of openness and humility we have yet to cultivate, let alone master. When a world leader advocates for the creation of a militaristic Space Force to exercise "dominance" in the heavens, we are moving further than ever from Gene Roddenberry's United Federation of Planets.

Instead, our exploration into the unknown should cause us to examine who we are as sentient beings, and science fiction as a tool for social change makes for a most welcome companion on our journey. You are about to read one of the finest collections of short stories from the world of speculative fiction I have ever encountered. The stories contained within will delight your sensibilities, inspire your wonderings, and connect you to your humanity, which is the point of good storytelling—but, you don't have to take MY word for it!

THE GALACTIC TOURIST INDUSTRIAL COMPLEX
Tobias S. Buckell

WHEN GALACTICS ARRIVED at JFK they often reeked of ammonia, sulfur, and something else that Tavi could never quite put a finger on. He was used to it all after several years of shuttling them through the outer tanks and waiting for their gear to spit ozone and adapt to Earth's air. He would load luggage, specialized environmental adaptation equipment, and crosscheck the being's needs, itinerary, and sightseeing goals.

What he wasn't expecting this time was for a four hundred pound, octopus-like creature to open the door of his cab a thousand feet over the new Brooklyn Bridge, filling the cab with an explosion of cold, screaming air, and lighting the dash up with alarms.

He also definitely wasn't expecting the alien to scream "Look at those spires!" through a speaker that translated for it.

So, for a long moment after the alien jumped out of the cab, Tavi just kept flying straight ahead, frozen in shock at the controls.

This couldn't be happening. Not to him. Not in his broken down old cab he'd been barely keeping going, and with a re-up on the Manhattan license due soon.

To FLY INTO Manhattan you needed a permit. That was the first thing he panicked about, because he'd recently let it lapse for a bit. The New York Tourism Bureau hadn't just fined him, but suspended him for three months. Tavi had limped along on some odd jobs; tank cleaning at the airport, scrubbing out the backs of the cabs when they came back after a run to the island, and other muck work.

But no, all his licenses were up to date. And he knew that it was a horrible thing to worry about as he circled the water near the bridge; he should be worrying about his passenger. Maybe this alien was able to withstand long falls, Tavi thought.

Maybe.

But it wasn't coming up.

He had a contact card somewhere in the dash screen's memory. He tapped, calling the alien.

"Please answer. Please."

But it did not pick up.

What did he know about the alien? It looked like some octopus-type thing. What did that mean? They shouldn't have even been walking around, so it had to have been wearing an exoskeleton of some kind.

Could that have protected it?

Tavi circled the water once more. He had to call this in. But then the police would start hassling him about past mistakes. Somehow this would be his fault. He would lose his permit to fly into Manhattan. And it was Manhattan that the aliens loved above all else. This was the "real" American experience, even though most of it was heavily built up with zones for varying kinds of aliens. Methane breathers in the Garment District, the buildings capped with translucent covers and an alien atmosphere. Hydrogen types were all north of Central Park.

He found the sheer number of shops fun to browse, but few of them sold anything of use to humans. In the beginning, a lot of researchers and scientists had rushed there to buy what the Galactics were selling, sure they could reverse engineer what they found.

Turned out it was a lot of cheap alien stuff that purported to be made in Earth but wasn't. Last year some government agency purchased a "real" human sports car that could be shipped back to the home planet of your choice. It had an engine inside that seemed to be some kind of antigravity device that got everyone really excited. It exploded when they cracked the casing, taking out several city blocks.

When confronted about it, the tall, furry, sauropod-like aliens that had several other models in their windows on Broadway shrugged and said it wasn't made by them, they just shipped them to Earth to sell.

But Galactics packed the city buying that shit when they weren't slouching beside the lakes in Central Park. If Tavi couldn't get to Manhattan, he didn't have a job.

With a groan, Tavi tapped 9-1-1. There were going to be a lot of questions. He was going to be in it up to his neck.

But if he took off, they'd have his transponder on file. Then he'd look guilty.

With a faint clenching in his stomach, Tavi prepared for his day to go wrong.

TAVI STOOD ON a pier, wearing a gas mask to filter out the streams of what seemed like mustard gas that would seep out from a nearby building in DUMBO. The cops, also wearing masks, took a brief statement. Tavi gave his fingerprint, and then they told him to leave.

"Just leave?"

There were several harbor patrol boats hovering near where the alien had struck the water. But there was a lack of urgency to it all. Mostly everyone seemed to be waiting around for something to happen.

The cop taking Tavi's statement wore a yellow jumpsuit with logos advertising a Financial District casino (*Risk your money here, just like they used to in the old stock market! Win big, ring the old bell!*). He nodded through his gas mask as he took notes.

"We have your contact info on file. We're pulling footage now."

"But aren't you going to drag the river?"

"Go."

There was something in the cop's tone that made it through the muffled gas mask and told Tavi it was an order. He'd done the right thing in an impossible moment.

He'd done the right thing.

Right?

He wanted to go home and take a nap. Draw the shades and huddle in the dark and make all this go away for a day. But there were bills to pay. The cab required insurance, and the kinine fuel it used, shipped down from orbit, wasn't cheap. Every time the sprinklers under the cab misted up and put down a new layer, Tavi could hear his bank account dropping.

But you couldn't drive on the actual ground into Manhattan, not if you wanted to get a good review. Plus, the ground traffic flow licenses were even more whack than flying licenses because the interstellar tourists didn't want to put up with constant traffic snarls.

Trying to tell anyone that traffic was authentic old Manhattan just got you glared at.

So: four more fares. More yellowed gas mixing into the main cabin of the cab, making Tavi cough and his eyes water. The last batch, a pack of wolflike creatures that poured into the cab, chittering and yapping like squirrels, requested he take them somewhere serving human food.

"Real human food, not that shit engineered to look like it, but doctored so that our systems can process it."

Tavi's dash had lit up with places the tourist bureau authorized for this pack of aliens that kept grooming each other as he watched them in his mirror.

"Yeah, okay."

He took them to his cousin Geoff's place up in Harlem, which didn't have as many skyscrapers bubble-wrapped with alien atmospheres. The pack creatures were oxygen breathers, but they supplemented that with something extra running to their noses in tubes that occasionally wheezed and puffed a dust of cinnamon-smelling air.

Tavi wanted some comfort food pretty badly by this point. While the aliens tried to make sense of the really authentic human menus out front, he slipped into the hot gleaming stainless steel of the kitchens in the back.

"Ricky!" Geoff shouted. "You bring those dogs in?"

"Yes," Tavi confessed, and Geoff gave him a half hug, his dreadlocks slapping against Tavi. "Maybe they'll tip you a million."

"*Shiiiit*. Maybe they'll tip you a *trillion*."

It was an old service job joke. How much did it cost to cross a galaxy to put your own eyes, or light receptors, on a world just for the sake of seeing it yourself? Some of the aliens who had come to Earth had crossed distances so great, traveled in ships so complicated, that they spent more than a whole country's GDP.

A tip from one of them *could* be millions. There were rumors of such extravagances. A dish boy turned rich suddenly. A tour guide with a place built on the moon.

But the tourism bureau and the Galactic-owned companies bringing the tourists here warned them not to overpay for services. The Earth was a fragile economy, they said. You didn't want to just run around handing out tips worth a year of some individual's salary. You could create accidental inflation, or unbalance power in a neighborhood.

So the apps on the tourist's systems, whatever types of systems they used, knew what the local exchange rates were and paid folk down here on the ground proportionally.

Didn't stop anyone from wishing, though.

Geoff slid him over a plate of macaroni pie, some peas and rice, and chicken. Tavi told him about his morning.

"You shouldn't have called the police," Geoff said.

"And what, just keep flying?"

"The bureau will blacklist you. They have to save face. And no one is going to want hear about a tourist dying on the surface. It's bad publicity. You're going to lose your license into Manhattan. NYC bureau's the worst, man."

Tavi cleaned his fingers on a towel, then coughed. The taste of cinnamon came up strong through his throat.

"You okay?"

Tavi nodded, eyes watering. Whatever the pack out there was sniffing, it was ripping through his lungs.

"You need to be careful," Geoff said. "Get a better filter in that cab. Nichelle's father got lung cancer off a bunch of shit coming off the suits of some sundivers last year, doctors couldn't do nothing for him."

"I know, I know," Tavi said between coughs.

Geoff handed him a bag with something rolled up in aluminum foil inside. "Roti for the road. Chicken, no bone. I have doubles if you want?"

"No." Geoff was being too nice. He knew how Tavi was climbing out from a financial hole and had been bringing by "extras" after he closed up each night.

Most of the food here was for non-human tourists, variations on foods that wouldn't upset their unique systems. Tavi had lied in taking the tourist pack here; the food out front was for the dog-like aliens. But the stuff in the bag was real, something Geoff made for folk who knew to come in through the back.

Tavi did one more run back to JFK, and this time he flew a few loops around the megastructure. JFK Interspacial was the foot of a leg that stretched up into the sky, piercing the clouds and rising beyond until it reached space. It was a pier that led to the deep water where the vast alien ships that moved tourists from star to star docked. It was the pride of the US. Congress had financed it by pledging the entire country's GDP for a century to a Galactic building consortium, so no one really knew how to build another after it was done, but the promise was that increased Manhattan tourism would bring in jobs. Because with the Galactics shipping in things to sell here in exchange for things they wanted, there wasn't much in the way of industrial capacity. Over half the US economy was tourism, the rest service jobs.

Down at the bottom of JFK, the eager vacationers and sightseers disgorged into terminals designed for their varying biologies and then were kitted out for time on Earth. Or, like Tavi's latest customer, just bundled into a can that slid into the back of a cab, and that was then dropped off at one of the hotels dwarfing Manhattan's old buildings.

When the drop-off of the tourist in a can that Tavi couldn't see or interact with was done, he headed home. That took careful flying over the remains of La Guardia, which pointed off from Brooklyn toward the horizon, the way it had ever since it collapsed and fell out stable orbit.

Land around La Guardia's remains was cheap, and Tavi lived in an apartment complex roofed by the charred chunk of the once-space elevator's outer shell.

"Home sweet home," he said, coming in for a landing.

There was a burning smell somewhere in the back of the cab. Smoke started filling the cabin and the impellers failed.

He remained in the air, the kinine misters doing their job and preventing him from losing neutral buoyancy, and coasted.

Tavi wanted to get upset, hit the wheel, punch the dash. But he just bit his lip as the car finally stopped just short of the roof's parking spot. He had the misters spray some cancellation foam, and the car dropped a bit too hard to a stop.

"At least you got home," Sienna said, laughing as he opened the doors to the cab and stumbled out. "You know what I think of this Galactic piece of shit."

"It gets the job done."

Sienna poked her head into the cab, holding her breath. Her puffy hair bobbed against the side of the hatch.

"Can you fix it?" he asked her.

"It was one of the dog things, with the cinnamon breath? That gas they breathe catalyzes the o-rings. You need to spend some money to isolate the shaft back here."

"Next big tip," Tavi told her.

She crawled back out and let out the breath she'd been holding.

"Okay. Next big tip. I can work on it if you split dinner with me." She nodded at the bag Geoff had given him.

"Sure."

"There's also a man waiting by your door. Looks like Tourist Bureau."

"Shit." He didn't want anyone from the bureau out here. Not in an illegal squat in the ruins of the space elevator now draped across this side of the world.

THERE WAS NO air conditioning; the solar panels lashed to the scrap hull roof top didn't pump out enough juice to make that a reality. But the motion sensitive fans kicked on and the LED track lights all leapt to attention as Tavi led the beet-faced Tourist Bureau agent through the mosquito netting.

"Your cab is having trouble?"

The agent, David Khan, had a tight haircut and glossy brown skin, the kind that meant he didn't spend much time outside loading aliens into the back of cabs. He had an office job.

"Sienna will fix it. She grew up a scrapper. Her father was one of the original decommissioners paid to work on picking La Guardia up. Before the contract was canceled and they all decided to stay put. Beer?"

Tavi passed him a sweaty Red Stripe from the fridge, which Kahn held nervously in one hand as if he wanted to refuse it. Instead, he placed it against his forehead. The man had been waiting a while in the heat. And he was wearing a heavy suit.

"So, I am here to offer you a grant from the Greater New York Bureau of Tourism," Kahn started, sounding a little unsure of himself.

"A grant?"

"The Bureau is starting a modernization campaign to make sure our cabs are the safest on Earth. That means we'd like to take your cab in and have it retrofitted with better security, improved impellers, better airlocks. For the driver's safety."

"The driver?"

"Of course."

Tavi thought it was a line of bullshit. Human lives were cheap; there were billions teeming away on the planet. If Tavi ever stepped out, someone else would bid on his license to Manhattan and he'd be forgotten in days.

Maybe even hours.

"Take it," Sienna said, pushing through the netting. "That piece of shit needs any help it can get."

Tavi didn't have to be told twice. He put his thumb to the documents, verbally repeated assent into a tiny red dot of a light, and then Kahn said a tow truck was on its way.

They watched the cab get lifted onto its back, the patchwork of a vehicle that Tavi had come to know every smelly inch of.

"What about the dead alien?" Tavi asked.

"Well, according to the documents you just signed, you can never talk about the... err... incident again."

"I get it." Tavi waved a salute at the disappearing cab and tow truck. "I figured as much when you said you had a 'grant.' But what happens to the alien? Did you ever find the body?"

Kahn let out a deep breath. "We found it, downstream of where it jumped."

"Why the hell did it do that? Why jump out?"

"It was out of its mind on vacation drugs. Cameras show the party started in orbit with a few friends, continued down the JFK elevator all the way to the ground."

"When do you send the body back to its people?"

"We don't," Kahn looked around, surprised. "No one wants to know a high profile cephaloid of any kind has died on Earth. So they didn't. The video of the fall no longer exists in any system."

"But they can track the body—"

"—already fired off via an old school rocket aimed at our sun. That leaves no evidence here. Nothing happened on Earth. Nothing happened to you."

Kahn shook hands with Sienna and Tavi and left.

The next morning a brand new cab was parked on the roof.

"Easier than scrubbing it all down for DNA," Sienna said. "The old one's probably on a rocket as well, just like the body, being shot toward the sun as we speak."

He scrambled up some eggs for his ever-hungry roomie, and some extra for the Oraji brothers next door. There were thirty other random clumps of real and found families living in welded together scrap here. Several of them watched the sun creep over the rusted wreckage scattered from horizon to horizon as they ate breakfast. Tavi would head back into the drudgery of flying tourists around, Sienna would work at trying to pry something valuable out of the ruins.

Just as they finished eating, a second cab descended from the clouds. It kicked up some dust as it settled in on the ground.

"Hey asshole," Sienna shouted. "If we all land on metal we don't kick dust into everyone's faces."

Grumbling assent rose into the morning air.

The doors slid open, and Tavi felt his stomach drop.

Another octopus-like alien stood on the ground looking up at them.

"I'm looking for the human named Tavi," the speaker box on the exoskeleton buzzed. "Is he here?"

"Don't say a thing," Sienna hissed. Sienna, who had all the smarts built up from a lifetime of eat or be eaten while scavenging in the wreckage.

"I am Tavi," Tavi said, stepping down toward the alien.

"You're an idiot," Sienna said. She walked off toward the shadows under a pile of scrap and disappeared.

* * *

THE ALIEN CROUCHED in a spot of shade, trying to stay out of the sun, occasionally rubbing sunscreen over its photo-sensitive skin.

"I'm the co-sponsor of the unit last seen in your vehicle when it came down to your planet for sightseeing."

Tavi felt his stomach fall out from under him. "Oh," he said numbly. He wasn't sure what a co-sponsor was, or why the alien's language had been translated that way. He had the feeling this alien was a close friend, or maybe even family member of the one he'd witnessed jump to its death.

"No one will tell me anything, your representatives have done nothing but flail around and throw bureaucratic ink my way," the alien tourist said.

"I'm really sorry for your loss," Tavi said.

"So, you are my last try before offencers get involved," the alien concluded.

"Offencers?"

The alien used one of its mechanized limbs to point up. A shadow passed over the land. Something vast skimmed over the clouds and blocked the sun. It hummed. And the entire land hummed back with it. Somehow, Tavi *knew* that whatever was up there could destroy a planet.

Tavi's wristband vibrated. Incoming call. Kahn.

The world was crashing into him. Tavi felt it all waver for a moment, and then he took a deep breath.

"All I wanted to do was the right thing," he muttered, and took the call.

"Very big, alien destroyers," David Kahn said, in a level, but clearly terrified voice. "We at the Greater New York Bureau of Tourism *highly* recommend you do whatever the being or beings currently in contact with you are asking, while also, uh, acknowledging that we have no idea where the missing being they are referring to is. Please hold for the President—"

Tavi flicked the bracelet off.

"What do you want?" Tavi asked the alien.

"I want to know the truth," it said.

"I see you have an advanced exotic worlds encounter suit. Would you like a real human beer with me?"

"If that helps," it said.

*   *   *

"You have such a beautiful planet. So unspoiled, paradisiacal. I was swimming with whales in your Pacific Ocean yesterday."

Tavi sat down and gave the alien a Red Stripe. It curled a tentacle around it, pulled it back towards its beak. They watched the trees curling around the La Guardia debris shiver in the wind, the fluffy clouds ease through the pale blue sky.

They deliberately sat with their backs to the section of sky filled with the destroyer.

"I've never been to the Pacific," Tavi admitted. "Just the Caribbean, where my people come from, and the Atlantic."

"I'm a connoisseur of good oceans," the alien said. "These are just some of the best."

"We used to fish on them. My grandfather owned a boat."

"Oh, does he still do that? I love fishing."

"He started chartering it out," Tavi said. "The Galactics bought out the restaurants, so he couldn't sell to his best markets anymore. They own anything near the best spots, and all around the eastern seaboard now."

"I'm sorry to hear that."

"About your friend," Tavi took a big swig. "They jumped out of my cab. When it was in the air. They were in an altered state."

There was a long silence.

Tavi waited for the world to end, but it didn't. So he continued, and the alien listened as he told his story.

"And, there were no security systems to stop them from jumping?" it asked when he finished.

"There were not, on that cab."

"Wow," it said. "How authentically human. How dangerous. I'll have to audit your account against the confessions of your bureau, but I have to say, I am very relieved. I suspected foul play, and it turns out it was just an utterly authentic primitive world experience. No door security."

Overhead, long fiery contrails burned through the sky.

"What is that?" Tavi asked, nervous.

"Independent verification," the alien said. It stood up and jumped down to its cab. It looked closely at the rear doors. "I could really just jump out of these, couldn't I?"

It opened the door, and Tavi, who had hopped over the roof and down the stairs, caught a glimpse of a pale-faced driver inside. *Sorry, friend*, he thought.

There were more shadows descending down out of space. Larger and larger vessels moving through the atmosphere far above.

"What is happening?" Tavi asked, mouth dry.

"News of your world has spread," it said. "You are no longer an undiscovered little secret. Finding out that we can die just in a cab ride—where else can you get that danger?"

The cab lifted off and flew away.

Sienna came back out of the shadows. "They're over every city now. They're offering ludicrous money for real estate."

Tavi looked at the skies. "Did you think it would ever stop?"

She put a hand on his shoulder. "Beats them blowing us up, right? They do that, sometimes, to other worlds that fight it."

He shook his head. "There's not going to be anything left for us down here, is there?"

"Oh, they'll never want this," she spread her arms and pointed at the miles of space elevator junk.

"And I still have a new cab," he said.

She put a hand on his shoulder. "Maybe these new Galactics coming down over the cities tip better."

And for the first time in days Tavi laughed. "That's always the hope, isn't it?"

DEER DANCER
Kathleen Alcalá

"HA!" SHE SAID, jiggling the wrench. "I've got you!"

The pipe came loose with a grating sound, and she reached in and unscrewed it the rest of the way. Rusty water dribbled out the end as she scuttled from under the house, waving the pipe section in the air. Brownish water spattered her shirt. It felt good.

"Found it! It will be easy to fix!" she said, wondering if they could find pipe the same diameter, and long enough to repair the plumbing.

This was the fifth house she had helped rehab, and Tater was beginning to think of herself as an expert in the undersides of houses.

Shonda took the pipe from her and fingered the rusty hole. "How you going to find the right size?"

"We've got a whole pile from the other houses around here. One of them must have used the same size, maybe even the same plumber in the first place. All these houses were built about the same time."

The sun, mother sun, blazed down, and Tater pulled her hat forward from where it hung down her back on a string.

"We'd better get home."

It was five bells since first light, and unless they planned to spend the rest of the day under the house, they needed to get back. Walking single file, Shonda took the lead, poking any suspicious-looking soil with her walking stick before proceeding. Tater carefully set her feet in Shonda's prints until they came to a place where the houses were lively with people preparing for midday siesta.

Chia was just pulling protective burlap sacking back over a patch of taters after digging up a few. The grey nubs did not look like much as they sat steaming on the ground, but washed and sliced into brilliant purple disks, they would glow. Tater's mom had named her after the naturalized Ozettes. Brought from Peru by long ago voyagers, the potatoes had taken to the northwest like, well, no other plant or animal. Tater was proud of her unusual name, and secretly hoped she was like them, ordinary at first look, but gem-like on the inside. Rooted.

Tater was still carrying the pipe. "What you going to do with that?" asked Chia.

"Match it, then recycle. The rest of the pipes held up good. This one is far enough gone Re-use might be able to smash it into dust for the iron."

Tater splashed some water on her neck and hung up her hat. Out of the sun now, she rolled up her sleeves and served herself soup she found cooling on the stove. Chia would stay up cooking so that the Day crew would have something to eat when they woke from their midday slumbers around sundown.

Nights worked second shift. It used to be called graveyard shift, but that made too many people sad.

What to think when the sun goes down and every light takes on a spectral aspect?
My eyes, my eyes – ever deceitful, ever necessary for one who relies on visual cues, who only trusts the stimuli she takes in through the range of light and motion.

The angular bounce of light at the solstice, of sun streaming directly into our eyes as though to make up for all the days when we see no sun at all. How our limbs loosen and we tilt back our heads with a slight smile, drinking it in.
Who can deny the intoxication of sunlight, the touch of gold as it runs down our arms from our fingertips. Our thighs grow slack as our lips part to drink in the pearly heat.
Our pens rest on their tables as our minds glide away from the task at hand.

*   *   *

TATER READ A page in her aunt's diary, then set it aside. She had been given it years before, but had not tried to read it until being assigned to housing rehab. She found it hard to sleep out here on the Edges. Reading the old diary helped. She loved imagining what it was like Before, when the sun was scarce. Tater liked stroking the soft edges. It was the only book she owned herself, and she found herself fingering the pages like worry beads. Tater lay back carefully in her hammock so as not to flip over, afraid of and grateful for the distance from the floor. Not that rats wouldn't jump or climb up onto the hammock if they felt like it. But Tater still felt better this way.

Now she tried to imagine Aunt Ceci's life when water stayed in its place and the sun was a welcome embrace against the damp cold. She could barely remember being cold.

"Not sleeping?" asked Shonda as she came in.

"Not yet."

Shonda unhooked her own hammock from where it hung coiled on the wall and took it outside. She preferred to sleep under the giant Doug fir that sheltered their house, a tree they had defended with guns and clubs early on. Tater could smell the taters cooking. There was an herb with them, something she could not quite place as she drifted off to sleep.

LATE AFTERNOONS WERE for domestic chores. That included upkeep on the house where they homesteaded. If they could defend it for seven years, the house was theirs.

Most people stayed on waitlists until a house opened up in the Center. But that could take forever. Homesteading on the Edges offered larger properties, enough to grow food. And also, dangers. But even for the Edges, there were waitlists of people stacked sky high in mass housing. Tater barely remembered Before, and there were some things in between that she could not think about at all.

Shonda gently shook Tater awake. It felt as though she had just dozed off, a dream of deer picking their way across a clearing fading gently from her mind.

"Your turn to wash."

Tater dragged herself back to the waking world. She might have been having a True Dream, but if that's what it was, it would come back. She would need to let the others know if it did.

When she was a child of eight, it became clear that Tater got the Dreaming. When she was fourteen, she was given her aunt's journal. Ceci was an original Dreamer, born in Mexico, raised in the US in secrecy by her family. Given every advantage to learn the language, the ways of these people so that she could rescue the rest of her family from the label THEM. Everyone in Ceci's family, including Tater's mom, worked every waking moment to keep Ceci, the youngest, in school and living long enough to pull her family through the tortuous knots of the legal system. She succeeded, and her nieces and nephews became US as well. But that was all Before.

Dream
Salal, salal, thimble berry, grass.
Smell of humans. Water. Stillness. Stillness.
Light slanting in for longer days.

HUMANS TOOK THEIR cues from the animals, and had become diurnal. Afternoons were for chores, but night was for guarding. Second shift got up and had breakfast with the day shift's dinner.

Tater could spot Nights on sight. Like her, they had a dreamy look, with large eyes and slightly larger nostrils. There was a lot of talk about whether this was adaptation, after so few generations, or just an affinity of Nights for Nights as partners, since that's who they got to know anyway. Every household had a combination of Days and Nights.

Tater joined the table next to Ana, one of the few Nights she spoke to regularly. "'Sup?"

"Not too much. Just talking about the bears spotted at the north end."

"Again? They've no fright."

"Sorrel's pretty sure she heard them talking again."

"You mean, like people talk?"

"Yeah. She swears she can almost understand them."

Sorrel was at the other end of the table describing the bear sighting. She stood up and lumbered down the length of the table, stopping to smell each of their plates, setting them laughing.

"Are the bears changing, or is it just you?" someone called out.

Sorrel took her seat. They were eating eggs tonight, gathered from the summer chickens.

"Could just be me," she said honestly. "I've got so I can smell people coming, even tell sometimes who it is." Sorrel flexed her powerful hands and set to her meal.

"Tater and me are going to need a full crew tomorrow," said Shonda. "Five people. Time to replace the roof on the Denny Way house so we can start on the inside. Plumbing's almost done. Tater's fast."

"Who will you work with next?" asked Ana.

Tater blushed and looked down. "Not for me to say."

"All in good time," said Chia as she began to clear the table. "She might have other dons she wants to develop."

Tater thought about that. Sometimes she forgot that she could choose what she wanted to work on, who she wanted to work with, as long as it was for the common good. It hadn't been like that Before, or even for awhile After. Again, she had the strong feeling of the deer in the ravine nearby, and when she looked up, Sorrel had stopped eating and was staring down the table at her, still and alert.

Tater pushed out her chair and stood up. "I've got to dream now," she said. Shonda pointed at Ana and Chia, who flanked Tater and escorted her out of the kitchen.

TATER'S TEAM DID not have a room set aside just for Dreaming. She was the only one in their household, and they all agreed it was a waste of space in their small but ship-shape house. But there was a bed in the main bedroom that was set aside for her. It folded out of the wall to offer a deep, safe space, and a clerestory cast a diffuse light in the room during the day.

The bed was lowered, and Tater climbed out of her day clothes into a soft cotton gown that did not inhibit her movement. That gown, of pure cotton from Before, was probably the most valuable thing the team owned. Tater was humbled by their goodness to her every time she put it on.

Ana got a mug of water, and Chia a towel. Sometimes the dreams could be rough, and Tater lost control of her body.

By the time they had tucked Tater into the bed and settled into chairs on either side of her, she was no longer seeing the room and people around her. It had been a few months since she had last dreamed, and the household was in some ways relieved to see what further instructions they might receive. She could still faintly hear their comforting voices.

"Duermete, duermete," Ana urged.

Sometimes the dream was clear and direct; other times, they could only speculate at what it meant, and what they were expected to do with the information. But no one doubted the authenticity of the dreams.

TATER WAS TRYING to run through the forest. This was big forest, not trash trees and overgrown Scotch Broom. Vines grabbed at her legs as she ran, causing her to stumble. Snatching at a handful of leaves to break her fall, she felt the painful jolt of nettles in the palm of her hand. Tater gathered all her concentration into her thighs and leaped, now! clear of her human body, bounding without effort through the underbrush.

Something was behind her, but she could not see it. The smell was pungent, like fire, like chemicals burning a hole in a metal container. Her human thoughts soon fled as she spotted another of her kind and followed, leaping sideways and forward so as to throw off any pursuers. She crashed through salal and salmonberry, fiddlehead fern and seeps where freshets rose when it rained. This was the damp country she remembered, the Before of her childhood, when everyone had enough to eat, clothes to wear, homes to live in. When children went every day to school to learn to live in a world that no longer existed.

TATER HELD THE raised sides of the dream bed and rode it like a little boat, rocking and bucking as she moaned and made strange noises. Ana and Chia were there to try to keep her from hurting herself, as she had on occasion, and to take note of anything she might say out loud while in the grip of her dream. They made themselves comfortable, and didn't have to say that they were pleased to have finished their dinners ahead of the Dream.

WHEN TATER WOKE, it was dark and very quiet. She was alone. She listened to the silence for a few minutes before rising. Climbing out of the bed, she walked out to the kitchen. A single lamp burned on the table. The dishes lay scattered, some with food still on them, as though abandoned shortly after Tater left. She stepped in something wet and looked down to see a dropped mug. Walking carefully, she returned to the bedroom and climbed back into the dreaming bed.

When Tater woke again, it was deep night, and again, she was alone in the house. She listened to the silence for a few minutes before rising. The lantern still burned in the kitchen.

Tater took a flashlight and walked out on the porch. The night shift should have been out on the perimeter, making noise, but Tater heard nothing. A strong smell of bear filled her nostrils and she returned inside to bolt and bar the door. Tater could not tell if she was Dreaming or not. This happened sometimes. Her surroundings felt real, but where was everyone? Wouldn't she have heard something if there had been an attack? Wouldn't they have taken her with them, even if she was in the throes of a Dream? Tater climbed back into the Dream bed once again, just in case.

Tater woke a third time, her left hand sticky where it had gripped the raised edge of the bed. When she lifted her hand and opened the palm, it was sticky with blood.

Tater woke at ten bells. Chia snored daintily in the chair beside her. Voices came from the kitchen, laughing and the sound of dishes and cooking. Tater pulled on her clothes, folding the gown gently across the coverlet. Chia woke and helped return the little bed to the wall.

In the kitchen, they were greeted with the clatter of dishes being dried and stored. Ana sang a high, silly song, and the smell of nettle soup bubbling on the stove filled the kitchen. Sorrel walked up to Tater and reached out. Tater flinched, and Sorrel stopped before gently bringing her hand down on Tater's shoulder.

"You've got news for us."

Tater opened her hand to show Sorrel where the stiffened blood had resolved into the outlines of a map, their own settlement at the center, the Edges stretching beyond.

THEY GREETED THE night with a collective roar. The members of the house were in full regalia, Tater wearing her inherited cocoon rattle leggings. She lifted her canes, one in each hand, and set the tip of each down the way a deer daintily makes its way through the forest. She turned her gaze this way and that in mimicry of the deer, careful not to lose the antlers strapped to her head. The drummer beat a bowl with two sticks turned upside down over a larger bowl of water, creating a booming sound that carried for miles. Ana's voice wailed a descant. The dancers made their way forward and back, forward and back, turning sideways in unison to appear larger to the unseen enemy.

Arise, arise fair sun, and kill the envious moon...

Dancers from other houses flanked them, creating a front of noise and light against the Outside. Tater felt vulnerable in her soft doe-skin clothing, conscious of how exposed her throat was each time she turned her head, knew that the bandage on her left hand showed she might be wounded. This is how they took back the world – step by step, song by song. At the end of the night, new fence posts would be pounded into place, new fences strung.

Tater lifted and set her canes carefully. The extra points of support allowed her to keep her feet close together as she pounded the ground with them, directing her energy deep into the earth. Tater realized that if she ever had a daughter, she would name her Ozette. This was new, the consciousness that she might have a future beyond herself. Tater's face shone in the flickering light. It was good to be alive.

THE VIRTUE OF UNFAITHFUL TRANSLATIONS
Minsoo Kang

THE GRAND PHILOSOPHER Ancient Leaf once expounded that a man who kills another out of passion or greed is condemned as a murderer, and one who kills ten people is reviled as a maniac, but one who causes the death of hundreds of thousands in pursuit of personal glory is often revered as a great personage. The Grand Historian Silver Mirror utilized the quote in describing the senseless nature of the Wars of the Four Princes and the Six Grand Lords, how the acts of all the kings, ministers, and generals throughout the long conflict achieved nothing in the end. The cycle of events from unity to disunity to chaos, then chaos back to disunity and finally to a new unity, only resulted in countless cities, towns, and villages falling into ruin. And the corpses of ambitious leaders, obedient soldiers, and powerless civilians lay in numbers like grains of sand upon a blood-soaked shore. Silver Mirror opined that a country that has reached the age of wisdom would stop building monuments to the warmongers of its history, but rather erect them for its peacemakers, those who saved lives by preventing the course of events from descending into a time of sword and fire.

One could point to such a monument that actually exists, namely the great mural painting known as "Peace of Five Peaks Island," which can be found on the southwestern side of the Phoenix Tower in West Capital of the Empire of the Grand Circle. When General Heavenly Whirlwind brought down the Radiant dynasty to ascend the throne as the first emperor of the Pure dynasty, he justified his coup by claiming, based on specious evidence including forged clan records, to be a descendant of the imperial family of the previous Primal dynasty. By asserting that the founders of the Radiant illegitimately usurped the authority of his ancestors, he portrayed himself as an avenger who was reclaiming what was rightfully his. He then moved the center of the Grand Circle to West Capital not only to force the surviving members of the Radiant aristocracy to abandon their feudal lands in the east but also to establish a historical connection between the Primal and the Pure. He also summoned the best artists of the realm to decorate the walls of the rebuilt imperial palace with pictures in the grand proto-elaboratist style depicting the glories of the Primal dynasty. Most of them portray scenes of military victory, including the unnecessary, unjustifiable, and unrighteous slaughter of the pacific people of the southeast plains, which is falsely pictured as a defensive action against bloodthirsty barbarians.

"Peace of Five Peak Island" is a remarkable exception in that it celebrates the avoidance of what was certain to be a devastating war that would have cost the lives of hundreds of thousands. It depicts the meeting of the Sixth Emperor of the Primal dynasty and the warlord of South Ocean known as the Great Sea Dragon, on a hill that is magnificently illuminated by an auspicious sun at midday. The Lord of the Grand Circle is in his gold and yellow splendor, surrounded by ministers in red robes and high hats, while the Master of the Endless Waves is in full armor and flanked by his sea lords. The former is grand and haughty and the latter is sturdy and proud, but they face each other with respect as they are there to establish peace rather than to challenge each other to war. Once they finish exchanging formal greetings, they will enter a splendid pavilion of many colors, pictured at some distance behind them, where they will sit and share precious liquor while their ministers and generals finalize the treaty between the empire and the fleet. On the far right side of the picture, a flock of seagulls dance above a luminous sea, as if in joy over the event.

The achievement of peace on Five Peaks Island has baffled historians for centuries as a miraculous last-minute aversion of a war that appeared inevitable to everyone concerned. The Great Sea Dragon, who began his life as a kidnapped child slave, then a galley rower, then a pirate, and then a pirate captain, emerged as an unprecedented genius of naval warfare as he battled and slaughtered his way to dominance in South Ocean and all its islands. With his fleet of ten thousand ships and an ambition that knew no bounds, he meant to take the greatest prize of them all, the Empire of the Grand Circle. But the Sixth Emperor was a man of war himself, as he was raised on the rugged northern frontier where he also served as the lord commander of fortresses. Even after his ascendance to the imperial throne, he was happiest on the campaign trail, extending his domain, punishing his recalcitrant subjects, and delighting in the destruction of those who defied him. In his endless greed for military glory, he left much of the running of the state to a group of eunuch secretaries, which led to what would later be referred to as the Rule of Fifty Half-Men. By all accounts, he was eager to face the barbarian upstart of South Ocean, whom he referred to as Pirate Fish Stink.

The initial meeting of their envoys was not an opportunity for a serious negotiation but for the ritualized issuance of challenges as a prelude to war. To the surprise of everyone, however, the talks on Five Peaks Island became protracted, as the emperor and the warlord communicated via numerous letters that were written, translated, and transported over the course of weeks. It ultimately resulted in the Great Sea Dragon receiving the imperial title of the Grand Guardian of the South Ocean with the responsibility of overseeing the affairs of the southern seas. In return, the Great Sea Dragon recognized the emperor's authority and swore to safeguard all merchant ships under the protection of the imperial monopoly. It culminated in the personal meeting of the two on Five Peaks Island, which the mural depicts, in which the warlord ceremoniously received the jade tablet of officialdom, acknowledging his status as the emperor's subordinate. And the emperor, in turn, granted him the singular honor of submitting on his feet, rather than prostrating himself on the ground. The peace treaty was duly agreed upon, stamped with great seals, and a celebration of feasting, dancing, and musical performances followed. Then the Sixth Emperor and his ministers returned to West Capital, the Great Sea Dragon and his ships sailed back to South Ocean, and the war that was thought to be inevitable never happened.

In recent decades, new discoveries made by junior historians at the

Hall of Great Learning have provided startling insight into the event. Through their painstaking search in many archives across the country, they have unearthed documents of disparate natures that have revealed a hidden history of the Peace of Five Peaks Island. They include some discarded source material for the *True Records of the Primal Dynasty*, an early draft of the incomplete *Preliminary Discourse on the Fall of the Primal Dynasty*, a batch of official correspondences that was housed at the Hall of the Imperial Secretariat that were thought to have been destroyed during the burning of the palace by the Radiant army, and, most revealing of all, some personal writings of the two translators who worked on behalf of the emperor and the warlord. In addition, findings from a secret storehouse at the Temple to the Primordial Nothingness in Sundown Archipelago, relating to the events from the perspective of the advisors to the Great Sea Dragon, have provided support for the newly revealed narrative.

The mural of "Peace of Five Peaks Island" depicts some fifty people, most of whom can be identified as important personages whose presence at the event is verified in the historical records. Immediately behind the emperor are the high minister of military affairs and the chief imperial secretary, and at a little distance to their left is a noticeably tall official whose sharp-eyed attention is on the Great Sea Dragon, not his sovereign. While the red robes of all other officials are decorated with the insignias of a pair of cranes or a pair of turtles, his is the only one with a pair of flounders, marking him as a temporary appointee to a position at court. The figure represents the scholar given the honor name of Diviner Supreme, a grand master of learning at the Forest of Brushes Scholastic Academy who acted as the imperial translator and interpreter during the negotiations.

Diviner Supreme came from an illustrious family of scholar-officials, his father attaining the position of the high minister of rituals, but he was somewhat of a wayward younger son in his early life. He passed the civil examinations at a young age, but before he could receive a government appointment, he had to go into mourning period as his father died from falling off a horse. At its completion, he not only declined to pursue a career in officialdom but left West Capital to travel the world.

In the course of his many adventures, he proved to be a veritable genius in the learning of languages, as he ultimately mastered no less than twenty-four living tongues and the reading knowledge of twelve defunct ones. After wandering the world for over twenty years, he finally returned to his family home in West Capital barely alive, after suffering a near fatal wound in a pirate raid in Middle Ocean. He eventually recovered, but the permanent damage done to his right leg made him unfit for prolonged travel. He was subsequently appointed as a master at the Forest of Brushes, becoming the greatest scholar of languages and linguistics of his time.

Although the exact origin of the warlord known as the Great Sea Dragon is obscure, he spoke a dialect of the language of Sundown Archipelago used in the southernmost islands. He forced all the sea lords of his fleet to adopt the tongue, even those who did not come from the archipelago. When he achieved dominance in South Ocean, the obscurity of the language became a major problem for the imperials in trying to assess his threat. It turned out that in the entire officialdom of the Grand Circle, Diviner Supreme was the only one who had knowledge of the Sundown tongue from his sojourn on the islands. Consequently, when the negotiations on Five Peaks Island was set to begin, he was given a temporary appointment as the imperial translator and interpreter.

In the painting "Peace of Five Peaks Island," standing to the right of the Great Sea Dragon, half hidden in shadow, is a slight figure in a nondescript gray robe, a young woman who is the one and only female figure in the picture. Despite the important role she played in the event as Diviner Supreme's counterpart who interpreted for the warlord, very little can be affirmed about her identity due in great part to the deplorable lack of information about women from that particularly sexist era. Even her original name is unknown, as Upright Lotus is an amity cognomen given to her well after the event. What can be reasonably theorized from the historical context is that she was probably a member of a prominent merchant family of the south, one who likely worked as an assistant to her father or some other patriarch of the clan after demonstrating a talent for languages.

Due to the highly restricted nature of the imperial trading monopoly in the seas under the control of the Grand Circle, merchants of South Ocean were effectively shut out of the area. As they had little choice but to deal with intermediaries of Middle Ocean, few of them bothered to learn the imperial tongue. What must be remembered is that the Great Sea Dragon's ascendance from the pirate captain of a single ship to the master of a fleet of ten thousand was remarkably fast, the speed with which he dominated South Ocean taking everyone by surprise. When he decided to take his fleet north, he had limited time to look for someone who could act as his interpreter and translator. It is unknown how Upright Lotus came to serve him, but the fact that she was one of precious few in the south who could speak the imperial tongue must have come to his attention under some particular circumstance.

What the newly unearthed documents reveal is that Diviner Supreme and Upright Lotus systematically mistranslated all essential communications between the imperial court and the leadership of the Great Sea Dragon's fleet, and in all likelihood did the same in their interpretive work. The documents also show that this was not the result of ignorance or incompetence but a deliberate act, pointing to the remarkable fact that the two translators colluded in the production of unfaithful renderings. Some examples of such mistranslations follow.

In the *True Records of the Pure Dynasty*, in the entry to the fourth day of the fourth lunar month in the nineteenth year of the Sixth Emperor's reign (Year of the Snake), it is written that on the occasion of the first round of negotiations on Five Peaks Island, the emperor sent a letter of admonishment to the Great Sea Dragon. While it is described as a "stern warning" to the warlord to refrain from challenging the Grand Circle and to submit himself to the authority of the emperor, its exact contents have been unknown until the recent discovery of a batch of imperial correspondences. What is immediately apparent from perusing the letter is that the Sixth Emperor did not assign the Office of the Imperial Secretariat to write an appropriate letter but rather composed it himself, as is apparent from his eccentric calligraphy in red ink. Far more than a "stern warning," it was an insulting missive designed to provoke certain war, as the Great Sea Dragon is addressed throughout as Pirate Fish Stink. In addition, there is no way to describe its nature other than as the ravings of a madman. The Sixth

Emperor promises not just defeat and annihilation in battle but the sexual violation of corpses, the magical tearing apart of souls, and the mass execution by extended torture of all the women and children of Sundown Archipelago as sacrifice to the god of war. He describes the entirety of South Ocean turned red with blood, the sinking of the southern islands by means of geomantically raised earthquakes, and the descent of all his defeated enemies into an underworld realm of eternal rape. The original letter was kept at the Hall of the Imperial Secretariat while a clean copy was sent to Five Peaks Island where it was delivered to the envoys of the Great Sea Dragon.

At the secret archive at the Temple to the Primordial Nothingness in Sundown Archipelago, a text has been discovered with a note indicating that it is the translation of that letter from imperial ideograms into the phonetic script of the south, rendered by the Great Sea Dragon's interpreter Upright Lotus. While it contains the gist of the Sixth Emperor's admonishment, it takes such liberties with the contents of the original that it can hardly be considered a proper translation. Its tone has been moderated and formalized to such an extent that the "stern warning" became more of a "respectful caution," with no mention of the name Pirate Fish Stink. The crazed quasi-religious ravings have all been cut out, replaced with a reasoned discourse on the sheer military and logistical difficulties the Great Sea Dragon would have to face should he dare to attempt an invasion of the Grand Circle proper. What is especially striking about the text is the insertion of numerous references to and quotations of the Grand Strategists, from such classic works as *Rules of Warfare*, *Expanded Rules of Warfare*, and *New Rules of Warfare*, with detailed expositions on why victory would be practically impossible to achieve for the Great Sea Dragon, and how even if he managed to initially take over significant territory through a number of victories on the battlefield, he could not hope to hold on to it in the long run with the limited resources as his disposal. Since it is implausible that the daughter of a South Ocean merchant would be so familiar with such military texts, this almost certainly points to collaboration with an imperial official.

After the Sixth Emperor's initial letter was dispatched, the Great Sea Dragon sent a number of his own missives to the imperial court, all of which have survived along with Diviner Supreme's translations. The messages in the original southern phonetic are aggressive, confident, and proud, declaring the warlord's intention to conquer the Grand Circle as he conquered the entirety of South Ocean. Diviner Supreme's translations are generally faithful, except for a glaring and mysterious alteration that appears in almost every fifth or sixth sentence, which is the mention of the color green. The waves upon which the Great Sea Dragon's fleet rides are described as green, the light emanating from his great curved sword is green, his green cape flies in the wind as he speeds forth toward the Grand Circle (he did not wear a green cape but a red one), and so on. He is even made to describe himself as the Great Green Sea Dragon and the Green Master of the Endless Green Waves who is destined to establish the Green dynasty after the downfall of the Primal. In the original letters, the word "green" does not occur once.

To give yet another significant example of such distortions, in the picture "The Peace on Five Peaks Island" the Great Sea Dragon holds the jade tablet of officialdom which he received from the Sixth Emperor, acknowledging his status as an imperial subject who rules over South Ocean in the name of the emperor. The color of the jade is red, which is the second to lowest of the six ranks of jade. Tablets in the two highest ranks, dark green and light green, were given on the extremely rare occasion that the emperor acknowledged a ruler to be his equal (*tablet of brotherhood*). For instance, the penultimate emperor of the Radiant dynasty gifted one to the Mountainous Father of the Golden Horsemen of the North in a futile effort to forestall their catastrophic invasion of the Grand Circle. Tablets in the next two ranks of jade, yellow and white, were given to rulers who were granted "subordinate but independent" status, kingdoms and lordly territories that were expected to pay tribute but whose internal autonomy was respected (*tablet of honored lords*). Tablets of the lowest jade ranks of red and black were granted to those whose dominion over certain territories were temporary, subject to review, and conditional upon pre-established imperial rules (*tablet of officialdom*). One who received such a tablet was expected to relinquish his power any time the emperor ordered him to.

During the final negotiation over the peace treaty, it is most certainly the case that Upright Lotus knowingly lied about the jade ranks. In the records of the Great Sea Dragon's advisors, they express great pleasure after learning from the translator that the emperor has capitulated to their demand that he recognize their lord as his equal. The acknowledgement is to be affirmed through the granting of the highest rank of jade in red. In the imperial records, on the other hand, the ministers affirm that if the Great Sea Dragon acknowledges his subordinate status by accepting the tablet of officialdom, their sovereign will allow him to submit on his feet. In others words, through Upright Lotus's lie, both sides came to regard the final outcome as a diplomatic victory.

There are many other examples of such deliberate mistranslations perpetrated by Diviner Supreme and Upright Lotus in apparent coordination with each other. They were able to do so without being discovered because Diviner Supreme was the only official in the Grand Circle who knew the language of Sundown Archipelago, and Upright Lotus was the only speaker of the imperial tongue in the leadership of the Great Sea Dragon's fleet. No one, in other words, was capable of checking their work.

After the successful completion of the Peace on Five Peaks Island, the Sixth Emperor's interpreter was granted the special honor name of Diviner Supreme, awarded with precious gifts, and offered a permanent position in the Imperial Secretariat. He humbly begged off officialdom with the respectable filial excuse that he had to take care of his ailing mother as his oldest brother was serving as the governor of the faraway province of Abundant Mountains and his second older brother had died in the previous year from an illness. Six months after, his mother passed away, and so he went into his mourning period. But after its completion, Diviner Supreme not only refused a position in the imperial court but he left the Forest of Brushes and West Capital, moving to a small town all the way in the southeastern plain, the last long journey he undertook. Not much is known about the life he led in this remote place, other than that he operated a school and produced some of the most important scholarly works on linguistics and cultural studies. For instance, his massive volume on his adopted homeland is still to this day the best source of information on the language, culture, and history of the region at the time. In particular, the record of his conversations with the survivors of the horrific massacre that was perpetrated on them by the Sixth Emperor in the early part of his reign provides a wholly plausible counter narrative to the official imperial account of the atrocity.

Toward the end of his life, he wrote what is his only known poem, a long narrative work in the neo-antique style, which may also have been his last writing. While many have marveled at the evocative beauty of its natural imageries, they have also found the work's overall meaning utterly obscure. It tells the story of a traveler who is lost in a dark forest, who becomes prey to a fierce tiger on one path and a pack of wolves on another, while he is also chased by poisonous snakes. At his most dire moment, he comes across a pristine lotus flower of many changing colors that becomes personified as a beautiful young woman. The traveler and the lotus woman plot together to evade the beasts and to escape the forest. They employ a variety of magic spells and clever tricks to evade the tiger, wolves, and snakes. The woman then becomes luminous and lights their way as they walk out of the forest.

One scholar theorized that the poem is in the mode of the so-called "dark cloud lyrics" written by scholars during the time of the repressive Legalist Emperors. They employed coded language, especially in the use of specific imageries with hidden meanings, to communicate with one another under the scrutiny of the Imperial Censorate. That notion has been proven to be correct through the discovery of some letters at the site of Diviner Supreme's final home. They were written in the southern phonetic script, on strips of bamboo that were tied together, sent to him by the interpreter for the Great Sea Dragon, to whom Diviner Supreme gave the amity name of Upright Lotus, which is also the title of his poem. The contents of the letters provide enough clues for decoding the work which reveals a remarkable account of what actually occurred on Five Peaks Island.

In the first days of negotiations on the island, the envoys of the Sixth Emperor and the Great Sea Dragon exchanged belligerent demands as both sides conducted their meeting as a prelude to war. Diviner Supreme, after spending an entire morning interpreting for the imperial officials, took a walk on a beach, filled with dread and melancholy at the prospect of the dark, violent times to come. There, he encountered Upright Lotus, who appeared to be in a similar mood. They walked together, spoke of each other's lives, their work, and their concerns for the future. In the course of a single day, as the sun set and they rested at a beachside tavern to share liquor, Diviner Supreme fell in love with the southern woman. As he gazed at her luminous eyes that shone with sad intelligence, he could not bear the thought of never seeing her again after the conclusion of the fruitless meeting, and of her becoming lost in the bloody war that was coming. Without considering the matter, he found himself committing high treason by revealing to her vital information that would have given the Great Sea Dragon a crucial advantage if he became privy to it. Diviner Supreme told Upright Lotus that the Sixth Emperor was hopelessly insane.

For almost five years, the Lord of the Grand Circle had neglected the affairs of the state, spending his time running around the palace in bizarre costumes and raving endlessly at his appalled officials and servants. All those who tried to remonstrate with him to correct his behavior were dismissed from their positions, exiled, or executed, until none was left in court except for sycophants, cowards, and mediocrities. He sent his best generals on impossible military operations, and when they returned unsuccessful, he executed them all, leaving no experienced and competent commanders at the Ministry of Military Affairs. One day, he accused his queen and all twelve of his concubines of conspiring against him, and had them and all their attendant ladies strangled to death, their corpses mutilated, and their remains spread across the empire to be fed to pigs and dogs. He hardly slept, was drunk most of the time, and ate only the vital organs of rare animals. And he was anxious to go to war, to turn South Ocean red with the blood of Pirate Fish Stink and his people. The eunuchs who served under him would be much vilified later as the Fifty Half-Men who all but usurped the power of the throne, but recent revisionist historians have pointed out that they had little choice but to take charge of running the government in the mad ruler's stead and actually did the best they could under the difficult circumstances. They were also successful in keeping the knowledge of their master's lunacy within the palace, as they scrupulously and, in some cases, violently suppressed any possible leak of the information.

It was only after Diviner Supreme revealed this to Upright Lotus that he began to dread the consequences of having exposed the great secret. He knew that if the eunuchs found out what he had done, he would be immediately recalled to West Capital and executed. Three generations of his family would be eradicated as well, as was the punishment for a traitor to the throne. So he was both astonished and relieved when his counterpart returned his gesture by revealing crucial information as well. It was that despite the Great Sea Dragon's bluster, he was wracked with doubt about the whole enterprise, as he had never conducted a major military campaign on land before. He was undoubtedly invincible on water, as he had never lost a naval battle since he took command of his own ship, but he had only lately began to familiarize himself with the basics of large-scale warfare on land from mercenary officers whom he hired as advisors. He was as ambitious as ever and genuinely wanted to find out if he could be as good a strategist on land as he was on the waves, but that was not the main reason he was challenging the Grand Circle.

Once he successfully established dominion over South Ocean, he realized that many of his sea lords, fierce martial men who had known nothing but raiding and warring all their lives, were getting restless. In addition, those who did not come from Sundown Archipelago, which was most of them, had submitted to him out of necessity and calculation, but resented his authority over them. He knew that he had also exacerbated their discontent by ordering them to learn and use his native tongue, wear the costumes of his people, and follow the political and ritualistic ways of the archipelago. Many of them had been part of a loose confederation of pirates in which the highest leader was the first among equals, so they found it humiliating to kneel while paying fealty to the Great Sea Dragon as their supreme lord. He was certain, therefore, that they would conspire against him sooner or later, unless he directed their energy elsewhere, to an enterprise that was dauntingly difficult as well as long-lasting, but one that also promised rewards beyond measure at its successful completion. The invasion would also give him the opportunity to get rid of some of his most untrustworthy subordinates on dangerous missions. But all that would work only if he proved to be victorious, as failure would lead certainly to the loss of his authority.

Diviner Supreme realized that if the Great Sea Dragon knew of the Sixth Emperor's madness and the empire's current lack of competent commanders, his self-doubt would disappear and he would launch an all-out assault as soon as possible. It was Upright Lotus who first suggested that the two of them were the only people who could stop the war. And so the conspiracy of unfaithful translations was born.

When Upright Lotus received the Sixth Emperor's raving letter to the Great Sea Dragon, she essentially rewrote the entire text as a polite warning from a calm and intelligent sovereign who was so supremely confident that he deigned to gently lecture the upstart on the foolishness of his course, providing a detailed and reasoned discourse on the many insurmountable difficulties he would face in taking on the Grand Circle. It was undoubtedly Diviner Supreme who provided her with the appropriate quotations from military classics. The profuse use of passages from the works was designed to intimidate the Great Sea Dragon by exposing his lack of knowledge on conducting a large-scale campaign on land, so further undermining his confidence. The letter gave the impression that the Sixth Emperor was surrounded by learned generals who provided him with such expertise, which they would deploy against the warlord in battle.

As for Diviner Supreme, the inclusion of the word "green" in his translations of the Great Sea Dragon's letters was inspired by his knowledge of his sovereign's early life. The emperor was born and raised in the northern frontier where his father, a member of a tertiary branch of the imperial family, was the lord commander of fortresses, a position his son inherited following his graduation from the Forest of Spears Military Academy. Given the large number of possible candidates to the throne, he had no expectation of attaining it when the sickly and impotent Fifth Emperor died without naming his successor. So he was taken completely by surprise when officials from the High State Council came to his headquarters to announce that they had designated him as the next ruler.

In that harsh region of frigid winds and rocky hills, there was a folk tradition about a figure who was called the Green Visitor. Parents of disobedient children would leave a window open for the creature, a macabre monster with rotting skin and bladed fingers, to come in at the darkest hour of the night. It would sneak over to the side of a sleeping child, rip off the skin on their face, and gobble it up. His coming was announced by the stench of fish, and he was sometimes depicted as having the head of a fish. Parents in the region corrected the behavior of recalcitrant children by threatening to invite the Green Visitor or by claiming to smell rotten fish in the air.

The Sixth Emperor was apparently subjected to such warnings during his childhood. With the onset of his madness, he became tormented by the recurring appearance of the Green Visitor in his dreams. The emperor became so terrified that he avoided sleeping as much as he could, so worsening his condition. He also banned fish from the palace, forbade the presence of green objects, and ordered that all things painted green be covered up with a different color. His reference to the Great Sea Dragon as Pirate Fish Stink made Diviner Supreme think that his sovereign harbored the suspicion that the warlord was the Green Visitor incarnate.

In the last letter Diviner Supreme translated with the numerous additions of the word "green" to frighten the Sixth Emperor, he added one original sentence at the end, promising that the Great Sea Dragon would go away without eating his skin if given the three gifts of title, jade, and liquor. The successful conclusion of a peace treaty with a foreign ruler usually ended with the emperor granting an official title, a jade tablet of the appropriate rank, and finally, precious liquor that they shared.

The Sixth Emperor surprised everyone with the order to offer the Great Sea Dragon peace. And they were surprised anew when the warlord agreed, on the condition that he was given the highest official title possible. A problem arose when the emperor refused to grant the jade tablet in the rank of green, as he would have nothing to do with something of that color. So his officials offered red jade, with room to negotiate up to white or yellow. The counter offer they received was that the Great Sea Dragon would accept red jade if he was allowed to submit standing up rather than having to prostrate himself on the ground, as was required of those receiving anything below the green. This was agreed upon. The negotiation over the jade color was entirely a play put on by the two translators. Diviner Supreme made it seem as if the Sixth Emperor got the better of the Great Sea Dragon by getting him to acknowledge his subordinate position in accepting the low grade of jade. Meanwhile, Upright Lotus told her master that the tablet of red jade was the mark of the highest recognition of equal status demanded by him, as demonstrated by the fact that he was to accept it on his feet.

And so the war was averted, with the Sixth Emperor relieved that he had appeased the Green Visitor, and the Great Sea Dragon thinking that he had avoided what was sure to be a disastrous land invasion against an able opponent. Within three years, both of them fell precipitously from power.

What the Great Sea Dragon thought was the Sixth Emperor's recognition of his equal status brought him no honor among his sea lords and led to a crisis of confidence. As he had feared, many immediately conspired against him, as they considered the peace he had made with the Grand Circle an act of cowardice. In the ensuing war in South Ocean, his nephew, whom he was grooming to be his successor, was bribed by rebellious sea lords into assassinating him. The Great Sea Dragon managed to escape the attempt and kill his beloved nephew, but his spirit was broken. In the next naval battle, he jumped into an enemy vessel by himself and fought a multitude of soldiers until they brought him down. South Ocean then fell into bloody chaos for the next five years, until the Peace of the Sixteen Sea Lords brought a measure of order back.

At around the time of the Great Sea Dragon's final battle, the Sixth Emperor expressed his desire to visit his original homeland in the northern frontier. He confided to one of his eunuchs that he did not fear going there to pay respects at the graves of his ancestors because the Green Visitor was no longer there. The monster had been pacified and sent far away, acting as his official in charge of South Ocean. It was also rumored that he meant to establish a North Capital and move his court there permanently. On the night after he arrived at the central fortress where he was born and raised, he used a secret passage to sneak out of his chamber in the middle of the night. He ventured outside and walked until he came to the house of a goatherd where he asked for directions to the path up a nearby mountain. When the goatherd suggested that he wait till daylight to travel, the emperor told him that he needed to get to the summit by dawn so that the first light of the new day would transform him into an immortal spirit. After he was shown the path, he granted the goatherd his cloak of radiant worm fabric and went on his way. He was never seen by anyone again.

The next day, when his eunuchs realized that he was missing, they kept it a secret at the fortress but mobilized the soldiers of a nearby garrison and sent them out in every direction to search for him. When the eunuchs were informed of the goatherd's story, the soldiers were dispatched up the mountain, but they eventually returned without having found any sign of him. In their panic, the eunuchs fabricated an imperial order and activated the troops of the fortress to slaughter all the soldiers of the garrison as well as the goatherd and his family under the false charge of fomenting a rebellion. In what came to be called the Rule of the Fifty Half-Men, the eunuchs continued to run the state while hiding the emperor's disappearance for almost a year, hoping in vain that he would show up somewhere.

They thought that they had killed every member of the goatherd's family but one of the boys they had executed was actually a neighbor's child who had come to the house to play. The real son was returning from an errand when he witnessed the killing of his family and hid inside a rotten tree. After the soldiers were gone, he begged all the way to the neighboring province where he was taken by some bandits and sold off as a slave. After a few months of working as a water carrier, he managed to escape and reach a town where an uncle on his mother's side of the family lived. He told the uncle his story, and the uncle told a local official who brought the tale to the magistrate. It eventually reached the ear of the governor, who sent a letter to the Sixth Emperor's nephew who was returning to West Capital from a pacifying expedition to the New Frontier of the far west where barbarians ate their food raw. He diverted his force to the town where he personally interrogated the goatherd's son. Enraged by what he learned, he gathered more soldiers and marched to the north, where he arrested and executed the fifty eunuchs. Within a month he arrived at West Capital, got rid of the Sixth Emperor's children by his murdered concubines, and ascended the throne as the Seventh Emperor. He also adopted the courageous and resourceful son of the goatherd who went on to have an illustrious career as a military officer, eventually becoming the commandant of the Forest of Spears.

There is one last element of the secret history of the Peace of Five Peaks Island to be told, though it can only be related in a speculative manner. The recently discovered letters that Upright Lotus sent to Diviner Supreme show that in the aftermath of their conspiracy to manipulate events through deliberate mistranslations, they planned to reunite at some point in the future. They knew that they had to be extremely careful, since it would raise suspicion if they were seen together by someone who knew their identities. For that reason, Diviner Supreme planned to decline the offer of a position in the imperial court and leave West Capital as soon as possible to settle in some remote place in the southeast, as close to South Ocean as possible. But then his mother died and he had to go into mourning period during which he could neither receive nor send correspondences, which caused a delay in their plan. When he was finally able to leave the capital and establish a home far away from the scrutiny of government officials, it was Upright Lotus who met with difficulties as she tried to arrange a passage into the Grand Circle.

Despite the remoteness of Diviner Supreme's last home, he did not lead the life of a hermit. He had his school, and many scholars who journeyed all the way there to meet and consult with the famed linguist reported that he led a rich social life surrounded by students and friends. The Seventh Emperor himself sent envoys to offer him a position in his court on no less than three occasions, but he declined each time, claiming to be too ill to travel, an apparent lie as he lived a very long life. It is most unfortunate that none of the visitors have written of the presence of Upright Lotus at his house. There is actually no reason to expect any of them to have done so, given the low status of women in this period. Men of the time would have hardly deigned to distinguish between a wife, a concubine, or a servant maiden who served them liquor and meals, but then withdrew to the women's quarters. Consequently, we cannot know if Upright Lotus ever managed to make her way to him.

When he wrote the narrative poem *Upright Lotus* toward the end of his life, was it a celebration of how he came to first meet his beloved with whom he shared a long, happy life together? Or is it a work of melancholy remembrance, of the one who was never able to reach him, leaving him to lead the rest of his life in solitary longing? I confess that it pains me deeply that we will, in all probability, never know.

The great mural painting "Peace of Five Peaks Island" is indeed the kind of monument to peacemakers that the Grand Historian Silver Mirror dreamed of in a civilization that has reached the age of wisdom. Yet it was not the gloriously attired Sixth Emperor or the proudly standing Great Sea Dragon who were the true heroes of the event. What all people who value peace and humanity should celebrate is the secret but truly great achievement of their interpreters, barely visible in the background of the picture as well as of history itself, who quietly and subtly saved the lives of hundreds of thousands through the virtuous use of unfaithful translations.

[Marginal Note: *My true and dear beloved, how well you have weaved the story together from so many disparate documents across the ages, in different scripts and genres. How you have rendered the invisible visible, how you brought clarity to the obscure, and how you shed light on the hidden. Yet, I must express disappointment at one aspect of your narrative.*

My true and dear beloved, could you really only have told the secret history of the unfaithful translators from the point of view of the man? I already know what your response to that will be. As you point out more than once, the events took place during a historical period that was a particularly low time for women, when they were subjugated, marginalized, and rendered invisible to such an extent that it is almost impossible for historians to gather much reliable information about their lives. This was true even for women of the highest status families, who were forbidden from learning, restricted to their quarters, and kept away from the social life of the larger community. Having made forays into research myself, I understand the difficulties involved.

But I must ask you, my true and dear beloved, have you tried hard enough? Or did your knowledge of the paucity of historical evidence on women of the Primal dynasty make you give up too quickly? Did you even attempt to read around the absence of information? To put it in another way, were you not bothered enough by the question of who Upright Lotus was to look further in search of her identity? Even her name is one that was given to her by a man.

For instance, you speculated that she might have been a member of a southern merchant family who worked as an assistant to her father. We know that indeed women played a greater role in South Ocean and its islands, a few even heading merchant concerns. Beyond merely theorizing about the origin of Upright Lotus, have you delved into that historical context? Even if you were not able to find any information about her before the Peace on Five Peaks Island, the research may have shed light on the life of such an intellectually gifted woman who worked for her family's business and then for a powerful sea lord.

But, my true and dear beloved, what bothers me the most is your lack of a detailed analysis of the letters Upright Lotus sent to Diviner Supreme. You say that they provided the essential clues that allowed you to decode Diviner Supreme's poem. How did they do so? Also, what exactly do the letters say, what is her writing style, what do they reveal about the character of the writer? You wrote, on that day on Five Peaks Island when Diviner Supreme fell in love with her, "he gazed at her luminous eyes that shone with sad intelligence." How did he look to her? Did she also fall in love with him? Or did she have her own reasons for her actions? After they successfully averted war, did she really want to be with him? Would she have wanted to take the enormous risk of traveling by herself to the Grand Circle, just so she could live in a society where she would have to lead a restricted existence? Would she have indeed done all that just to be with him, or could she have made her own way and led her own life? Even if they were never reunited, leaving Diviner Supreme to lead a life of, as you say "solitary longing," that doesn't necessarily make it a tragedy for Upright Lotus. She may have found happiness in a different world.

I assume, my true and dear beloved, that the letters do not provide direct answers to those questions, as otherwise you would have revealed them. But you must see how your neglect of their specific contents deprives the reader of what may turn out to be clues to another alternate view of the events. A secret history within the secret history of the Peace of Five Peaks Island, if you will.

You have done well, my true and dear beloved, but you can do better and you must do better. We all must, in our never-ending task of rendering the invisible visible, bringing clarity to the obscure, and shedding light on the hidden.

My true and dear beloved...]

COME HOME TO ATROPOS
Steven Barnes

EDITORIAL NOTE TO Carver Kofax:

I understand that monies have been exchanged and that the Atropos account has been good for us in the past. However, I'm not entirely certain that we want to continue working with this project beyond this point. There are certain legalities (yes, this infomercial can be placed upon the internet through offshore servers) and moral questions that have to enter the equation. I'm not entirely certain that our finance department has considered the implications though I do acknowledge and respect the time and effort already invested. We agreed to the contract and I suppose we must continue, but I wish to formally register my discomfort with the situation. I am also puzzled about the stipulation that the infomercial be promoted to primarily white upper class markets. Isn't this racist?

—Adrien Stein, President, Stein and Baker Advertising

[The following is rough script submitted for your approval. The Art Department can be trusted to add their own input and illustrations as we continue the process of development. Musical accompaniment is not my forte, but perhaps some of the more celebratory tunes by their native group *Los Muertos*?

— Carver Kofax, creative operations
Stein and Baker Advertising]

* * *

INFOMERCIAL SCRIPT, PROJECT ATROPOS

[Image: Crashing Caribbean waves beneath a summer moon. FX to enhance silvery reflection on the romantic waves. Narrator's voice should have that "this is a cola nut" quality. Is that guy still alive?]

Narrator: Come home to Atropos, my friend. Here in the Caribbean you will experience a paradise of golden beaches and sunny days, enough to fill your senses and melt away your cares and woes.

[Image: Friendly brown-skinned natives. And should we change 'days' above? Technically, the average stay is less than 24 hours, after all.]

Narrator: We understand your very special situation and our smiling, happy guides will welcome you from the moment that you step off the plane—

[Image: St. Atropos airport. (Please FX wipe hurricane damage. Make it look good!) Can we get B-roll of arrivals? And for God's sake, clean them up. Drooling and wheelchair-bound just isn't sexy.]

NARRATOR: —surrounding you with love and support as you approach your final experience. While others may have mocked and discouraged you, telling you you haven't the right to do as you wish with your own bodies, we understand that all journeys come to an end, and that choosing the moment for that is one of the greatest rights a human being can enjoy. We are a people who remember a time when our bodies did not belong to us, when we were told that there would be divine judgement for the ending of pain and sorrow. Understanding is the birth of compassion.

The history of Atropos has made us accepting of a wide variety of choices. We learned to take sadness in stride, to find the freedom within what others might consider oppression, and we know that despite whatever diagnosis you may have received there is still joy for you to be found in our smiling faces and cheerful eyes.

[Note: here our employers wished us to insert a specific clip of natives dancing in the street around three elderly, wheelchair bound euthatourists. I have to admit that the dancers seemed more than just welcoming and supportive. There was something... gleeful? Yes, that might be the right word. They seem too happy. Isn't this a little inappropriate? Can we not find some alternative images? C.K.]

Narrator: Here you will find the shepherds you have sought to lead you to your destiny, from the moment you step off the plane or cruise ship near the docks, as so many of our ancestors did prior to reaching their final destinations, working in the Americas—

[Note to Image library: is *Gone with the Wind* in public domain now? There are some great possibilities there. Can we license?]

NARRATOR: —or enjoying any number of wonderful opportunities in Central America. Whether enjoying the sunshine raising cotton and textiles in the Carolinas, or treasure-hunting for gold and diamond deposits in the mountains of Brazil's *Minas Gerais*, these migrant workers left their homes centuries ago with hope in their hearts, and were rewarded beyond their imaginings. We invite you to celebrate their first view of the New World from the same perspective.

[Note to Image Library: We need shots of the transport ships arriving. Happy workers disembarking, eager for adventure. It shouldn't look EXACTLY like "vacation," but let's stretch the analogy as far as it can go, shall we? And for the Brazilian mines, can we find pictures of black kids digging in sand at the beach? Let's keep it light, while respecting historicity, please.]

NARRATOR: Our people happily perform dances and rituals celebrating these arrivals and departures, playing their roles with practiced ease, and the weight of their papier mâché chains is lightened by the twinkle in their eye, knowing that as in all such delightful play, the slave is actually the master, forcing their supposed captors to provide all food and shelter and entertainment, allowing them to enjoy life as few ever have, or will again. But we hope to give you a tiny taste of their joy!

[Image library: Use your judgement. We need a variety of images of the beautiful people of Atropos, and the hospitality they can provide. Certainly we can find some who don't look hungry? And no amputees, please.]

NARRATOR: Surrounded by love and comfort in air-conditioned buses, you will tour our beautiful island. You will of course see the extensive hurricane damage you have heard of. Do not be alarmed by the lack of water and power to these regions: our people are resourceful, and although your leaders felt it would be best for us to rely upon our own resources, our people feel only welcoming toward you, and will cheer you on your way. And considering that obesity is a plague of the modern world, you will be delighted to see so little of it here. In fact, the World Health Organization recently declared the Atropians to be among the least obese people on Earth.

You will see closed factories due to American embargoes and power outages, but as your great philosopher Napoleon Hill once said, "In every disaster is the seed of an equivalent benefit." "Think and Grow Rich!" Had we but known that was all it took! We are a resourceful people who can be trusted to find other means of generating revenue. You are "living" proof of this yourself!

You will have the opportunity to visit the many locations where our ancestors learned to work in the sun through long hours and with modest caloric intake. Not for nothing are we called "The Spa of the Caribbean"! Our fortunate forebears found plenty of opportunities to learn the new chattel system, the one where our work could be transformed into good hard American money. What luck that we, who had not developed such systems, were able to take advantage of preexisting structures. What a blessing to simply slip into them, receive our new names, languages, and religions, say goodbye to the cares and woes of personal responsibility. How can we possibly show our gratitude to the descendants of these wise ones?

The depth of that gratitude cannot be expressed in mere words. At the end of your wonderful day you'll be taken to your hotel, where you will have an opportunity to meet more kindred souls on a similar journey. Those still ambulatory enough to enjoy dancing may do so, while others can listen to our local musical troupe *Los Muertos* until dawn, or be wheeled out to watch the sun rise while savoring specialized tropical drinks with our well known coconut-pineapple phenobarb infusions, a new spin on an old favorite! Holothane inhalation and ketamine injections are also available on request, as well as trademarked Tetrodotoxin specialties hand-harvested from the "Zombie Cucumber" sea urchins for which our island neighbors are so famous! By special request we can also provide Acepromazine, Propofol, or Medetomidine, in combinations guaranteed to usher you gently to your eternal reward.

While our trademarked concoctions can protect your taste buds against any bitterness inherent in the medications offering the relief you crave, we respect that some are conflicted, and wish the bite of Socrates' hemlock, an old favorite given a modern twist, served in a coconut shell with a tiny festive umbrella. For those even more convinced that voluntary exit is a sin, concoctions infused with potassium chloride can help purge your soul with intensity even a martyr would envy. We promise a truly stimulating passage.

Custom-designed exits are also available, and our expert staff is eager to consult with you on any refinements you may desire.

A variety of ministers, priests, and even a rabbi are on call for your prayer needs. We accept all major credit cards, but require cosigners for other deferred payment plans, of course.

Watching one final sunrise, you'll be able to close your eyes knowing that you have ended your pain and suffering in the hands of those who have much reason to wish to assist you.

Isn't it time?

THE FINE PRINT
Chinelo Onwualu

RED DUST SWIRLED about the black vehicle as it slid silently into the village. Nuhu was sitting among the other men under the giant flame tree in the village square, sipping sorghum beer and gossiping aimlessly. He watched with dread as the driverless car hummed to a stop just beyond them. Its clean, glossy lines looked out of place in the desiccated landscape. A crowd of children gathered to look at the car, but scurried off when the door opened.

The woman who emerged was not exactly what Nuhu was expecting. Tall and fair, she wore a modest red hijab and black abaya. It was not until she was close that he could tell that her kohl-rimmed eyes had no irises or pupils.

"Who is Nuhu Aliyu Danbatta here?" she called out. Nuhu's beer turned to mud in his mouth. The other men suddenly found reasons to be elsewhere and crept away hastily. He was tempted to feign ignorance and pretend he was another, but that never worked. The question was merely a formality; she knew exactly who he was. They always knew.

"I am he," he said, standing.

She regarded him without expression. "I am your final notice," she said. Nuhu felt the cold hand of despair grip his heart. His legs felt weak and he forced himself to remain upright. "You have three days."

"Wait, wait, let's discuss this," he said, unashamed of the note of desperate pleading that had crept into his voice. "Please."

"There is nothing to discuss. The terms of the contract are clear."

"But he's my son..." his voice trailed away as he stared into her blank face. This was futile, he realised. How could she, a spell made flesh, possibly understand? She turned to walk away and a surge of anger rose in him.

"This is not fair!" he screamed at her retreating form.

She paused and turned back. A flicker of something passed over her face.

"Fair?" she echoed. There was an air of detached anger to her, as if the ire that briefly distorted her features was not her own. Nuhu knew he was hearing the voice of the elemental being that animated her. "How is this not fair? When you sealed the contract, just what did you think would happen?"

A sudden hope surged through him. This was the first time any of them had ever spoken to him beyond their protocols and he lunged at the slim chance this invited.

Crossing to close the space between them, he dropped his voice to a pleading whisper. "Please, ask me for anything else; I will give it. Don't do this."

"Three days," the spell said. "Give him up peacefully or I will be forced to fulfil my mandate."

The woman strode back to the driverless car and got in. With a near silent whoosh, the car drove off.

Nuhu's stomach roiled and a wave of nausea overcame him. He barely had time to lurch to the space behind Mallam Bello's hut before he vomited the sorghum beer. Wiping his mouth with the edge of his keffiyeh, he began to cry.

GRANDFATHER'S HOUSE WAS hard to miss. Its three stories of whitewashed marble dwarfed the mud brick-and-thatched-roof homes around it. Built in the style of the old masters, it boasted a red tile roof and marble pillars over the veranda. One had to look closely to notice that more than a few tiles on the roof had already rotted through—they were unable to withstand the heavy deluges of the rainy season—and that the white plaster was peeling and cracking. The date palms that lined the long driveway looked majestic, but provided little shade.

As Nuhu walked up the long drive, the noon sun reflecting harshly off the grey flagstones, he remembered the massive fruit trees that had once surrounded his grandfather's compound, before the Catalogues came. He and his friends would spend hours climbing them and picking mangoes, cashews, guavas, and oranges, each in their own season. As beautiful as the palms were, he could not recall any of them ever bearing fruit.

Grandfather was seated among the other elders of the town in the main room of the house. The floor was covered with colorful carpets of the finest weave, and the old men lounged on leather cushions decorated in gold and silver thread. One did not have to look closely to see that the carpets were already going threadbare in parts and the leather was cracked from use.

Nuhu greeted the men, performing obeisance at Grandfather's feet. The old man wore a djellabiya of fine white cotton, and his beard was freshly oiled and trimmed. Like the others, he was fat and sleek with good food and care, and Nuhu lost the resolve that had brought him here. Instead, he exchanged pleasantries with the old men, asking after their health and families. He thought to leave quietly, but his plan was forestalled by one of the elders.

"I hear you received your final notice today," said Mallam Garba, shifting his bulk as he adjusted the voluminous sleeves of his sky blue babban riga. Nuhu nodded glumly. "You should not wait so long to make your payment; you might lose your next Catalogue."

Nuhu could not think of what to say to this. Instead he turned to the man who had raised him after his parents' death and asked: "Grandfather, what does the Djinn want of us?" He fought to keep the tears out of his voice.

"Wants? The Djinn *wants* nothing. He is the benevolence of God. His only desire is to serve mankind," said Grandfather in his deep, sonorous voice. The old man settled into his seat and lit his fine clay pipe. Nuhu recognised his storytelling pose and sighed inwardly—he would not be leaving for hours. "You know, I was there as a child the day the Djinn first came among us. I saw him with my own eyes. A wanderer from the land of spirits, he had been trapped by an evil being and forced to do great harm to mankind. When he was finally set free of his prison he sought only to serve and make amends for the wrong he had once done. So he asked us each to name our single deepest desire, and in return he asked each for only one thing—a gift of his own choosing.

"You do not remember the cruelty of the masters, Nuhu. How their thugs would raid our humble village, beating men and dishonoring our women, taking our food and animals under the pretence of collecting taxes. Those were dark times, my child. We were slaves, forced to do the bidding of those no better than ourselves. Worse, for the masters did not know God.

"I remember the day the last of their machines were driven from our streets, never to return. The Djinn had set us free, Nuhu. And do you know what he asked of us in return?"

"A cow—"

"A cow!" thundered Grandfather, continuing as if Nuhu hadn't spoken. "A single cow in exchange for our freedom. No more would our women be incited to disobedience and prostitution, filled with the false ideas of the masters' teachings. No more would our young men labor under the yoke of another's desires. And after he freed us, did he abandon us to the vagaries of fate? No! He remained at our service, offering us his protection and benevolence. And today we have the Catalogue," Grandfather hefted the enormous book that appeared on the doorstep of every man once he turned sixteen, "that once a year we may come to him with our deepest desires. And in return what does he ask?"

"A boon," Nuhu whispered.

"A boon," Grandfather lowered his voice. "A thing so small, it would not trouble you to give it. After all he has given you, would you deny him this?"

"But my child—"

"Nuhu Aliyu!" Grandfather called out in his booming voice, "Are you the first man to give a child to the Djinn?" Nuhu shook his head. No one knew exactly when the Djinn had first begun to ask for children. It was usually a girl child—unfortunate, but since every family had sons these days, not too much to bear. Though there would be no dowry for the child taken, a man could always have more daughters. Plus, it was one less mouth to feed. The mothers did not always agree, but then women were unnecessarily sentimental about such things. On the rare occasion that a boy child would be taken, it was always a youngest son—the kind who would only cause trouble for a family by disputing his inheritance, or bring shame by running off to become an entertainer.

"Besides, what will become of such a child?" asked Mallam Daudu with his characteristic gentleness. "A child that cannot even be brought out for its Naming Day?"

Nuhu hung his head in shame. A son's Naming Day was normally a time for celebration. The family would slaughter a goat and there would be village-wide feasting. But his own child's naming ceremony had been a quiet one: no feast had been held and none but Grandfather had attended the blessing. This was usually reserved for children with deformities—and girls.

"Nuhu, think of what your father would say," Grandfather pitched his voice low and placed a warm hand on Nuhu's shoulder. "You were his greatest wish—his only desire. Is this how you want our line to end? In the hands of that... child? Fulfil your contract and the Djinn will ensure that you always have more sons—just as he did with your father."

This was a familiar refrain to Nuhu. For as long as he could remember, Grandfather never hesitated to remind him that the responsibility for continuing the family lineage lay solely on him. His elder sister had died at birth, and though his father had married and divorced many other women, Nuhu was the last of his living children, and the family's only son.

He could barely speak, and Grandfather took his silence for assent. Satisfied, Grandfather clapped his hands and his newest wife entered the room balancing a tray of delicacies. At sixteen she was in full bloom, with round cheeks, clear skin, and straight white teeth that spoke of robust health and good feeding. She even had the luminous, blue-black complexion that was all the rage these days. But her beauty was only human. In a few years Grandfather would tire of her. By the time next year's Catalogue came out he would be finding fault with her and eyeing the newest models. Nuhu doubted she would see her eighteenth year in this house.

Grandfather was right; the Djinn had indeed given him a great treasure. His own fox bride had only been offered once—not before and not since.

There were none to compare with her, Nuhu thought wryly.

IT WAS GRANDFATHER who first told him about fox brides, when he was still a child. After dinner, when the women were clearing away the dishes and the men of the household settled down to smoke their clay pipes, the old man would regale Nuhu with tales he himself had heard from the masters of impossibly beautiful women who never aged, never spoke out of turn, and cooked and cleaned without complaint. Women who looked upon their husbands with absolute devotion and birthed only sons.

And so when Nuhu had gotten his first Catalogue on his sixteenth birthday and saw her entry, he knew exactly what his wish would be. He had placed the order and she had arrived by shuttle bus within the week. Of course he had been warned that her cost would be high—he had signed the contract after all—but nobody ever reads the fine print.

Everything Grandfather had said was true, Nuhu mused as he trudged up the hill to his house. Hana was the perfect bride. Five years later, she still possessed the same otherworldly exquisiteness that had captivated him in the Catalogue. Her flawless complexion was still porcelain-pale, her large black eyes never needed kohl, and her tiny bow mouth was perfection itself. Beneath her hijab her hair was a straight black waterfall, and she would always be as slender as the day she arrived. Yet as he spied her waiting for him by the low mud wall of their compound—she waited for him whenever he went out—Nuhu felt a familiar weariness settle in his bones.

When she caught sight of him her face lit up in joy. She almost broke into a run to meet him, but she stopped herself. She was finally starting to remember, Nuhu noted.

"Husband, you're home!" she said, and she rubbed at his arm as he stepped through the low wooden gate built into the compound's wall. "I have missed you."

Nuhu forced a smile. The stories had not mentioned that all the attention she gave grew draining after a time. Such devotion was acceptable from a pet, but from a human—even if it was only a fox spirit wearing human form—it was unsettling. Hana was always eager to do his bidding; she never questioned or disagreed with him, but neither did she advise or correct him. She had no interests or opinions of her own, and her temperament never varied. There were no bad moods to be cautious of, no minor sulks to coax her from. The only time he had ever displeased her was when, a year into their marriage, he told her that he had decided to take another wife.

For the first time, he witnessed the true wildness of the fox in her. Crying and howling, she had vowed to kill herself and any other woman who came near him. She had scratched at her face and chest with her claw-like nails until they were bloody with gouges. It took all night to calm her. By the next day, Hana's wounds were healed as if they had never been, and her sweet disposition had returned. But Nuhu had not forgotten his terror. He never spoke of taking a second wife again.

Now he gritted his teeth as she washed his feet in rosewater, an elaborate ritual that she performed every time he came into the house. He suffered in silence as she offered him plates of snacks and treats that she had prepared especially for him, but when she asked after his day he had to draw the line. The encounter with the spell was still too fresh with him.

"*Habibi*, I am tired," Nuhu said, forcing a light tone. "Could you perhaps draw me a hot bath? Make sure to fetch the water from the forest stream, just how I like it."

"Of course, my love," Hana said in her sing-song voice and she darted off. It would take her a few hours to hand-draw water from the stream on the far side of the village, but he made sure to see her to the door and out of the compound. Only then did Nuhu call for a servant to bring him his son.

Umar was just two months old but Hana had already stopped nursing him. That was another thing they hadn't told him. Fox spirits did bear only male children, but they rarely raised them. All their devotion was reserved for their husbands.

He could not believe how tiny the baby was, even at this age. And it was still a shock to see the two-month-old's fine down of dusty red fur and his sharp yellow eyes. To hide his pointed ears, they kept a woollen cap low over his brows, even in the heat. But Umar gurgled like any other child. Nuhu waggled a finger at the baby's face, careful not to let the child grab at it; his tiny teeth were already needle-sharp. He cradled the baby until it fell asleep in his arms. As Nuhu watched his son's tiny face slacken, a warmth spread through his chest. He rubbed a finger against the soft fur on the baby's cheeks. The spell's words came back to him with force and he drew the child tighter to him, causing it to fret a little. He didn't care what Grandfather said; no one would take this baby from him. No one.

THE DJINN'S HEADQUARTERS was located on the top floor of a massive obsidian-faced building that dwarfed the skyline at the center of the capital city. After the spell's visit, Nuhu had spent the next three days deep in thought. Finally, on the day he was to give up his son, Nuhu had persuaded his cousin Mohammed, who owned a commercial motorcycle, to make the two-hour journey from the village to the city.

It was nearly noon when they arrived and the city was winding down for afternoon siesta. Nuhu knew the Djinn never took siesta—and his business was too urgent for protocol. They wove through the busy traffic of the capital, dodging cars, minibuses, and tricycles until they got to the tower. After promising to meet with him in front of the revolving doors in a few hours, Mohammed drove off.

Nuhu spared a moment to take in the massive structure, a black finger whose tip was lost in the clouds. It was said the building had appeared overnight, and he marvelled at the power required to do something like that. Then remembering his purpose, he squared his shoulders and strode in.

The lobby was as stark as the exterior. The walls were paneled in a dark wood and the carpet was an industrial iron grey. A row of black leather chairs lined one wall under a series of monochrome paintings that provided the only real color in the room. A spell in a black hijab sat behind a desk of white marble with a single bright red phone on its surface. She looked vaguely familiar, but Nuhu didn't have time to parse why.

"Excuse me," Nuhu greeted politely. She turned her pupil-less eyes to him and he suppressed a shudder. "I would like to see your master."

"Do you have an appointment?"

"No."

"I'm sorry; without an appointment I cannot grant you entry."

Nuhu thought hard for a moment.

"But I have a complaint."

The spell stared at him for a long moment. Clearly, no one had ever come in with a complaint before. Finally, she graced him with a wide mechanical smile and pressed a number on her phone.

"Customer Service is on the thirtieth floor. Thank you for visiting us, Mallam Danbatta."

The lift slid open with a soft ping and Nuhu stepped on. Only as the doors slid closed did Nuhu realize he had not given the spell his name. A cold wave washed over him just as the door clicked open at the thirtieth floor.

Nuhu hesitantly stepped out of the lift and took a moment to observe the quiet efficiency of the spells sitting at their cubicles as they conducted their duties. With a start, he realized they were all women. Come to think of it, Nuhu didn't think he had ever seen a male spell. A long row of tinted windows at the far end of the room let in just enough light to signal daytime, while soft fluorescents above supplied the rest. The carpet here was a soft blue-green. It was hard to believe that unremarkable rooms like this controlled the lives of thousands of people who ordered their wishes through the Djinn.

A spell in a grey kaftan and matching hijab walked up to him. Her pupil-less stare seemed to carry a hint of curiosity.

"I understand you have a complaint?" she asked.

"Yes, but I would like to see your supervisor," Nuhu said.

"I am head of this department. Perhaps I can help you?"

"I am sorry. My complaint can only be resolved by your manager."

The spell's face went blank for a moment, like a radio that had been turned off. When she became animated again, it was as if she had shifted to a different frequency.

"My manager is unavailable at the moment," she said cheerfully. "Why don't you come into my office and we can discuss the issue?"

Without waiting for his answer, she turned and glided deeper into the maze of cubicles. Nuhu had no choice but to follow.

The office was a glass enclosure at the end of the room with only a desk, two chairs, and a file cabinet in the corner. On the desk was a manila file folder, and a red phone. She indicated that Nuhu should sit in the chair in front of the desk and took her place behind it. Clasping her hands together, she fixed Nuhu with an unblinking stare. "Would you please explain the situation?"

Nuhu briefly considered apologizing and leaving, but he caught himself. This was his last resort. If this didn't work, he would lose his baby. He explained as best he could, watching the spell for any signs of sympathy or understanding. Her expression of cheerful concern never wavered; she simply nodded. "Tell me more."

When he was done talking, the spell gave a final nod. "I am so glad you have brought this to our attention. What would you like to see happen here?"

"I-I want to keep my son," Nuhu said, blinking in incredulity. Hadn't he been clear?

"Let us review your file; perhaps there is something we can do."

Joy bloomed in Nuhu's heart as he watched her open the manila file in front of her. From it she drew out a slim sheaf of papers. Nuhu had never seen it before, but he knew what they were. His contract. Signed before he was born, it was every wish that he or anyone in his family had ever made on his behalf. He watched as she scanned through the papers, fighting the urge to wipe his sweaty palms on his trousers. He had worn his Friday best.

"It seems you have not made a wish in four years. Why is that?" The spell fixed him with a look, and Nuhu quailed. Before getting his first Catalogue, he had only ever had one wish, and by the time his next Catalogue had come the following year, Nuhu had lost his taste for wishes; his fox bride was enough.

"Well-well... that is... well, I-I already have everything that I need," he stammered.

The spell arched an eyebrow. The look of distant curiosity had returned. "You have no desires?"

"Only to keep my son," Nuhu said quickly.

The spell frowned and looked through the sheaf of papers again. "The terms of the contract indicate that you are to yield your first-born child in payment for your bride. Normally, I would be able to offer you some compensation, but you have not placed enough wishes to qualify for any of our promotions or rewards. I'm afraid there's nothing I can do."

A lead weight settled in Nuhu's stomach. Desperation overwhelmed him; he wanted to leap to his feet and scream. Then a thought struck him.

"But my son is no child. He is not human."

The spell blinked at him, her face slack with astonishment. Just then, the phone on her desk rang. The spell picked it up and after a moment or two, put it back down.

"I think you may need to speak with my manager," she said.

THE ROOM WAS white. Floor to ceiling, it was covered in some sort of sheet or tile that fit seamlessly and gave no impression of angles or perspective. It was like stepping onto a blank canvas, and it made Nuhu's head hurt to look at it. Ambient light from no direct source filled the room. In the center of it—or what Nuhu assumed was the center; he had no real way of judging distance in this space—a small man in a white djellabiya floated in mid-air, his legs crossed in the lotus position. He was tiny, no bigger than a small child, and though his face was seamed with thousands of wrinkles, he seemed ageless.

"Welcome Mr. Danbatta," said the Djinn. "Please, come in."

Nuhu realized he was still standing in the lift. The spell had ushered him into it and pressed a red button which was on its own pad, separate from the bank of other buttons. He stepped cautiously into the room. Behind him the lift slid shut, and the room became a featureless white space once more.

He took off his cap in deference and greeted politely. The small man returned the greeting and waved a hand at a red armchair in front of him. Nuhu was certain the chair hadn't been there a moment before. The Djinn waited for Nuhu to sit before speaking again.

"I understand you want to discuss your account," he said. Nuhu shifted uncomfortably, his throat suddenly dry.

"I have come to beg you: Please, spare my child," Nuhu said. He could feel a lump of tears at the back of his throat.

The Djinn sighed and tugged at his long white beard.

"Would that I could," he said. The boredom of a thousand lifetimes leaked through his voice. "This is all in the contract, Mr. Danbatta. That child is mine by rights."

"He is not even human. He would be of no use to you."

The Djinn laughed, an oddly hollow sound. "For a moment, I thought you might have something new to say... Look, *you* may have sullied yourself through your animal union with the fox, but your abomination of a child is still a human spirit. I can always find use for him. The contract stands, I'm afraid."

Nuhu thought of his tiny, beautiful, helpless son as nothing but a tool in the Djinn's employ. Anger flared in him and he stood.

"No! I refuse to accept this!" he shouted. "You promised us freedom, yet you are no better than the masters. Nothing has changed. We are slaves to you as surely as we were to them."

The Djinn cocked a shaggy white eyebrow. "How so? I provide you everything you desire through the Catalogue."

"You fulfil our desires, but not our needs."

The Djinn shrugged at that. "What can I say? Humans are such short-sighted creatures..."

"You will not take my baby," Nuhu said. "You will have to kill me first."

The Djinn was suddenly standing in front of Nuhu, his face inches away. His expression grew ugly and Nuhu saw the ancient creature behind the human mask.

"I cannot kill you, Mr. Danbatta, but I can hurt you," it said with soft menace. "And should you try to stop me from taking what is mine, I will."

"If you could hurt me, you would have done so already," Nuhu said, and he felt the truth of his words as he spoke them. "You have no power over us. None except what we give you, year after year. That is why you send us the Catalogues."

The Djinn stared hard at him for a moment, then he burst into laughter. He laughed so hard his tiny frame shook.

"Well done, Mr. Dambatta. I knew there was a reason I liked you," the Djinn said when he could finally catch his breath. A chair matching Nuhu's appeared behind the Djinn, and he sat down on it. "So, now you understand. But that still does not free you from the contract you signed. Your child is due for collection today."

"No. You may have our liberty, but you have no claim on my son." As Nuhu spoke, another realization hit him.

"Why is that, Mr. Danbatta?" The Djinn seemed genuinely eager to hear Nuhu's next statement.

"I saw my file, and I saw that my parents made a wish for me—a boy child—and in exchange, you took their only living daughter. She's still here, isn't she?"

"Perhaps..." The Djinn leaned back and steepled his fingers, a smile creeping over his face. "I have so many employees."

"You signed a contract with Nuhu Aliyu Danbatta the son of Ahmed Mahmood Danbatta—but I am not his son, am I?"

The Djinn's smile grew into a grin of ghoulish glee. "No, you are not. Your father could not sire sons, no matter how many wives he took. And I can do many things, but even I cannot create human spirits."

"Who am I, then?" Nuhu asked, his mind reeling. "Whose child am I?"

"No idea. When I first started, I'd take the children myself. But the organization has grown so quickly, and your people are so eager to give up your children for a bit of material comfort..." The Djinn shrugged and spread his hands. "I don't really handle the paperwork anymore."

"It doesn't matter," said Nuhu, sadly. "Your contract with me is void. Take back your fox wife, leave me my child."

"Of course," The Djinn stood with an inexplicable air of satisfaction. "After all, my purpose has only ever been to serve the desires of men."

From somewhere behind him, Nuhu heard the lift ding open. The spell he'd seen in the lobby emerged; she was holding his son, Umar. Face to face, Nuhu could see how much she resembled his father in a way he never had. She smiled as she handed the child to him.

"Is she happy here? With you?"

"Happier than she would ever have been among your people," the

Djinn said. "*I* have always known the value of women."

Nuhu didn't know what to say to that, so he nodded dumbly. He wasn't sure what was what anymore—and he realized that he no longer cared. Cradling his precious son, he turned and went home.

UNKIND OF MERCY
Alex Jennings

IT TOOK JOHNNY a long time to find work after we moved to the city. He is kind of set in his ways, and more than anything he likes to have a beer and watch the game, you know? Comedy hadn't been going so well, and it had been a while since I went to see him at one of his shows because God knows I work an awful lot. I mean I literally clean up shit for old folks at the Home down on Magazine Street, and we've only got the one car, and being on the goddamn bus for that long can be just exhausting.

At first, even the bus seemed all glitzy and glam, but Johnny was just like, "A bus is a bus. You sound like Clotile." You know. From the Boudreaux and Thibodeaux jokes? She's married to one of them, I can't remember which, and hearing him say that made me feel like a bumpkin. Sure enough, getting on the bus the next morning was not glitzy *at all*. I had to admit to myself that I am what you would call one of the working poor. Still, that is my choice. I didn't grow up poor—my daddy wasn't an astronomer or nothing, but he had a good job working cranes offshore.

Don't misunderstand. Johnny is so not a negative person. He does not take the air out of things or crap all over stuff just to do it. He was just not feeling good about things because he was doing mics five and six nights a week, and Bill Camden had moved out to L.A. sooner than anyone expected so he wasn't here to book Johnny on his show, and his partner, Kenny, never thought Johnny was all that funny, and so Kenny was not all hot to book Johnny on Laughter's

Lane or on Three Phony Cacophony like Bill would have done.

People think Johnny is doing a character, but he's not. Not quite. I mean he was a Juggalo when we met, with the greasepaint and the Faygo and all, but the smoke from those bonfires in the woods got in his bones and so to me he smelled like a party. The moment we met, I looked in his eyes and saw that even though he was nobody, he was a fucking star. People just needed to change the right channel in their brains to see his shine. And he'd make them.

ANYWAY, AFTER JOHNNY said that thing about the bus, I started noticing little things that kept my feet on the ground. Like, it didn't take long to start saving money for a car with what I make at the Home, and I can *feel* that car getting closer, you know? But, for instance, the *litter*. People litter more here in a way that they don't in Laffy, and definitely not in New Iberia, right? It's like a *right* here. In his act, Bill says it's a sign of manhood or something—? *Virility*. I was waiting for the bus awhile back and this black guy dropped a cold drink can next to the trashcan and this older black guy started giving him a hard time about it, and then they both stopped short and just laughed like it was the funniest thing. The attitude was, *Wouldn't it be* hilarious *if we cared about this?* It bothered me and it bothers me still.

So things like that started adding up, and Johnny wasn't working for a while, and he wasn't making money off comedy at all, and I was kind of carrying us. I still had enough to save, and it's not like either one of us was big eaters, and we don't have no kids, so it wasn't the end of the world, but god damn. And then he was like, "You see this bullshit?"

I was folding laundry. I don't like to say it like that, because I don't want people to think that Johnny doesn't help out around the house because he does. Neither of us is big on chores, I fucking *hate* them, and he feels the same way, so what we do is any time we can, we break up the chore into parts and we mix and match. Like I'll wash the dishes and put the laundry in and maybe even take it out, and then Johnny will fold it and put it away, and put the dishes away, too, but actually, the day I mean, it was the other way around. I was doing the putting-away, but that was because Johnny had washed and dried, so I was just doing my part.

Of course, I knew what Johnny meant because it was all over the news and everywhere. You know how it was last summer with the monuments, and with the football players and I know I'm supposed to have an opinion on it, but the right opinion depends on who you are talking to and I feel like I don't have that much skin in the game, you know? I mean, sure, we were taught that the monuments are there to remind us of our heritage or whatever, but people act like our heritage can't be bad, and like taking them away would dishonor the dead or something, but I feel like a statue is a statue is a statue. My Uncle Russ says what's next, they take down Mount Rushmore? But didn't we kill up all the Indians and take their holy ground and carve a bunch of Great White Fathers into it? So, like, maybe take that down, too, but Jesus Christ if I ever said that, I would get an earful, and the truth is I don't even care that much.

I remember when Dale Lubin got shot right in his fucking face and they ruled it a suicide, but come on, his hands were ziptied behind his back. Dale was just as white as me and Johnny, but he grew up poor and he was still poor, and when I think about the cops who shot him like that just going home to their families like nothing happened and just living their lives, I get real mad, and I have to stop thinking about it. That's what Johnny brings up every time someone mentions all the black kids getting shot in the news and he says, well, you didn't see fuckin' Dale's face all over CNN, and I mean, he's not wrong, but he's not right either.

Anyway, Johnny was talking about the football players kneeling during the "Star-Spangled Banner" and how when we were at Sunday dinner with his cousins last week everyone was talking about how disrespectful it is to the flag and the troops and that's what a lot of people are saying on TV and stuff, too, but I been watching football all my life, and since when do the players come out for the Anthem? Not since always, I'll tell you that much.

But I listened to Johnny gripe about it a minute while I folded clothes, and really, I was folding too slow because the smell of clothes fresh out the dryer is maybe the best smell in the entire Earth except for the smell of a baby's scalp.

Johnny said, "It's a goddamn disgrace is what it is," and that's the first time I felt it. Like I remember when I was real little, and my family would go up to see my Uncle Russ in Chicago at Christmas time. He had this big old house just all piled on top of itself. Like you'd go up a flight of stairs, and you'd think to yourself, that's it. No more house. Nobody would put more house on top of this much house. But when I started, I started on the ground floor where we always came in at the side door by the garage, and *of course* there was more house, because for one thing, stairs led down from there into the basement, but there was always more house. I would wake up in the twin bed at like five in the morning, and I could just feel the whole house full of family sleeping way above me and below me, and I knew I wasn't by myself and I knew that if criminals or monsters or like enemy soldiers busted in, there were a bunch of people who would literally fight to make sure they couldn't get at me and kill me, and it was the warmest feeling, and that was how I knew what love and family were. It was that kind of occupiedness-of-our-surroundings with other quieter folks.

Right then, it was like there were two of me. One of me was normal and listening to Johnny grouse about millionaire football players with so much money that they could take the time to disrespect the Flag before doing their goddamn job, but the other me was like a twin sister, a Siamese twin that had been asleep my whole life, but she was awake now, and she could feel that not-aloneness. She could feel someone else, and she did not know if that Someone Else would be willing to fight criminals or whoever to save her.

And Johnny said, "Honey. Hey. Earth to Alaina-Rose. Where you gone to?"

And I said, "Nowhere. I'm right here with you, Johnny Lamarque." Because it feels so good to hear him say my name, and it tastes so good to say his.

THE NEXT TIME I noticed was at work maybe a week later? There is this one guy named Ronald who is not even that old. He has MS, and also he's not right in the head, but I think the not-rightness is connected to his condition? Well, as soon as I started working there, my supervisor

Yvonne told me that Ronald doesn't believe a healthy person should have a bowel movement more than once a week, so he would just fight to hold it in as much as he could and when it came out, it was just god-awful. Yvonne showed me what to do and how to do it, and let me tell you, I will not mention any more of that because Christ alive. Anyway, I only mention it now because this was one of those days where Ronald lost the battle and actually went and I was getting rid of the stuff into the toilet, and trying not to really look at it, let alone smell it because like I said: Christ alive.

And I was in the middle of reaching for the toilet handle when I knew there was somebody else in the bathroom with me. That feeling of not-aloneness was stronger this time, and I mean, I know I'm only nineteen, but you know how it is when you experience something that's not in any of the movies or books that you've ever read or anything like that. Like, I mean, the hair did stand up along my arms, and I felt a sensation like cold wet fingertips touching the back of my neck, but there was more to it than that. There was kind of a sound that wasn't a sound like I read one time about this deaf guy who was near an explosion, and the closest he ever came to hearing anything was feeling the vibration of it through his feet? It was like that. It was like there was this sense that I wasn't born with, and something was trying to connect with it and had to translate itself to my body some other way.

And so I knew someone was with me, but I also knew that person wasn't paying any attention to me. Like I knew they were focused on themselves so that if I could see them, they would be standing at the sink staring at themselves in the mirror, but they were as aware of me as I was of them—but not quite, because I knew that if I turned around to look at the mirror, I would not see anyone there, and also there was not anybody there because the person I sensed was not a person.

I asked Yvonne about it when we were smoking together out back. I love her so much. She is an older mixed lady whose hair is so nice it looks like a wig. Like seriously, someone should take her hair and make wigs just like that in every color and sell them to drag queens at Fifi's and to anybody who wants to have just killer hair.

Yvonne tossed her fake-but-not-fake hair and was like, "You mean, like ghosts?"

And I said, "Yes. No. Yes, but not like ghosts." And I searched for an explanation with my free hand. "I mean, like, working here, did you ever feel like you weren't alone when you were sure you were alone, but not like there was a person there with you. Like, something that's not a person, that never was a person, but also isn't bad or scary?"

And she was like, "Girl, *what?*"

And I laughed, you know, and I said, "*Shit*, girl! You should see your face right now!"

And she didn't buy it at first. She was like, "Is you joking me?"

And I cackled, but realer than before, and I said, "*Come on!*"

BUT I KNOW there's no ghosts. Like, I *know*. If ghosts were a thing, my mom or my Grandma Rall would have come to me by now, and not only have they not contacted me, but I've never even felt them watching me. Any time I've seen them or talked to them in dreams, I could tell it wasn't them, that it was just more of me, you know? Like, in that one psych class I took at the community college back in Lafayette, Mr. Charm taught us about how other people in dreams aren't really other people, they're just also you representing people and other stuff to yourself. It makes sense because can you imagine if all the things and places you dreamed about were real? Where would they go when you wake up? Who would be responsible for clearing them away and storing them like the sets for high school drama productions and stuff?

I talked to Johnny about it, and he was like, "Those things and people aren't you. They're just projections created by your mind, and when you wake up, they're uncreated, and so they're just *not*." We were *punishingly* high.

But that makes even less sense to me. *Un*created? What is that? I took physics in high school, and my God, what a shit-show that was, but at least I know that you can't just *uncreate* matter or whatever. Like, it has to *go* somewhere. It has to become energy or something.

I think about that, sometimes. About what it would be like to be unborn. Uncreated. You would too, if you saw what I've seen.

*   *   *

OKAY, SO JOHNNY started picking up some work here and there. Like he would go in and be an extra on TV shows and in movies, and then Christy Darmody posted on Facebook that somebody dropped out of his monthly showcase he does at the Joy, *We There Yet* at the last minute. He needed anybody who could do a solid ten, and Johnny was the first one to step up, so just like that, he got on the show. This was a big deal. It was the first showcase Johnny got since we moved here, and it pays two hundred dollars.

I came home from work that night, and Johnny was in his greasepaint. He looked just like he did in high school, but without the dreds, and it blew me away. He was wearing a pineapple shirt and cargo shorts and sandals with socks, and I was like, *What...?*

He just looked me straight in the eye, and he was like, "I'm Hemi Boufee the Parrothead Juggalo. Gimme some Faygo and a cheeseburger, and *I'll eat that shit in paradise!*" I can't do it right, but it was a *scream*.

What Christy didn't tell anybody is that Vinny Doppler was in town doing that Stagecoach Mary movie and that he was doing half an hour to close. By the time we got to the Joy, word had gotten out, and the place was packed. Johnny did his ten, and people were howling. I looked at the crowd, and I saw the lights go on behind everybody's eyes the second he did his intro, and he leaned on that catch phrase without being hacky about it. He *destroyed*. Then Vinny came out and killed even harder. It was—God. It was the best.

In the green room after the show, Vinny saw Johnny after Johnny washed off his paint and was like, "Holy shit. I remember you from Laffy, my dude! Who turned you into a *comic*?"

Johnny was like a plant in one of those timelapse videos. He *unfurled*. He'd been eating shit at open mics for months, and now Vinny. Fucking. *Doppler* was calling him a *comic*.

VINNIE TOOK US everywhere that night. We went to *Titties and Ditties* at Candomble's. We went to the back room at Troy's. Johnny was beyond thrilled. He didn't even get a big head or anything. He just listened to everything Vinnie had to say.

I felt more of them, though. Beings like the one at work, like the one in the house that time. They were everywhere. All over the streets in the French Quarter. They threaded through the crowds on Frenchmen outside the jazz clubs and restaurants. They stood in with the audience at every club. They crowded into every bar. They are aware of us. They see us when we think we're alone.

The one at the apartment wasn't there when we got home. I don't know where it was, but it was just us in our little shotgun that night. I called in sick to work. I'm not one to do that. I'm not one to call in just because I'm hung over, but I was jumpy and out-of-it, and I knew there were more at the Home than the one that was with me in the bathroom.

"Hon, you okay?" Johnny asked me right before we turned in. "You seem a little weird."

"This has been the greatest night of your life," I said.

"Uh, yeah," he said. "Probably. Definitely. Definitely."

"Well, I'm your person, and I'm happy for you," I said. "More than happy. I'm ecstatic."

He looked at me for a long time, like he was trying to figure out if I was telling the truth. I was, though, and he could see it. He just nodded.

"So, let's talk about it in the morning."

I DREAMED OF Grandma Rall that night. Except it wasn't her. It wasn't me, either. It was one of them. We were back at Uncle Russ's house, and the smell of Christmas dinner cooking was all through the house. Seafood dressing. Dirty rice. Etoufée. Mirlitons. And pies: mincemeat, strawberry rhubarb, chess pie.

Grandma Rall sat at the kitchen table, her back to me. She was naked, and I could see the rolls of fat at her sides. I knew it wasn't her, but I felt bad for her. I felt bad that the thing had her body just *out* like that. She would have been so embarrassed.

I asked it what it wanted from me.

It turned in the chair, and I almost saw its face. I backed up against the dishwasher and the dishwasher turned on. Startled me. It started gesturing with its hands, with both its hands—and I couldn't quite see everything it was doing. I understood just like it was speaking clearly like you and me right now.

no

"What do you mean? Why are you watching us?"

nearby

"What are you watching for? What are you hoping to see?"

nothing seek nothing except

"Except? Except what?"

for under the blown apart without wholeness unkind of mercy

"What?" An aching feeling stole over me then. It was like loneliness, but not. It was like a song I'd heard but didn't quite remember. It was like being at the wrong end of a telescope, and then being crowded out of myself.

It stopped answering. It was—The whole time, I felt like it was extremely difficult for it to communicate with me. Like, it would pause for a long time after everything I said, and then it would answer, like it was translating my words to itself. When it stopped responding, it was like it had reached the end of its ability to understand or to make itself understood, and so it just dropped its borrowed hands to either side of the chair and waited.

I willed myself awake and there was blood on both sheets. My period had started in the night.

JOHNNY WAS GONE all day and into the evening. It didn't occur to me until he texted around four that he was with Vinny on the set. In the meantime, I tried to go for a walk in City Park, but *they* were everywhere. They stood on the neutral grounds, staring at traffic. They were out front of every home and every business, and I knew they were inside, too. There are so many of them. So so many.

I called my friend Eileen from JP's and asked her if she'd felt anything weird. I explained.

"Naw, baby, that's fucked up. So they like ghosts, but not ghosts?"

"They're not ghosts. They're—They were never alive. They're too alien, but I don't think that's even the right word, because I think maybe they've always been here."

"Damn. But, like, they out of phase, or some shit? Like they live at a angle to us?"

"Right! That's right!" I said. I almost jumped up and down. "Like if you could turn in exactly the right direction, or see from exactly the right angle, they'd be there. But you can't, because the angle doesn't exist."

"You should talk to my cousin Pharell. He teaches astronomy at Tulane. He know all about Planck signals and baryons and shit."

"What the fuck is a baryon?"

"Girl, don't start me to lying," Eileen said. "That's some shit he mentioned at Mamaw house don't make a lick of muhfuckin sense."

TALKING TO EILEEN made me feel better. She was always good for a laugh, and it didn't solve my problem, but I put her suggestion in my back pocket, you know? Like it made me feel better that there was a thing I hadn't done yet that I could do. Once I had that, I didn't feel like I even needed to come see you. I couldn't stop thinking about the thing from my dream, and I knew I'd have to talk to somebody—like some authority or something, eventually. I just wish I'd—I wish I'd talked to someone before it happened.

nothing seek not except

Word salad. Like you hear from a schizo street person, but—except I knew it wasn't. I knew it had told me something important.

Johnny was lit when he got home. It was no big deal—he'd earned himself some leeway, the way he'd been busting his ass. He kissed me hello and plopped down in front of the TV and started flipping through channels. More of the same. The President daring North Korea to nuke us. Pundits yelling at each other on the news. Shootings. Beatings. Rapes. Torture basements. I couldn't take it. I went to bed early.

*   *   *

I WOKE TO Johnny standing in the bedroom doorway, blinking at me through a haze of pot smoke and too many beers. "Hey," I said.

He didn't answer right away, and in the silence, I realized that something—some thing—stood between us. And you know what? It wasn't so bad. For the first time, I was as aware of one of them as I would have been of anybody else, and it wasn't frightening or off-putting. It just *was*.

"Hey," Johnny said, finally.

"Come to bed?"

"Have I...? Have I been a asshole?" he said.

"What?"

"Did I ignore you?" he said. "Did I get too wrapped up in my shit?"

"No," I said. "You didn't do anything wrong."

I reached out to him, and he took a step toward me. I don't know. It can't be as simple as he bumped into it. It must be more than that. We bump into them all the time. We *must*.

Do—Did you ever draw? You know how you'll make a mistake and go to erase it right away, but you're using a shitty pencil eraser instead of one of those good ones? And you're kind of mad at yourself for making the mistake in the first place, and you'll do a shitty, hasty job? It was like that. There was no blood or anything, it just smeared him into the air.

He tried to scream, but he didn't have a mouth anymore. Not quite. He reached for me.

I didn't move. I didn't make a sound.

It bore down harder, and then he was *gone*.

So, HERE I am, for all the good it'll do. I came to you because it was a thing I could still do. I'm sorry to unload like this, but there's nothing else—what else can I do? It's okay that you don't believe me. There's not going to be any trouble. The cops aren't after me. The world has already altered itself so that Johnny was never anything or anyone. My memories of him are fading. I probably won't remember his name by the time we're done here.

When it happens to me, you'll forget me, too. Everyone will. I'll make a wrong move, and one of them will erase me, and the world will reorder itself, and that'll be it. I'm telling you this because I think I know what the thing in my dream was trying to tell me. They see us, and they—they—they don't know what to make of us one way or the other. We're here and they're here, and it's like whatever. But Juh—Juhh—my boyfriend—my fiancé—? He did something one didn't like, and it decided about him, and it removed him. It could happen to any of us any time. It does.

What will we do if they all decide at once?

BURN THE SHIPS
Alberto Yáñez

THERE ARE NO obsidian blades in the camp. The Dawncomer guards have learned enough to make sure that no ritual knives get smuggled in. Without obsidian, Quineltoc can't spill blood properly—he can't keep the law, can't observe the rites of the Living Lord as a man of God must. The ghost-colored invaders who came from beyond the rising sun trust in their vigilance and in their cold technology to protect them. It does.

The People make do. They've had to, for over a decade now—ever since the Dawncomers laid aside any pretense of friendliness and openly usurped the Emperor's power. But there is always the Lord.

Quineltoc keeps faith.

It'll be enough.

Surely.

But tonight, need drives him, as relentless as a snakedriver's whip. He sneaks into a tight corner between the latrines, hidden from the sight of the guards. The stench of watery shit and piss is thick despite the cold, dry winter night. It's long after curfew and he'll be shot on sight, but Quineltoc is alone for the first time in months. In an overcrowded hell, solitude itself is almost worth the risk.

The wind picks up and moves the clouds across the blue-black sky, revealing stars glinting like frozen tears on the bruised face of night. The waning quarter moon gives little light, and Quineltoc shivers as he contemplates the dark between the stars. His copper brown skin, sallow from poor rations and exhaustion, tightens and prickles as he shivers. The *Tzitzimimeh* dwell in the vast emptiness.

He doesn't precisely *fear* the dark goddesses, orthodox man that he is. *God's sisters made willing sacrifices,* he reminds himself. *The Bone Women gave their lives for the Living Lord, for His law.* The law itself keeps the People safe, and he keeps the law.

Their blood, their flesh, to nourish Him.

The grey hair on the back of his neck stands up. He tells himself it's the biting wind that makes him feel small and naked under the pitiless stars.

Quineltoc steels his faith and straightens his back, ignores the cold, and starts to softly chant the bloodletting prayers. He takes a shard of bone out of the pocket of his thin grey pants. Carefully, he doesn't think from who that bone came, and focuses on the prayers he uttered as he honed the shard's point, whetted on hope and dismay. He shivers again, harder—shudders—and pulls the sleeve of his dirty smock back, slicing the flesh of his left forearm. The red blood is black in the shadowed starlight.

He *should* call out, proud, happy at an offering given, voice ringing like a bronze temple bell to proclaim his bloodletting, but the guards would hear him. After a long moment trembling in the cold, Quineltoc is able to focus. The year's count is ending soon, and with the power of time turning behind his prayers, Quineltoc hopes that the Lord will listen despite the lack of incense and obsidian.

Maybe provide a different answer.

The wind dies down and Quineltoc hears nothing beyond himself and the blood surf, deafening, in his ears. The pounding of each heartbeat one more note in a space where experience and grace have taught him to expect to hear the voice of God.

Ba-dum.

Ba-dum.

Silence.

Ba-dum.

Even with no incense to carry his pleas surely God will hear him? *Answer!* he thinks deep inside himself, and then stifles the demand.

Ever since he was newly a man and became the youngest lawspeaker of the People of the Starry Codex, the voice of God has answered him at prayers. More than forty years. Now, with the scent of misery the only incense, Quineltoc dreads the reply.

Silence.

Ba-dum.

Exhorting the Lord is difficult, but hopelessness is harder. Quineltoc prays, silent words shaping his cracked lips in curves of agony and devotion.

Ba-dum.

He lets out a mangled cry, barely remembering to muffle his despair with his dirty, chapped hands. A dog barks on the other side of the camp.

The lawspeaker, who had been called to walk before the Living Lord, falls to his knees in the icy muck. In fragmented silence between heartbeats, Quineltoc hears a small, still voice, giving him the answer he has heard before:

Guide the People to Me, Quineltoc. Help them be willing. I am so hungry. Nourish Me.

Ba-dum.

Ba-dum.

"No."

Cital has heard that word from her husband more times in the last week of arguments than in the nearly forty years spent together before it. She can tell that the argument feels ancient, endless, to the both of them.

"What other choice do we have?" Cital demands. Her voice is thick with stowed rage writhing like a fire axolotl in her guts, with the tears that she's refused to shed since she watched a Dawncomer guard shoot their daughter Shochi four months ago. Her dark eyes are dry in her prematurely-lined brown face. Three decades since the massive invasion fleet turned their world inside out on a fine spring dawn. The new sun had been huge and red, staining the sky, the Sunrise Gate opening from an old, strange world.

The Empire of the Land Between the Waters had grown accustomed to the almost random trickle of small refugee boats over the previous century, their half-drowned sailors bedraggled like mangy golden rats fleeing chaos from an unfathomable somewhere behind the sunrise. The Dawncomers had just been pale, yellow-haired jetsam on the eastern shores, easily welcomed curiosities. But then they came in great blazing ships teeming with their survivors, unwelcome arrivals with guns and plague and their foreign god, slowly taking over everything.

Citlal has lost almost everyone she's cared for in a long and fortunate life except her husband, her godly man who refuses to understand what must be done. They are in one of the warehouses the Dawncomers use to keep up the pretense that these are *work* camps. The other captives ignore their whispered argument out of respect and familiarity. The scent of old boots and cloaks stripped off at gunpoint makes the chilly air musty as the stolen goods move down the conveyer belt with typical Dawncomer efficiency. The usurpers brought cold mechanical technology with them, and it was impervious to the living magics the People use. Their casual illnesses had killed multitudes throughout the Empire, hitting magebloods the worst, eviscerating the effectiveness of the People's priests and magicians. Centuries of order toppled, the Emperor's power turned into empty ceremony and yea-saying.

"So we just *wait* for God to save us?" Citlal is so beyond frustration with her husband that it's hard work to remember anything but her anger. "How long do we cling to prayer? Do we just *wait* for God to kill the Dawncomers? We could *act*—"

"And if we *were* to do it... if we commit that *sin*, what will we be?"

"Alive."

Quineltoc closes his eyes. Citlal's point is sharp, like all of the cactus spine reasoning of her arguments across their lives. As sharp and relentless as her anger is, she knows that he argues reasons—*truths*—that he devoutly hopes she'll accept. She fights the urge to count them off on her fingers as he repeats himself, his tone a perfectly logical hammer to knap away the flint of her resolve. "The face of the Living Lord would turn from us! The Sunset Gate would be closed shut to everyone we would 'save.' No reunion with our people in the next world beyond the west! The *Tzitzimimeh* will eat our souls!"

"And probably make dresses out of our bones, too!" she retorts, childhood story truths made glib and fierce by the effort not to yell.

Quineltoc stops sorting dead women's shoes for a moment, breathing hard at her. As a wisewife of the People, Citlal knows the laws that bind magic since the Living Lord rose. She understands the way order limits chaos, like the stars fixing the dark sky. She *knows*, bone true, the reasons for the laws that forbid the action she urges. Invoking the Dead Sisters *is* dangerous, especially with the Temple Major— the place where the divine presence of utter night could safely touch mortal earth—now rubble under Dawncomer boots.

Quineltoc sighs and enunciates clearly at her, as if to a foreigner: "Every one of us lost."

"What good is salvation if the spirit of the People is dead, Quineltoc?" she counters. She sorts a feathered green hat out of the hodgepodge, twiggy fingers nimble but aching in the cold. "They captured every single mageblood on orders from their Hierophant."

"The Lord saved us before. We need to trust and obey." His earnestness is painful. It reminds her of the kind young man who won her heart with marigolds and poetry during the first years of their marriage.

"Quineltoc, it isn't half-dead refugees begging for sanctuary!" She repeats her own list of inarguable facts. "*All* of the Dawncomers remaining have come now, and they're tired of *us* living in *their* new home. *They burned all their ships*. They *can't* go back through the Sunrise Gate. And there's only room for themselves in their vision of the world," Citlal spits the words out like cactus gall. "And God doesn't care."

"Of course He does, but it's not for us to decide how He shows it! We made a pact: He gave men magic, and we swore that we were His! If the Lord chooses that we die here... we'll sing hymns to His light as we do it."

Citlal knows that her husband's faith is straight and true. He's heard the voice of God. He knows what certainty is.

Doubt is new, and grown bitterly familiar.

It's ash, she thinks. Black ash falling from the sky on the days when the People's corpses are burnt, ash on her tongue that God says nothing to her husband now.

"We can only do it during the Dead Days, Quineltoc. End-Year comes in two days, and we *won't* last another year. If you help, all the People will rise up!" She takes a breath and then she whispers, "Please." He purses his lips together so tightly that they almost disappear and looks away, pretending absorption in sorting stolen shoes.

Citlal counts to five, and five again, and exhales. Her anger settles, like a pot of chocolate moved off—but still near—the flame. She continues, admitting to heretical magic, "I used women's blood and the night wind to speak to the wisewives in the other camps and reservations." *There are so few of us left.* She continues. "The Dawncomers are planning another purge in three days, through *all* of the camps. They won't burn the bodies for at least a few days after that. They dole out our misery to feed their own god, damn them. I think they're offering *us* as a sacrifice, but we can appeal to the *Tzitz—*"

He shakes his head no, grey hair a scraggly storm about his head. "Citlal, *no*. The other lawspeakers in the camp agree with me."

She snorts, and throws a fine turquoise spidersilk shawl into a sorting bin. "You mean none of them dare disagree with the great lawspeaker Quineltoc! We will *all* die." She pauses, deliberate. "*They killed Shochi.* And if they *are* feeding us to their god, do any of our souls even make it past the Sunset Gate to the next world?"

He throws out his hands, negating the possibility. "Shochi *is* in God's keeping," he says, almost reasonable. Then his voice hardens. "And I refuse to be the one to keep us apart for eternity."

Citlal's shoulders slump and her head dips, lank black hair streaked with silver-white obscuring her face. She knows that tone in her husband's voice. He won't countenance the magic that could save them, not if it embraces the dark between the stars.

She reminds herself that he's a good man, a godly man. The Living Lord has spoken with him. The People use his name as another word for rectitude, for devotion, for wisdom.

She reminds herself.

A good man who only sees God.

She will not be so blind.

* * *

THERE ARE FIVE Dead Days between End-Year on the night of the Festival of Gates and the start of the new year. Five days when the doors between the worlds of the living and the dead are open and the skeletal Dead Sisters of the Living Lord stride unhindered across the living world. Then, with the sunrise start of the Day of New Fire, God sets the divine glyph on the lists of the living and the dead after making the year's bargain with His sisters, and shuts the gates.

One of the prayers the People sing to guard them in the dark tells of the grim and beautiful bat-winged Obsidian Butterfly, the Lady of the Knife, eldest of His sisters. She is set to mark down all the living and list, as God so decides and the *Tzitzimimeh* agree, the deaths in the coming year: *who by fire, who by water, who by old age...*

They are the Living Lord's People, praying and keeping God's laws with the magebloods to guide them. *Who by falling, who by plague...* Citlal has never liked that prayer. She doesn't find comfort in its cosmic certainty.

The People have kept the laws as best they can, watching the Dawncomers abandon slyness and rise to real power over the past decade. *They're* the strangers now, forbidden to rebuild the great pyramid Temple Major in the heart of the old capital. Still, the People have adapted.

Who by strangulation, who by thirst, who by willing sacrifice...

Quineltoc hid his face when the guard shot their daughter Shochi, and murmured the prayer recited upon receiving news of a death in the stillness after the gunshot: *Blessed be the Living Lord, the keeper of life.*

The guards tossed their daughter's body on a pile with others: grandmothers, the gold stolen from their teeth to make wire for machines; children, stomachs distended and arms stick-like with hunger; lame men, who could not work fast enough, bludgeoned to death with rifle butts... A daughter, beloved.

Who by gunshot... she whispers, adding a new death to the ancient litany.

She will never forgive Quineltoc for looking away.

*   *   *

END-YEAR GATHERS ITSELF in the rising dusk, the prayers of the magebloods exhaling softly into the night. Across the Empire, the rest of the People—less devout and free enough, if burdened and afraid—accommodate the usurpers' orders for no public ceremonies. But in every camp and reservation where they have been packed into across the Land, the magebloods of the People of the Starry Codex observe the rites as best they can, makeshift and brave.

It's a ragged chant. Voices falter as physical weakness from short rations and exhaustion robs their breath, yet the chant is kept. The guards don't bother to forbid them song with so many voices unable to ring out.

East-facing, the barracks' door is in direct sight of the guards, so Citlal crawls out under the women's barracks on the west side of the camp.

A few of the other women have guessed at Citlal's plan. Some of the mothers and elderly nanas even approve. One, an old kitchen witch from a fishing village on the sunset coast, gave her a blue silk purse smuggled out of the sorting line so that Citlal could gather the earth and ashes she needs.

Citlal clings to the shadows and makes her cautious way to the women's barracks on the north side of the camp, carrying the full purse next to her heart. The remaining wisewives in the camp have berths in the northern barracks. In the other camps across the Empire, every wisewife left gathers as well. They hope to accomplish the task, together.

Borrowing a sliver of the rising power of the first night of the Dead Days and retracing the initial steps of the *Tzitzimimeh*'s dance, Citlal says a word and cloaks herself in a bit of darkness and misdirection. The guards don't look her way; their dogs whine, but don't bark. She passes through the northern barracks' door and it doesn't creak. As thin as she's become, she doesn't have to open it very far.

The cutting night wind blows her along. Ce-Mishtlin and Yoal, the other two wisewives still alive in their camp, are waiting just inside the door. Ce-Mishtlin is short, dark brown, pretty, an aquiline-nosed young woman from one of the southern tribes of the People. Her spectacles are wire-rimmed, and the right lens has a small asterisk crack flaring in from the outer edge. The cheekbone underneath is bruised and inflamed. Citlal recognizes the marks left by a heavy fist and is careful to kiss a greeting on Ce-Mishtlin's other cheek.

Yoal is several years older than Citlal, with the pale fawn skin and plaited black hair of the northern tribes, and her skin sags, missing pounds. She had once been tall, beautiful and fat, but now Yoal is deflated and slack from six months in the camp. Citlal meets Yoal's agate-dark eyes and takes her hand, nodding her respect. Determination glints like starshine in Yoal's eyes.

The wisewives head to a dark corner of the barracks, passing crowded bunks full of women chanting softly. As they walk by, the women fall silent and then resume praying after they pass, an exhalation that carries them aloft like a murmuration. Citlal is glad that they haven't reached the portion of the rites where they'll sing of the Obsidian Butterfly.

Once the three women reach the vacant bit of floor against the western wall that Ce-Mishtlin and Yoal have claimed as workspace, they sit down in a triangle, propped on knees bent, legs underneath them. They are as alone as they can be in the stuffed barracks; the women berthed in the near bunks have all moved away to the other side of the building to give them respectful privacy, or out of fear of their power.

Ce-Mishtlin pulls a sheet of soft brown codex bark-paper out from underneath her grey smock and places it between them. The camp sub-commander had drafted her to be his secretary and bedwarmer. Unwelcomed but useful, the positions give Ce-Mishtlin access to some supplies and news from outside the camp, which is how they learned that the purge was coming.

Yoal lays three steel pins next to the sheet of paper. They're mismatched hatpins stolen from the sorting lines. One has a brass butterfly for a head, another a coral bead, and the third has a cloisonné sun in blue-green, a turquoise solar disc worked against a black background. A symbol of the People's faith, it must have belonged to a pious woman. Citlal opens the blue silk purse and sets it down next to the other items, careful that the earth and ashes don't spill.

They prepare the sheet of the bark-pulp paper first, taking turns with a small, sharp letter opener that Ce-Mishtlin stole to create a lacy cutout frame a couple of finger's breadth from the edge of the sheet. Then, they join hands and wills to charge the sheet with potential and promise, and link it to the other items. It's the simplest part of the magic, linking an object to another so that they entwine fates. It's legitimate, even sanctifying, as when the lawspeakers write out the marriage contracts for a new couple. The paper will bind whatever contract is written upon it with the other items.

The pins are next. Ce-Mishtlin takes up the red-beaded one, Yoal the butterfly. Citlal's lips compress briefly in hollow black humor at picking up the devout woman's hatpin. Her grandmother, who was pious and god-fearing, had an obsidian pendant marked in the same way. Citlal accepts her own apostasy.

The women murmur words of binding, followed by a kitchen prayer of blessing, and each pricks her wrist with her pin, a minor bloodletting so the red blood beads up and coats the steel stem. A moment later, the pins gleam bright again, the blood absorbed into their metal hearts. Each pin is now an instrument of the will of the wisewife who fed it her blood. This magic is ambivalent in the eyes of the lawspeakers... and as such, forbidden.

Moving quickly to slay doubt or fear, Citlal commits to the next, darker working, and stabs her still-bleeding wrist with her pin to make the blood flow freely. She grits her teeth against the pain and places her wrist above the purse to let the blood stream into the thirsty earth and ashes. Yoal and Ce-Mishtlin do the same. This willing sacrifice of blood and life force is deeply profane and terribly unwise outside of the safe and sanctified bounds of the destroyed Temple Major. They keep their wrists there until the blood stops flowing. When they remove their wrists, their skins are whole and clean; each bears only a faint scar.

Inside the silk purse, the earth and ash and blood are liquid, a black ink that smells incongruously of hearth smoke and mortuary incense as it slowly churns with the power the women channel from the death of the year and the dark between the stars and their beating hearts. What's writ in this ink will be inscribed upon the world. The stories the wisewives teach one another say that this knowledge was shared by the *Tzitzimimeh* when they danced out of the void. It happened long ago, before the Bone Women gave up their lives so that their stillborn younger brother could become the Living Lord. The magic is grim, and all the more so for the ashes of those who were once their kin.

Citlal chants the first line of the wise-work, and Ce-Mishtlin repeats it as Citlal starts the second, and Yoal joins the round as Citlal reaches the third line.

Each chants the song three times through, and as Yoal's voice finishes ringing out on the last phrase, the three jab their pins into the night's blood. There's a small glimmer like faint starlight and slowly the inky stuff is absorbed by the pins in the same way as their blood was. The hatpins can write in the language of the world now, each stylus an instrument of dark and needful magic. Outside, the night wind howls, in fury or approval, and then shushes as if silenced.

Citlal looks at her sister-magicians and sees the exhaustion she feels mirrored in their faces. Yoal's face droops, wrinkled more deeply than before. Ce-Mishtlin is greyish, the dark brown of her complexion sallow and drained, the bruise on her cheekbone a vivid purple.

There's one more major part to the wise-work that's left, which will have to wait until after the purge.

It's that portion of the wise-work, Citlal knows, that will damn them. Ce-Mishtlin and Yoal accept it, and so does she.

THE PURGE IS quick.

The Dawncomers are nothing if not efficient. In the late morning sun, old men, howling women, the remaining small children, girls who don't look at the guards, boys who glare, men who aren't broken quite enough—they all are chosen and pushed forward into ranks. In every camp, the Dawncomers form a line, raise their rifles, and shoot. Most of the soldiers aim for the head or heart, but a few enjoy taking gut shots.

The prisoners don't run—where would they hide, what darkness would cover them?

Some of the People are defiant, looking straight into their murderers' eyes. Others wail in despair. A few sing, the ancient doxology their last words:

Hear the Living Lord: the Living Lord is God. The Living Lord lives!

Thousands die.

It cuts Quineltoc to watch, but he does it. He looked away once, and he can't do so again. It's part of his duty to bear witness, to acknowledge the beauty of the People's faith and the Living Lord's plans, even as it hurts his soul. Most of the People never speak directly with God, never hear His terrible reply, but every child of the People grows up believing that God will always hear that prayer.

Hear the Living Lord: the Living Lord is God. The Living Lord lives!

Quineltoc wills himself not to question, and repeats his prayer.

As THE RETORTS of the rifles sound across the camp, Citlal and Yoal and Ce-Mishtlin are mostly alone in Citlal's barracks. Facing each other with hands linked one to one to one, the blank contract and the charged hatpin styluses in the middle, the three women raise their arms and sing out, capturing the power of the deaths of their murdered people and adding it to their joined will.

In other camps, other wisewives do the same.

None have any pretense that this is anything other than necromantic abomination, perhaps even an invitation to the skeletal Dead Sisters to come and claim them all. But it must be done if any of the magebloods—the sacred heart of the People—are to survive and make the People whole again.

The Emperor has abandoned them, and the Living Lord has abandoned them, and the lawspeakers would rather the magebloods die unprofaned than take this step. But the women all spoke together through the night wind and the power of their own blood, and although a few wisewives dissented or abstained from condoning the plan, they concur: if God will not understand, what good is God?

The power streams like silent black lightning, rising above them in a column of energy holding up the stars. Their faces are skull-like in that light, the littlest dead sisters. With a final unison shriek, they bring their arms down, and the power slashes down, too, concentrating on the paper and the pins.

Written in a hand not any of theirs, the glyph for *night* appears on the sheet of codex paper. It's the glyph of the *Tzitzimimeh.*

Nodding in grim satisfaction, Citlal kneels to pick up her pin and wields it to write a word on the signed contract. It's the glyph for *fire*. It means *life*. The dry hatpin stylus leaves rich black ink behind, fathomless in its depth.

The other wisewives write out the same glyph, Ce-Mishtlin in careful block marks as neat as a printed sign, Yoal in spidery, old-fashioned scribe's hand.

They based their wise-work on the story of Lotli, the lawspeaker who centuries ago defended the People in the outland jungle city of Braj against the persecution of a mad king. The People were wanderers then, having not yet reached the Land Between the Waters. Lotli animated a man of clay and wood to fight the king's soldiers.

Braj was a small city, the quarter assigned to the People easily defended by one protector. There were trees and plenty of clay on the shores of the river that ran through the city's heart.

The bare prison camps are each much larger than Braj, and have no clay.

But the wisewives have other material at hand.

IT'S WOMEN'S WORK to prepare the dead amongst the Dawncomers, just as it is amongst the People. No one notices that Citlal, Ce-Mishtlin, and Yoal are late to join the other women, and no one comments as they mark the bodies with their styluses. The black ink is just another stain, one more splatter, before it sinks past the skin and into the bones of the dead.

The men keep laboring in the warehouses. A few are ordered to help the women drag the bodies into stacks. As thin as the corpses are, they pile comfortably, like cordwood.

The dead lie there.

One of the men, a young dropout from a *kalmekak*, the traditional schools of the law and magic, does notice Yoal marking the body of a half-blood musician who used to play trumpet in the capital symphony. He objects: "What are you doing? That's—" but a look and a whispered word from Yoal render him mute. He may never talk again.

The power the wisewives now carry is awful, equal parts terror and glory. Each might destroy a battalion with a gesture and four words, but she would die doing it. That could leave the *Tzitzimimeh* dancing free across the flesh of the land, limitless, and the magebloods would stay in the camps until the Dawncomers killed them all. And there are no guarantees: the Dawncomers integrate their tiny mechanisms into their bodies, their technology leaving them mostly spell-proof.

Citlal knows that they are all a little drunk with the power. It's headier than agave liquor after a fast. She could make the Dawncomers pay a steep blood price right now, but she knows that the power will grow if they wait. Each day that draws nearer to the Last Night before the Day of New Fire will increase their strength. Each night, unseen by human eyes, the Bone Women dance with greater frenzy. Pinpoint blooms of light burst and die in the wisewives' dark eyes, and even the fiercest old women in the camps, who long for blood and vengeance, avoid meeting their gaze.

Meanwhile, the dead lie there.

THE DAYS PASS quickly, the weather turning colder. The thin barracks walls whistle when the wind blows. The chill keeps the stacked bodies from bloating, although watchful eyes would note that there has been no decay.

Listening ears might hear a susurrus coming from the piles of the dead.

The sound is a prayer.

Any of the People could tell them it's the song of the Obsidian Butterfly, but none of the Dawncomers notice it.

"IT'S DONE, QUINELTOC," Citlal tells him. Her voice is a little hoarse with strain.

He's not looking at his wife. He's trying to take in the quality of the light. The sunlight is golden in the hour before sunset. Standing in the open gravel lot in the middle of the camp that the Dawncomers use for ranking up the prisoners, the light is beautiful. It's the exact color of the dress Quineltoc's daughter was wearing when they were herded onto the train cars, and it lends the dirty pall of the killing ground an unexpected dignity. Seen in a reflection of Shochi's beauty, even this place is momentarily transformed for him.

Then he understands Citlal's words.

A hole in the world opens under him, the shape of his faith, of his heart, of his daughter. He could feel the power moving on End-Year night, enormous, but he couldn't read it. He recognized it as wisewife magic, beyond the bounds of orthodox knowledge.

The power raised from the executions of their people had gone unnoticed in his own grief. Necromancy was so foreign to lawspeaker magic that he couldn't have discerned its shape against the glare of souls departing.

There is no way for him to stop it. The power Citlal has used is outside the scope of the law. The pact between the Living Lord and the People of the Starry Codex is broken. It must be.

He blinks back tears—the light is still golden and is in his eyes—and says, "Thank you for telling me, Citlal." Then he walks away back to the men's barracks on the east side of the camp.

The light remains golden until he reaches the barracks.

LAST NIGHT FALLS; the Day of New Fire will begin with sunrise. The Living Lord will affix His divine glyph on the lists of the living and the dead after haggling with the *Tzitzimimeh*. The Dead Days will be over. Once, the new year's first holy fires would have been kindled atop the Temple Major with crystal lenses under the noon sun.

Citlal huddles for warmth with Ce-Mishtlin and Yoal in the twilight. They exchange tired hugs, then walk down the path to where the bodies of the murdered remain stacked. Ce-Mishtlin read orders that tomorrow the Dawncomers will make the prisoners take the corpses to the mechanical pyres. For so many reasons, tonight is the time to act.

Ce-Mishtlin has had proud, sleepy word from the man whose bed she's been forced to warm that the Hierophant himself is touring the camps and the reservations. The wisewives will be glad to receive him.

*   *   *

QUINELTOC THE LAWSPEAKER stands in the entrance to his barracks, the wood-framed building creaking loudly in the sudden wind. He recognizes that the wind isn't natural, that it's the movement of numinous power reflected in the physical world. The Dawncomers claim that their cold technology prevents such things, but there is power and then there is *power*.

Nothing in the course of the bitter years between their peoples would have prepared the Dawncomers for what is about to happen. They do not know the *Tzitzimimeh*.

He hears the high sound of a single sustained note from across the camp. It shouldn't carry that far, but it does. It's the trained voice of a wisewife in full exercise of her magic. It's Citlal, singing in a high, clear soprano. Quineltoc hears another voice join in, an alto harmonizing; Ce-Mishtlin, he thinks. Then, the crystalline clarity of Yoal's voice, slightly deeper than Citlal.

Wordless, the voices braid power between them. Quineltoc can't see the energy the way he can see the glow of the lawspeaker script he uses to write his own magic, but it would be impossible for a trained magician not to register some sense of this. He crosses the threshold and walks toward the singing.

He thinks he knows what to expect, but there's no being ready for the sight of the corpses of their people rising and moving as if with their own volition. Each one, he can see, has been giving a bit of life, marked with the glyph for fire. He thought that Citlal had hoped to get him to animate protectors from whatever materials they could find or steal, but this...

Quineltoc spies Citlal and her companions standing together, a sheet of codex bark-paper glowing to his lawspeaker's vision. Even at a distance, he can read "fire," *life,* inscribed upon it in three different hands. He stumbles when he sees the glyph for *night*. He recognizes the contract, and understands how the wisewives have been able to animate so many. The part of him that's a scholar admires his wife's genius. The part of him that insists he trust the Living Lord is afraid and wants to beg forgiveness for Citlal's transgression.

Dawncomer soldiers arrive in confused clumps, and don't notice the three women in the midst of the chaos. When they realize that the milling crowd is made up of the murdered, they close ranks and ready their guns.

The women's song changes and shifts into the wordless melody of the song of the Obsidian Butterfly—the litany of deaths. It sounds like the music of skeletons dancing.

The animated People begin to walk toward the Dawncomers, their dead eyes shining with a cold starry light. The faces of the dead are grim: there is no burning revenge in their expressions, no glint of justice. There's only enough life in them to make clear the certainty of death for the Dawncomers before them. Somewhere in the silence between heartbeats, a teasing ribbon of skeletal laughter is heard by everyone in the camp.

Quineltoc wants to clamp his hands over his ears, but he knows that won't stop the sound. He hears a frightened soldier call out to his foreign god and another cry out for his mother. Another starts to shoot at the closing crowd, releasing them all to do the same. They yell obscenities as they fire.

The bullets do not stop the dead.

One of the guards, a tall red-bearded man whom Quineltoc recognizes as a mostly decent man, for a killer, shakes his head in denial at what's happening. The guard shoots the animated corpse of a woman marching toward him, but the bullets don't stop her, nor does his wildly hammering rifle butt once he runs out of bullets. When she closes with the red man, she grasps him by the shoulder with one hand and throws him down. Rising up on his knees, the man keens in fear, but with a hooked strike, the woman rips his jaw away and his cries are lost in blood. A revivified child aids her with little hands that rip clothes, skin, intestines. Quineltoc wants to look away as his murdered folk begin tearing the soldiers apart, but he doesn't. Eyes open, he focuses on his wife singing, audible to him over the soldiers' screams.

Lifetimes later, once the sounds of tearing flesh stop and the screaming ends, the raised dead move on, swifter now perhaps that they've tasted blood. They head toward the stream of Dawncomers attempting to get away. The usurpers don't get far before the dead catch them.

It goes on like that for hours.

IN THE MORNING light, the carnage is incredible. Limbs and heads and feet are strewn about like the aftermath of an explosion in an abattoir. The stench of blood and spilled bowels is a foul blanket, heavy even with the wind that has not stopped since last night. Quineltoc stood witness the entire time, watching the soldiers trying to evade the righteous dead. They all failed.

Inside the camp administration building, other former prisoners are using the wireless radio to contact the other camps. The wisewives' plan worked in all of them, but there were many casualties. Quineltoc mourns all the lives lost, even the Dawncomers', but does it quietly. Privately, and with weightier grief, he mourns the aching silence: the absent small, still voice. He doesn't have the heart to explain to his people that while they might be alive, they are damned.

Even illusory joy is a blessing after the horror they've endured. It'll be soon enough that he'll need to tell them that they are no longer the Living Lord's own and will never see their loved ones who have already passed through the Sunset Gate into the next world beyond the west.

Quineltoc takes a deep breath and goes to search for his wife. He finds her outside the soldiers' mess, sitting on the wide green fender on the back of a Dawncomer armored car.

Citlal looks proud and defiant and strong to him, sitting there in her dirty grey prison smock. He thinks about the first time he'd met her, eighteen years old on the day before their wedding—their parents had been old-fashioned and arranged it all—and how beautiful she'd been, golden brown and flush-cheeked, clear brown eyes dancing. He'd thought himself very lucky, a student of the law to whom God had already spoken, about to marry a beautiful girl with power and learning of her own. He has loved her for almost forty years. But the words come of their own accord, the impulse deeper than reason: "*Quineltoc-ne amo-namictili Citlal-te.*"

They're in the Nawa, the holy tongue, the one the People use for blessings, rites, and spells.

"I, Quineltoc, divorce you, Citlal."

He's a lawspeaker. His words are enough to make—unmake—a blessing, a curse, a rite, a marriage.

It's simple enough.

He's shocked himself, but Citlal just laughs. It's a deep, appreciative laugh, the kind only long-time lovers or intimate friends who know each other's every secret can laugh. It's the laugh of delight that comes when someone does exactly what you know they'll do, and you love them for it.

It's a wife's laugh at the folly of her husband, and that's when Quineltoc knows that he can accept the silence of God if he can but hear Citlal laugh like that for the rest of his life.

AFTER SPENDING AN hour with Quineltoc not really saying much aloud, Citlal goes to the communications room in the camp headquarters. Yoal and Ce-Mishtlin are sitting there talking quietly at a small table. Ce-Mishtlin holds the contract in her hand, unwilling to let it out of her grasp, her magicked stylus serving as a hairpin to keep her tight black curls in a semblance of order. Yoal drinks a cup of black coffee she liberated from the Dawncomer officers' mess, her pin holding a thin blue wool blanket around her shoulders like a shawl.

"Did they get the Hierophant?" Citlal asks.

"Yes," Ce-Mishtlin replies smiling, tears glimmering in her warm black eyes.

"He was visiting Mazaán," Yoal explains with quiet viciousness. Mazaán was the largest of the reservations, where the People were kept before being shipped to one of the work camps. "Ometzin and Chinueh died, but they got the bastard."

Citlal closes her eyes briefly, mourning two of the five wisewives who were imprisoned at Mazaán.

"There's more: the Emperor has sent word that none of the magebloods of the People will be imprisoned by the Dawncomers any longer," Yoal continues. "It seems that the Miktlán dead"—the

Miktlán camp was small, but it was just north of the capital—"paid a visit to the Imperial Palace in Zochimílc. He's sending away his Dawncomer 'advisors' and calling for rebuilding the Temple Major."

"Nice to see that His Majesty has a spine after all, no?" Ce-Mishtlin grins, hope and hurt in equal measure in her eyes.

Citlal laughs and joins them at the table. She knows that the People won't ever be free of the Dawncomers—there are too many of them, and a growing number of mixed blood children—but the scales are no longer so unbalanced now that the usurpers know that the People can retaliate in ways that cannot be evaded even with their cold technology and guns.

"Thankfully, they don't understand the bounds of the wise-work. Typical Dawncomer ignorance, but I'm grateful for it this time," Ce-Mishtlin says.

Smiling, Ce-Mishtlin holds up the contract for Yoal and Citlal to see. Then the southerner dips her head in farewell, takes a deep breath and uses her stylus to add a line to the fire glyph, changing the word's reading to *cold: death*. Ce-Mishtlin exhales and stills forever, cold, cold. The air freezes around her, wintry steam rising from her like the memories of benedictions. All of the righteous dead she had marked are now just corpses again.

Yoal sighs, and tears come to her eyes as she murmurs something that might be the prayer for the dead under her breath. She pulls her stylus out of her improvised shawl and changes her fire glyph with it and says to Citlal, to the empty husk that once was Ce-Mishtlin, to the morning light, and to the memory of the skeletal dancers in the dark, "Thank you." Then Yoal, too, dies.

Dry-eyed, Citlal nods her deepest respect to the bodies of her sister-magicians and pushes herself away from the table. She takes their contract, and walks out of the building, needing a moment alone under the winter sky.

She continues past the Dawncomer officers' housing to a small green garden, planted with roses and lilies forced to grow out of season by Dawncomer technology. It had been where the camp commandant liked to take his afternoon tea.

It's deserted now.

Citlal sits down on the grass, the new year's cold sun an indifferent blessing. Alone and safe for the first time since Shochi was murdered, she cries. They aren't easy tears. Each sob pulls a barbed thorn of pain from her heart. The absence of Shochi is a void she knows will not be filled. Citlal will not cross through the Sunset Gate to find her daughter beyond the west, if Shochi has made it to the next world. But perhaps the People will find a new home, now that they'll have the chance.

After a while the tears calm, and she is quiet. The wind has died down, and she is perfectly at rest. She takes a deep breath and stands.

It's then that she hears the voice of the Living Lord. It is not a small, still voice: it's the roar of a hurricane, the tumult of a mountainside falling. The sound knocks her to her knees. Even through the din, it's everything that the Starry Codex and the stories and Quineltoc said it is. It's bliss and grace and fulfillment and balm, sweet balm on Citlal's battered heart.

Daughter, blessed are you. You are truly the mother of your people. I grant you life for proving it.

It's warmth and light, a bonfire lit and blazing. It's the peal of conch trumpets heralding joy. The sound is like receiving judgment and being found worthy.

Through you, the People will live on to nourish Me. Feed Me, daughter.

Her anger is incandescent. It leaves no room for shadows, for doubt: whatever test she's passed, whatever plan she's fulfilled, whatever blessing this might be, it *isn't* right and it's *not* enough. They all are owed more than this. The countless dead, Quineltoc, her sister-magicians, *Shochi*, are all owed more than *this*.

Citlal shouts, a piercing scream that assaults the vaults of heaven. The sound of skeletal women, dancing, fills the cold winter sky and the void beyond. "No," she says. "Better the anxious night than a certain path down your monstrous gullet. Better that we live and die by our own choices than at your whim. Better the night and all the cold stars than your hunger."

The warmth and light retract, surprised, afraid.

Citlal takes the contract and her stylus and carefully adds a line to the remaining glyph: *life* becomes *death*. Elsewhere in the camp, the last of the righteous dead lie down, all animation fled. She tries to let go of her anger, of her injured sense of justice, with her last breath, but doesn't quite. The sense of responsibility for the People remains, but she knew that it would. Her body falls to the ground.

Visible only in the dark between the stars, the newest Bone Woman gets up and walks off. The fulfilled pact between the wisewives and the Dead Sisters blows away in the cold wind that howls. Bones rattling, the *Tzitzimimeh* continue to dance.

THE FREEDOM OF THE SHIFTING SEA
Jaymee Goh

Superpredator

> *E. aphroditois is a polychaete marine worm that grows up to three meters or ten feet long and swims using bristle-like appendages, called parapodia, along the length of its body. It has a reversible pharynx and long mandibles with which it catches prey.*
>
> *—An Introduction to the Deeper Sea*

SALMAH MET MAYANG on a sunny day in an isolated lagoon. Astonishing, as tourists had devoured the beaches near her coastal town. Even more astonishing: Mayang's lower body. Salmah was repulsed by the waving legs at her sides, but drawn to the iridescence of the segments of her body, like a centipede's, glinting rainbows in the midday sun.

Mayang had shrunk back underground—underwater underground, Salmah marveled—but her face was still uncovered, her hair drifting like seaweed. Salmah should have run away; instead she pulled on her goggles and got on her knees to investigate the sharp little face, broad nose, lush lips, beguiling eyes. Salmah's hand hovered over Mayang's face, wondering if she dared touch it, but decided she didn't. Besides which, Mayang looked like she wanted to be left alone.

So Salmah left, and immediately went to the library to find out what the creature could be. Not a mermaid: mermaids were not half woman, half centipede like that. (Not even a centipede, but some sort of worm.) Not a spirit: she was too real. She went through a list of all the female monsters she knew and then some, but still came up with nothing.

She returned the very next day, to enjoy the quietness, and to find the stranger sitting on a rock, eating a fish. The stranger receded into the seabed a little when Salmah approached, but Salmah held out her hands as non-threateningly as possible, with a gift: homemade kuih.

"Asalamualaikum," she said, wondering if the creature was Muslim. "My name is Salmah."

"Walaikumsalam," came the cautious reply. A pause. "Mayang."

With this firm introduction, Salmah made friends with the first non-human creature she had ever known. By the end of the dry season, Salmah had learned a great deal about Mayang, like Mayang's age (Mayang could remember a time before British imperialism), Mayang's favorite fish (stingray), Mayang's length (twenty meters), and Mayang's favorite hunting grounds (a beach off the coast of Thailand popularly considered haunted). They sometimes swam out into the ocean, Salmah with a precious snorkel and mask she'd saved up for, holding gently onto Mayang's shoulders as they investigated reefs far from shore. Salmah watched Mayang hunt: swift movements too fast to see, mandibles slicing creatures in half. Salmah found herself unable to turn away from the sight.

In turn, Salmah told Mayang about changes in the human world, and the latter listened with a patient disinterest, expression flickering at odd moments that Salmah thought completely boring. She confided in Mayang: troubles at home, college applications, job seeking, boyfriends. Mayang was not always good at listening: she hated humans generally, men specifically.

"I don't really see any problem," Mayang replied for what sounded like the hundredth time to Salmah's complaint about a recalcitrant boyfriend who refused to call. "If he doesn't want to be with you, then you're free."

"But that's not what I want. Have you ever liked anybody?"

The ensuing silence was punctuated by the sound of thunder in the distance. Mayang bobbed in the water, staring into the distance as the tide came in. Salmah began picking up her sarong to go when Mayang said, "I like *you*."

Salmah almost slipped. She was about to respond when lightning crackled across the sky. Mayang reached out to shield her. Salmah hugged her in return, feeling the cold skin, the almost-human skin, slick-smooth.

"I've loved many," Mayang said into Salmah's ear. "Many many. I've lost them all, to men, to marriage, to murder. And I will lose you too, someday. You're too full of this world, of life on land, for the sea."

Salmah opened her eyes to find that Mayang had been bearing her closer to the shore, making sure she was in shallower waters. "Don't say that. I will always come back." Shyly, she kissed Mayang on the mouth, before running off, face hot in the cold wind.

The monsoon season beat down, flooding schoolyards and fields, blowing off roofs as it had done for generations. Salmah went out on the better days to look for Mayang, but with little luck. Mayang's last words echoed in her ears like a portent, an omen.

The lagoon lost a sandbar near its mouth, opening into a dense mangrove swamp. In low tide, the tree roots were visible, with curious curves: too petted, too cultivated. Salmah waded past mudskippers and fish, until she found Mayang's body, half-buried in the sand, shining in the dappling sunshine. Panicked, she ran along the trail of legs, screaming Mayang's name.

Mayang rolled over with a grumpy groan, and blinked sleepily at Salmah. She smiled. "Hello. How was work?"

Salmah clung to Mayang tightly, shaky with relief. She kissed Mayang's forehead, cheeks, and mouth. Mayang drew back, hissing, and Salmah saw the inside of Mayang's mouth: the mandibles in her cheeks uncurling a little, the tiny teeth that looked disturbingly normal, and a looseness of skin behind them. "I'm sorry! Was I too rough?"

"I just woke up." Mayang stroked Salmah's hair gently. "But I missed you, too."

Just like that, their friendship continued as before, but Salmah could not stop thinking of the inside of Mayang's mouth, her soft cool skin, her vestigial breasts. Mayang's eyes glittered with amusement when she caught Salmah staring, permitted the human woman's hands to linger on her waist, shoulders, even the frond-like legs on the sides of her wormbody. Their arms entwined as they swam together, Mayang swimming on her back to kiss Salmah's belly, knees, toes. Salmah would whine as they returned to Mayang's grotto about unfairness, because Salmah couldn't return the favor.

"I'm not like you," she groused, coming to rest under a mangrove tree.

"You are not," Mayang agreed, pointedly staring at Salmah's fine-haired legs. "Not with those useless things anyway."

"I can do things with these that you can't with yours."

Mayang tilted her head, raising an eyebrow.

Carefully, Salmah hooked her legs around Mayang's waist, drawing the wormwoman closer to her. Then she wrapped her arms under Mayang's arms, determined to make sure the latter couldn't slip away. She blushed, but grinned through it anyway.

Mayang brushed a tendril of hair from Salmah's face, kissed her temple.

"Have you ever kissed a woman?" Salmah asked.

"Many," Mayang replied.

"Who?" Salmah thought maybe she sounded too demanding.

"Have *you* ever kissed a woman?" Mayang asked, not deigning to answer that question.

Salmah nodded. Her school had been an all-girls' school, although she now dated men. "But... not someone like you."

Mayang tasted like saltwater, like the sea. Salmah ran her fingers through Mayang's hair and down her back. Mayang smelled like warm winds over the ocean. When Salmah pulled Mayang closer, she let her legs slide down, and resisted a giggle when the arches of her feet brushed against the bristles along Mayang's sides.

Mayang tasted Salmah, with what felt like multiple tongues down the length of Salmah's neck, clavicle, chest. In horrified fascination, Salmah watched as Mayang's jaw unhinged, pharynx extending a little to encompass the whole of one breast, and teeth at the back of Mayang's gullet tickling her nipple. Hard nubs lined Mayang's mouth, massaging, grazing. Oral membrane still extended, Mayang worked her way downwards, tickling Salmah's belly, pausing right before the cleft between her legs.

Mayang's eyes shone with an inner light, ghostly and still, her arms curled around Salmah's thighs. Salmah tried to breathe evenly, the thudding between her legs growing and growing, her alarm at the seams on Mayang's cheeks coming apart also growing and growing. But Mayang's mouth—the inside of it, Salmah reminded herself—pressed among the soft hairs there. Internally shrieking, Salmah nodded.

The pharynx pressed in, rubbing itself all over trembling muscle within and labia without. Salmah gripped the tree roots above her head, staring up into the sky beyond the leaves but not focusing, feeling the tide coming in around her body, feeling a tide coming inside.

Mayang curled her body underneath Salmah, keeping their torsos above water, for Salmah to catch her breath after. She held the human woman through the ragged breathing and occasional gasps—Salmah sat right on top of some of Mayang's legs, that had to keep moving to steady them—and stroked Salmah's hair, singing an ancient song.

"You don't—how do I—" Salmah frowned.

Mayang laughed. "No, you can't. Not now, anyway."

"This seems unfair."

"I have the freedom of these shifting seas in exchange for this small pleasure."

"I don't think—" But Salmah's thought was cut off as it began to rain.

"You should go home," Mayang told her.

The season passed: thunderstorms and lightning displays crashing across the skies made it too dangerous to go to the beach to look for her lover. Salmah moved into the nearby town to work at her family's behest. She thought about Mayang often, but like a dream, an unreal experience with an untrue creature, as her work as a clerk took up her days. University abroad seemed even more possible than before.

Then there was the fact that Salmah could not speak of Mayang to anyone. What could she say? *I am seeing a woman*—to a family who would frown on the idea and assume she hadn't met a nice man to marry yet. *I am seeing a sea creature who is half a centipede*—to whom? And if one could not speak of a love, was it real? Salmah thought about her aunts and friends involved with married men, and was vaguely envious: at least those men had identity cards to prove their existence.

I will lose you too, someday. The pronouncement almost made Salmah angry to think about. By the time the monsoon season was over, Salmah had convinced herself not to go looking for Mayang again. She sent out her university and scholarship applications, received acceptances, and weighed her options carefully. Let Mayang be right if she wants to be.

But she felt guilty. Perhaps she should at least say goodbye. This was harder than it looked, since as soon as she had made her decision, her family suddenly clamored for her attention: endless going-away dinners, visiting relatives, crying grandparents. When she finally found some time to look for Mayang, she worried that perhaps she had been gone too long.

His name was Amir, she would find out later in the newspapers. She barely noticed him as she waded through the mangrove mid-tide looking for Mayang, dismissed the swishing of waters behind her as the waves coming in. She was about to give up, turn around, and head home, when he grabbed her hair at the nape of her neck and slapped a sandy, sweaty hand around her mouth.

Oh God, not here, not now. Salmah thrashed. She was too young to die, had too much to do, she was here to say goodbye to Mayang, not the world. She wrenched away from him, screaming, and ran. He was too close behind, and Salmah turned to see his hand too close to her face—

Then he yelped and disappeared under the water. There was a cloud of sand where he had been.

Salmah screamed and cried and screamed and cried all the way home.

*　　*　　*

Aphrodite

E. aphroditois buries its long body in the ocean bed, where it waits to ambush its prey. It moves with such speed that sometimes it slices its prey in half, and drags its catch into the seabed to prevent it from escaping.
—Predators of the Sea: the Worm Edition

SIMON SAW HER from a distance first, sitting pretty on boulders far from the beach where he had taken his daughter for a long walk. Eunice had pointed her out first, and he had to squint to really see the figure, looking to the shore forlornly, like Hans Christian Andersen's mermaid in Copenhagen. They had seen the Malay mermaid on occasion since, on their beach excursions.

His wife refused to join them on their walks. Salmah had seen some crazy stuff that he wasn't sure he believed. Mermaids? Cannibal mermaids? He loved her, but she was insane sometimes. He'd thought he was going to marry a nice moderate Muslim girl. If she'd turned out a fundie terrorist, that would at least be understandable, but no, he got weird confessions about some lesbian relationship with a mermaid. She probably made that shit up to make him jealous, get back at him. He couldn't help being a huge flirt; she'd liked that, way back when. And what was wrong with him flirting with other women? It was just flirting, and it wasn't like he was divorcing her.

In fact, Simon took really good care of her, all things considered: roof over her head, grocery money, and all the love a woman could ask for, even if sometimes she was fucking ungrateful. Unreasonable. He had to keep her in line at times. Luckily her father understood him. Some things are shared, even cross-culturally. He supposed that with some other family they would have interfered in the marriage by now, so he counted himself lucky, and put up with their mat salleh jokes.

He kicked a seashell into the distance, still mad at the latest fight they'd had. Wasn't she getting a trip home every year? It was expensive, flying over the Pacific every winter. She hated the idea, claimed that monsoon season was too dangerous for Eunice to be near the sea. That was the latest sticking point. He admitted that he'd been a little careless; he'd been so caught up talking to that really interesting musician on the beach he hadn't noticed little Eunice getting lost. Salmah had screamed at him for hours while they lodged a police report, and then stormed out in a crying rage. He'd been too tired to keep her from going out. Let her complain to her neighbors or friends or whatever. He'd tell his side of the story eventually, and he would at least sound sane about it. He liked her friends. All of them pretty, like she'd been before bloating up like a whale.

It was maybe a bit mean of him to hope that she would go missing too. That would take care of that craziness without the business of divorce, and maybe he could marry someone else who wouldn't be so damn shrill. Nope, she'd come home with Eunice in her arms, both of them damp and stinking of rotting fish. He hadn't asked Salmah where she'd found Eunice, but now Eunice was babbling about mermaids too, and that was two crazy women in his house.

There she was again, arms resting on a shelf at the far end of a line of beach rocks. She stared at him with an intensity that made him wonder. She wasn't that far out from shore. He waved at her, smiling. She ducked a little behind the rock, but bobbed up again, smiling back, he hoped, waving coyly.

Simon waded into the water, a little experimentally. Monsoon weather made the sea cold at times, but it had been a hot day. But it wasn't too bad, and besides, that woman on the rock looked lonely. As he approached, he realized, she also looked fine as hell: cheekbones like they'd been cut by diamonds, large dark liquid eyes, and her arms were toned, like she worked out regularly. And her hair! At first he thought it was black, just like basically everybody else here. But it seemed to have a rainbow sheen to it, as if she had an oil slick in her hair, or maybe as if her hair was an oil slick.

"Oy," he called.

"Salaam," she replied.

"Mind if I hang out with you?"

It took her a moment to answer, as if his accent was a problem. "You may."

She was in waist-deep water, and he counted himself lucky to be tall. Being a mat salleh had its advantages, he thought as he leaned over the rock to look down into those amazing eyes. Not only that, but clearly he'd lucked out with a freaky girl: she wasn't even wearing a top. Women here wore t-shirts and sarongs at the beach out of modesty, and with the growing Arabization, more of them were buying those swimsuits that covered everything. It was a crying shame; that had never been the case when he visited Asia in his youth. Also a crying shame: the water was cloudy, so he couldn't check out whether she was wearing a bottom. He thought he caught a glimpse of one, a scintillating waistband, but the water sloshed up and he lost sight of it.

"So... you live around here?"

"I move around a lot. You?" Her Malay had an odd accent. He'd heard that the northerners had a different dialect of Malay, but he'd never met anyone who spoke that way before. Still, it gratified him that his Malay was passable enough that a stranger thought he was local.

"I'm from Amerika Syarikat."

"How interesting. Your Malay is very good." Her hand reached up to touch his face. "Is your hair really that color?"

He grinned, bending his head down for her to touch his curls. His naturally blond hair fascinated locals. Her fingers were tentative, and she wrapped a lock around her pinky. Now that her arms were away from her breasts, he could see that they were small, almost flat, but cute all the same.

"So soft," she cooed, letting her hand slip down the back of his head, his neck. "So nice."

"Thanks," he said, about to share his shampoo-and-conditioning routine (women loved that sort of thing) when he noticed her hand dropping downwards even further. Her fingertips drifted across his chest and even lower. "Oh, wow." He didn't protest as her hand tugged at his waistband, pulling him around the rock. He stepped around, let her guide his hips so he leaned back.

She was fast in unbuttoning and unzipping. Some sort of freaky slut, he thought, aware that he had the same stupid grin from earlier on his face as she got to work on his erection. He gazed down at her rainbow-black hair, amazed at how fast she deep-throated him. And what the fuck was her tongue, even? It felt like it was swirling all around his cock, or that maybe she had multiple tongues. He'd have to investigate it after, because it felt so goddamn good.

Thunder rolled across the sky, and the waves came in harder. He was impressed; she wasn't stopping even though the tide was obviously coming in, lapping higher around his hips now, spraying her cheeks.

"Water's coming in," he croaked, gently but regretfully pushing at her shoulders. She took his hands and put them on her head, on her dark hair, and pressed him against the rock even more firmly.

She did not stop, even as the tide came in higher, but he was beyond caring, because this was the best blowjob of his goddamn life and he wasn't going to let something like nature get in the way. At the back of his mind he was maybe worried that maybe she might drown if she kept on going, but he gripped her hair and kept thrusting into her throat. Who knows when he might ever meet her again—maybe he'd get her number.

"I'm gonna come," he gasped, out of courtesy. Vaguely, he realized that he was knee-deep in the sand. When had that happened? Maybe it wasn't the tide coming in after all, but them sinking into the water. He'd ask Salmah about it later.

He glanced down—what the fuck, she was underwater, dark eyes meeting his—and—no, what!—mandibles protruded—no, unfolded—from her cheeks and clamped down around his hips. He screamed.

Oh shit, oh shit, oh God, oh God. He scrabbled at the rock behind him—the water was higher than before—pulled at the mandibles—sweet Jesus, *mandibles*—but they dug into his flesh deeper, and her arms were wrapped around his legs, and she was sinking into the sand—what the fuck—and pulling him with her. Every effort he made to get out of her grasp made her mandibles dig in further

"Help!" he shrieked, drowned out by another clap of thunder.

Water roared around his ears. She was pulling him underground underwater, he realized. What the fuck was she? He pushed at the seabed, gasped when she bit down hard—he yelled, oh shit, underwater—but he was still sinking, the sand was up to his chest now. His lungs burned, his hips were scalding.

As the seabed came up about his ears, he swallowed. Water tickled his fingers. Rough sand engulfed them.

*　*　*

Eunice

Contrary to its popular name of "bobbit worm," named after the famous case in which Loreena Bobbit cut off her husband's penis with a scissors, E. aphroditois do not have penises, as they are broadcast spawners. Little is known of their mating habits, as very few individual specimens have been found.
—*Mysterious Marine Matings*

EUNICE DREAMED THE same dream for a long time: she drifted in the waves, frightened and tired of swimming, and saw a long, large worm, swimming towards her. Then a human face, and human arms, grasping her tightly, lifting her to the surface, allowing her to gasp for air. Eunice rode on the worm-woman's back towards shore, but not towards where she had lost her father. She'd dreamed of falling asleep, dreamed she'd awoken to her mother's cries of relief. In these false awakenings, half-lucid with the awareness that she was not really awake, Eunice clung to the worm-woman tightly, trying to ask questions, impossible ones like "Why does Mom hate me?" or "Why didn't I get Dad's blue eyes?" or "How come the other kids look at me weird?" or "What are men even?"

When she was older, she fought with her mother over the details: her mother insisted that she had found Eunice half-drowned and asleep on the beach; Eunice knew that the worm-woman was real, and she half-remembered a conversation between the woman and her mother. It was hard to forget that musical voice, almost like whistles in the dark. She didn't know what the details were anymore, but someone had cried.

Eunice plodded along the beach, squinting into the distance. It had taken years, but she was sure that she had finally found the right place. Her mother had tried to throw her off the trail several times: "Oh no, it was at Seberang Ris," she'd say. "Maybe it was at Pulau Redang, very popular there." After several fruitless road trips, as well as much rifling through her mother's old documents, Eunice found a relative's phone number that worked—one of many who had shunned her mother after the disappearance of Eunice's father. She had to listen to a long religious screed about the pernicious effects of black magic and a roundabout accusation of her mother, but she finally got the information she wanted. The family had moved far and wide across the Peninsula, and no one would balik kampong to where her mother had grown up, but they still remembered the name of the town.

There was an isolated lagoon, a tiny one, encroached on all sides with trees growing in the accumulated silt. They weren't even mangrove trees, but evergreens, angsana, and saga, probably brought there by the ocean. Eunice sat down for a while, taking in the sight. There was an opening to the side, and a sandbar that blocked off the lagoon from the ocean. Rocks of all sizes were scattered here and there, beachrocks now obscured by the trees.

Something twinkled beside a rock on the edge of the lagoon. Eunice jumped up to investigate. She had to stomp on some saplings, but when she got there, there was nothing but water. Interesting, though: the rockline held back the sand on one side, but on the other, the water looked deep. She kicked off her sandals and pulled on her snorkel.

The water was cold for that time of year; it seemed to swallow her. She blew out the water from her snorkel, and began to slowly explore along the rockline. Soon she was bumping up against the tree roots of a mangrove swamp. She had half a mind to get out; no telling what poisonous snakes or crocodiles could be living there. But there was something so incredibly familiar about the place, something that twigged at the back of her mind. The silt was so loose here that any little disturbance stirred it up, so Eunice drifted carefully.

There, half-buried, a woman's body facing up. Eunice clung to a tree root tightly to stare. Was she dead?

A flurry of silt went up, and the woman was gone. A dark shadow circled around Eunice, and from the sandy cloud, a pair of brown arms reached out to her. Eunice froze, letting the hands touch her face, drift over her snorkel mask, brush her bangs back. The sand parted, and the woman's face came into view, achingly familiar. She had a broad nose and large dark eyes, and her cheeks seemed to have scars. She swam by, a hand trailing down Eunice's side, dipping into the small of her back.

Eunice sucked in her breath at the sight of the long segmented body beginning from the woman's waist. The bristles on the sides waggled independently of each other, navigating the water. The worm-woman swam above Eunice's legs, and under, running her hands up from her hips, to her waist, the sides of her breasts, and cupped her cheeks. She gently prised one of Eunice's hands from the tree root and tugged, smiling.

Eunice let go, let herself be pulled along by this woman. They passed under tunnels of mangrove roots, towards open sea, and along the coastline to a rocky beach. Eunice pulled herself onto a shelf, water sloshing around her hips as the waves came in. The woman wrapped herself around a rock, leaned forward with a beaming smile.

When Eunice pulled off her mask, the smile faltered a little.

"You're not Salmah." She wasn't exactly unfriendly, but there was a slight wobble in the music.

Eunice shook her head. "I'm Salmah's daughter." She hesitated. "You saved me, when I was little."

The woman's gaze swept over her, then she lowered her head to rest her chin on her arms. "Has it been so long?"

"Sorry."

"It's not your fault. I just thought—but never mind. How is she?"

Eunice's mind ran through a thousand possible answers. *She's fine— she's busy with a new business—she seems lonely—she hates swimming now—she seems happy—she's got a new husband.* She went with the most honest answer. "I don't know. I haven't really talked to her in a while." She pursed her lips. "She never told me your name."

Those large eyes seemed to glitter in the sunlight. "Hm." Everything about her seemed iridescent with the sunshine. The brown of her skin had a reflective rainbow sheen, and the curls of her hair resembled an oil slick.

The waves rushed to shore. In the distance, herons cawed.

"My name is Mayang."

Eunice smiled. "Eunice."

"Eunice. It sounds nice. American name?"

A nod. "My father named me."

"I see."

Mayang said nothing further about Eunice's father, even when Eunice casually mentioned him later in the conversation, as in "that time when Dad got mad about—" and watched Mayang's reaction carefully. But save for a flicker on Mayang's face, he was as good as irrelevant. They wouldn't talk about him after that, on further visits, resting after a long swim around the reefs and nearby islands, drilling holes into the bottoms of rich men's yachts with screwdrivers and drills Eunice brought. Mayang would confess to Eunice the fates of former lovers, devoured by sea predators, dead by the poison of pollution, or simply lost to the worldly concerns of humans. Eunice would tell Mayang about the new technologies that had arisen, the advancements scientists were making in space and deep sea explorations, and the new wars. When they made love, Eunice was torn between jealousy and satisfaction, that her mother had this before she did, and would never have it again.

"You never talk about yourself," Mayang interrupted Eunice one day as they lazed in a nest of rocks, Eunice in Mayang's arms. Mayang was not an interrupter, but she couldn't help herself in that moment. "Why is that?"

Eunice shrugged. "I'm not a very interesting person." And went on describing memes.

Mayang let it pass until Eunice was done talking. Then she stroked the young woman's hair. "*I* think you're very interesting."

Eunice caught Mayang's hand, and kissed its palm. "I think you're more interesting than me. You live forever under the sea. You see things no human ever could." She thought for a moment about her never-mentioned father. "Also, you eat people. That's really cool."

Mayang laughed so loudly Eunice was afraid someone would hear them, discover them and their secret. The seams in her cheeks loosened a little, mandibles almost unfolding in her mirth. But Mayang sobered as quickly as she had laughed. "There is a price to the freedom of the seas."

She was so serious, Eunice had to know. "What is it?"

"Everything amazing you tell me, every change in the human world, will be lost to you," Mayang answered, hands still stroking Eunice's hair, drifting down. "Death is still a constant danger. There are so few of us, torn apart by the tides, I don't even know where the others are anymore."

"I found you easily."

"I like to stay put. Fishing here is easy. There are so many more tourists than before." She smoothed the fabric of Eunice's panties. "But no more this feeling good here. Because you won't have it anymore."

Eunice let Mayang's hand linger, weighing the truth of the statement. Eunice's wormbody explorations had turned up nothing sensitive. She parted her knees a little, and pressed the hand further down. Mayang's fingers played with a stray hair, but withdrew after a moment.

"You're so young, Eunice. Go live a full life. The sea is for bitter old crones like me."

Eunice turned to kiss Mayang's cheek, and trailed her lips along a mandible seam. "You're not a crone," she murmured, brushing sand off Mayang's brown skin, flicking a cake of silt off a breast. It was small, mostly vestigial muscle leftover from years of swimming in the ocean. "And I'm not that young." She kissed Mayang, working her fingers into the worm-woman's mouth to reach places her tongue could not reach. Mayang's mouth—the loose membrane, the soft muscles—pressed down, not to push Eunice out, but to draw her in. In a busy embrace, Eunice straddled Mayang, stretching the length of herself along to brush against the bristles that fluttered in a way Eunice noticed only happened when they kissed.

The epidermis along Mayang's body cracked as it dried. It did not happen often, Mayang had told Eunice, and really only meant she had a new segment to her body. Eunice helped peel the old skin off, and marveled at the polished iridescence beneath. She ran her fingers across the new skin, soft for now until it toughened over time, and grinned to hear Mayang moaning. She carefully stripped the length of Mayang's body, fingers dancing between parapodia to a startling cacophony from Mayang. When she reached the final segment, throbbing with its newness, she embraced it, showering it with kisses, while Mayang arched her back, mandibles unfurling wide in a long, ragged cry.

The afternoon sun had gone down by the time they rested. "When there were more of us," Mayang whispered, eyes closed in dreamy afterglow, "we met during molting season. What a shame there are so few of us now."

Eunice went home and quit her job. She closed her bank accounts, all social media possible, wrote several letters that were along the lines of, "Don't look for me." Her mother tried to withhold her car keys and her identity card, as if those were things Eunice needed anymore. Concerned acquaintances tried to call, but Eunice turned off her phone and removed the SIM card.

Off the shore of Terengganu, where it was still dark enough for moonlight to set the white sands aglow, Eunice rode Mayang's back to an island of rocks too small for development, too rocky for trees.

"Will it be painful?"

"Very." (Mayang actually couldn't remember anymore.)

"Will you be there when I wake up?"

"Yes." (Mayang lied, because anything could happen.)

They tumbled onto a bed of sand together, kissing and licking and tasting, Eunice wrapped around Mayang. Mayang ran her pharynx over the length of Eunice's neck, chest, belly, while her fingers found the human cleft and thrust deep, feeling along the lines of the wet walls for throbbing muscle. Eunice gripped Mayang's hair, a little alarmed at the sudden engorgement from Mayang's mouth, raking teeth across her clavicle, the round of her breasts, and every sensitive spot Mayang knew. She swallowed the bile of terror as Mayang's head settled between her legs, mandibles unfurling and foaming at the edges. Water rose around her hips.

Mayang bit deep, seeking the second heartbeat, splitting skin and flesh. Eunice screeched as Mayang's teeth-lined pharynx burrowed around her clitoris, nerve endings shattered and ripped apart. The froth turned bloody, burning, blazing as seawater rose. Eunice clamped her legs together, almost catching Mayang's neck, and Mayang ducked away to let the transformation begin. Eunice squeezed her legs shut, gasped in shock between sobs, while Mayang rubbed her arms up and down and stroked her hair and crooned an old song: the blood from Eunice, the foam from Mayang, the salt of the sea, all would bubble together to form a cocoon, so sleep, so fade away, let the warm blood go. The water rose, and Eunice felt the moonlight ebb from her vision. Everything grew cold and dark and silent except for Mayang's voice.

Eunice dreamed of entwining with Mayang over and over, of exploring the ocean depths and each other, of the freedom of the shifting sea.

* * *

Coda

DO YOU KNOW, Eunice? I cannot remember the last time I witnessed a metamorphosis. When the water covered you, the foam turned into a thin film that reminded me of bloody cauls over babies. Unpleasant memories. When you wake up, I hope you will not mind having been buried in the silt of the mangrove, because I had forgotten how much men are prone to roaming in their boats these days, their mastery over the ocean allowing them a greater range. You will also have more food around when you wake up, and I will be there to catch them with you, and teach you how.

And I can already sense that you will not be happy in this sleepy little beachside, so we will drift across the oceans to find old shipwrecks and waylay unhappy boats. We will delve into the trenches to find the methuselahs who feed on whales and deep sea squid in between their slumbering aeons. Maybe we will find others like us. Maybe we will make more like us. Maybe in the far future you will leave me anyway, but it will not matter by then.

Sleep easy, my little Eunice.

THREE VARIATIONS ON A THEME OF IMPERIAL ATTIRE
E. Lily Yu

THEY NEVER TELL the story right. The Danish must have their heavens and happy endings, and Andersen's tales are meant for children. We, however—you and I—know that people are people, and every one of us capable of—

But the story.

Once there was a vain and foolish emperor, who made up for his foolishness by a kind of low cunning. As such rulers do, he drew to himself a retinue of like men and women, who told him he was wise and humble, gracious and good. The emperor would smile at their flattery, which in his wisdom he knew to be the truth, and lavish gold and gems and deeds upon them. Thus was everyone contented within the palace walls. And those outside got on as well as they could.

Eventually, with narrative inevitability, two men with knapsacks and pockets full of thread came knocking at the palace gates.

"We are tailors," the first one said, "wise but humble tailors, who seek to offer our boutique services to men of might, such as yourself."

"Here is a list of our bona fides," said the second man. "Sterling references, one and all."

"The very best, I'm sure," the emperor said, looking at the ruby buttons on their vests of gilt brocade.

"What we'd like to offer you is an exclusive deal—"

"—the latest in fashion, which no one else owns—"

"—designed in collaboration with a distant country's military-industrial complex—"

"—top secret and cutting-edge—"

"—the Loyalty Distinguisher line of couture."

"What a mouthful," the emperor said, looking askance. "Call it something I can pronounce."

"What a brilliant suggestion! The Thresher, how's that? Since it sorts the wheat from the worthless chaff."

"Powerful," the emperor said. "I like it."

"Now, the key selling point of the Thresher line—what a wonderful name!—is that it'll let you sort at a glance your loyal, meritorious, and worthy subjects from—well, the useless ones."

"At a glance, eh?"

"Indeed! When we dress you in Thresher fabric, cut to the height of style, those subjects of noble character will see you as you truly are, with all your hidden virtues displayed. They'll swoon at your intellect, marvel at your power, gape at your discernment and understanding. You'll know them by their raptures and fits of joy. Then you can place them in positions of authority. Judging village disputes and distributing grain, for example. Or tax collecting."

"Good," the emperor said, rubbing his chin. "And the rest?"

"The Thresher fabric will reflect their true ugliness. They will pale and shrink back and avert their eyes."

"They will scream and faint."

"They will whimper at the sight of their deepest selves."

"And thus you will know your traitorous subjects."

"Hard labor would be too good for them."

"Make me this suit at once!" the emperor said. And his court, whispering amongst themselves, wondered how the marvel would be managed.

Well, you know how. The tailors placed loud orders on the phone for Italian leather and French wool, Japanese silks and bulletproof thread; had conspicuously large boxes airlifted to their quarters; and all day and all night they cut and sewed the air with an industry that was inspiring to see.

The appointed day came, red and hot. Crows rattled in the palace trees. In the emperor's chamber, before his cheval glass, the tailors presented their work with pride.

"Our finest piece."

"A triumph."

"A breakthrough in fashion."

"But let us see what it looks like on you. Habeas corpus is the haberdasher's true test."

The emperor looked at their empty hands—swallowed—scowled—thought—and said, "Bravo!"

"Is the jacket not to your liking?"

"Hm, yes, the pants are a little long."

"I'll fix that in a minute, never you worry. There."

"How's that?"

"Perfect," the emperor said, gazing at his reflection.

"Now you must show it to your subjects. Your courtiers have assembled and are waiting."

When the emperor strode into his court, a ruby-buttoned tailor at each elbow, his courtiers stared. Then one, then another hastily applauded, and the stamping and cheering shook the walls. A little color came back into the emperor's cheeks, and he whuffed through his blonde whiskers in relief, though what terrible worry he had been relieved of, no one watching could say.

"You chose your court wisely," the tailors said. "Now ride throughout your kingdom and sift the wicked from the good."

And the emperor, glancing dubiously at the saddle, mounted his horse and rode through the city streets. His stomach billowed with every bounce. Before him rode his courtiers, shouting the people forth to praise the craftsmanship and glory of these new clothes, which would divide the loyal from the perfidious.

The people, who had not survived six decades of imperial whims and sudden prohibitions on various fruits, fats, and hats without acquiring a certain degree of sense, observed the wind's direction and vociferously admired the blinding gleam of the cloth-of-gold, the shimmer of silks, the cut and fit of everything.

Children, however, who through lack of life experience have not yet learned the salubrious lessons of unjust pain, while quite disposed to lie to avoid immediate punishment, are also inclined to speak inconvenient truths at the most inconvenient times.

"Ma, the emperor is naked."

"No, he's not. He's wearing the finest suit that I ever did see."

"Ma, I can see his *dick*."

At this the goodwife clapped her aproned hand over her son's mouth, but it was too late. The emperor had heard. He turned a pitying eye upon them, as their neighbors immediately began to point and hiss. Why, they'd always known—an absent father—single motherhood stirred up evil, that's what they'd always said—but the emperor's getup was magnificent—truly unparalleled—only a stupid blind woman couldn't see that—

The emperor nudged his horse with his knees and serenely continued upon his way.

In the morning the boy and his mother were gone. Their little stone-and-thatch cottage had burned to the ground. Their neighbors and their houses had vanished as well. Only a few cracked teeth and a fistful of phalanges were found.

The emperor retained the tailors on an exclusive contract at astronomical rates and took to riding out among his people on a weekly basis, since it was now clear that there was treachery in the land. People fell over themselves to report their parents, in-laws, rivals, classmates, colleagues, never failing to praise the newest suit of clothes themselves, until the streets turned black with blood and soot.

When the emperor was finally stricken with a fatal case of pneumonia—which happened far later than one might imagine, because he was a corpulent and well-insulated man—his former subjects, one after the other, dazed by the news, picked up the phone by habit to denounce their friends, and heard, on the other end, the dusty silence of a dead line.

UNNECESSARILY GRIM, YOU say? Unrealistic? Scenes this bloody no longer occur in the civilized world? I agree with all your criticisms, most erudite of readers. There's nothing for it but to try again.

Here then is a more charming tale, one that will better suit your taste.

Once there was a body politic that, through happy geographic accident, had avoided any number of devastating wars, and was thus left the most powerful government in the world. On the basis of that evidence, it thought itself the most enlightened body politic that the world had ever seen. It kept its citizens under surveillance, arresting or ejecting those who did not agree, and as a result enjoyed unanimous approbation.

One day, two men, sons of a vast clothing empire, who had recently been elected to the body, presented a sheaf of invisible bills.

"See how stylishly we've cut, trimmed, and hemmed taxes! How popular you'll be with the tastemakers of this realm—how perceptive and attractive you'll seem—if you pass them!"

"See how they funnel the vast majority of money to the military, which is always fashionable. How powerful you'll look to your enemies!"

"Look how your children will benefit, leapfrogging into elite universities, flourishing in the compost of your trusts and estates!"

"All honorable members of this body politic will see the good, glorious vision these bills represent. All citizens of discernment shall agree. The others? Well, they are not citizens, or they are fake citizens, voting without proper identification, and we should divert a portion of our security budget to uncovering these traitors and deporting or imprisoning them, as our fathers did in their day."

The platforms and proposals were trotted before the country with pleasing pomp and ceremony. The true citizens applauded them so loudly you couldn't think, and trained in militias to hunt down the fake citizens, and rammed cars into the bodies of fake citizens, and phoned in denunciations of their neighbors, ex-lovers, grandchildren, pets—and before too long the streets ran black and red with—

Ah.

That didn't go very well, did it? Heavy-handed, on the nose... it's hardly even a story. The artistic error was choosing a plurality as a subject. It's difficult to create complexity of character, complete with inner conflicts and landscapes and unique worldviews, when one's protagonist is an amorphous group. Especially when the members are as slippery as politicians. I understand now why Andersen chose to write about an emperor rather than, say, the Rigsdag. Artistically, that is, never mind that the first Rigsdag convened twelve years after his fairy tale was published. That detail will be conveniently left out of my forthcoming treatise on art. It is a treatise written for a very select few, and will be scorned by the unenlightened masses. Only a humble and wise reader such as yourself, magnanimous and perfect in character, will understand the secrets I disclose therein.

So a character study is what's needed, it seems.

ONCE THERE WERE two tailors—

YOU KNOW WHAT? You're right. We don't need both of them. They're hardly distinguishable as it is. Andersen might have wished to signify the multitudinousness of such men, or illustrate how well they work together, once they recognize each other, but we can take that for granted as something the reader already knows.

ONCE THERE WAS a man who called himself whatever was suitable to his purposes at the time. If it profited him to say he was a soldier, then he was a soldier who had served with distinction. If it furthered his aims to call himself beloved, then someone's sweetheart he was. By speaking the words that another person wished to hear, whether those words were flattery or promises or blame, he could insinuate himself into most others' trust.

He had few talents besides this one, and a loathing for honest work besides, but this one talent proved enough to feed and clothe him until such time that the trick was plain. By then, of course, the man was long gone.

He fed at first on the labor of farmers, progressing at length to literate merchants and clerks. Over and over his living proved to him the moral by which he compassed his world: that the slow and stupid existed to be ruled and robbed by cleverer and better men than they.

But the smell of damp wool and the low burr of laborers came to displease him; the damp, wormy odors of ancient books soon bored him; in short, there are only so many times a bright man of tremendous worth can fleece the same kind of idiot. The reward is small, the dupery tedious. One must establish trust, perform small favors, establish rapport and commonalities, and so on and so forth, and that routine grows repetitive. The man longed to leave a mark on the face of history, as a result of which he could no longer be ignored.

And to do that, one must be proximate to greatness.

So the man who would call himself anything stashed away the profits of his cleverness until he could move to the valley of kings and queens, where starry fortunes were built upon a vastness of sand. Like pharaohs these men and women lived, erecting monuments and pressing whole hosts into hard labor; and word of their power and wealth had come to his ears.

The man bid farewell to the women who all thought themselves his one and only love, with haste and without many tears, since he did not expect to see them again. He did not kiss the infant boy that one held, with his own dark hair and dimpled cheeks. Time and space did not chain our storyteller, for the stories he told disregarded both as soon as they became inconvenient. And so by steamer and coach, Greyhound and plane, the man made his way to the valley of sand.

And where money flows and ebbs in deep tides like the sea, shifting mountains, crashing, storming, drowning, the humblest barnacle is sufficiently wetted if it only clings to a firm surface. So the man lived, studying the landscape, until he heard the clack of dice in every two shells rolled along by the sea. With adjustments to his former patterns, he crabbed small fortunes with the wire cage of his smile and landed wish-granting carp with his tongue for bait.

A little empire he eked out, nestling against the greater fortunes and powers that ironed the land flat, effacing a neighborhood there, shredding communities there. From the kings of that land he learned to spin his silken webs to catch not one fly but a thousand. Once stuck in his flatteries, they squirmed to be sucked, pleading to be wrapped in his glorious silks. And he, like a spider, was glad to oblige.

Dining on every rare delicacy, traveling to white-dusted parties by limo and helicopter, he was contented for a time.

Then, as he listened, as he grew familiar with that land, he learned that these kings were clever but lesser, that an emperor ruled over them, and that this emperor was a fool. The kings simpered and groveled when they came before the emperor, just as this man did before them.

Bit by bit, the glitter of the valley of kings faded. The man grew restless and hungry once more. Late at night, he spun plans to weave himself into the imperial court and staff. Favors were asked here, a rumor murmured there. A few careers had to be ended to clear the way, but what of it? Soon an invitation on cream-thick paper made its way into his hand.

All was ready, the story staged, waiting only for the curtain and the lights.

On the morning the man walked out of his old apartment for the last time, a plane ticket clutched in one hand, he found a boy no older than fifteen, dressed in the clothes of another era, standing in the building's entryway.

"Excuse me," the man said, stepping around the boy.

"You're my father," the boy said.

"I don't have a son."

"Here's a picture of us. I was three at the time."

"That could be anyone."

"It's you. I didn't come to bother you. I only wanted to ask—"

"You're making me late."

"—why you left. Why we weren't enough for you."

"Nothing personal. Nothing to do with you. But look at your mother. Was I supposed to grow old—with that? In that small, ratty house? In that backwater of a time and place? No, I am meant for greater things."

"She said you were a tailor."

"I do stitch, weave, and spin."

"Will you teach me to be a tailor too?"

"In ten minutes, I'm going to miss my flight, which will cause me to miss a very important appointment. See, I'm on a tight schedule. Call me another time."

"But," the boy said, looking after him, "I don't have your number…"

"So sorry, your imperial grandiloquence," the man said, several hours later. "Encountered an unavoidable delay. But now that I'm here, my various skills as a tailor are at your praiseworthy self's disposal. I can sew you an outfit, invisible, that all your subjects must nonetheless kiss the hems of, and admire. Sew half-truths and falsehoods together, until a listener can't tell head from tail. Weave tales to turn brother against brother, snipping all bonds of loyalty except to you. These matters make my trade."

"Be welcome here," the emperor said. "I can tell that you are a gifted man."

And the emperor threw a fistful of peas at him.

"Quick, a suit that will make me irresistible. I need it in five minutes. The Queen of Sheba is coming."

"Immediately," the tailor said.

But when the tailor returned after four minutes, carrying a suit of exaggerations, the emperor was already pawing at the Queen, who resisted with an expression of deep distaste, extracted herself, and stormed off.

"Where were you?" the emperor said, mashing a handful of gravy into the tailor's hair. "I told you to be done in two minutes. You took ten."

The tailor said, "That's right, O golden sun of wisdom."

"I didn't get to fuck her because of you."

"To make amends for your disappointment, may I offer you this suit of Impregnable Armor?" And he held out again the invisible clothes that mere minutes before had been an Irresistible Suit.

"Don't be stupid. I can't get pregnant."

"Ah, but this suit protects you from all harm."

"Gimme," the emperor said, and was quickly dressed.

Even though his wares were intangible, producing enough of them to please the emperor and thus avoid the latest flung dish of baked beans proved exhausting for the soi-disant tailor.

He spun the Three-Piece of Plausible Denial, the Vest and Cravat of High Event Attendance, the Cufflinks of Venality. Each time, the emperor toyed with his work, tried it on, pronounced himself satisfied, and promptly forgot it existed.

"May I suggest," the depleted tailor said, "stripping the populace of their rights, so that no one has rights but the most righteous of all, which is to say you, our rightness, you who are never wrong."

"Why not?" the emperor said.

That was carried out, despite demonstrations and strikes and scathing newspaper columns, and then the tailor had to invent a new diversion.

"What about setting neighbor against neighbor and stranger against stranger? Tell the old story of the dark-skinned foreigner with his knife dripping blood. A little chaos does for power what warm horseshit does for weeds."

"Whatever you like," said the triply-clothed emperor. "Next."

And those foreign-born or born to foreigners or born to those born to foreigners were rounded up, accused of crimes, and variously punished.

"May I suggest plucking the flower of youth before it grows strong enough to revolt?"

"Let it be so," the emperor said.

Across the realm, children were mown down like green grass ahead of the mower's scythe. Even the onion-eyed kings in their silicon towers felt their quartz hearts crack and said, "No more." But they spoke it softly, so the emperor would not hear.

And while the tailor measured and spun and snipped, the murmur of the people rose to a roar. For there remained some of intelligence and clear thinking and good judgment among them, and these had gently taught the rest to put on new eyes and see.

On a day when the emperor was deliberating between the empty suit of Universal Belovedness on the tailor's left arm and the trousers and blazer of Religious Authority draped over his right, a herald ran in with the report that a mob had smashed through the palace gates and was headed toward the emperor's palace.

Indeed, through the window they could see a dark storm of humanity swelling on the horizon. All that stood between that flood and the doors was a line of police with loaded rifles. Most of the mob was children, with some old women mixed in, and some young, as well as a few brave men, and they stepped over the bodies of those who were shot and pressed forward to the palace, inevitable as death.

The tailor, with the instinct of a hare, twitched and backed toward the exit.

The emperor said, "Sit."

And the tailor sat.

At a snap of the emperor's fingers, servants tugged the curtains shut, so that they could no longer see the cresting wave. The lights were switched off. They waited in darkness.

"Bring me a bottle," the emperor said, and poured two fingers of sixty-year-old liquor into two glasses. One he drank. One he emptied over the tailor.

"That suit," the emperor said, "that prevents all harm—I'm wearing it now. But what will you do, clever tailor, when they come through these doors?"

Distantly, over the gunfire, they could hear the children singing, and the song rose sweet and clear on the wind. Soon there began, at the palace doors, a heavy and fateful thudding, like that of a heart under terrible strain. All the world, it seemed, kind and cruel alike, had come to beat down the palace doors.

If you'll excuse me, I am now going to join them.

Heaven help the children.

Heaven help us all.

BLOOD AND BELLS
Karin Lowachee

THIS BE HOW *my mother died.*

Outside there be gunfire and voices. Maybe it's rain, or maybe the sound of rain hitting the dirty windows be her worlds at war with each other. The smell of blood bloats the air to bursting. She be bursting in this room. She be locked away. Her home be a small cold apartment in the heart of the Nine Nations. The paint peels. The walls cry from leaks in the pipes. The broken-tiled floor spreads hard and slick. Her brother's friend Yascha kneels in front of her open legs, as if he's praying to her. Or preparing a sacrifice. She holds onto her brother's hand. But he's not the only one she wants. She hears his voice coming closer from outside, demanding, worried, a gushing wound of love and anger. Maybe she deserves both of these emotions.

She be fifteen years old.

There be something inside of her that makes violence where there was peace, makes traitors in the place of lovers.

That something be me.

The door opens, but too late. There be a rush of blood.

I come screaming into the world at the same time my mother leaves it.

MY SON TZAK has tiny bells in his hair, just like the Opike killer standing across from me in the puddle. Their mothers came from the same Opike band, but wan't related. Still, all Opikei males wear bells in their hair. My son be only a half-blood, but he wears the bells. His mother would have wanted that so I give her that, even though she be dead now.

The Opike in the puddle has many bells, many skinny braids, and a dissatisfied face. He be nervous like me but don't want to show it. So instead he looks like this be all a waste of time. The unusual night rain pours down behind him in sheets, echoing steel music on the flimsy, slanted roof of the abandoned clinic. Water collects in tiny lakes on the black pavement and makes liquid fingers in the uneven ground, reaching toward us. Garbage flows down with the water like drowning souls: bits of aluminum, cracked syrettes, broken chain links. Shell casings. The round white light shining from my leader Jeriko's black lapel makes shadows and reflections collide.

Jeriko and Aszar, the Opike leader, continue their rough conversation. There was a murder yesterday in a stylehouse on Backbone Street, in Opike territory. Aszar thinks Jeriko might know something because the murderer supposedly fled to our band. But the murderer din't. This be what Jeriko is trying to explain, but Aszar in't listening. The victim was his cousin Yascha. The murderer even took the body. Aszar be a running rage. Even other Opikei be heard to grumble over Aszar's foolishness and the blood it brings them sometimes.

Tonight, Aszar brought five from his Opike warband. Jeriko brought six from our Domani band, including herself. We all got weapons, an hour wet from rain, and I want to go home. I watch the Opike standing directly across from me. His hands are in his pockets. The bells in his hair chime lightly. All of the Opike make music when they move or talk, and they can't talk without moving. Right now Aszar's hands cut the air like his words cut off Jeriko's words.

My hand is in my pocket and my gun is in my hand.

We don't know about that murder. No Domani were on Backbone when it happened. No Domani would keep a murderer from Opike justice. The Domani and Opikei are blood nations.

All of this fails to penetrate Aszar's gimpy brain.

Just behind me on my left stands Roon. I can almost hear her eyes moving from one Opike face to another. Hesi, Yei, and Pomjo make no sound. They stand on Jeriko's right. The Opikei across from us look straight at us. We've picked our opposites. The argument escalates. Sounds echo. We shift, and lights on our leaders' lapels flicker, shining on faces and half-destroyed walls.

Aszar flips open his gun, out of his pocket in a flash of steel.

They all come out, a unified snapping of impending murder. The guns whir as the bullets come alive, their narrow tips shining blue-white, like hot stars. They make the muzzles glow.

Jeriko stands with her hands flat out. She laughs.

"This be gamey, Aszar. You won't find the murderer, much less your dead cousin's body, by lighting me. You'll only make yourself a target."

There are seven other bands in the Nation. Some of them prefer the Domani to the Opike. Aszar should remember it.

The Opike across from me doesn't blink. Only his bells twinkle and chatter in the rainy breeze. Moisture runs into my eyes but I don't take off my target. I can't tell if he recognizes me as the mate of one of his dead bandsisters. I don't know if he knows that I hate Yascha, the dead one. Aszar knows though.

Aszar says, "If you're keeping my cousin's murderer, the Nations won't stand in my way."

Right. Aszar walks wide of the Council, even though he's on it. He's pulled the wrong noses in his time.

"I'll unroll who did it," Jeriko says. "But I need to be alive and so do you."

Aszar doesn't say anything for a stupidly long time. Our arms stay out and our guns pointed. But finally he sees the wisdom in Jeriko's words. His gun lowers. He flicks his wrist and flips it into safety, a spiral flourish. Small brains like his want to show off when they can.

The other Opikei follow suit. Jeriko never pulled a gun. When she lowers her hands we flip ours to safety.

Aszar signals his band with a brief jerk of his barely bearded chin. They peel into shadows behind him. He keeps looking at Jeriko. Then he looks at me. His eyes are gray and clear and murderous.

He turns in a whip of coat. Jeriko's white light points at his back like a laser sight. Aszar tests her. He be that bold.

The Opikei pass through the sheet of rain at the crumbled end of the wall and disappear.

I pocket my gun.

"Get on the street," Jeriko says to us. Her gaze flickers to me like a subliminal. "Unroll who did it."

We nod and murmur agreement.

"Taiyo," my leader calls.

My bandbrothers and sisters glance at me but separate like grenade fragments, bleeding into the downpour. I go closer to Jeriko.

"This wan't you." It's not a question in sound, only words.

"I din't light his mudfaced cousin."

Jeriko sighs. "No end to drama since Tzakri's mother dead."

I chew the inside of my cheek before I let some words fall out that I can't pick up. I say nothing.

"It be simpler on all of us if his little bells be back in Opike territory."

"He be *my* son!"

"Shut yourself. I speak truth and you know it. Prove to the Nations you din't light Yascha."

"As you say." Like I need to prove something I din't do.

I turn and kick the garbage at my feet as I step through the wall of water, right into little bullets of rain. I jog through puddles and pools of lamplight, heading back to my son.

SOMETIMES, LOSA AND me, we jawed about leaving the Nine Nations. Sometimes we jawed about dreams that we knew were too high to ever land. "Imagine the green," she'd say. "Imagine the sun. Does it feel different outside of the city?"

When I saw Losa dead in that room, the bedding all bloody beneath her and her neck slack on the pillow, every part of me in that moment went somewhere else. Someplace up and above but it wan't no freedom angel gone to such great heights. All my breathing went under and my body went up, like tumble-end in storm sea. Death was the scent of iron and electricity. I tried to shoot Yascha, but Losa's brother stopped me. Everybody crying, everybody mud-tears, and little Tzakri the loudest, this little wrinkly thing. A skinned cat, ugly gray, and for a second I hated him too.

But when Yascha reached for him I knocked that bastard back and took the boy myself. I took him up all blood and squall. Because he was mine.

He be mine.

THE ABANDONED CLINIC be five blocks into Gim band territory. The Gim band be neutral so both Jeriko and Aszar agreed to meet there. That was good because I don't want to go into Opike territory if I can help it. Some of them do remember me. But it be not good because Gim territory be five long blocks from my higher, through rain and polize streets. The polize patrol heavily in Nation territory. Their crawlers whir from corner to corner like mechanical cockroaches. The arthritic buildings and erratic lamplight sliced by the storm help me evade them. I'm soaked to the skin by the time I reach my higher. The broken main door swings open from the growing wind and slams shut behind me like a flapping mouth. The front floor be a shallow pool of grime and water. I'm already wet so I walk through it without care and up the slippery stairs, holding the metal rail. The lights here flicker too, buzz blue and black, on and off like code. I pass lines of shut black doors on either side. Muffled voices and sharp sounds weave through the rumble of the storm—vis or reality, who knows.

I pass a hand over the scan on my door then punch in the letters and numbers. The lock lights green, and immediately my son jumps up from the floor when I enter.

"Dehhh," he whines, "Kujaku was mean to me."

I shut and lock the door before the whole higher hears the complaint. The vis blinks in the shallow room, an old romantic prog that's all I have in storage. Something Losa liked. The windows be tinted black like I always keep them, but the track lights are bright. They reflect on my son's brown flat belly and his skinny legs. He keeps tugging at the waist of his too-big shorts. Little brown frog, all excited. He manages to hop over the toys and clothes on the floor and jumps into my arms.

"Kujaku's been mean, ah?" I keep one hand around him while he hangs off my neck like a sling, legs dangling.

"Kujaku han't been mean," Kujaku says from the couch, where he sits sprawled and barefoot. "Kujaku be tired and wants Pup to go to bed." He sacrificed a night of work for me because Jeriko called on me personal.

"Sorry," I tell him, and sit on the couch. Tzak the Pup climbs over my lap and sits himself between me and Kujaku. I belong to him when I'm home; infiltrators beware. "Aszar was being an ass. It took Jeriko smack-talk to calm him down."

"Moron Opike." Kujaku tilts his blonde head back at me, sinking deeper into the faded cushions. "Least you be alive."

"Deh," Tzak says, loudly, to interrupt us. "Kujaku was going to pick me upside down and throw me in bed. That's what he said."

I'm wet and sitting on the couch, making damp everywhere. Tzak be damp too, now, but he don't care.

"Kujaku won't have to throw you, 'cause I will." I stand and grab up my son, flip him upside down under my arm and cart him to the bedroom.

"Deh!"

I make small puddles as I go, all over the floor. It needs a clean anyway. Tzak wiggles ruthlessly. He has my doggedness and his mother's defiance. I get bruised. I dump him on the bed and he bounces. The tiny bells in his hair make scattered music.

"Ouch, wild boy! You abuse your deh."

He's a tumble of free-flying hair, half a dozen thin black braids, bells, and baggy shorts.

"You're all wet." He bounces now out of his own volition. The bed can barely take it. Soon it will fall through the floor and the neighbor will kill.

"That's because it's raining." I shake my hair and flick some droplets onto his face. He wrinkles his eyes and wipes at his nose, grinning. Such a little frog, easy in dry or wet. I struggle out of the heavy, soaked jacket. My shoulders sigh in relief. I hang up the jacket on the closet door handle where it will make a lake on the floor. Ah, I don't care. "Come on, Kujaku be right, it's way past your sleeptime. Get under the blanket."

He crawls beneath like a spider. I squish across the floor and sit on the edge of the bed and tuck him in tight like a mental patient.

"Deh!" He squirms.

I laugh and untuck him a bit. He flops his arms over the blanket, wild noodles. His smoke blue eyes blink, getting heavy with sleep. I knew he would stay up until I came home. Kujaku always has it hard when I'm late.

"Go to sleep." I use my father tone.

He holds out his arms. So I lean down and kiss him and let him hug my neck. I pat his hair and smooth it. The bells tinkle.

"Sleep."

He rolls to his side and tucks in. I put his favorite bunny-soft in his arms and he holds onto it, eyes squeezed shut in obedience. It's a rare thing and I don't question it. I get up and take off my wet clothes, dump them in a corner and go to the bathroom to dry off. Then I pull on an old sweater and zipper turfs, take the gun from my jacket pocket and go out to the couch and Kujaku, who be dozing in front of the maudlin vis. He's earned it. I slip the gun in the waist of my turfs and kick his bare feet before I step over them to the kitchen square.

"You want to stay here, Kujio? It's still raining."

"Eh," he mutters, already half-asleep. He has nobody to go home to anyway.

I turn up the kitchen lights and call down the light over Kujaku. The vis screen flickers over him like glowing eyes. I put a package meal on the counter to flash, lean against the fridge and light a smoke. It dries the rest of the rain inside my skin as I pull on it. The smoke rises to the ceiling like a prayer, making me sleepy to watch it. Kujaku be my bandbrother all my life, before I met Losa and before she had Tzak. Losa be dead. Tzak be three years old already.

I feel more than seventeen.

THE LITTLE FROG wakes me up. He climbs onto my chest and pats my face with his small cold hands.

"Deh, I'm hungry."

"Mmn, go to sleep."

"I slept already!"

The sun beats at my eyelids and my son beats at my cheeks. I blink into light, grab him, and roll him into the pillow to tickle him like a tickle killer. He screams and kicks and laughs. It's a mêlée of limbs and the sound of bells. One wild foot gets my knee.

"Ach! That needs revenge." I chomp his bony elbow.

"Deh!" His fist flies. He has sharp aim and my ear be a stationary target.

I pin him in a truce hug, with my back to the window and the early sun. That window doesn't tint for some reason anymore. Still, more time for sleep, just a minute or ten before Domani business. Tzak pats my face some more, pinches my nose, but I keep my eyes closed.

"Deh just wants a few more minutes, beba."

He's a warm squirmy thing, then he settles with his head under my chin. His hair smells like sleep and sunrays. I don't know when, but the morning passes.

"DEH, SOMEONE'S AT the door."

There's a pounding outside of my head. Tzak shakes my shoulder. The sun has moved, or a cloud has walked up my alley of the sky. Tzak kneels on the bed beside me, little face wrinkled in worry. He doesn't like visitors who don't know the code. Kujaku is the only one besides me who knows the code.

"Someone's at the door," my son says again.

"Stay here." I roll out and grab the gun off my bedstand. The air hits the skin on my arms and torso. I shut the bedroom door behind me and my feet get wet on the way to the front door. Overnight in't long enough to dry the rain inside. Kujaku in't on the couch or in the kitchen, but the windows are still dark.

I lean a shoulder on the front door. "Who is it?" My optic's been broken for a week. I keep forgetting to fix it.

"Romko. Open up."

Romko, Losa's blood brother. Full blood Opike. I han't seen him since she died.

I talk through the door. "What do you want?"

"It's too gamey in the hall, Taiyo. Open up."

My son be in the bedroom. I flip open my gun and unlock the door, aiming the weapon head-high.

"Whah, hold on!" Romko raises his beringed hands. His braids tinkle as he steps back. "I come to jaw, not scrum."

"What do you want?"

"Will the whole higher hear it?"

I watch him. He has Losa's exact eyes, inconstant blue. When he smiles it's like Losa come back. I let him in but don't safety the gun. I shut the door and lock it again. He stands in a little puddle from last night.

"Ach, Tai, han't you housebroken Tzakri?"

"Third time asking, and my last."

Romko folds his arms and spreads his feet, standing like a chief of an overturned apple cart.

"Street jaw say you lit Aszar's cousin."

Rumors travel like garbage to a gutter.

"Street jaw needs to be broke." I go to the kitchen, but keep my edges on the Opike. Romko and the cousin were friends. Yascha. Stupid dead bastard. I won't rain on my face for him.

"Aszar believes the street jaw," Romko says, cutting off the ends of his words.

I put my glass under the dispenser, dribble some ice water into it and sip. "Aszar's an idiot."

Romko straightens. "Don't say so, Tai."

"I've said it. I've always said it."

"You know lies serve selfish wonders. He might avenge Yascha on your disrespect."

"I sho've avenged Losa on Yascha's incompetence."

Romko looks away first, toward the couch. His gaze finds interest in the menial mess. "Aszar han't forgotten your threats on his cousin."

I shrug. "Let him remember. Jeriko don't chain me like Aszar whips his band. I might prove a little more than slightly entertaining."

"Don't you think this gone on long enough?"

"What this?"

"All this fight. Yascha *tried*, Taiyo. I know you hate to hear it but he hated himself more than you can for Losa's end."

"I doubt that."

"Tai, Losa be dead."

I look at him and his earnest face. Face, that's all it is. Maybe he's here to warn me. He really in't here to give revelation. "I wan't sure she was," I tell him. "Thanks."

"Listen," he says. "Your Losa wan't so full of grace."

I feel the gun in my hand. "What you say now?"

The thoughts rotate in his eyes like a siren. And he backs down. Of course. "Aszar wants the murderer. Opikei don't like you and some jaw say your own band blames you for this ongoing. I got my balls in a bind to tell you this."

"Good thing you don't need 'em."

"You stupid fool, Tzakri be my little bandbrother. I want him to be safe!"

"He has a father," I say slowly. "And a band."

"There an't no good end in this world for him."

I step close up to him, fast. "You threatening my son?"

His hands rise, weak defense. "All I say, Tai. The Nations an't all there be in the world."

I stare at him. Wonder for the first time if Losa's dream found brotherly ears.

I see his thought flip over like a card. His tone hardens. "The Nations won't back a thief forever."

"Or a murderer."

His gaze be crooked and we don't meet. For all I know he started the street jaw. The set up can run deep. Opikei are notorious. No Domani turns a back on an Opike.

Then again, no Domani should bed an Opike either. Jeriko had warned me. Even Kujaku.

"Good luck," I tell him. "There be a trail of tragedy following Opikei these days."

His eyes get mottled.

"That be all?" I smile. "The day ages and so do you."

Romko don't smile. "They be your waking hours, for however long they last." He goes to the door.

I follow. "I'll relay that to Jeriko."

He glances at me and steps out, maybe a bit fast. He's not a coward but he's got a mind. And eyes. He saw the gun in my hand.

"Deh, who was that?"

I lock the door again. "I told you to stay in the bedroom, Tzakri."

"But I'm hungry." He stands on the threshold, a shoulder against the jamb, one foot on top of the other. He needs a good scrub.

I tuck the gun into my turfs. "Go shower, beba. I'll flash something."

"Who was that, Deh?"

"Nobody, beba. When I say to stay in the bedroom, I mean it. You know?" I look at him hard. His eyes are larger than they need to be in such a small face. When he smiles it's Losa come back.

It's Romko.

I don't smile and neither does he. His lip sticks out. "I know, Deh."

That pout can move staunch mountains and a father's heart.

I MEET KUJAKU on the crowded corner in front of my higher. I called him but didn't tell him about Romko. Those aren't things you say over a call. I hold Tzak's hand and smoke with my other. Kujaku trots up from a daybar across the street, weaving through a slow pass of scuffed, gem-tone crawlers. It's a cool day after a long night of rain. The sky be deep blue. The sounds of a blinking city seem to suction to the painted walls of the highers and other buildings.

Emidit be a big city. I only know the portions that belong to the Nations, which an't as shiny as those of the Regierun. Friends of the polize, the Regierun. They put us here and they keep us here, among highers and shops and streets that bend and snap from lack of nutrition, like sickly kids or wrinkled old women.

Tzak leans away from me, anchored by my hand, a tilted tree in a breeze. He's playing, but I don't trust the mash of people—the drunks, the kneelers, and the palmers. They will all make my son older than he is and I'm in no great hurry to let him lose his youth. So I yank him back and he bumps my side.

"Ah," he says, working up to a howl.

"Stay still, Tzakri."

"Ah ah," he says, jiggling.

"Here comes Kujaku. Look."

But Tzak in't interested in Kujaku. He steps on my foot.

"Enough." I grab him up, one scoop into my arm. It's what he wants anyway. His arms go immediately around my neck and suddenly he's perfect.

This child be spoiled.

Kujaku stops under the dead lamp, where I stand, and pokes Tzak's stomach.

"Hei Pup."

"Don't." Tzak flies a foot at Kujaku.

"Last time," I warn him. He turns his head to peer over my shoulder and ignore me. Every year he gets heavier. My arm earns it.

Kujaku thieves a cig from my pocket. "You heard the street jaw?"

I light it for him and we walk. Most of the people step aside without touching. In our territory they know the signs, the black collar that means Domani.

"Romko visited."

Kujaku's pale eyebrows lift. "This sunup? All the way from Opikei mudholes?"

"All the way."

"Well technically we an't at war." Kujaku shrugs and puffs. Streeters watch him go, even though he's clearly not on duty. He has a look that makes fugitive eyes: low-lidded blue stare, large flexible lips. Losa wandered his way once, but only with her gaze. Her feet knew better and walked to me.

"I think maybe I should stay off the street." I'm only half-serious.

"Might be," Kujaku agrees. "Aszar in't known for his agile logic."

"He won't get far. All Domani can smell Opikei. They might do the deed but they won't leave our territory alive."

"Tai." Kujaku flicks his ashes. "I know your ears an't sweet on these words, but not all Domani like your Losa years."

I look at him hard. Tzak dozes on my shoulder. It in't a good thing to have to walk your own street with an eye to your wake. Or for your bandbrother to echo an Opike. "So they'd side with Opikei lighting me?"

Kujaku frowns. "No. Jeriko won't, you know. But the Nine Nations might just call it even and part."

"Jeriko *and* the Nations stood by my side with Tzak."

"You already had stole him, Tai."

"I didn't steal my own son!"

Kujaku touches my arm. "It be only frank jaw. I in't saying I agree."

"There be a wrongness in the understanding of the Nine. Just 'cause Losa died and the Opikei braided Tzak, it don't mean they should own him. He be my blood."

"And theirs, they say."

"He be more my blood than any but a corpse's." Romko may have tied that braid to his wrist when he be born, but I be in his veins. "Jeriko stands by it and it should be enough for the rest of the band."

In truth, the rest of the band can go to mudfire if they think I should abandon Tzak to the Opikei.

"We stand by you, Tai," Kujaku says. "All who count. I said only *some* Domani."

"And the Nine?" Nine bands across Emidit. Each one of them with their own pride.

"The Nation be full of people like Aszar. There be no help for them but death by stupidity."

"I'd marshal them along if they stood in my way."

Kujaku glances up at me. He blows out a stream of smoke. "I know it, bandbrother. And sometimes it be a heavy thought."

ROON TAKES TZAK from my arms. We stand in her doorway, in the narrow hall of her higher. A city of scented candles burns behind her in a gauze-shrouded room. A blue haze. She's got flaky tastes but she's Domani dependable. She coos over Tzak like a cresty fountain bird. I see the bulge by her waist; her gun. She'll look out for Tzak. Tzak be half-asleep and the handover wakes him.

"Deh," he moans.

"I have to go somewhere," I tell him. "Roon will keep you today."

"Dehhh." He's set up for a tantrum. Children and feral dogs, never wake them from a nap.

"Go on," Roon says, holding firm while Tzak builds up for a bawl.

"Be good," I tell my son, and rub his braided hair.

"Not with you as a deh," Kujaku puts in.

"Shut up, kneeler."

I wrinkle fingers at Tzak, trying to ignore his crumbling face, and walk down the bare hallway with my bandbrother. Tzak's wail follows me like a polize siren, echoing among the gut pipes above.

It be a daily abandonment.

"So how are we to find this murderer?" Kujaku yawns.

"We ask," I say.

We move through the midday streets like nose-poking polize. But here, in daylight, we *are* the polize. The power and the Regierun of Domani territory. Polize know better than to scrum with us in view of witnesses. Streeters here may have little voice, but enough of them can out-boom a bomb. They have no near affection for the Regierun on the rich side of Emidit. No Domani and few Nation bands are stupid enough to scrum in broad daylight, anyway. So it's our haven, here on the street, bold with our black collars.

Emidit stinks, like it always does with the heat of the sun to expose its lower skins. The tall dark buildings suck up tight weather and hold it in, but there's still ample sky to rain down daggers of light. Clouds be rare in these summer months; last night was a fluke. In this clime, what isn't swallowed by steel gets spat up by gray pavement and vomited in the sweat of sardine bodies. Even my short-sleeve shirt, open at the neck, is a layer too much.

"Who're we going to ask?" Normally Kujaku's in his doorway at this hour, scoping hopefuls. This morning he scopes with me. Jeriko ordered an unrolling, so all of us pull.

We pass the gaping mouth of the Hank Street subterrain and hear the rumbling anger of its passing beneath our feet.

"Let's catch it to the house." I motion to the stairs leading down.

"Can we eat first?" Kujaku elbows me toward a pockmarked vendor box, strategically placed beside a guaranteed flow of flesh traffic from the sub. "You pay, of course."

"Me of course? You make more living than I do by theft."

"You be in the wrong thieving biz," he says, with a kneeler's grin. He's the kind of pretty that rubs elbows with repulsive.

"I prefer to stay on my feet." I punch in our unhealthy orders on the console and scan my ring. Mysterious workings rattle in the wide silver interior of the anchored vendor, then our spiced meat buns pop out of the gap at the top of the cart, steaming. I hand Kujaku his, with a nice swat upside the head, no extra charge, then take my own and head toward the subterrain.

Our rocking ride makes unsteady digestion, but it's a short stint, only ten blocks. At least it be steely cool and we have our pick of seats from streeters with smarts. Rush hour tends to have little effect on a Domani. Up on the corner of Backbone and Dye we take the murderer's alleged route to the scene of the offense, a high-end stylehouse with a long reputation. *Pagoda.* It looks like one, all bright blues and reds and golds, a peacock building. It be Opikei protected and routinely patronized. But not Opikei run. Regierungi living greases the palms of this place.

"Now this here be an opportunity," Kujaku says.

"We're on the roll for Jeriko," I remind him. "Keep your soles flat."

"Eyes can scope."

There's no reforming him.

I glance up and down the sidewalk, mindful of Romko's words, but no Opikei gunmen spring from the crowd. It be one thing to talk of war, another to do it. So we said when Losa died.

I go in the stylehouse first, and my feet sink. There be carpet all over the interior; even the walls be thin engraved velvet, blood red. Gold-tasseled couches and glass partitions broadly divide the space. Everywhere be hollow rich. The bar be stacked with colored glass bottles and private lacquer drawers. A tall smooth woman attends to them all with a swan-necked scanner in her hand.

I step down into the social pit, through expensive cool air and the faint scent of previous nightly decadence, straight to a man in a white shirt. He be seated at the bar with an activated slate set on top. His pink, smooth fingers tap the screen expertly.

The woman looks up first. Her face be holo perfect, but it be plastic flesh. She in't surprised. Somewhere in one of the back rooms, through the curtained doors at the edges of my sight, guards watch me and Kujaku, probably right down to the pores on our skin.

"Mr. Ong," she says.

The man looks up and he in't surprised either. He has an emotionless powdered face and small black eyes. They find our black collars and linger.

"What can I do for you?" A rounded Regierungi accent.

"An Opike man was shot here recently," I say. "What do you know about it?"

He looks back at his slate, but it's blank now. Protected. "I told the Opikei everything I saw. You can ask them."

"I'm asking you."

Kujaku walks around, grazing a hand on the ornate workmanship of the glass separators. The designs be all curlicues and vague entwined bodies.

"I have no association with the Domani." The mole above his left eyebrow twitches. "But I do with the Opikei. So ask them."

I can be patient. "The Opikei claim it was a Domani who did the deed. So you see we have a right to ask."

These things sometimes take plateaus to reach. If he pushes me to the next flat then I will go there.

The woman's eyes follow Kujaku like a trigger finger.

"I know your face," Mr. Ong says. "They say you're the one who killed the Opike. You're the one who stole their child."

Kujaku stops in my periphery with a hand on the velvet wall.

Maybe Mr. Ong knows how thin his life is. "Who says I lit Yascha?"

Mr. Ong doesn't answer. He's an uncreased Regierungi.

The sight of my gun wrinkles him slightly.

"You see how this can be, Mr. Ong."

"Everyone knows you stole their child."

"Who says I lit Yascha?"

He shrugs. "Everybody. Words," he waves a hand, "they travel through the air like dust."

I can kill a Regierungi every day and still not be filled. I take one stride and push my gun against Mr. Ong's right nostril.

"Someone want to start a war?" I ask.

"Tai," Kujaku says.

People have materialized from the walls. Tall men and women with hidden hands. Mr. Ong holds up his palm.

"The friend shouted Domani," he says. "But in truth the killer was hooded."

"Friend? Of Yascha's?"

"The same."

I ease back the gun a little, but not enough that he can't still smell the steel. "Romko said it be Domani. Specifically me?"

Mr. Ong shrugs. "Aszar was in the back, playing and having some poke. The cousin and his friend were in the pit with some drink. A hooded man shot one of my guards and stormed in. He knew just where to look and where to shoot. He was good." The black eyes look down the silver of my weapon, then flick back to my face. "The cousin died. Romko said he saw a black collar beneath the overshirt before it fled. He said it was Domani. Aszar drew his own conclusions."

"This be how it fell out? A Regierungi rolls the truth?"

"A Regierungi with a gun up his nose will roll his tongue like a kneeler."

The man be a survivor. I lower the gun. The room breathes slightly.

This information was too easy to come by.

I look at Kujaku and head to the door. He treads in my wake, backward to watch the room. Not one of them moves. We hit the sidewalk and street stink, hot from the cool indoors.

"What do you make of that?" I ask Kujaku.

He spits on the pavement. "They twisty their words like intestines. But they be gutless."

"I wouldn't put it past Romko. He ups and sees me for the first in three years? To warn me Aszar wants my blood? This in't revelation."

"Romko be no gymnastic mind."

I nod. "True. He's always been someone's pawn."

Kujaku says, "His king be dead. Who directs him now?"

So sits the question. But we can't sit here.

"Let's get out of this Opikei shade."

Kujaku follows me to the subterrain. "The goods an't so hot here anyway."

*　　*　　*

WE CALL A report to Jeriko of what we unrolled from Mr. Ong, but she don't believe it either, at least not the surface. "Dig deeper. Romko might plant the seed but someone else laid the dirt."

And dirt stinks worse in the hot temperature of an Opikei agenda.

It's back to Roon to check on Tzak, though. Except when we get there the door be blasted open and inside all the candles be upended, the blue gauze torn down, everything shredded. I run through the flat but no Tzak, and Kujaku hollers at me from the kitchen. When I join him, there be Roon face down on the tile, paralyzed. Her hand clutches her gun. It still buzzes live.

Silent, Kujaku leans down to flick it off.

"I found these." I hold out my hand. Beads and bells in my palm. From my son's braids. "They took Tzakri."

JERIKO SAYS NOT to do anything but Kujaku and me both know we're going to ignore. End the call. Who else would take my son but a wide-armed Opike? Specifically Romko. Romko and his generous warning that Aszar wants me dead. Before Aszar wanted me dead, Romko had me marked. Before even Losa died, Romko wanted me dead just for walking my feet to his sister. It goes back that far and further still if you count all the years in the Nation when Domani outsmarted Opikei and won the Council's favor.

There be only one place Tzak can be—in Opike territory.

Kujaku and me hop back on the subterrain. But half-way through our ride, four black collars come up on us. Our bandbrothers. Pomjo and three novii, younger than me with their yellow training collars. But they all be loaded up.

I stare up at Pomjo from my seat. "You light me if I don't?"

"Jeriko's orders. Don't make this tough." He almost looks apologetic.

"Roon be shot," Kujaku says. "Not dead, but someone got at her to get the boy."

The air around Pomjo sinks. "You still gotta come."

Jeriko's dog. So at the next stop, me and Kujaku unboard with our bandbrothers. They walk us like prisoners back through the streets, back to Domani territory, full on every side. No borders but Domani.

I don't see the familiar streets, just Romko's face and his lying mouth. All I feel is an itch to pummel it into the ground. To get Tzakri back.

We go to the Domani clubhouse, empty at this hour. There be Jeriko sitting at her usual shimmer blue table, arms wide as the white leather. White liquor sits in front of her in two tall bottles.

To me: "Sit." And to Kujaku: "Get."

So the game sets and everybody takes up their places. Pomjo in't far, bulldog staunch.

Jeriko pulls a sip of her drink. "You an't going to Opike territory."

"You going to get my son back?"

Her hand lands on the back of my neck. Squeezes hard. "Taiyo. We an't starting a war over your little belled bastard."

I jerk my head but she holds on.

"Your ears be open, Tai?"

I say nothing.

Out the corners of my eyes, more bodies come through the door. Closer and they be three band leaders. From Gim, Sashasa, and Moj. Collars all flashing their colors, two sisters and a brother.

I count their meaning. Territories all closest to Opike.

"You an't going to get your son," Jeriko reiterates. "An't nobody here be letting you cross. Their band be ordered to shoot you on sight. Your ears be open now?" She shakes me. "I need to hear it!"

I press my jaw together. "Ya."

She lets me go. "Good. Now make peace in your heart and maybe one day the Opikei will let you visit your boy."

I gather Kujaku with a glance and we exit the clubhouse. Sun hits my eyes hard, but I don't rain on my face. I let it burn.

"Now what?"

He gives me a smoke and I spark it. "Gutless Jeriko think she can chain me? That an act of war to take what's mine!"

"The point be it was always disputed he be yours, Taiyo. Family outrank where any of us put our pokers."

I be sick and tired of everyone telling me what's so. Like band rules sound better than what's in the blood of my heart.

"What you be thinking?" Kujaku asks with some hesitance.

I walk and smoke.

"Tai."

I tell him nothing. These days who knows who be listening on the open street. Instead I take Kujaku back to my higher. Everybody expects me to go there, so I go.

There be my weapons anyway.

BROWN PAPER ON the floor, the kind they use to wrap fish. Who uses paper these days but for stink purposes? I wait until Kujaku shuts the door before I unfold it. It smells like something mud dwelling beneath a bog.

Five words scrawled by hand: *Losa's den. Take the roofs.*

"WHO ELSE IT be but Romko? What else but a trap?"

Kujaku doesn't answer. It be not a question that needs jaw. Of course we go. We walk the roofs like birds at seed, peck and follow, from rim to edge and flat and back to rim again. Frog-hop high and light, swing from iron and jump to black gravel. I know this route, it be how I got to Losa back when we were kids and this journey felt like both romance and rebellion. Far below us, Emidit squeals life and rumbles threat, some animal storm resisting to be tamed. The sun be arching low, spreading blood light over all the jammed highers.

Losa's den be half-abandoned now, it was on its way when alive she be. Roof door bent enough to sport a broken latch and me and Kujaku squirrel down steps from floor to floor, where there be no light but what ekes through broken down sliver windows. The steps be slick and smell of piss and rain.

To the fifth floor, barely lit. Echoes bounce along the puddles like skip stones and I stop before number 555. We used to think the triple 5s be luck, Losa and me. We'd shut this door and pretend all the world was some other planet, something from fairy jaw and cast aside tech. Three years beyond those times, more from when we saw each other on the street as children and latched like parasites to the thought of each other, and it feels more like dream than any outlandish jaw so far flung it makes fantasy out of history.

She said once, "This can't always be."

I used to laugh her silent. Asked her why she be ruining what we got. Not what we got in Emidit, since that was next to nothing, but what we got in our dreams.

I try to put some dreams in Tzakri but they don't last the night.

"We go in?" Kujaku with his hand on my back.

I hold my gun at my side and shove the door in. It be broken like all else.

I expect Romko and my boy. That thieving bastard.

What I see be Yascha.

"PUT THE GUN down, Taiyo," he says, all calm like he han't be dead.

I want to shoot. But Kujaku spout behind me: "Where you come from?" He wants to hear this.

So do I. And there an't a corpse in this world who speaks.

I lower the gun. I walk a circuit around the room, walls all peeling like dry skin, pockmarked like disease. The bloody bed be gone. There be just Yascha and he wears no Opike collar. I pace back and forth.

"We needed some way to get out," the liar says.

The second part of that *we* comes through the door behind Kujaku. Romko and my boy.

"Deh!"

Good thing no Opikei blocks my son from running to my arms. I pick him up and hug him until his tears squeeze out. Until mine nearly do.

"So you blame me?" I turn so my back be to the corner and both Opikei in my sights. Kujaku steps outside of Romko's periphery. His gun be out too.

"You were the one that would make sense," says Yascha. "And we knew you'd come for Tzak."

"I come for you too." Not to collect except in blood debt.

"Open your eyes!" Romko moves to stand by Yascha. Aszar's cousin and here they be, doing something diagonal of their band?

"What game?" I look from face to face. Romko be earnest as usual. Yascha gray-eyed like his cousin but there be a stillness in him, no hands moving. "You leave the Nations?"

"Ya." He don't even blink. "Once Losa died, once Tzakri be born, we be planning it. But you had the boy and there would be war. We knew you wouldn't come by any other means than a theft. Losa used to tell me how you talked of going, but you never did. Me and her, we planned it for that night. You weren't supposed to be there."

But I had gone when she didn't answer my call. So many words and so little sense. My boy be wrapped around me, his face pushed in my neck. I feel him breathing. The bells be broken from his hair, no chiming when I touch the back of his head.

"Tzakri be my son by blood, Taiyo," Yascha says.

I feel my head shaking but no words fall out. Maybe it be my world instead.

Shaking and falling.

"I be not what you think I am, and neither was she. But you be the only father Tzakri knows so we want you to come with us. For him."

"This was her dream," Romko puts in. "And the bands won't war if they think you ran."

If they think I did it. Just like I ran diagonal of all Domani when I bed an Opike girl. Got a boy from her.

I got a boy from her. A boy with smoke blue eyes and his uncle's smile.

I stare into Yascha's eyes. He be so quiet and still, like no Opike I ever known. No bells, just blood.

This be where it started. How my world changed when the boy in my arms came screaming into the world. At the same time his mother left it.

Yascha could have taken Tzak and disappeared. Pin me with the murder. Watch our Nations stand in the rain and unfurl every weapon in anger. Become a muddy rage of revenge. This be all of what I think of him, like I think myself Tzakri's father.

This falling down room have a habit of changing lives.

I still be Tzakri's father. It in't all because of blood.

I think of my higher but it be just a place.

I think of the boy so solid in my arms.

I hand Kujaku my gun. In one look he says he be with me, like always.

What else do I need?

"There be a lot to unroll," I say to the Opikei. Though they wear no collars and no bells. For some reason I just notice the lack of music in this room. No chime from the past come to haunt us here. There be no Opikei in Losa's dying place.

No Domani either.

"We have to move," Yascha says. "Out of the Nine Nations."

Kujaku says, "Where we go?"

Imagine the green. I can hear Losa. I almost see her too. I see her in her brother's face, three years come back like that. So much blood and electricity.

"We go anywhere," I tell them. Chained to nobody, no leader, and no Nation. Tzakri's body clings to mine. Imagine the sun. "We be free."

GIVE ME YOUR BLACK WINGS OH SISTER
Silvia Moreno-Garcia

IT'S UNDER HER skin. It's an electrical current, an itch, a malaise that does not cease. At nights she rubs her hands against her arms and it is there, like pressing your hands on a vein and feeling its gentle thump. A river of emotion surges through her body; an old river.

Some ghosts are woven into walls and others are woven into skin with an unbreakable, invisible thread. You inherit the color of your eyes, but also this thread which chokes you and bites into your heart. If you look back into any family tree you find paupers and merchants and poets and soldiers, and sometimes you find monsters.

During the day, she manages not to think of it. She takes the subway to work, she sits at her desk, she surveys the city from her office window and she forgets about old phrases, old stories, legends that nobody remembers, washed away by the tide of modernity.

But at nights it's still there, under her skin.

There are warlocks and there are witches who are not what they seem. There are birds that are not birds and the flapping of wings and there is hunger. And it comes in the blood, it can skip a generation or two but it won't be washed away. But it's all in her dreams, all in half-forgotten tales of her childhood which she brushes away come morning, like brushing away cobwebs.

Child eaters. Devourers.

She boards the subway and puts on her headphones. The stations go by, there's the blur of people, and she exits the subway car and walks up the stairs, avoiding vendors and beggars. There's nothing to fear with the cellphone in her hand, the gentle music in her ears, the purse dangling from her shoulder.

She phones her mother every Thursday and they talk for half an hour and on Fridays she likes to watch a movie. Saturdays she goes grocery shopping.

There are no curses under fluorescent lights, nor can you find mysteries at the till while you swipe a credit card.

The city comforts her like a mother who coddles a child. It says, "You are an ordinary body among ordinary bodies, you are in fact no-body."

She likes that, just like she likes the neon of the signs downtown where nightclubs mushroom and the honking of cars fills the air while the pedestrian crossing urges pedestrians to walk.

One day a man sits next to her on the subway. He wears a suit and his black shoes have just been shined, and he has a watch on his right wrist, but she knows immediately he is a not man. She knows there is something under his skin.

She sits, rigid with fear, eyeing him from the corner of her eye while he remains immersed in his newspaper. She can smell his cologne, but beneath that there is another scent, the odor of raw meat. Meat left under the sun to spoil. It makes her think of the ranch where she spent her summers, of her grandmother chopping off a chicken's head.

It makes her think of blood. Makes her think of all those stories about the warlocks and the witches who turn into other things and how they fly through the air until they sneak into a child's room and bite into their neck.

Blood, thick and black, like the man's suit. He makes a motion with his hand, as if checking the time, and raises his head, looking at her and smiling. She can see his teeth – ivory white, old ivory kept in cupboards away from dust – and the smile, which is dark, and the eyes, which are like gleaming obsidian.

"I know you," he says.

Even if those that are not the exact words he says – because she is wearing the headphones, how can she hear him? – it is what he *means*. It's all meaning, all there, like the bones that hide under muscle and flesh. True even if they are out of sight. Like the veins and arteries running down her legs, mapping her body. Rivers of life which extend far beyond the single body and reach through time.

In the stories, there's always a moment when the warlocks and the witches know themselves, and when they do there is no going back. It's like lighting a match; such a chemical reaction will not allow the elements to return to their original shape.

When they know themselves they are forever changed.

"Sister," he says, with a conviction that will not be denied. He knows her, knows the atoms in her body and the hidden wings beneath the cage of bones. He knows her like they must all know themselves, gazing at each other in the moonlight with their flesh peeled off and their faces removed.

She is scared. She is paralyzed. She does not understand why none of the other passengers seem to notice her distress. Why do they keep looking at their cellphones, why do they keep chatting, why do they look down, bored, at their scuffed shoes? She feels she will die there, sitting in that cramped, stuffy subway car.

There. There is the stop. The doors open and the man stands up, holding out his hand to her. He wants her to go with him.

"Come," he says.

Something forbids her from considering such an action. It is the timber of his voice, which is deep and smooth, like tar. Or it is the smile, smooth too, and deepening, as if he already knows she'll agree to walk with him.

She clutches her purse and closes her eyes. The subway is in motion. When she looks again he is gone. The seat next to her is empty.

She rushes out the subway concourse, up the stairs, startling a dozen pigeons which fly up into the darkening sky and for a moment she holds up her hands, as if protecting her face from them, as if they would claw her and puncture her skin with their beaks in an attempt to expose her other, inner skin.

The pigeons fly off and she lowers her hands.

At home she turns on all the lights in the apartment, turns on the TV and does not watch it. She paces until midnight, then slips into bed.

She breaths slowly and tries not to think about the way her heart is beating, loudly, loudly, loudly, in her chest, and the way the blood drifts in her veins, and she bites the inside of her cheek and tells herself there is nothing under the skin.

She dreams a different dream that night. It's not a dream, but a memory, of long ago, long buried and forgotten like a child's discarded toys.

She is ten years old in the memory. Her grandmother is making chicken stew in the kitchen; there's much plucking and feathers and boiling of water. She feels hungry and grandmother says the food will be ready soon. It is taking far too long.

She should be helping the old woman, but instead she drifts into the nursery. Her baby brother is asleep. She looks at him, gentle and tiny, his breath soft, and then she reaches a hand into the crib.

That is it. The end of the memory, the end of the dream. When she wakes up she is shaken and can hardly look at herself in the mirror. She is afraid of what she'll see.

Her brother has been long dead. Crib death. He passed away before reaching his first birthday. She seldom thinks of him; he's not brought up. Once a year there is a gloomy mass for the child which her mother organizes, like clockwork. She does not normally attend the mass. The last time she went to the church, she recalls her mother's cold stare.

Just a look, a few seconds long. A look of loathing.

I know what you are, said the look. I know what you did.

That look of pure hatred.

But there's also love in the look. How could there not have been love, too?

A love that had kept certain secrets or had ignored the truths under the skin.

Slowly she gazes in the mirror and lets out her breath.

The mirror shows nothing. Her eyes are dark, but not the color of obsidian and her face is a simple face, just a couple of acne scars left from her teenage years to mar its surface. She applies lipstick and mascara, brushes her hair, and steps out of her apartment.

The city makes her forget her worries. The large ads on the bus shelters, the guy at the newspaper stand arranging his merchandise, the scent of cigarettes wafting towards her as she walks by a café: these details ground her and return her to this ordinary life, this ordinary moment.

She sets the purse on her lap, enjoying the presence of the other commuters, their voices in her ears, the movement of the subway car. A woman with a baby sits next to her.

The baby is wrapped in a fluffy yellow blanket and it gurgles.

She looks at it.

It's such a pretty little child, like the Christ in a Nativity scene, soft like porcelain, this baby at her side.

But her mouth salivates and she feels a terrible hunger and something stirs under her skin, and she presses her knuckles against her teeth to keep them from chattering. Outside, there's the flapping of wings.

THE SHADOW WE CAST THROUGH TIME
Indrapramit Das

[*Archive reconstruction; lore record, The First Demon, as re-told by Truthteller Surya*]

IT IS TOLD that the first demon was born when a young human child from the first village on this world wandered out into the forest nearby to explore. This was so long ago that no human had yet died on this world, in the village within the great winged hulk of the first starship that came down from the first world. What the child wandered into was no forest, of course, because the forest is a thing of first world, and back then, no humans had planted any trees in the cold soil of here. But to the forest the child went with their lantern, because humans see what they want to see, and everyone called the shaggy dark on the horizon a forest, though no one was prepared to find out what it was until that day. As the child came closer, they saw that the trees of this forest were in fact a city of clay spires from which flowed rivers of hair that blew in the wind, hair without heads, without humans, growing out of towers that reeked like excrement and coiled with jagged black spikes. But this child knew no fear, having known only the deathly void of space outside their starship's windows, and the distant tales of first world, so they ventured into this strange city, drunk on freedom, on finding their own world to name and gift with the blessing of human witness. They were clever, and knew that these towers had to be houses, which, for humans at least, were starships that did not move through space, and simply sat on a world to transport humans through time instead. The child wanted to find out who lived in these houses on this world. They went up to one of the towers, which they realized had a doorway into darkness. Raising the lantern to the impenetrable mouth of this doorway, the child asked the darkness, "Does someone live here?"

The darkness answered, "Yes."

The child asked, "Who are you?"

The darkness said, "I am the shadow that you have cast from across time, from the first world to this one."

The child asked, "What does that mean?"

The darkness said, "It means that you belong under a star far away in the night sky, too far to cast a shadow here. It means that *nature* abhors a *vacuum*, but there is no nature here."

The child said to the darkness, "I'm sorry, but I still don't understand. Can you explain it better?"

The darkness said to the child, "It means that you cannot be good in a world that has seen no evil. It means that I will be your shadow under the new stars. It means that I will be the gift of evil. It means that I am the kal, and I have waited long aeons for you."

And then the child realized that they had indeed come too far into this strange new wilderness, their lantern a tiny star in this city now grown dark as space with the new sun Umi below the horizon.

"But we have left evil behind on first world," said the child.

And the darkness laughed, because outside of the endless void, a shadow needs something to cast it. The wind grew sharp as poison, as the locks of headless hair blew on the spires, and it grew cold as the skin of a starship drifted far from a sun, and the child had no choice but to enter that doorway where the darkness lurked. Lantern and child were swallowed, never to be seen again in the village of the starship.

When at dawn what used to be the child emerged from the spire, they were not human, for their bones had turned black as distant time. The child was no child any longer, but first of demons on this world, Death Walking, because all worlds need death if humans must tread on them. From that day onwards, the humans of our world began to die, as humans must, as we did on first world, and as we have done on all the worlds.

* * *

[*Archive reconstruction; personal record, Death Letter of Truthteller Surya*]

IN THE CHILL air, the doorway to darkness breathes a humid heat. Umi, the great lighthouse, is at the horizon, about to be swallowed by night's tide. The doorway is an orifice under a spined arch, at the base of a spire of bones and living clay that rises a hundred feet into the air, jagged with curling black spikes. One of this monument's many names (none given by those who built it) is hagtower, for the long white snarls of hair and grey membranes of skin that grow around the skeletons that compose it, making them look like ancient humans pickled in time and spacelight. Hags from Farhome, the first world, handmaidens of Death Walking dancing down (or up?) in a pillar from the sky. Hair and skin; fibers of exomycelial lifeforms sewn into the bones by its builders. There is lore that says the hags are our dead, going back to the ancestral grounds of Farhome—they will climb the glowing bridge of deadmoon in the sky, and leap off it into the ocean of spacetime to swim the waves back to the beginning. There is lore says the reverse—the hags are the dead of first world climbing out of the ocean, dancing down here to cast our shadow and bring death here. Our village favors the former. It is our ancestors whose bones dance in these towers, who bodies make the demons that live in them, breathed to life by the black flame of the kal.

If I try to hurt the hagtower—with fire, or weapons—it is said that it will wake and tear me apart with its many calcified claws and stony teeth. It will not. The skeletal walls are lifeless bones, even though the tower itself is a colony lifeform. If there were demons nesting in the tower, *they* would kill me. But even if the tower were empty of a demon mother of contagion, the hag-skin that sheathes the dancing skeletons, translucent and grey under the light of the stars and flaring sunset, is sensitive. Disturbing it can release potent toxins. I have my gas mask and fiber pelts and gloves. But why *would* I hurt the hagtower, and the kal inside it, even if I could? I don't touch the curtains of hag-skin or locks of hag-hair, or disturb anything in this sacred place. Up in the sky,

Archive passes in the darkening sky, a tiny moving star. I chose this.

In the etched shadows of Umi's fall, the hags of the tower do come alive to my eyes, their hair stirring in the cold breeze from the mountains far to the northeast. This doesn't scare me, because I have come to see the hags—they are built of the bones of my people, my guardians, my friends, my lovers, my offspring. I have come to join them.

All these things are known to my people. They are not known to many of you in the sky, beyond the fallen gate, so I speak them to you and to the demons that surround me, in case time's river snuffs our flame from the world. In case the gate opens again, and you find this letter, and need guidance to understand what's transpired here. My words will go to Archive, because I must bear witness. There is more happening here than just my insignificant death.

FOR MANY YEARS of my life, I was a mother by profession. I was twenty years old (by our sun, and no others) when I grew the first of fourteen children inside me. By then it had been years since we realized the gate in the sky had collapsed. We'd seen the ripples of spacetime warp the constellations, sending stars dancing on an invisible tide through the sky. Archive told us too—the gate was closed, and all the worlds gone. No more starships, no more trade missions, no more precious cargo of star-borne human genes to feed our gestation pods. Our village's dragon spirit Eko, the starship that brought my ancestors here, could perhaps be revived one day, but it has slept long, and deserves its rest. It is ancient, and it would take much to learn how to steer it again. Even if Eko did set sail again after the long centuries, without an open tunnel to head to we'd be lost, drifting forever on the black ocean of space. We have no way of knowing when the gate might be opened again from the other side—it could be decades, centuries, millennia, forever.

Already my generation barely remembers the days when the gate was open, of visiting season, when arriving starships made new constellations in the sky. People from other worlds came down to crowd the world with new looks and tongues to bewilder and delight, their starships' bellies full with precious cargo, foods we've long forgotten the tastes of, rice and wheat and tea and coffee, grown in climes milder than ours. Guardian Geyua, who was a teacher and Truthteller like I became once my mothering days expired, told us of these days, of the markets that sprung up in the village commons, bustling with life from other solar systems, of the Ambassadors who came from far off islands in the cosmic ocean. Some of them carried the words of Farhome, the promises of terrible machines, of mining bots and fueled vehicles and guns long forbidden on our world, in return for mineral, flora, fauna, and knowledge unique to this corner of the universe. We traded, but only for food and materials. They gave us much less than those other promises would have gotten us, but it was still a life-giving supply. But once the tunnel collapsed and the gate fell, visiting season became memory, not expectation.

We were alone, like first world once was at the dawn of exo-time.

So I offered my body for the service of the village, of my people, so that we might keep our flame alit here a little longer. The gestation pods can only do so much when there will be no new humans coming here to trade new genes, perhaps ever—our wellspring, contained in the belly of our starship, grows dry under the inexorable drought of passing generations. Sex was not new to me. So I went to the fertility rite once I was of age, with my hair let down and my body bared, swathed only in space—charcoal for the void and rock salt for the stars, to honor the ocean of space and time that now threatened to drown us. One with the night sky against the bonfire, camouflaged, I could still recognize the silhouettes of the people I had grown with, and loved all my life, my fellow villagers, but if we saw each other, we said nothing. It was late summer, with the tunnel's death still visible above us, a celestial wave streaking the stars. The bonfire was high and sparking, licking the throat of our village starship. Across the peaty sentinel grounds and mutant pines cloaked in summer's mist, from the kal forest, we could hear the ululating cries of demons as they saw the blaze. We sang back, and danced our hearts to thunder. There were young and old there, all the village's clades, the eldest, beyond birthing age, clothed not in space but in white ash, as handmaidens of Death Walking in their benevolent aspect, come to bless the rite and partake in its pleasure if they wished. Even some who declined to take part in the sex danced naked, to give the rest of us strength—others watched the children in the nurseries, who had been put to sleep. We drank bitter sap mead until the ground moved, and our swaying orbits brought us clashing into each other.

Having tasted each other's honeyed mouths, we entered the ancient starship's inner sanctum, and made love there to herald our true independence from Farhome, under the great arches of our dragon spirit's metal ribs, under the impassive eyes of sculpted titans that once held the cosmic darkness at bay for our ancestors on their carbon-fiber shoulders. Long ago, our Ambassadors, sent to the stars from a village far to the east, where the world's largest spaceport lies, had crossed the cosmic ocean to declare that this world was not a Protectorate like so many others in the sky. They told Farhome that our union here was of independent peoples on a world given to us by the bountiful universe, not by the leaders of first world. It had always been a tenuous agreement, with first world's attempts to establish a protectorate stretching over generations. There is enough unique resource and knowledge here to keep the attention of Farhome, despite our colder climes and the threat of contagion. With the tunnel gone, the agreement was truly sealed. On the night I attended my first fertility rite, a tradition heralding our freedom and our potential doom, I fucked Saya of my clade, a village protector by profession, and a friend to my heart.

If you will abide, I can tell you of Saya's way with bow and spear, how her weapons sculpted her arms like wind against rock, revealing the rivers of her veins. I often brought her skaelg-broth during night watch, and watched the stars with her, watched how they were replicated in the eyes of demons emerging from the kal forest to stalk the sentinel grasses closer to the village. She never let a single arrow fly the many times I kept her company in the watchtowers. But I felt safe around her, even when I could hear the rattling whisper of demons echoing through the night. I admit this sometimes thrilled me, to watch their crowns of shadow breach the mists around the village wall, hunting for creatures to take back to their hagtowers. I never saw their faces, though I tried—they wear the faces of the dead, we are told, and I wanted to see if I could spot the faces of anyone I had lost to Death Walking. In breeding season, we saw demons roam far from the kal forests, approaching perilously close to the walls of the village and battling each other under the gene-crafted pines. Their horns clashing to release spores that travel on the wind, and bring the song of contagion to animals like us.

We were told from the time we are children: if you are called to the kal forest while young, you will enter the doorway to darkness, and your body will be given to the shadow to become a demon everlasting, a kalform. All through the summers, the spores will call the young to the kal forest, and you must resist the song of the handmaidens in their towers with discipline and pain, unless you are deemed unfit for the society of your fellow humans. When you give yourself to the kal forest as an elder, you will enter the doorway to darkness to be digested by the hagtowers. You will be one with the ocean of space and time, and your bones will give the handmaidens of death form in this world. Protectors are told during training to never kill a demon unless they put a human in direct danger, because every demon is an immortal kalform. To end the existence of one is to destroy something that might have lived for generations, having swum in the same waters of time as our ancestors, carrying their death masks.

Saya and I had played as children in our clade's communal hall, running over the dirt ground shrieking with the other children—each of us had been demon or human in those games, chasing or chased. But as adults, in her watchtower, I knew Saya had come face to face with the real thing, that she had ushered humans to the kal forest to *become* demons.

ONE OF SAYA'S earliest duties as protector was to be part of an escort party for a rapist among our clade. For taking a young woman by force, he had been sentenced to be given to the kal forest, to become either food for the hagtowers or a body for a new demon. I remember watching in terror among the gathered crowd, before the exile. Saya's young face had hardened, the waters gone from her flesh, like I'd never seen her before. She lashed her fist into the rapist's face. The sound was like a stone hitting a tree-bark, the blood bright with oxygen in the misty morning. Another protector, older, put a hand against her shoulder, firm. "No need for that," he said. Unspoken: *Exile is enough.* Saya gave a jerky nod. Sick with worry, I watched the protectors put on their gas masks and take the condemned man through the village gate, into the peaty sentinel grounds, out towards the dark horizon of the kal forest. Saya did not hesitate, her bow slung across her shoulder, her spear held firm.

They returned in the evening without the rapist. I tried hugging my friend, but she avoided it, instead briefly squeezing my hand and walking away. I said nothing, just relieved that she had no wounds from the mission. When I joined Saya that night in the watchtower, she didn't want to talk about it. When I kept asking if she was alright, that drought of tenderness returned to her face, like in the morning, and I recoiled. She asked if I wanted to know what Death Walking looked like, up close. I don't remember her exact words, but she said many things that frightened me. She said she'd expected the rapist to struggle, scream as they got closer to the kal forest. But he'd just gone quiet. Saya said that even with her mask on, she could feel the pull of the hagtowers, especially when she saw the peace in that man's eyes. When they came close enough, he just ran all by himself, into the mists of the forest. She didn't even see the demons.

"I recognized," she said. "That what we are doing is sacrifice. He was a gift." Then she looked at me, this part I remember. "I saw your judgment, Surya. When we left. When I hit him," she said.

"You think I would judge you for taking a rapist to the kal forest?"

"What if it had been a thief? A food hoarder? We'd still send them." We haven't sent minor criminals out there for a long time, but this was right before the gate's collapse.

"It's not my place to judge," I said. She smiled, with bitterness, though it was gone quick.

"It just made me think we don't belong. Here, on our own world," she said. "That the kal is doing us a favor, taking us away. Demons don't rape, after all."

I don't remember what I said to that. Maybe that demons kill. Maybe that they don't have sex at all.

What I remember is that even in those days of youth, Saya seemed aged beyond her years after that trip out there. I remember the creases of her scars, like mine, dotting the lines of her cheekbones and temples, sinuous along her arms, where we pierced ourselves with hot needles during the fruiting seasons, when the kal spores are strongest in the air, and we feel the pull of the kal forest, the handmaidens of death singing from beyond time in our blood. That is when all the pubescent young in the village are sealed in the starship, where we drank bitter tincture to dull the call and threaded our skin with metal and string so the pain kept us from walking away to the kal forest. If we weren't careful, we could wade out of time's river and straight into the ocean of shadow, before the current of life carried us there. I knew that protectors who skirt the edges of the kal forest sometimes abandon their masks and venture inside, never to return.

I've known since childhood that I would visit the forest when my body's time in the world waned. Since then I've known that our guardians, and friends, all the members of our clade, would walk there eventually, when their bodies made the decision to send them to exile. But at that moment, talking to Saya in the watchtower, I grew terrified that Saya would go on exile before time's river brought her to the doorway. That she would heed the song early and leave me without my dearest friend. I told her not to go early into the dark woods. I asked her not to.

Saya said nothing, leaving me out in the cold.

And then, years along the current, the gate in the sky collapsed.

We had never fucked before, though we had fought in the mud as children, but we did that night, when I first joined the fertility rite, because I felt that Saya's warmth and strength would be good for the child-to-be in my belly. When that bend in the river came, all us mothers gave birth in the belly of the starship, because it is the safest place in the world. The air vibrated with our spilled blood, our screams. I watched many of this new generation of womb-born emerge before mine came. It hurt like falling to the world. For the first time, I became a mother. I don't remember the name of my first daughter, but I remember her tender face devouring the air, fresh from my body, no different than the infants plucked from the membranous embrace of gestation pods. Saya came to see me, with our other clade-members. Because we were dressed in the dark of space when we made love together, all of us villagers, Saya was no different than anyone there. But I knew that it was her seed that had grown into that first child. She winked at me, and carved a thin line in my bicep with an arrowhead to mark the first birth. "Today you are one of the Atlax above," she said, looking up at the statues gripping the ribs of the starship. "Pushing the dark back," she said, near drowned by the choral wails of a new generation. She didn't hold the baby, because she was no more a guardian to it than any other there. She had every right to, as part of the clade, but I know Saya. She didn't want to seem possessive.

I HAVE FOURTEEN small scars on my arm now, carved by different members of my clade each time I gave birth in the starship's inner sanctum. After the first, they were much less painful, because I asked for the tinctures. I have one half-scar, for one infant lost to miscarriage. And another, longer line of pale tissue across my lower abdomen, where four of fourteen were cut out of me. I have been lucky, fertile as the gardens under our climate tents. My body is striped like that ancient fire spirit of first world, the taigur, scarred not just by my clade-members' work but by the babies that have stretched my belly like a drum with their limbs and heads, pushing against my flesh and skin so that they too are the Atlax, holding back the tide of time so that they might meditate, timeless, within me, before facing the turbulent river.

MANY OF THE children have left with trading parties to other villages, never to return, to keep the human flame lit, delicately dancing on the oily surface of our gene pool on the world. If the gene pool becomes too shallow, too stagnant and polluted, that flame will flicker, wane, and disappear. The gate in the sky, after all, still remains closed, though we have danced many times around Umi. I can only hope that the little ones who went away with the surly traders on their solar buggies and gliders loaded with goods, found peace and bountiful lives under the sign of a new starship beyond the wilds. We get supplies, or other children to be swapped for ours, in return. Sometimes news comes—

of trade caravans lost in the wilds and gliders crashed because of storms—but I choose not to remember the details.

SAYA AND I took many lovers in the years of rites to follow, on those summer nights with blazing bonfires under Eko's throat. The two of us never had sex with each other again, that I can remember, though our love has never waned. She found great fellowship in her protector group, fucking many of them, and making companions of them as they went hunting and foraging. By the time she was middle-aged, her back and gut were drawn with scars from the spearheaded tails and horns of demons, for coming too close and being too bold along the edges of the kal forest. I was always in awe of her courage, that she had been so close to demons and survived. I asked her many times, have you seen them wearing the faces of our dead? Of Geyua and the elder guardians who have walked away? And she always said no, I've seen only the faces of strangers from distant bends in the river of time, our ancestors preserved by the kal.

She was proud, though, never to have killed a demon in all her time as protector. Because she was one of my closest clade-members, I made friends of her fellow protectors too. One of them, Keliyeh, I loved for a while. He had killed a demon once, or so he said, to defend himself from an attack. I believed him, because he'd lost an arm because of it, replaced with a beautiful prosthesis of carbon-fiber painted black as the horns of the creature that took that part of his body. But no protector can ever have proof of such a killing, because demons killed must be left for their kin to collect and take back to the hagtowers to be digested as food. Demon and human; we all go to the hagtowers in the end, to the shadow of the kal. It is a sign of respect, of our bond.

ONCE SAYA RETIRED from the protectors she become a Truthteller like me, teaching the children by my side and thrilling them with tales of her adventures. Just as she had taught me so much about the kal and its many forms, about the demons, I taught her along with the children of Farhome's lores. I showed her ghostlights from other worlds, paintings and video and statues and art, archives, pictures of demons long before they came to be on our world. She was amazed by these unimaginably old visions of horned creatures, demons imagined at the beginning of time by people who'd never seen one. "The lens of spacetime can be like a telescope. Even now, perhaps our ancestors watch us," I said once (or something like that). She laughed, but she was agog with wonder. These times, the two of us aging together in safety, teaching archives, stretching and tanning hides, smoking meats, were precious to me.

In this time of her life, she confided in me in ways that made me think she still wanted to go early to the kal forest. That fear of mine never quite went away. I knew she, like many protectors, suffered sleep walks and vivid dreams that drew her towards the hagtowers. She told me once, drinking mead in the banquet hall, that on her foraging patrols she had twice seen demons embracing in each other's arms within the gloaming of a hagtower's doorways. That they had been making love, like humans, like their bodies once had when they were used for human lives, for singing and dancing and talking and eating and fucking.

"Death Walking, making love?" I asked her, my disbelief clear.

"Fucking, if you prefer," said Saya. "Would that make it more believable? I know what I saw. Demons, fucking like humans. Rutting behind the curtains of hag-hair."

"The kal reproduces by taking bodies, making kalforms, not sex. You probably saw two demons during fruiting season, clashing horns to release spores, that's all."

"Oh, are you the one who has looked Death Walking in the face now? Why are you explaining what I've known since I was a child?"

"You think *I'm* still a child, to be made a gullible fool."

Saya cackled then, shook her head, and hurled the last of her mead down her throat. There was sweat beading on her forehead. The hall was chilly, despite the fires inside. As she'd grown older, she drank more, not less, to numb the call of the forest. We probably fought some more that night about what she saw out there, but in good nature. She never brought it up again, though. She is a proud woman, and doesn't take accusations of foolishness well.

I should say now that Saya has already walked here to the kal forest to meet Death Walking, like so many I have loved, like all my guardians, and some of the children I birthed, who did not heed the warnings. The dirt roads of the village feel empty these days, haunted by mist or sunlight, the shadow cast by Eko long. Do not be sad for Saya—she lived a long life, with many to love in it. My fear, that she would leave me to come to the forest early, did not come true. Like a true friend, she waited, waited long, until there were cataracts in her eyes and she was braving spasms of longing for the forest. Too much exposure to kal spores during her time as a protector, despite the masks she had worn. She finally heeded the call in dark of night, alone, taking a solar skiff. I've long known we were approaching the end. I thought we would go together, but I should have known she wouldn't have wanted to say farewell in person, or have to watch me die with her. For all her strength, she couldn't take such things. The first time we watched one of our elder guardians go on the final exile, she cried for days, barely eating unless I spooned broth into her mouth.

I cannot begrudge her the silent departure. She *did* leave me alone, but she waited as long as she could. It has been two days since she left the village. So now I come to the doorway as well.

I TAKE OFF my backpack and open it. Inside are scrolls of printed meat from the village's bioreactor cauldrons, wrapped in twine, their flesh marbled violet under deadmoon's glow. It's cold enough that they have kept through the day's journey on the solar skimmer, which I've left by forest's edge for protector patrols to retrieve later. I unwrap one of the scrolls, tearing off pieces of it and carefully leaving the pages of meat pierced on the black spikes emerging from the bony walls of the hagtower. I leave these little offerings, prayer flags of succulent DNA from first world, as decoration around the doorway. I came through the forest with a necklace of dead rabbits taken from the village hutches, tossed behind me to keep demons at bay until I reached a hagtower. Three rabbits are left hanging over my heart, and I give them as gifts as well, hanging them by the doorway. The hagtower seems to stir, a rustling from far above. In the village, the scrolls would be smoked over spiced peat flame and eaten in strips with porridge, the rabbits skinned to make pelts and turned to stew or kababs. Here, the offerings are left raw.

I speak into the darkness, as the child who became Death Walking did.

"Who lives here?" I ask the dark.

The darkness doesn't answer, but the mother of contagion at the top of the spire does, their voice the death-rattle of the demon they are. Their cry is powerful, audible over the wind despite being so far above me. It is not the scream that precedes attack, but the ululation that signals a space, a warning, for me.

So I kneel on my swollen knees, and bow my head low to the hag-webbed ground, sending pangs up and down my back. My old heart beats like it is young again. I haven't been slaughtered swiftly by the mother at the top of the hagtower because of my age. I have proven my lack of speed, and brought gifts.

I keep my forehead to the cold ground for ten seconds, my own grey hair mixing with creepers of hag-hair. Then, still kneeling, I look up at the sky, and see the mother crouched high above the bony hags, a demon against the stars, horns silhouetted against the twinkling arch of deadmoon.

"I have come to leave this tributary, and swim out to the great ocean of spacetime above. You are the shadow we've cast, and our guide to darkness. I offer myself freely to your kal, mother of contagion," I say, looking up while still kneeling.

The horned head retreats, becoming one with the spikes and bones of the hagtower. I look down again, and wait for what seems an eternity, my breath hissing in my mask. Then, the hags of the tower sing to me, a haunting wail that raises my body up. Something is moving through the hagtower's cavities, the kal inside responding like an intricate machine, turning the entire colony lifeform into a musical instrument as the wind runs through it. The song stops. The demon emerges from the doorway to darkness in front of me, parting the curtains of hair.

At first, the mother of contagion looks like a human, skin white as a star, etched with scars just like me, dressed in diaphanous robes of hag-hair that hang off them like moonlit water. They wear a chain of black bones around their hips, which ends in a living spearhead. It is their tail—the most visible part of the mutated kalform skeleton inside their ante-human flesh. Then, as the demon walks out of the hagtower, emerging from the writhing, unseen grasp of the kal inside, their crown of shadows slides out of the dark doorway. The horns curling out of their head; two daggers of dark slicing out of the temples, two spirals curled with all the grace of the universe itself behind their pointed ears. There are smaller horns decorating their bald scalp, bristling down their neck like jet flames. The black fire of deep space, and the water of time.

I am face to face with Death Walking, like the first child to come to the kal forest. The demon's eyes are the burnished scarlet of dying stars. And in their pale arms, nestled in the folds of the demon's white robes, is a sleeping infant, small black pinpricks like drops of blood decorating its hairless scalp—the beginnings of horns, a crown of shadows. This cannot be, of course—Death Walking cannot give birth through womb or machine, only humans can. I assume I'm hallucinating this star-carved child out of fear and euphoria.

But the demon pays my disbelief no heed, walking up to me, their bare clawed feet caked in dirt, sinking into the mulch. They bend down, a rattle in their chest and throat, mouth parted to reveal fangs black like their horns. Like me, the demon kneels, but only on one knee, their powerful legs sliding out of the robes. Their thighs are crisscrossed with scars where the kal inserted its shadowjacks all along the given body, to mutate it into this kalform. I was so surprised to see the baby in their arms that I barely looked at their face. *They wear the faces of the dead*—perhaps I will see the death mask of one I have loved. But this demon wears the face of someone I have never known, though they are very beautiful in their own way, their cheekbones and temples sharper than any human because of their kal-mutated bones, growing into their crown of horns. But how can I be disappointed, here at the end of my life, when Death Walking holds out this strange infant to me, as if to show me a miracle.

"Is this your baby?" I ask, my voice trembling through the mask's speaker.

There is kindness in the demon's face, if only because my human brain wants there to be—recognizes something in the death mask of a human from hundreds of years ago, turned to something else. Behind them, the hags of the tower smile their toothy smiles, my people from across time laughing at this unexpected ripple in the river. I laugh as well. The mother of contagion has become a mother. The demon does not laugh. The demon extends their arms so that the baby is near my own chest, head and buttocks cradled in their elongated hands, stirring memories of holding so many of the village's babies to my breasts, years and years ago. I notice that the baby has genitals, which look the same as a human's. Instinctively, I reach out to take the baby, the thought that the demon wants me to feed it suddenly growing amid the blossom of memories within my skull. I am too old, and have no milk in my breasts, but my hands reach out anyway.

I think of Saya, refusing to take from my arms the first baby I birthed for the village, even though she knew there was something of her in it.

The demon steps back lightly. There is a lash of movement that starts at their waist and shimmers around them. A razored flower of agony in my back, brief and powerful enough to buckle my legs and send me tumbling to the ground. The pain subsides quickly, but I can barely move. The demon looms over me, returning the infant to their chest, where the robes have parted to show small breasts leaking rivulets of dark, viscous milk like ink. Just as the hagtowers feed the demons with their hagmilk, so does the demon feed this child. I see their tail slither around their body again, curling against flesh leaving a trail of my blood with its spearhead. It reminds me of another spirit of Farhome, the serpent, seen in many lores I've learned from Archive. I remember that, to many peoples across the sky, our world would be seen as punishment for the wrongdoings of humanity. Hellhome, because *here be demons*. I laugh. Another demon moves towards the mother of contagion who felled me, climbing down from another hagtower nearby. They squat by the mother's legs, watching me. I can't see their face well, just the blazing pinpricks of their eyes reflecting the deadmoon. I imagine that this one wears the face of Saya, even though Saya is too old to have been used to create a demon, and is now being digested inside a hagtower. I may as well imagine her face, though. I wonder whose body grew whatever mutant seed that created the baby in the demon's arms, derived of DNA spiraling out of the stars and into the shadow of this world. The infant starts to cry, and it is a sound I've never heard before—a higher, sharper rattle than that of the demons. It is one of them. This is a real child of demons, offspring of Death Walking. I am witness to a great turbulence in the river of time, a bloom of life springing from the depths.

Saya was right all along. She *had* seen what she'd seen. All these generations of taking human bodies to create new kalforms, and the kal has finally learned how to use the bodies as we do. Death Walking has evolved to reproduce sexually. I laugh, and wonder if that's the taste of blood at the back of my throat.

The mother of contagion wasn't asking me to feed their infant, but showing me, the human, their antecedent, what they have learned from us. Tears blur my vision. As I was mother, they are too. I, we, are a mirror to them, and always have been.

PERHAPS ONE DAY the humans of our world will die out completely, leaving only Death Walking. As I send these words up to Archive, a demon watches, lets me speak. I have no pain, their tail's spearhead slick with anesthetic to numb the gash in my back. They seem remorseful, but that is because they have a human face, and once again, I see what I want to see in its scarlet eyes. I startled them by reaching for the infant. There are others, their eyes glittering atop the hagtowers and their swirling hair. Is this the first of their children that I hear suckling at the breast of the demon, like the first child that walked into the doorway to darkness and created their race? Was this baby truly created through sex, through that ancient dance of bodies forged from the echoes of Farhome? I cannot know these things. It seems a pity to die now, at the cusp of such realizations, though it doesn't sadden me. These demonic poisons are intoxicants; how else to explain this ridiculous poem I have narrated to my killers, reliving the last moments of my life to you, to them?

Even as my life leaves this body, I feel it raging in my brain, as if the language demons don't yet have must be expressed through me, the waters of time muddied by my glorious flailing. I can barely feel this body, which will be dragged into a doorway to darkness and turned to hagmilk.

These demons, that surround me as I die, no longer seem like aliens. They never were aliens. This is their home, the home of the kal. Perhaps the kal has been trying to hold us by the hand all along, and bring us to its world, not ours. If the gate in the sky never opens, it may not be such a tragedy for us all to die, as I will soon. The strange cry of the demon infant proves this. Our flame may waver out on the world, but our shadow will remain. It isn't possible, is it, for shadow to be cast without light, but here I have witnessed a miracle unthought of in all my days of praying by the Reactor of our ancient starship Eko, may it never crumble so that the children of demons may play on its weathered flanks.

I've taken off my mask, so that I breathe the same bitter air as the demons. This tributary ends, and I clamber out wet with lived time. The handmaidens sing, and Death Walking feeds their child with the black milk of space. I walk with them now across the bridge of deadmoon, studded with roiling gemstones of ice and rock, alive with Umi's light. The ocean above is dancing with starry surf. I dive into it.

WHEN AT DAWN what used to be the child emerged from the spire, they were not human, for their bones had turned black as distant time. The child was no child any longer, but first of demons on this world, Death Walking, because all worlds need death if humans must tread on them. From that day onwards, the humans of our world began to die, as humans must, as we did on first world, and as we have done on all the worlds.

THE ROBOTS OF EDEN
Anil Menon

WHEN AMMA HANDED me Sollozzo's collection of short stories, barnacled with the usual fervent endorsements and logos of obscure book awards, I respectfully ruffled the four-hundred page tome and reflected with pleasure how the Turk was now almost like a brother. Of course, we all live in the Age of Comity now, but Sollozzo and I had developed a friendship closer than that required by social norms or the fact that we both loved the same woman.

It had been quite different just sixteen months ago; when Amma informed me that my wife and daughter had returned from Boston, the news sweetened the day as elegantly as a sugar cube dissolving in chai. Padma and Bittu were home! Then my mother had casually added that "Padma's Turkish fellow" was also in town. They were all returning to Boston in a week, and since the lovebirds were determined to proceed, it was high time our seven-year old Bittu was informed. Padma wanted us all to meet for lunch.

I wasn't fooled by Amma's weather-report tone; I knew my mother was dying to meet Sollozzo face to face.

I wasn't in the mood for lunch, and told my mother so. I had my reasons. I was terribly busy. It was far easier for them to drop by my office than for me to cart Amma all the way to Bandra, where they were put up. Besides, they needed something from me, not I from them. Some people had no consideration for other people's feelings—

I calmed down, of course. My mother also helped. She reminded me, as if I were a child, that moods were a very poor excuse. Yes, if

I insisted, they would visit me at the office, but just because people adjusted didn't mean one had to take advantage of them, not to mention the Turk was now part of the family, so a little hospitality wasn't too much to ask, et cetera, et cetera.

Unlike his namesake in *The Godfather*, Sollozzo was a novelist, not a drug pusher (though I suppose novelists do push hallucinations in their own way). I hadn't read his novels nor heard of him earlier, but he turned out to be famous enough. You had to be famous to get translated into Tamil.

"I couldn't make head or tail," said Amma, with relish. "One sentence in the opening chapter is eight pages long. Such vocabulary! It's already a bestseller in Tamil. Padma deserves a lot of the credit, naturally."

Naturally. Padma had been the one who had translated Sollozzo into Tamil. And given herself a serving of Turkish Delight in the process.

"If you like Pamuk, you will like him," said Amma. "You have to like him."

I did like Pamuk. As a teenager, I had read all of Pamuk's works. The downside to that sort of thing is that one fails to develop a mind of one's own. Still, he was indelibly linked to my youth, as indelibly as the memory of waiting in the rain for the school bus or the Class XII debate at S.I.E.S college on "Are Women More Rational Than Men?" and Padma's sweet smile as she flashed me her breasts.

Actually, Amma's lawyering on the fellow's behalf was unnecessary; my Brain was already busy. My initial discomfort had all but dissolved.

I even looked forward to meeting Sollozzo. Bandra wasn't all that far away. Nothing in Mumbai was far away. Amma and I lived in Sahyun, only about a twenty-minute walk from my beloved Jihran River, and all in all I had a good life, a happy life in fact, but good and happy don't equal interesting. My life would be more interesting with a Turk in it, and this was as good an opportunity as any to acquire one.

However, I knew Amma's pleasure would be all the more if she had to persuade me, so I raised various objections, made frowny faces, and smiled to myself as Amma demolished my wickets. Amma's home-nurse Velli caught on and joined the game, her sweet round face alight with mischief:

"Ammachi, you were saying your back was aching," said Velli in Tamil. "Do you really want to go all the way to Bandra just for lunch?"

"Yes wretch, now *you* also start," said Amma. "Come here—*arre*, don't be afraid—come here, let me show you how fit I am."

As they had their fun, I pulled up my schedule, shuffled things around, and carved out a couple of hours on Sunday. It did cut things a bit fine. Amma was suspicious but I assured her I wasn't trying to sabotage her bloody lunch. I really *was* drowning in work at Modern Textiles; the labor negotiations were at a delicate stage.

"As always, your mistress is more important than your family," said Amma, sighing.

Amma's voice, but I heard Padma's tone. Either way, the disrespect was the same. If I had been a doctor and not a banker, would Amma still compare my work to a whore? I had every right to be furious. Yes, every right.

I calmed down, reflected that Amma wasn't being disrespectful. On the contrary. She was reminding me to be the better man I could be. She was doing what good parents are supposed to do, namely, protect me.

"You're right Amma. I'll make some changes. Balance is always good."

Unfortunately, I was as busy as ever when the weekend arrived, and with it Padma and Bittu, but I gladly set aside my work.

"You've become thin," observed Padma, almost angrily. Then she smiled and put Bittu in my arms.

I made a huge fuss of Bittu, making monster sounds and threatening to eat her alive with kisses. Squeals. Shrieks. Stories. O, Bittu was bursting with true stories. She had seen snow in Boston. She had seen buildings *this* big. We put our heads together and Bittu shared with me the millions of photographs she had clicked. Bittu had a boo-boo on her index finger which she displayed with great pride and broke into peals of laughter when I pretend-moaned: *doctor, doctor, Bittu better butter to make bitter boo-boo better*. It is easy to make children happy. Then I noticed Velli had tears in her eyes.

"What's wrong Velli?" I asked, quite concerned.

She just shook her head. The idiot was very sentimental, practically a Hindi movie in a frock, and it was with some trepidation that I introduced her to Padma. They seemed to get along. Padma was gracious, quite the empathic high-caste lady, and Velli declared enthusiastically that Padma-madam was exactly how Velli had imagined she would be.

Eventually, with Padma guiding the car's autopilot, all of us, including Velli, set off from Sahyun. At first we kept the windows down, but it was a windy day, and the clear cool air from Jihran's waters tugged and pulled at our clothes. Amma had taken the front seat, since Bittu wanted to sit in the back, between Velli and me. We would be gone for most of the day, and so Velli had asked us to drop her off at Dharavi so that she could visit her parents. We stopped at the busy intersection just after the old location of the MDMS sewage treatment plant and Velli got out.

"Velli, you'll return in the—" I began, in Tamil.

"Yes, elder brother, of course I'll be there in the evening, you can trust." Velli kissed her fingers, transplanted the kiss onto Amma's cheek, and then said in her broken English: "I see you in evening soon, okay Ammachi? Bye bye."

The signal had changed and the car wanted to move. Velli somehow forgot to include Padma in her final set of goodbyes. She ran across the intersection. "She's an innocent," said Amma. "The girl's heart is pure gold. Pure gold."

"Yes, she is adorable," said Padma, smiling.

"She was sad," observed Bittu. "Is it because she is black?"

Amma laughed but when we looked at her, she said: "What? If Velli were here, she would've been the first to laugh."

Maybe so. But two wrongs still didn't make a right. Amma was setting a bad example for Bittu. It was all very well to laugh and be happy but the Enhanced had a responsibility to be happy about the right things. Padma explained to me that Bittu actually had been asking if Velli was sad because she wasn't Enhanced. In their US visit, Bittu had noticed that most African-Americans weren't Enhanced, and she'd concluded it was for the fair. Velli was dark, so.

I met Padma's glance in the rear-view mirror and her wry smile said: did you really think I'd taught her to be racist?

"No, Bittu." I put an arm around my daughter. "Velli is just sad to leave us. But now she can look forward to seeing us again."

I too was looking forward, not backwards. Reclining in the back seat, listening to the happy chatter of the women in front, savoring the reality of my daughter in the crook of my arm, meeting the glances of my wife—I was still unused to thinking of Padma as my ex-wife—I realized, almost in the manner of a last wave at the railway station, that this could be the last time we were all physically together.

When she'd left for Boston with Bittu, I had hoped the six months would be enough to flush Sollozzo out of her system. But life with him must have been exciting in more ways than one. The Turk had given her the literary life Padma had always craved, a craving it seemed no amount of rationalization on her part or mine could fix.

With Padma gone for so long, I'd had to look for a nurse for Amma. It quickly became clear that I could forget about Enhanced nurses, since all such nurses were employed everywhere except in India. Fortunately, Rajan, a shop-floor supervisor at Modern Textiles, approached me saying his daughter Velli had a diploma in home care, he'd heard I was looking for a home-nurse, and that he was looking for someone he could trust.

Trust enabled all relations. As a banker, I'd learned this lesson over and over. I was enveloped in a subtle happiness, a kind of sadness infused with a delicate mix of fragrances: the car's sunburnt leather, Amma's coconut-oil loving white head, Padma's vétiver, Velli's jasmine, and Bittu's pulsing animal scent. The sensory mix wasn't something my Brain had composed. It must have arisen from the flower of the moment. I savored the essence before it could melt under introspection, but melt it did, leaving in its place the residue of a happiness without reasons.

Somewhat dazed, I leaned forward between the front seats and asked the ladies what they were talking about.

"Amma was saying she wanted to come for my wedding in Boston," said Padma. "I want her there too. I'll make all the arrangements. My happiness would be complete if she were there."

"Then I will be there," announced Amma. "Just book the plane ticket."

"Amma, you can barely navigate to the bathroom by yourself, let alone Boston."

"See Padma, see? This is his attitude." Amma employed the old-beggar-woman voice she reserved for pathos. "Ever since you left, I've become the butt of his bad jokes." Then Amma surprised me by turning and patting my cheek. "But it's okay. He's just trying to cheer me up, poor fellow."

"That's one of the hazards of living with him," said Padma, smiling. "Amma, seriously, I'll book your ticket. If he wants, your son can also come and crack his bad jokes there."

"Yes, the more the merrier," said Amma, good sport that she was. She then stoutly defended Padma's choice, pooh-poohing moral issues no one had raised about Turkish-Tamil children, and saying things like what mattered was a person's heart, not their origins, and that love multiplied under division, and wasn't it telling that he loved red rice and *avial*. "I always thought Mammooty looks very Turkish," said Amma, her intransigent tone indicating that Sollozzo, whom she had yet to meet, could draw at will from the affection she'd deposited over a lifetime for her favorite south-Indian actor. That's how much she liked Turks, yes.

I liked him too. Sollozzo wasn't anything like the gangster namesake from the classic movie. For one thing, he had a thin pencil moustache. I could have grown a similar moustache, but I couldn't compete with his gaunt height or that ruined look of a cricket bat which had seen one too many innings. He came across as a decent fellow, very sharp, and his slow smile and thoughtful mien gave his words an extra weight.

He had brought me a gift. A signed copy of Pamuk's *Museum Of Innocence*. It was strange to think this volume been touched by the great one, physically touched, and the thought sent an involuntary shiver down my spine. A lovely, Unenhanced feeling. Two gifts in one. The volume was very expensive, no doubt. I touched the signature.

"My friend," said Orhan Pamuk in my head, from across the bridge of time, "I hope you get as much joy reading this story as I had writing it."

I touched the signature again, replaying its message. I looked up and saw Padma and Sollozzo watching me. It was touching to think they'd worried about finding me the right gift.

"I will cherish it." I was totally sincere. "Thank you."

"Mention not," said Sollozzo, with that slow smile of his. "You owe me nothing. I *did* take your wife."

We all laughed. We chatted all through lunch. I ordered the lamb; the others opted to share a vat of biryani. As I watched Bittu putting her little fingers to her mouth, I realized with a start that I'd quite missed her. Sollozzo ate with the gusto of a man on death row. Padma shook her head and I stopped staring. My habit of introspection sometimes interfered with my happiness, but I felt it also gave my happiness a more poignant quality. It is one thing to be happy but to *know* that one is happy because a beloved is happy makes happiness all the more sweet. Else, how would we be any different from animals? My head buzzing with that sweet feeling, I desired to make a genuine connection. I turned to Sollozzo.

"Are you working on a new novel? Your fans must be getting very impatient."

"I haven't written anything new for a decade," said Sollozzo, with a smile. He stroked Padma's cheek. "She's worried."

"I'm not!" Padma did look very unworried. "I'm not just your wife. I'm also a reader. If I feel a writer is cutting corners, that's it, I close the book. You're a perfectionist; I love that. Remember how you tortured me over the translation?"

Sollozzo nodded fondly. "She's equally mad. She'll happily spend a week over a comma."

"How we fought over footnotes! He doesn't like footnotes. But how can a translator clarify without footnotes? Nothing doing, I said. I put my foot down."

I felt good watching them nuzzle. I admired their passion. I must have been deficient in passion. Still, if I'd been deficient, why hadn't Padma told me? Marriages needed work. The American labor theory of love. That worked for me; I liked work. Work, work. If she'd wanted me to work at our relationship, I would have. Then, just so, I lost interest in the subject.

"I don't read much fiction anymore," I confessed. "I used to be a huge reader. Then I got Enhanced in my twenties. There was the adjustment phase and then somehow I lost touch, what with career and all. Same story with my friends. They mostly read what their children read. But even kids, it's not much. Makes me wonder. Maybe we are outgrowing the need for fiction. I mean, children outgrow their imaginary friends. Do you think we posthumans are outgrowing the need for fiction?"

I waited for Sollozzo to respond. But he'd filled his mouth with biryani and was masticating with the placid dedication of a temple cow. Padma filled the silence with happy chatter. Sollozzo was working on a collection of his short stories. He was doing this, he was doing that. I sensed reproach in her cheer, which was, of course, ridiculous. Then she changed the topic: "Are you, are you, are you, finally done with Modern Textiles?"

"I am, I am, I am not," I replied, and we both laughed. "The usual usual, Padma. I'm trying to make the workers see that control is possible without ownership. Tough, though. The Enhanced ones are easy; they get it immediately. But the ones who aren't, especially the Marxist types. Sheesh."

"Sounds super-challenging!"

On the contrary. Her interested expression said: Super-tedious. I hadn't intended to elaborate. As a merchant banker, I'd learned early on that most artists, especially the writer-types, were put off by money talk.

It didn't bother me. I just found it odd. Why weren't they interested in capital, which had the power to transform the world more than any other force? But I was willing to bet Sollozzo's novel wouldn't spend a comma, let alone a footnote, on business. Even Padma, for all the time she spent with me, had never accepted that the strong poets she so admired were poets of action, not verbiage.

"I hate the word posthuman!" exclaimed Sollozzo, startling us. "It's an excuse to claim we're innocent of humanity's sins. It's a rejection of history. Are you so eager to return to Zion? If so, you are lost, my brother."

Silence.

"I know the way to Sion," I said finally, and when Padma burst out laughing, I explained to the puzzled Sollozzo that Sahyun, where I lived with my mother, had originally been called Sion and that it had been a cosmopolitan North-Indian intersection between two South-Indian enclaves, Chembur and Kingcircle. Then Sahyun had become a Muslim enclave. Now it was simply a wealthy enclave.

"Sahyun! That's Zion in Arabic. You are living in Zion!"

"Exactly. I even have one of the rivers of Paradise not too far from my house. Imagine. And Padma still left."

"There's no keeping women in Zion." Sollozzo gifted me one of his slow smiles.

"Of course," said Padma, smiling. "The river Jihran is recent. There wasn't any river anywhere near Sion. The place was a traffic nightmare. Everything's changed in the last sixty years. Completely, utterly changed."

"On the contrary—" I began, leaning forward to help myself to a second helping of lamb.

"My dear children," interrupted my mother, in Tamil, "I understand you don't want to, but you mustn't postpone it any longer. You have to tell Bittu."

"Yes, Bittu. Break her heart, then mend it." Sollozzo didn't understand Tamil very well, not yet, but he had recognized the key word: Bittu. This meeting was really about Bittu.

First, the preliminaries. I took the divorce papers from Padma, signed wherever I was required to sign; a quaint anachronism in this day and age, but necessary nonetheless. With that single stroke of my pen, I gave up the right to call Padma my wife. My ex-wife's glance met mine, a tender exchange of unsaid benedictions and I felt a profound sadness roil inside me. Then it was accompanied with a white-hot anger that I wasn't alone with my misery. The damn Brain was watching, protecting. But there is no protection against loss. Padma—Oh god, oh god, oh god. Then, just so, I relaxed.

"There's a park outside," said Padma, also smiling. "We'll tell Bittu there."

It began well. Bittu, bless her heart, wasn't exactly the brightest crayon in the box. It took her a long time to understand that her parents were divorcing. For good. She was going to live in Boston. Yes, she would lose all her friends. Yes, the uncle with the moustache was now her step-father. No, I wasn't coming along. Yes, I would visit.

Et cetera, et cetera. Then she asked all the same questions once more. Wobbling chin, high-pitched voice, but overall quite calm. We felt things were going well. Padma and I beamed at each other, Sollozzo nodded approvingly.

Amma was far smarter. She knew her grandchild, remembered better than us what it had been like not to be fully Enhanced. So when Bittu ran screaming towards the fence separating the park from the highway, Amma, my eighty-two year-old mother, somehow sprinted after her and grabbed Bittu before she could hit the road. We caught up, smiling with panic. Hugs, more explanations. Bittu calmed. Then when we released her, she once again made a dash for it. This is just what we have pieced together after some debate, Padma, Sollozzo and I. None of us remember too much of what happened. But it must have been very stressful, because my Brain mercifully decided to bury it. I remember flashes of a nose-bleed, a frantic trip to the hospital, Bittu's hysterical screams, Padma in Sollozzo's arms. I remember Bittu's Brain taking over, conferring with ours, and shutting down her reticular center. Bittu went to sleep.

"Please do not worry." Bittu's Brain broadcast directly to our heads. It had an airline-stewardess, voice, and it spoke first in English, then in Hindi. "She can be easily awakened at the nearest facility."

I remember the doctor who handled Bittu's case. She was very reassuring. I remember everything after the doctor took over. She was that reassuring.

"Bittu was Enhanced only last year, wasn't she?" said the doctor.

She wanted to know the specifics of the unit. Did Bittu's Brain regulate appetite? How quickly would it forget things? What was our policy on impulse control? That was especially important. How did her Brain handle uncertainty? Was it risk-averse or risk-neutral? Superfluous questions, of course. The information was all there in the medical report. I listened, marveling, a soaring happiness, as Padma answered every question, and thus answered what the doctor really needed to know: are you caring parents? Do you know what you have done to your child with this technology?

The doctor asked if we had encouraged Bittu to give her Brain a name. Did we know that Bittu referred to it as a "boo-boo?" Newly-

Enhanced children often gave names to their Brains. Padma nodded, smiling, but I could tell she was worried. Boo-boo?

We got the It-Takes-Time-to-Adjust speech. Bittu was very young, the Brain still wasn't an integral part of her. Her naming it was one symptom. Her Brain found it especially difficult to handle Bittu's complex emotions. And Bittu found it difficult to deal with this *thing* in her head. We should have been more careful. It especially hadn't been a good idea to mask the trial separation as a happy vacation in Boston. We hung our heads.

Relax, smiled the doctor. These things happen. It's especially hard to remember just how chaotic their little minds are at this age. It's not like raising children in the old days. Don't worry. In a few weeks, Bittu wouldn't even remember she'd had all these worries or anxieties. She would continue to have genuine concerns, yes, but fear, self-pity and other negative emotions wouldn't complicate things. Those untainted concerns could be easily handled with love, kindness, patience and understanding. The doctor's finger drew a cross with those four words.

"Yes, doctor!" said Padma, with the enthusiasm all mothers seem to have for a good medical lecture.

We all felt much better. Our appreciation would inform our Brains to rate this particular interaction highly on the appropriate feedback boards.

Outside, once Bittu had been placed—fast asleep, poor thing—into Sollozzo's rental car, the time came to make our farewells. I embraced Padma and she swore various things. She would keep in touch. I was to do this and that. Bittu. Bittu. We smiled at each other. However, Amma was a mess, mediation or no mediation.

"Was it to see this day, I lived so long?" she asked piteously in Tamil, forgetting herself for a second, but then recovered when Padma and I laughed at her wobbly voice.

"That lady doctor liked the word 'especially', didn't she?" said Sollozzo, absentmindedly shaking and squeezing my hand. "I had a character like that. He liked to say: on the contrary. Even when there was nothing to be contrary about." He encased our handshake with his other hand. "Friend, my answer to your question was stupid. Totally stupid. I failed. I've often thought about the same question. I will fail better. We must talk."

What question? The relevance of fiction? I didn't care. So. This was it. Padma was leaving. Bittu was leaving. My wife and daughter were gone forever. I felt something click in my head and I went all woozy. The music in my head made it impossible to think. I was so happy I had to leave immediately or I would have exploded with joy.

Amma and I had a good journey back to our apartment. We hooked our Brains, sang-along with old Tamil songs, discussed some of the entertaining ways in which our older relatives had died. She didn't fall asleep and leave me to my devices. My mother, worn out from life, protecting me from myself, even now.

That evening, Velli made a great deal of fuss over Amma, chattering about the day she'd had, cracking silly jokes, and discussing her never-ending domestic soap opera. Amma sat silently through it all, smiling, nodding, blinking.

"Thank you for caring," I told Velli, after she had put Amma to bed. "You look tired. Would you like a few days off next week?"

"I'm not going anywhere!" she burst out in her village Tamil. She grabbed my hand, crushed it against her large breasts. "You're an inspiration to me. All of you! How sensibly you people handle life's problems. Not like us. When my uncle's wife ran away, you should have seen the fireworks, whereas you all—Please don't take this the wrong way elder brother, but sometimes at night when I can't sleep because of worries, I think of your smiling face and then I am at peace. How I wish I too could be free of emotions!"

It is not every day one is anointed the Buddha, and I tried to look suitably enlightened. But she had the usual misconception about mediation. Free of emotions! That was like thinking classical musicians were free of music because they'd moved beyond grunts and shrieks. We, the Enhanced, weren't free of emotions. On the contrary! We had healthy psychological immune systems, that was all.

I could understand Velli's confusion, but Sollozzo left me baffled. We chatted aperiodically, but often. Padma told me his scribbling was going better than ever, but his midmornings must have been fallow because that's when he usually called. I welcomed his pings; his mornings were my evenings, and in the evenings I didn't want to think about ESOPs, equities, or factory workers. It was quite cozy. Velli cutting vegetables for dinner, Amma alternating between bossing her and playing Sudoku, and Sollozzo and I arguing about something or the other. Indeed, the topic didn't matter as long we could argue over it. We argued about the evils of capitalism, the rise of Ghana, the least imperfect way to cook biryani, the perfect way to educate children, and whether bellies were a must for belly dancers. Our most ferocious arguments were often about topics on which we completely concurred.

For example, fiction. I knew he knew that fiction was best suited for the Unenhanced. But would he admit it? Never! He'd kept his promise, offering me one reason after another why fiction, and by extension writers, were still relevant in this day and age. It amused me that Sollozzo needed reasons. As a storyteller he should've been immune to reasons.

When I told him that, he countered with a challenge. He offered two sentences. The first: *Eve died, and Adam died of a heart attack*. The second: *Eve died, and Adam died of grief*.

"Which of these two is more satisfying?" asked Sollozzo. "Which of these feels more meaningful? Now tell me you prefer causes over reasons."

"It's not important what I prefer. If Adam had been Enhanced, he could've still died of a heart attack. But he wouldn't have died of grief. In time, no one will die of heart attacks either."

Another time he tried the old argument that literature taught us to have empathy. This bit of early-21st century nonsense had been discredited even in those simple-minded times. For one thing, it could just as easily be argued that empathy had made literature possible.

In any case, why had empathy even been necessary for humans? Because people had been like books in a foreign language; the books had meaning, but an inaccessible meaning. Fortunately, science had stepped in, fixed that problem. There was no need to be constantly on edge about other people's feelings. One knew how they felt. They felt happy, content, motivated, and relaxed. There was no more need to walk around in other people's shoes than there was to inspect their armpits for signs of the bubonic plague.

"Exactly my point!" shouted Sollozzo. He calmed down, of course. "Exactly my point. Enhancement is straightening our crooked timber.

If this continues, we'll all become moral robots. I asked you once, are you so eager to return to Zion?"

"What is it with you and Zion?"

"Zion. Eden. Swarg. Sahyun. Paradise. Call it what you will. The book of Genesis, my brother. We were robots once. Why do you think we got kicked out of Zion? We lost our innocence when Adam and Eve broke God's trust, ate from the tree and brought fiction into the world. We turned human. Now we have found a way to control the tree in our heads, become robots again, and regain the innocence that is the price of entry into Zion. Do you not see the connection between this and your disdain for fiction?"

I did not. But I had begun to see just how radically his European imagination differed from mine. He argued with me, but his struggles really were with dead white Europeans. Socrates, Plato, and Aristotle; Goethe, Baumgarten, and Karl Moritz; Hugo von Hofmannsthal, Mach, and Wittgenstein: I could only marvel at his erudition. I couldn't comment on his philosophers or their fictions, but I was a banker and could make any collateral look inadequate.

In this case, it was obvious. His entire argument rested on the necessity of novels. But every novel argues against its own necessity. The world of any novel, no matter how realistic, differs from the actual world in that the novel's world can't contain one specific book: the novel itself. For example, the world of Pamuk's *The Museum of Innocence* didn't contain a copy of *The Museum of Innocence*. If Pamuk's fictional world was managing just fine without a copy of his novel, wasn't the author—any author—revealing that the actual world didn't need the novel either? Et cetera, et cetera.

"I have found my Barbicane!" said Sollozzo, after a long pause. "I need your skepticism about fiction. Fire away. It will help me construct a plate armor so thick not even your densest doubts can penetrate."

All this, I later learned, was a reference to the legendary dispute in Verne's *From the Earth to the Moon* between shot manufacturer Impey Barbicane and armor-plate manufacturer Captain Nicholls. Barbicane invented more and more powerful cannons, and Nicholls invented more and more impenetrable armor-plating. At least I was getting an education.

If his hypocrisy could have infuriated me, it would have. As long as his tribe had mediated for the reader, it had been about freedom, empathy, blah di blah blah. Sollozzo hadn't worried about mediating for the reader when he'd written stories in English about Turkey. Stories in English by a non-Englishman about a non-English world! Jane Austen[1] might as well have written in Sanskrit about England.

It didn't matter, not really, this game of ours. Men, even among the Enhanced, find it complicated to say how fond they are of one another. Sollozzo made Padma happy. I was glad to see my Padma happy. Yes, she was no longer mine. She'd never been mine, for the Enhanced belong to no one, perhaps not even to themselves. I was glad to see her happy and I believed Sollozzo, not her Brain, was the one responsible. Bittu was also adjusting well to life in Boston. Or perhaps it was that Bittu had adjusted to her Boo-boo. Same thing, no difference. Padma said that Bittu had stopped referring to her Brain entirely.

Padma was amused by my chit-chats with Sollozzo. "I am super-jealous! Are you two planning to run away together?"

"Yes, yes, married today, divorced tomorrow," shouted Amma, who had been eavesdropping on our conversation. "What kind of world is this! No God, no morals. Do you care what the effect of your immoral behavior on Bittu? Do you want her to become a dope addict? She needs to know who is going to be there when she gets back from school. She needs to have a mother and father. She needs a stable home. No technology can give her that. But go on, do what you like. Who am I to interfere? Nobody. Just a useless old woman who'll die soon. I can't wait. Every night I close my eyes and pray that I won't wake up in the morning. Who wants to live like this? Only pets. No, not even pets." She smiled, shifted gears. "Don't mind me, dear. I know you have the best interests of Bittu at heart. Which mother doesn't? Is it snowing in America?"

It's all good brah, as the Americans say in the old movies. As I ruffled the pages of Sollozzo's volume, *The Robots of Eden and Other Stories*, I wondered what Velli had made of the arguments I'd had with Sollozzo. I remember her listening, mouth open, trying to follow

[1] An English author, noted for her charming upper-class romances.

just what it was that got him so excited. She'd found Sollozzo highly entertaining. She used to call him 'Professor-uncle' with that innate respect for (a) white people, (b) Enhanced people and (c) people who spoke English very fluently. Sometimes she would imitate his dramatic hand-gestures and his accented English.

In retrospect, I should have anticipated that Sollozzo's suicide would impact Velli the most. How could it not? The Unenhanced have little protection against life's blows on their psyches. I had called Velli into my office, tried to break the news to her as gently as I could.

"Your professor-uncle, he killed himself. Don't feel too bad. Amma is not to know, so you have to be strong. Okay, Velli?"

I had already counseled Padma on the legal formalities, chatted with Bittu, made her laugh, and everything went as smoothly as butter.

Padma and I decided we'd tell Amma the next day, if at all. Amma got tired very easily these days. Why add to her burdens?

"I have to handle his literary estate," said Padma, smiling, her eyes ablaze with light. "There's so much to do. So for now we'll all stay put in Boston. Will you be all right? You'll miss your conversations."

Would I? I supposed I could miss him. I didn't see the point however. I was all right. Hadn't I handled worse? What had made her ask? Was I weeping? Rending my garments? Gnashing my teeth? Then, just so, the irritation slipped from my consciousness like rage-colored leaves scattering in the autumn wind. It was kind of her to be concerned.

"Why did professor-uncle kill himself?" asked Velli, already weeping.

"He took something that made his heart stop," I explained.

"But why!"

Why what? Why did the why of anything matter? Sollozzo had swallowed pills to stop his heart, he'd walked into the path of a truck, he'd drowned, he'd thrown himself into the sun, he'd dissolved into the mist. He was dead. How had his Brain let it happen? I made a mental note to talk to my lawyer. The AI would have a good idea whether a lawsuit was worth the effort. Unless Sollozzo's short-story collection contained an encoded message (and I wouldn't put that past him), he hadn't left any last words.

"Aiyyo, why didn't he ask for help?" moaned Velli.

I glanced at her. She was obviously determined to be upset. Her quivering face did something to my own internals. I struggled to contain my smile, but it grew into a swell, a wave, and then a giant tsunami of a laugh exploded out of me, followed by another, and then another. I howled. I cackled. I drummed the floor with my feet. I laughed even after there was no reason to. Then, just so, I relaxed.

"I'm sorry," I said. "I wasn't laughing at you. In fact, you could say I wasn't the one laughing at all."

Velli looked at me, then looked away, her mouth working. Poor thing, it must all be so very confusing for her. I could empathize.

"Velli, why don't you go down to the river? The walk will do you good and you can make an offering at the temple in professor-uncle's name. You'll feel better."

I had felt it was sensible advice, and when she stepped out, I'd felt rather pleased with myself. But Velli never returned from the walk. I got a brief note later that night. She'd quit. No explanation, just like that. Her father Rajan came by to pick up her stuff, but he was vague, and worse, unapologetic. All rather inconvenient. All's well that ends well. Padma and Bittu were happy in Boston. Perhaps they would soon return. I hoped they would; didn't want Bittu to forget me. Sollozzo's volume would get the praise hard work always deserved, irrespective of whether such work pursued utility or futility.

"You'll spoil the book if you keep ruffling the pages like that," complained Amma.

I returned the volume to Amma, marveling at her enthusiasm for reading. For novels. For stories. Dear Amma. Almost ninety years old, but what a will to live! Good. Good! Other people her age, they were already dead. They breathed, they ate, they moved about, but basically, they were vegetables with legs. Technology could enhance life, but it couldn't do induce a will to live. Amma was a true inspiration. I could only hope I would have one-tenth the same enthusiasm when I was her age. I started to compliment Amma on this and other points, then realized she was already lost in the story. So I tiptoed away, disinclined to come between my beloved reader and the text.

DUMB HOUSE
Andrea Hairston

"WHAT THE HELL would I do in a smart house but lose my mind?"

Cinnamon Jones shook a mop of salt and pepper braids at the sweaty characters panting on the side steps to her dumb house. She had to boost her farm's horror rep. This was the third time traveling *salesmen* had braved the path to her door in a week. The two slicksters in fluorescent suits and stingy-brim fedoras fumbled through bulky bags of samples, fronting like throwbacks from the 1950s.

Cinnamon waved them away. "You're wasting your time." Her hands were covered in dirt and grease from trying to fix a ventilator in the porch-greenhouse. Spider plants were trailing through the windows, enjoying an afternoon breeze. Daffodils busted out in yellow glory, scenting the air inside and out. "You're lucky." Doing Carnival this morning to welcome new leaves and first fruits had put Cinnamon in a decent mood. Otherwise, she'd have been cussing.

"We got just the smart house you need!" one fellow boomed. "Smart and sassy!"

"How'd you get up here?" The main road was blocked off—Co-op security for all the farms. The old African must have left the bike path gate open again, probably even invited the suits in. Cinnamon would have to talk to Taiwo. What good was a monster patrolling the farm perimeter if they didn't scare folks away? Carnival had sucked up Cinnamon's people-energy. She didn't want to see anybody. "I'm not buying. Nothing. I told you guys that online." Opening the heavy greenhouse door had been a bad idea. It was too hard to close.

"We came a long way on foot, sugar, to see you. In person." The talker had devilish dimples and misty green eyes—a tall drink of water with a broad chest and a faint accent. Very pale. Northern European? "That path meanders all over hell and back."

"Evil need a straight line." Cinnamon chuckled. "That's elder wisdom from Japan."

"Word." The *salesmen* exchanged glances. The talker cocked his head. "Good don't get lost in the twists and turns." He looked back at the maple, birch, and white oak trees hugging the hills. "And everything's better live, know what I'm saying?" A jewel-encrusted sword pin held his silk tie in place. Wispy white hair was tucked under the fedora. In the last century, maybe, he was a glamorous silver fox who hung out with black folks. Course everybody talked black these days. Twenty-first century English was a child of rap. "I know you been hip-hopping and show-stopping your whole life. And forward thinking too."

"Not any more, though." Cinnamon missed the wild person she used to be.

"A dumb house ain't you." The fox grinned and spun around, dipped low and jumped high, a dancer. A really sly algorithm had sicced this fellow on her. "Why get stuck in the old school now, girl?"

"Girl?" Cinnamon wasn't fooled by the hip masquerade. These were poor men—laid off, downsized, hedged out—pushing junk on other poor folks. Desperate, they'd walked two muddy miles to con an old black lady—live, since the online swindles failed. Rescuing her from her retro self was the script. Cinnamon muttered curses at Taiwo for too much African hospitality at the gate and not enough scary juju. "I'm glad I'm old."

"Me too. You have enough wisdom to appreciate our offer." The silver fox babbled on about the wonders of the new age. Cinnamon shook her head at his scam-speak and squinted at the short, silent one. He was thin, tan, and eight inches shorter than Cinnamon. He had features from all over the map. Or maybe that was make-up. Sensuous, quivering lips made Cinnamon nervous. Black opal eyes tracked her every move. He was mirroring her, like a theatre game. Slick. Folks moving and breathing with you made you let down your guard.

This was an altogether intriguing pair.

Cinnamon had to stay frosty. *Salesmen* could be spies, sussing out hackers and digital renegades for Consolidated Corp. She was two payments behind and owed several thousand dollars plus interest for basic access. Consolidated's profit-algorithm might cut her loose any minute or mess up her credit and bully the local bank. But sending out a live posse, two *salesmen* on this mission—in purple patent leather loafers and paisley ties? What deep correlation had she bumped up against?

The smooth-talking fox dropped his voice, rumbling and growling at her. "Upgrade for the people who love you, girl."

"Who you calling *girl* again?"

The fox stepped back, looked her up and down, and tap danced around the fieldstone terrace. "Still looking fine." The accent was faint, maybe imagined. The gleam in his eye was definite.

"Lines like that never work on me." Cinnamon wiped dirt and grease from her hands onto a gardening apron. Well, almost never.

"Come join us in the twenty-first century." He laughed good-naturedly, not a put-down and just shy of a come-on. He was good, a real showman. "You won't regret it."

Both *salesmen* broke out inflatables that whistled and squealed as they blew up. In two minutes Cinnamon's fieldstone terrace was the bouncy inside of a model smart house. "Stuff just fixes itself, before you even notice it's broke. Everything is hooked into everything else, a learning machine, a coordinated network, voice-activated and taking the cues from you."

"Right. Me, only better." Cinnamon sucked her teeth like her Gullah grandmother and ignored the giant balloons. "You sure you got the right ZIP Code? I can't afford this. Down in the Valley, rich folks in Electric Paradise just love this kinda—"

"Carlos Witkiewicz here." The talker bowed. His breath had gotten shallow. A vein throbbed at his temples. "My partner, Barbett Blues." Barbett Blues' lips quivered. His breath was ragged too. He shot a worried glance at Carlos. These guys were more desperate than the last fellow.

"Blues? Witkiewicz? Like that Polish playwright?" Cinnamon pursed her lips and scowled. Barbett followed suit, snarkier than Cinnamon could manage. "Are those your real names or company handles?"

"Company names, for security," Carlos sounded embarrassed or apologetic.

People tracked *salesmen*, even came after them, as if *salesmen* were responsible for the broke-down, planned-obsolescence crap they sold, as if *salesmen* were jacking the prices into the stratosphere. Barbett's and Carlos's names probably changed every day, maybe even a couple times a day. With makeup, contact lenses, hats—*salesmen* were ghosts, nothing to connect facial recognition to.

"You don't have a car, darling, just bikes, and living way out here, growing oats and rye for the Co-op." Carlos pointed at her sugar shack spouting smoke, and purred, "Maple sugaring all alone."

"Not alone," Cinnamon corrected him. She carefully curated her digital persona and backed it up during live encounters. Hiding in plain sight.

"I know a monster's got your back, a witch-dog too—Bruja?" Carlos grinned. "What about the *people* who love you? I mean, they're worried. An unenhanced house, at your age, that's flirting with disaster. You feel me?"

Cinnamon snorted. "How old are you?"

"Well, I'm—" Barbett slugged Carlos before he finished. They reminded her of folks she knew a long time ago, when she was full of beans and not so much salt-and-vinegar.

Cinnamon chuckled. "Sixty is on my horizon, but I got a ways to go." The *salesmen* could have been her age or close to it. Mostly younger folks out there hoofing it for Consolidated and other big corps—so what was their story? "We old farts are the ones who still know how to survive in the outback or when the power gets cut or when the rivers chase us up into the hills! My grandparents and great-aunt made sure of that for me. I can survive on weeds, use roots to heal what ails you, and make a fire in the rain."

"A root worker? Fire in rain?" Barbett Blues spoke! A throaty blues-singer rasp and a strange accent. He was another smooth character underneath the snark. He leaned close. "Still?"

"So much, just washed away." Carlos surveyed the hills again, stricken. "Up high is lucky."

"Oh. You were in the water wars. Sorry," Cinnamon said.

Carlos nodded, then cleared the storm from his face. He and Barbett were probably living out of a beat-up dumb car, driving themselves along the digital divide. The faint tang of hand sanitizer and rancid grease wafted from their clothes. Yeah, they were sleeping on the road and taking showers in the rain. It was work hard-sales or starve. The sly algorithm wanted her to feel sorry for the fallen middle class and spend big, like shopping would help save the world from itself.

Sleazy data miners were working her last nerve.

Cinnamon sighed and took off the greasy apron. No more repairs today; her concentration was shot. She needed imagination flow to solve a glitch and fix what was broken. The *salesmen* gaped at her snakeskin demon costume. Feathers and feelers reached toward them. Jewel eyes on her thighs broke the sun into rainbows and peered through the spaces between things. Carlos was dazzled, obvious desire on his breath. Acting unimpressed, Barbett slugged Carlos again, but took careful note of Taiwo's juju-tech.

"You should've seen Carnival this morning. We put on a show for the whole Valley." Cinnamon cringed. Did *salesmen* have time for Carnival? "You both water-war refugees?"

"Yeah, so?" Carlos snapped at her. "The past is not important."

Who else their age would be desperate enough to take this ridiculous job? Risky too—angry bad boys in the hill towns regularly went out hunting somebody to blame. *Salesmen* were low-hanging fruit.

Carlos gritted his teeth. "I'm living tomorrow now. So should you. Buy on credit."

"I like today just fine. Yesterday give me a good feeling too." Cinnamon let self-righteousness flow for a second. "Progress is an illusion. A marketing ploy."

Dirt kicked up behind Carlos. One of the inflatables had refused to blow up. Gas was hissing through the spring herb garden instead of doing its job on a wad of limp plastic. Carlos dropped to the ground, fussing and cussing at valves and tiny pumps.

Barbett Blues whispered sweetly to Cinnamon who didn't understand much except, "Old lady, alone, bad." He was talk-singing—an astral-bop riff in that unfamiliar accent. "Scared? You?" Barbett chanted.

"Should I be? You planning an ambush?" Cinnamon put her hands on hefty hips. The feathers on her shoulders curled into thin blades. Barbett's eyes got wide. "Some folks are more cloud than storm. Not me," Cinnamon sounded as country and throwback as possible. Not an act—she had Georgia roots by way of Chicago and Pittsburgh, transplanted to Massachusetts.

"Here come future." Barbett pointed at the inflatables. "Start small, lonely no more."

"I told you. I'm not alone," Cinnamon said.

"They pay us not to listen." Carlos pulled a tiny tool kit from his bag.

"Well, look." Cinnamon nodded at the spirit garden surrounding the fieldstone terrace. Coming up to the house, the *salesmen* had walked through a half circle of wooden statues—West African deities: Shango, Yemaya, Oshun, Obatala, and Eshu. Granddaddy Aidan carved these spirit figures for Taiwo. Barbett stood near Mami Wata, African queen mother of the waters, who soaked up sun for her ocean spray of LED lights. Cinnamon had built Mami Wata from a hunk of recycling junk.

"Voodoo-hoodoo." Barbett hopped from one foot to the other. Miz Redwood, Cinnamon's grandmother, had done hoodoo hot-foot spells all around the house.

"Nobody believes in that." Carlos checked valves and hoses on the pumps. "People be hoodooing their own selves." He sounded like Miz Redwood was talking through him for a moment. "Stop."

Barbett stepped out of the loafers into the crabgrass to cool his feet. The maple trees rustled in a private breeze. Everything else was still. Tiny red flowers and leaf buds glistened with late afternoon fog. Granddaddy Aidan and Miz Redwood built the dumb house in a warm hollow, near Great Aunt Iris's favorite spot to collect roots. A foggy clump of shade looked like Aunt Iris, hunched in dead weeds and talking wind words. Barbett and Klaus gasped. The elders had promised to haunt Cinnamon, and she let them. They haunted desperadoes and other fools trying to mess with her too.

"You'd be surprised who all keeps me company," Cinnamon said.

"I don't think so." Carlos tightened one last valve. Barbett stepped back in his shoes.

"You two met Taiwo at the gate." Cinnamon enjoyed telling this story. "Almost a hundred fifty years on this Earth. How long in other dimensions is an open question." Taiwo was out there, somewhere, doing who knows what, yet the old African and a brigade of warrior-women haints were never far when danger lurked. "Monster always on the case," Cinnamon whispered.

Carlos spritzed a tiny hose with sealant. "Word on the road is that Taiwo has totaled trucks, sent armed thugs packing, and brought comatose bad boys back from the dead. He? She? uses alien tech from another dimension and juju learned in West Africa from the Yoruba, Fon, and Igbo—tribes over there."

"You're well-informed." Cinnamon rubbed her nose. Too well-informed, really. Maybe these intrepid *salesmen* had come to check up on the wild stories. "Why did Taiwo let you through?"

"Green. No waste water." Barbett waved a flyer of stats for a smart toilet, talk-singing. "Why flush good data?"

"Fixed!" Carlos jumped up in front of a three-dimensional print shop bouncing close to the herbs now. "A home factory where you might make a doll of yourself or, or anybody you love."

"No way!"

Carlos clutched his chest and got paler. He looked like he might fall over.

"You guys got the wrong ZIP Code or the wrong sales pitch or both. I'm not your target audience." She shook her head at the inflatables bobbing in the breeze: a food processor, climate system, virtual shopping mall, game and entertainment center, med unit, and a sex suite with vibrators, massage slings, and purple dragon dildos. Mobile cameras, mics, and dust angels floated everywhere, sweeping up allergens, dead skin, and intimate data. The toilet was talking to the fridge and the microwave, and set to broadcast—Big Data laws be damned. Cinnamon groaned. They were selling ancient tech, from before 2020. This might be warehouse stock that never sold and cost too much to take apart and throw out. Or maybe it was toxic shit that got recalled. Cinnamon glared at a purple dragon dildo. It made her feel like a prude and a little horny, or actually lonely.

Carlos wagged a finger at her. "See anything you like?"

"No." Cinnamon folded her arms across her breasts, feelers flailing and feathers bristling. Barbett reached across Carlos, touched a sharp edge, and sliced a finger. Cinnamon jumped back. "Pack that crap up. Walk on back to the gate. Tell Taiwo I don't need company." She stomped up the stairs to the greenhouse. Taiwo would be up all night, sweeping the whole area for spy tech left behind, not Cinnamon.

"Leave. Now!" Cinnamon shouted over her shoulder. She'd wasted enough time and most of her decent mood. Feeling good was too precious, too rare. "Trust me. I do have a monster on call." She shoved the greenhouse door toward the sill.

Carlos stuck his foot in the crack and got up in her face. "What about a special offer tailored just for you?" He and Cinnamon were about the same height and he was as muscled and strong as she was. Fine wrinkles around his eyes and lips looked like he used to laugh a lot. No lips to speak of but they curved into a foolish grin. Cinnamon smashed the door against his purple shoe. Carlos yelped, and the door bounced back, almost knocking her down.

Cinnamon rubbed her forehead and smacked the door. "Whose side are you on?"

"Yours. Look." Carlos unfolded an array of tiny gadgets on a sheet of flexible plastic: beady little camera eyes on everything, ladybug speakers and mics, storage chips as thin as a strand of hair, or maybe those were sensors. State-of-the-art gear. A Wi-Fi virtual-reality rig had sleek silver goggles and plush ear cups on a sparkly tiara. A row of crystal data cubes made rainbows like the jewel-eyes on her demon thighs. These cubes were Cinnamon's design. Consolidated was still getting rich off her whimsy.

"Fifty percent off." Carlos was relentless. "This afternoon only." They were trying to sell her own tech to her. Irony was a killer. "You can't beat that."

Cinnamon shook her head.

Carlos was breathless. "Free installation plus we can waive the cable connection fee."

"No cable out here. It's the ancient phone line, a satellite, or that cell tower." She pointed to the nearby mountain range. A metal tree with antennae, receivers, and processors was camouflaged as a strapping elm giant. A ghost tree. "Consolidated owns the sky, the airways…"

She scanned above them for drones. "I have nothing worth stealing. What's your game? Who are you really?"

Carlos clamped a hand over the sword pin on his paisley tie. "Even the algorithm doesn't know who the fuck I am." He dropped his hand and got back on script, back on charm. "We can start installation immediately. Let us make your today great."

"I love my dumb house. My grandparents built it—straw bales, solar power, and hoodoo conjure. I don't let just every pushy body inside." Rage flared. "I'm the guardian of this gate." She shoved Carlos and Barbett down the steps. They scrambled to protect their newfangled electric delights. Bruja, border collie witch-dog, barged through the inflatables snarling and snapping at the bouncing wonders. She was late to the party. Some watchdog.

"Dog bite?" Barbette exchanged desperate looks with Carlos. "Witch-dog worse than ghost-dog."

"You know Spook?" Ghost-dog was Taiwo's eyes, ears, and nose on the prowl. Hardly anybody ever saw Spook. He was a creature of myth and legend. They'd done deep research. Cinnamon whistled. Bruja trotted over and looked her brown eye and blue eye at Cinnamon, ready to bust big balloons if given the command, ready to do worse too. "Bruja doesn't like strangers any better than I do." The *salesmen* didn't start packing up like they had any kind of sense. Whatever algorithm was running their mission had made unreasonable demands.

"Sixty percent off." Carlos let irritation leak. The mask was cracking. "Free upgrades for four months. No rate hikes for six months. No payments for twelve. A totally discount future!"

"I don't care if you're giving it away." Cinnamon offered a sweet smile. "You guys are worse than chewing gum and super glue."

Carlos clutched the sword tiepin again. "Just let us in. We'll explain everything." The accent came back. German. "Please."

Barbett clutched his tie-pin too. "Good story."

"You think I'm a fool?" Cinnamon was curious despite her suspicions. They dropped their hands. "You recording this right now and streaming it to home base?"

Carlos waved a hand in the air. "Quality control, to help improve service."

Barbett spit strange words in his ear.

"Why does he talk so weird? Tell me that at least."

"Not he. Gender free." Barbett was defiant. "Identity hard to hold in English."

Carlos talked over Barbett. "No payments for a year. Use all this gear, free. How can you refuse?"

"Nothing's free." Cinnamon shook her head. Why keep arguing with them? She did have a soft spot for old thespians and there was something else about them, something she should remember.

"Paranoia prevents you from enjoying progress." Carlos ventured too close. Bruja nipped at his heels. He danced away from her growl and tripped into the inflatable sex suite. The VR-tiara punctured a dragon dildo and the exhibit hissed and shriveled around him. Cinnamon gripped Bruja before she lunged. Carlos scrambled for balance. "They're firing us today, if we don't get a sale—" He clutched his heart and crumpled. His splotchy face landed in a cluster of bluebells.

Barbett crouched down quickly and turned Carlos over. The stingy brim fedora rolled into the forsythia bushes. Barbett brushed flowers and dirt from Carlos's face, put a pill under his tongue and an ear to his chest. The feathers and feelers on Cinnamon's demon costume softened, fluttering in the breeze. Bruja whined and struggled.

"So you like him now." Cinnamon let her go. The witch-dog ran to Carlos and licked blotchy cheeks. Cinnamon stepped close. Carlos's eyes rolled up in his head. Fear streaked across her nerves. This was real. "Is he having a heart attack or something?"

"Or something." Barbette ground gleaming teeth. "Dumb car blows out at gate."

"Ah, can't fix itself." Cinnamon squatted down and touched a clammy neck. She barely felt a pulse. "I don't have a car up here. You should call somebody."

"Cell wrecked." Barbett held up a mangled phone. "His too."

"Damn." Cinnamon's cell was in the microwave, dead to the world. The nearest Co-op neighbor with a car was a few miles away. This stupid scenario was the heart of their sales pitch. Cinnamon hated irony. "I'll call for help."

She sprinted to the garage. The landline and computer lived on a table among her pedal-people bikes and trailers. She'd haul Carlos to the gate if need be. Unblocking the main road would take forever. The dial tone was a relief. Bill paid, service yet to be phased out. She punched the emergency number then argued with a dispatcher half way round the world or maybe in Arizona. Consolidated never paid health expenses for *salesmen*. So Cinnamon lied and offered an Electric Paradise account. She still had an expense line from debugging the Valley security system last week. She slammed the phone down. An ambulance was going to cost a fortune and take forever to get there.

Carlos could die in the meantime.

Cinnamon raced back from the garage, smacking the inflatables out of her way. She needed a defibrillator, not a sex suite. The sun was still blasting heat, even at a low angle. Sweat collected in her hollows, curves, and creases. Bruja curled close to Carlos, panting to stay cool. Treading on Miz Redwood's spells, Cinnamon's feet burned. She was hoodooing herself.

"They're coming," she said. "Taiwo will let us know when they reach the gate."

"We can't pay," Barbett said.

"I paid for the wheels. The Co-ops set up a free clinic at the Ghost Mall. There's a bed for you in the shelter. You'll be fine." Cinnamon fought nasty suspicion with logic. *Salesmen* were amateur spies, dirt-cheap labor collecting random data. *Salesmen* wouldn't stage a heart attack on her steps. Live-action melodrama was for pros—corporate espionage. No reason to spend so many live minutes on Cinnamon.

"He is breath," Barbett talk-sang and patted Carlos's chest tenderly, as if they were more than colleagues. "All heart. Good heart."

"Uh huh." Cinnamon's heart pounded.

Carlos gulped a raggedy breath through bloodless lips.

"Oh, all right." Cinnamon relented. "The garage is an oven. We take him into the house to wait. It's cool."

She undid Carlos's tie and tossed it in a can of storm water and fertilizer dung. She snatched Barbett's tie too. "You look a little peaked yourself." She threw the spy gear into the birdbath. Barbette shook off the fedora. A mane of black and grey skinny braids tumbled free. A familiar smirk lurked behind an excellent make-up job. Recognition smacked Cinnamon so hard, she almost fell down next to Carlos. Name aphasia made her want to scream, but they were lifting Carlos and stumbling toward the greenhouse. He was heavy and hot and familiar too. Older yes, but how had she missed who they were? They recognized her for sure.

Cinnamon halted at the steps to the greenhouse. "Are you going to tell me what's going on?"

"Inside. Sun too hot. Too heavy for talking."

Bruja herded them up the steps and into the greenhouse. When they reached the irises, the witch-dog raced back and jumped against the door. The hinges creaked and hollered, then the damn thing closed easily behind them.

IT WAS TWENTY degrees cooler in the open room at the center of the dumb house—always temperate, thanks to straw bale walls. Pots of lavender and jasmine cleaned and soothed the air. Spider plants cascaded out of hanging bowls and snake plants crowded the corners, clearing toxins too. Creature and demon costumes hung from the mantle and molding hooks. Masks peeked from the shelves. Half-finished props were scattered across the dining table: birds, shields, wands, boulders, staffs, and a flying-carpet drone that broke more often than it flew. Photos and otherworldly paintings from Cinnamon's old life, her good life, graced the walls. Rag rugs from Aunt Iris cushioned tired feet. Granddaddy Aidan had crafted chairs, tables, and a big sofa. Miz Redwood stuffed the pillows. Cinnamon's demon mask perched on the back of the sofa, grinning as they deposited Carlos on the firm cushions.

Cinnamon sucked a deep breath and grabbed the mask. The hair was a scratchy thicket of brambles and thorns. Lightning bolts on the cheeks sparked and fiber optic eyes smoldered. She set the mask on the dining table and shut the hallway doors, revealing Taiwo's altar to Eshu, crossroads deity, trickster always messing in people's lives. Taiwo's chant still echoed through the house:

Who do you mean to be?
I am Guardian at the Gates
Master of uncertainty
The cat that be dead and not dead
The electron, the pulse, everywhere at once
And nowhere too

"What is that?" Barbett who wasn't Barbett said. "What am I hearing?"

"Taiwo." Cinnamon was about to burst.

The old African wouldn't waste words on just anybody.

"Taiwo, talking all the way from the gate?"

Cinnamon closed the sky light. "This morning's prayer. Lingering. Till there's another prayer." A constellation of LED lights on the ceiling and walls glowed softly and banished the sudden dark. "Inside here is a Faraday fortress. No signals in or out. We can say anything." But she didn't know what to say or think or feel. "Marie? Marie Masuda? Is that you?"

"Of course." Marie spat wads of cotton from her cheeks and mopped goop from her face onto a once-white handkerchief. "Damn! Who else would I be?" Marie was still snarky.

"So why the masquerade?"

"*Salesmen* can't reveal true identities. You lose your commissions and get fired."

"Oh." Cinnamon held out a recycling basket for make-up refuse. "Are you really genderqueer?"

Marie shrugged. "Probably, but I don't mind *she*. Too old for new pronouns."

"Not if you rehearse. Too lazy, maybe..."

Marie smirked and stuck out her tongue. Bruja plopped in front of Thunderbird and Dragon as they powered up between the sofa and the bookshelves—her favorite spot. Marie gawked. "Are those winged heaps of junk robotic lights?"

"Circus-bots," Cinnamon sputtered. "Carnival took all their juice."

Marie nodded. "Tin-can dragon and cellophane wonder-bird. Still putting on shows? I thought you were some big engineer."

Cinnamon wasn't going there. "Is that Klaus Beckenbauer with you?"

"Who else? He should come around soon." Marie peeled derma-wax from Klaus's nose and chin. "The pass-out heart-thing looks worse than it is. That's what Klaus says. I don't know if I believe him. Maybe dancing in this heat was a bad idea. He can still kick it, though."

"No, no." Cinnamon gripped a sweetgrass broom leaning against the sofa and let her theatre voice boom. "You two can't just sneak back into somebody's life in fucking disguises and then do idle chit-chat about pronouns and sexy dance moves."

"You looked right through us!" Marie yelled too. Bruja sat up and whined. "How could you not recognize us?" Marie was mad that their disguises worked so well. This was unreasonable, but Cinnamon swallowed an angry retort. Marie sniffled and stroked Klaus's chest again. "The air is better in here. Look at him breathe." She blinked contacts lenses into a plastic case. Familiar brown eyes glared at Cinnamon. "I'm still not nice, you know. I've never been nice."

"I remember." Cinnamon always liked how snarky Marie was. "You two are like, ghosts come to haunt me. Spooky."

Marie rolled her eyes, still a hardcore realist. "Is it spooky and nice at least?"

Klaus, Marie, and Cinnamon had been tight friends back in Pittsburgh, more than friends actually, teenagers in love, doing plays, dancing, and carrying on. Klaus and Marie were Cinnamon's first loves. She'd lost track of them. Her heart ached to see them again, on her sofa. The passion they'd professed for each other at sixteen and seventeen was stored deep in her heart—part of her algorithm for love. How could they be real?

"We were so sullen, ardent, and clueless." Loneliness crashed into Cinnamon, crushed her chest, made her gasp.

Marie eyed her. "What?"

"Nothing."

"Out there quoting Japanese wisdom from the old country—really?" Marie snorted.

"From Granddaddy Aidan's journal, not about you being Japanese-American."

"But you talk that crap to strangers? Jesus."

"I can't believe you're fussing over nothing, and after all this time." Marie softened. "I was joking."

"Ha, ha." Cinnamon's costume itched prickly skin. "What is it, thirty years?"

"Forty years and some change. And I recognized you right off." Marie pouted.

"Well, I'm not trying to hide my face, am I?"

"But you are hiding out here all alone! Taiwo is mad at you for that and for going country and throwback on us. Anti-technology, you?"

"Yeah. I've killed three AI assistants—Willy, Milly, and Geraldine—fussbudget spies, collecting my data, talking so sweet, and the bitches were steady using me against me." Cinnamon balled her fists. "How could you come as *salesmen*?"

Marie flipped her braids from side to side. "Hiding in the outback is no way better than masquerading on the road." Marie was always good on nailing her.

Cinnamon bent over Klaus. "What can I do?" She stroked his head. He loved that when they were young.

Marie clutched his hand. "He didn't really explain. He said don't worry unless it takes more than thirty minutes for him to come 'round."

"That's bullshit if I ever heard it."

"You know how he is."

"Still?"

Marie almost burst into tears. "Sorry. It is so good to see you. I can't tell you how good." She stood up and moved in for a hug.

Cinnamon backed away. She bumped into Taiwo's altar. A picture of Cinnamon, Klaus, and Marie as teenagers fell over, and the glass in the frame shattered. A thousand pieces sprayed across the floor. Marie dropped down, plucked the old photo from the shards, and shook it gently. Their teenage selves wore goofy smiles and colorful regalia from Africa and Georgia swamp Indians. They were hanging all over each other, love on public display. Cinnamon had forgotten the title of that play—a monster-with-a-golden-heart gig. Marie touched their eager, sweet faces. They were fearless, staring out at a grand future.

She held it against her chest and swallowed a sob. Cinnamon grabbed the sweetgrass broom again and swept up the glass, letting Marie collect herself. Marie hated *public display*. Cinnamon dampened a cloth in a water can and wiped up the tiny fragments.

Marie hovered over her. "So what are you doing?"

"What? Oh, you mean with my life." An awful question. "What are you two doing? *Salesmen*?" Cinnamon was disappointed and jealous. At least Klaus and Marie were in the muck together. She dumped the glass in bottle recycling. "Couldn't you find anything better to do?"

"You haven't been out on the road." Marie was ready to cry again. She set the photo back in the altar among cowry shells, red feathers, and giant acorns. "I like who I used to be. I miss her, and every day takes me further away, to, to—"

"To some cranky stranger with bad teeth and a foul temper." Cinnamon and Marie laughed and fell into a hug. It was awkward and itchy at first.

"What's this fabric?" Marie marveled as the demon feathers and feelers turned soft and silky.

"Second skin. Taiwo's juju-tech." Cinnamon pecked Marie's cheek, chaste and reserved suddenly. There was no protocol for old teenage lovers sneaking back in your life—gray, crinkled, and tough as nails. She bent over Klaus again. His eyes fluttered.

"A kiss would wake me right up." He grinned at her, cheeks pale and cool again.

"I guess you'll have to go on dreaming then." Cinnamon didn't resist as he tugged her close and kissed her forehead. He sat up slowly. She kissed his rough cheek and touched the pulse on his neck. It was steady, strong.

"I was listening to you two. It felt like a dream." He laid his cheek in the palm of Cinnamon's hand.

Marie poked his shoulder. "So what, you're fine now?"

"Almost. A little hungry, but otherwise fine." Neither Cinnamon nor Marie challenged him. "Dancing in the sun, I worked up an appetite."

"Uh huh." Cinnamon gave him the stink eye.

"My condition looks worse than it is." He raised his voice. "I'm a doctor. Trust me."

"Where's the potty?" Marie asked, scowling. Cinnamon pointed.

"Where's the kitchen?" Klaus jumped up, acting fit and frisky. "You got any food?"

Cinnamon jumped up beside him. "I'll get you something."

Of course Klaus had to come around the corner with her. A screen and a wall of DVDs hung opposite the refrigerator over a breakfast nook. Klaus stroked a row of old-fashioned jewel cases.

"You don't stream movies, I take it." He pulled out *Brother from Another Planet* and *The Shape of Water*. "Do you have *Black Panther*?"

"No streaming." Cinnamon fought a wave of self-righteousness. "Remember Aunt Iris busting up the TV?"

"During commercials." He pushed the films back in.

"*Why hand your enemies the keys to the kingdom?*"

He laughed as she smeared a fortune in cashew butter on a thick slice of three-seed rye. She added fresh strawberries from her greenhouse. Klaus scarfed the food down and chugged a mug of lukewarm green tea.

"So what's your story?" She tried to sound casual.

"I'm jealous. Marie didn't talk to me like to you and no snark. As if I don't have all the cups in my cupboard."

"Cups in the cupboard is a German thing; we say all the lights aren't on, or something."

"I didn't recognize Marie either. She was standing under my nose, grinning." He spooned the last of the cashew butter onto another hunk of bread. "We weren't expecting each other, not like walking up to your dumb house, knowing you'd try to kick our predatory capitalist asses." Delighted at this image of Cinnamon, he popped whole strawberries into his mouth and swallowed without chewing.

"You can't blame Marie. It's not like you talk unless we beat it out of you." Cinnamon passed him a hunk of soy cheese.

"Marie's as sad as you." Klaus ran his finger over Cinnamon's creased forehead.

She stroked his sparse hair. "Is Marie as sad as you?"

"I hear you all talking about me!" Marie yelled from the bathroom.

Klaus crammed cheese in his mouth and crept back toward the center room. Balance was elusive. He steadied himself against the wall and smiled at the props and sweetgrass baskets and fans. Bruja thumped her tail, encouraging him.

"You're a charmer," Cinnamon said. "Witch-dog prefers circus-bots to most people."

"What about you, you been good? You got yourself a magic haven, not a dumb house." He was on the sofa again, shivering. "Sit down so we can all talk, tell each other everything." He winked at her. "I got a chill in my bones. Warm me up."

Cinnamon wanted to let her heart go, let it fly to him and Marie, but folks dropping out of nowhere was a bad sign. Cinnamon was on somebody's radar. Marie swooped in from the bathroom and pulled Cinnamon down on the sofa with Klaus. After a few awkward moments, they squished close together and giggled like teenagers and old farts. Klaus popped out the misty green contacts. His silvery blue eyes were sad, tired. Cinnamon clutched their hands and looked across the room to the photo. It felt like looking across the years.

Klaus had been a Doctor Without Borders and Marie a Singer Without a Stage until the water wars. They stuttered, talking around the present, vague and protective. But stories about old times, magic times, tumbled out of everybody's mouths. Cinnamon wanted to hug them close and never let them leave. She also wanted to chase them out the house.

"So tell me, people." Cinnamon shook off a suspicious funk that could have paralyzed her and pulled them close. "You did deep research and ambushed me. I know zip about recent history. How long have you been hooked up?" Jealousy was better than depression.

Klaus and Marie pulled away from her. "We just met this morning." They spoke in unison as if they'd rehearsed this. "Nobody else—"

"Wanted to come out to my hoodoo-voodoo farm." Cinnamon chuckled. Forty years and they still finished each other's sentences, and she was still jealous for nothing.

Marie flipped her braids around. "Taiwo and haints, come on."

"A ghost-dog *and* a witch-dog." Klaus poked her demon second skin. "And this costume."

"A good horror-rep is the best protection against desperadoes." Corporate spies were another matter.

"Can we trust you?" Marie squinted, looking for signs of betrayal.

"Of course we can," Klaus blinked at Cinnamon. "Can't we?"

Marie reached over Cinnamon and slugged him. "Naïve people get killed."

"You all in some kind of trouble?" Cinnamon sucked her teeth. "Is that why you—"

"Came to see you? No." Klaus looked wounded.

"We're Whistleblowers," Marie whispered, proud and devilish, "not real *salesmen*."

"You told her, not me." Klaus held his breath.

Bold Marie stroked Cinnamon's braids. Klaus pulled one that curled tight at her forehead down to her chin. They were saying just what Cinnamon wanted to hear. "So you're warning folks about toxins, scams, and hostile takeovers."

Klaus nodded. "Any straight up evil mess."

Cinnamon licked dry lips. "People say the Whistleblower thing is an urban legend. Wishful thinking."

"*Scheiße*!" Klaus cursed in German.

"Yeah, shit," Marie groaned. "That's exactly what the big corps want you to think."

"*Die Arschgeigen*!" Klaus muttered.

"Ass-violins? Ass-fiddles? Really?" Cinnamon was laughing.

"People should believe, even if we are secret." Klaus hissed. "We should be possible."

"Join us. You'd be a great Whistleblower." Marie sounded excited.

"You're here to recruit me?"

"For a traveling show." Klaus was smooth. "We got inside info, sugar. Double agents gotta know what's what."

Consolidated or some other mega-corp was after Cinnamon's farm and the other Co-op farms nearby. A slick algorithm expected her to jump at fancy rigs, bug drones, and hair-thin sensors. Eighty percent chance that curiosity might bankrupt her, and a mega-corp could scoop up the entire region. One farm failing would start a cascade.

Cinnamon was flabbergasted. "My land, not information?"

"Co-ops are a threat." Marie shrugged like it was obvious. "Dumb houses are a nuisance, a gateway drug."

"To what? Revolution? You're kidding." Cinnamon had to get out more.

"Food, social resources, water," Klaus said.

"One system to rule them all." Marie did a wicked monster laugh.

"Shh," Klaus looked around. "Do you hear that?"

I am Guardian at the Gates
I have many plenty heads! You do not know me
I ask:
Which direction you goin' take?
Who you mean to be?

"Taiwo's morning chant, second verse," Cinnamon said.

"It echoes through the house all day." Marie shook Klaus. "Is that cool or what?"

Color painted Klaus's cheeks. "How does that work?

Cinnamon pointed. "Speak your heart to the Eshu altar that guards the house."

Marie tugged Cinnamon's arm. "So, you want to be a Whistleblower? Do guerilla traveling theatre?"

Cinnamon slumped. She wasn't ready for them or for all that. "I can't leave the farm or ditch the Co-ops."

Klaus and Marie looked crushed at this plausible excuse, then Marie spoke. "We thought you'd say that."

"The farm, the Co-op, that's good work," Klaus added.

A bell rang. It was like being wrenched out of a dream. Taiwo called them to the gate. Cinnamon was relieved. She shouldn't trust anybody too quickly, not even Klaus and Marie. "I'm sorry about getting you fired. The Ghost Mall infirmary is great. They'll patch you up, patch up your dumb car. Nobody will suspect you're Whistleblowers."

"We still got jobs." Klaus stood up. "Getting fired is part of the pitch."

"Can we leave a chant for you?" Marie asked.

"Why not?" Cinnamon went to the garage to get wheels for Marie and to hook up a trailer to her bike for Klaus. She'd hear the chant later, a surprise to come home to. Marie packed up the inflatables,

Bruja nipping at her heels. Klaus insisted on walking to the garage. He took precise steps, not a joule of energy wasted. Cinnamon stuffed the flatbed trailer with Miz Redwood's pillows.

He sank into them, stretched out his legs and sighed. "I'll be fine."

THE BIKE PATH wandered two miles through the woods. The pink-orange rays of the setting sun got tangled in stark black boughs and branches. The air close to the ground was blue-green and hazy. Cinnamon's pedal-people bike lumbered along like a tank. Klaus was no heavier than other gear she'd hauled. Cinnamon tried not to worry. Nobody's cover was blown. Maybe she'd have her old friends in her life or they'd disappear again. For sure she'd pay off Consolidated with the last of her savings.

Loud bangs and angry voices jolted her. She pumped the pedals harder. Bruja ran ahead, a silver streak vanishing beyond the trees. Cinnamon squeezed the brakes just before they slammed into the gate. Klaus groaned at the abrupt halt. She jumped from the saddle, peering at the road. Marie pulled up beside them. Klaus stepped out of the trailer. They pressed their faces against the iron latticework.

A short way down the road, a car exploded in flames, an old jalopy, what *salesmen* drove. Cinnamon shuddered and looked around for Bruja. Witch-dog had a secret passage to the main road. Cinnamon whistled for her.

"Not our car," Marie said, calm. "We wheeled if off the road and covered it in bushes."

A mob of men taunted each other beyond the burning vehicle. Their blood-smeared suits, raggedy jeans, and denim jackets could have been rival team jerseys. "Bad boys, desperadoes, and *salesmen*," Klaus sucked his teeth like Cinnamon. "The ambulance won't drive into this."

Taiwo jumped through the stringy yellow flowers and red leaf-buds of a white oak onto the blazing car. Muscled, scarred, and fierce, Taiwo looked like a buff African Amazon. A little more gray in the crown of braids these days, but not much change since Cinnamon was sixteen. Taiwo wore a black and red top hat from Carnival decorated with cowry shells and plumes. Lightning streaked across the storm-cloud cape as it fluttered around a cutlass. The men missed this grand entrance, banging and slashing at one another. Bruja barked and got their attention. They swallowed whatever they'd been yelling and froze.

Taiwo drew the fire from the car, sucking down blue and orange licks of flame. The mob was ready to pee themselves as Taiwo spit the blaze toward the orange ball of sun at the end of the road. Flames winked out or merged into the bright light. The blackened jalopy shifted under Taiwo's weight and belched ashes out broken windows. The mob was backing away. Bruja ran to Taiwo, who cut a fine figure backlit by the sun, storm-cape snapping in the wind: badass monster on the case.

"You must be willing to die in order to live." Klaus, Marie, and Cinnamon shouted a line from their old monster play in sync. "The lightning eater!"

Mangy desperadoes were the first to bolt, followed by hill town bad boys. Four *salesmen* gawked at Taiwo on the jalopy, uncertain. Bruja growled, and they jumped into a beat-up SUV and sped off.

"This spectacle should keep folks away for a month." Cinnamon opened the gate and ran to Taiwo. The old African stumbled off the car roof and leaned on her.

"Good day today, you three together. Fire, easier than lightning, only a night to recover." Taiwo enveloped Marie, Klaus, and Cinnamon in the storm-cape, holding them close until a driverless ambulance pulled up. Cinnamon had paid for a medic, but why fuss? Klaus and Marie waved from the back window. Cinnamon decided to visit them at the infirmary. Taiwo was right. It was good having folks tugging at her heartstrings.

"Don't scold me; I won't scold you," Taiwo said, and disappeared into a tree house.

BACK HOME, CINNAMON swept the grounds for spy-bots. Exhausted, she stumbled through the greenhouse into the dumb house. Klaus and Marie had left their prayer to Eshu behind:

I say:
Wrong road lead you to nowhere
Wrong road take your name, your face
Turn you downside up and outside in
Wrong road leave you heartless
I don't say
Which Road
Wrong Road
You the one know who you mean to be

ONE EASY TRICK
Hiromi Goto

MARNIE MORI HAD packed a couple of onigiri and a piece of chicken for her day trip so she didn't need to buy lunch or snacks, but she felt bad about just using the convenience store's washroom. And it was nice and clean, too. She was grateful. She exited the bathroom and walked down the aisle, pausing in front of the magazine rack. Maybe she would buy one… The glossy covers of women with their polished teeth, their svelte bodies, their chests, their long legs— gossip rags, fashion, housekeeping, bikinis, the whole shebang. There were men's magazines too: hunting, bodybuilding, fishing. But most of the publications were directed toward women and with the same old perennial message, shouting from every cover, for all the women to see.

More than Ten Ways to Lose Your Belly Fat! In fact, there were at least twenty effective tips on how to reduce belly fat. For those with less time and attention, there was always One Easy Trick.

Che! Marnie clicked her tongue. In gas stations, in the doctor's office, at the grocery store checkout, pop-up ads blooming on her screen when she clicked links on Twitter, looked up stuff on Google and listened to 70s songs on YouTube, the information, doctrine, religion, incantation, spell seemed to follow Marnie Mori wherever she went. The tall, lean white women with pony tails and rolled-up yoga mats who lived in her neighborhood did not help one bit. In time she grew numb to the refrain; she began to unhear and unsee it. If Marnie had never grown to love her belly fat, she had accepted it. They'd been part of each for so long, even longer than her marriage with her ex-husband and her previous committed long-term relationship with Cassandra, combined. Essentially, the past thirty years. And now she was alone, again. But belly fat was still with her.

Huffing with indignation, Marnie moved away from the magazines. She wasn't fucking buying one of them, that was for sure. She nodded at the middle-aged white woman who was working the till. Marnie squinted at her name tag—

June, maybe, or Jane. They were probably near the same age, but Marnie wasn't exactly sure. June had a really wrinkled face, from either too much sun, or smoking, or probably both.

"Mornin'. Almost good afternoon," June/Jane said. The country gas station was empty. Business was slow.

Marnie reached out and grabbed an overpriced tube of Pringles and set it on the counter. She was finally close enough to read the cashier's name tag.

"Those chips are tasty inside a sandwich," June said.

"Whoa!" Marnie said. "That sounds good! I'll try that next time." She wasn't faking being nice. It really sounded like it'd be pretty damn tasty.

June smiled wide. There was a Harlequin Romance novel next to the till, with the page marked with a stick of gum wrapped in silver foil.

Marnie grinned back. June looked like the kind of woman who'd be fun drinking beers with, while barbequing some steaks. It was a damn shame Marnie didn't drink anymore. She paid up, got her change. Tucked the stuff into her backpack.

"Thanks, come again," June said.

Smiling, Marnie turned toward the door. Caught herself in the glass.

Her eyes moved from her own smiling reflection, downward, to her belly fat.

She knew fat activists like her sister, Joan, would call her fatphobic for thinking her belly unattractive. Marnie resented that was she was supposed to feel ashamed of her own dislike, making it her bad exponentially. She had nothing to hide; she was a feminist and she wasn't ashamed of her*self*. She just didn't love her belly fat. And that was no one's business but her own.

Fuck those magazines.

The door jangled as she strode out the gas station store.

BELLY FAT HAD never stopped her from doing the things she loved. An hour later she was in her favorite Pacific Northwest forest, among the spicy sweet-smelling Douglas fir, pine, and cedar. Smiling, she picked her way through the land, breathing deeply, eyes scanning the ground, hearing the intermittent jangle of the bear bell hanging off of her backpack. There was a quality to being alone in the woods that felt safe and dangerous at the same time. Kinda like how the sound of the bell warned bears of humans in the vicinity, so it was meant to protect her, but it also reminded her of the possibility of the danger of bears... The overlay of these emotions vibrated inside her. Making her aware, alert, and grounded. It was good to be out of the city, and on land that wasn't mediated by concrete.

The thick soft moss buoyed her, even as decaying logs and broken branches obstructed easy passage. Marnie zig-zagged through the forest, scrambling over the smaller of the fallen trees, going around the larger trunks too big to straddle, the jangle of the bear bell a constant reminder. She placed her feet carefully; a sprained ankle in this terrain could happen as easy as one misstep on a damp log. There was no cell phone reception this far north of major cities, and she'd have to make it to the car if she got injured. She slowed down her pace.

Breath left her mouth in small puffs, sweat trickling from her armpits, moist heat spreading beneath the straps of the small backpack and her bra. She never sweated in the city. Walking through wild lands was the best kind of medicine. There was very little bird song. Now and then flocks of bushtits made their squeeze-toy noise, but otherwise the only sounds were what she created on her own. When she stopped moving, the quiet stilled around her like water in a pond.

Marnie scanned the moss, looking for hints of pale yellow flesh. Her vision wasn't what it used to be. The mostly coniferous trees were spaced widely enough apart for the light to reach the forest floor, but the day was slightly overcast and now that Marnie was fifty years old, autumn leaves, a discarded bit of decaying plastic bag, and a golden chanterelle looked pretty much the same from ten feet away. She supposed it was time to get prescription glasses. Blinking hard Marnie worked her way through the woods. She'd never taken orienteering courses, but she always knew in which direction she'd left the car. Her zigzag path ran parallel to the gravel road. She wouldn't go any deeper into the forest on her own.

When she'd been a child, about ten years old, her oto-san had taken her and her sister to look for precious matsutake, pine mushrooms. Her father had taught her how to identify them and she'd never forgotten. Huh, she thought. They could have traipsed past a thousand chanterelles without knowing. All her father knew was matsutake. It had been enough, back then.

In that first forest, how sweet the air. Sweet and spicy, wet and earthy. How thrilling, to be on an adventure with her father. How rare and special a thing it was. Her heart thumped with excitement and joy. Her sister, Joanie, less confident and younger, stuck close to their oto-san, but Marnie was a long-time tomboy and considered the forest her second home. As the afternoon skimmed over the tops of the trees they began walking at different paces.

Marnie raised her head and tilted it to one side. Had she heard something?

...a whisper

Marnie's eyes widened. She held her breath. Listened with her entire being. The hushhhh of air between the branches of enormous trees, the long hair strands of grey lichen wafting back and forth.

Come in... a little further...

Forest... Forest was speaking to her. Marnie nodded, and picked her way deeper among the trees.

Just a little more, Forest whispered. *Soon, very soon, you'll find the matsutake...*

Yes. She was certain. If she looked a little more, the matsutake would be there, and how happy her mother would be. Her father so proud.

Come in deeper, and you will find what you are seeking.

On and on she followed the voice, the pathless path, wending between tree trunks wider than her father's arms could span. The soft moss beneath her sneakers felt rich, thicker than the carpet at her friend's house, pretty Julia, whose father was a lawyer.

A small branch snapped beneath her foot. The sound spread out, across the deep stillness, like rings of water expanding on a dark deep pond. Her ears rang. Marnie slowly raised her head and looked all around. Trees, tall, and dark and moss. Pale grey-green lichen hanging from crooked branches. She was alone. And she had no idea which way was out...

Marnie grinned, and shook her head as she peered at the moss. Joan never developed a liking for the forest, the mountains. And her oto-san never had the time to take her out picking wild mushrooms again. So as an adult she'd begun going back alone. She didn't hear the forest's voice like she did that first time. Marnie didn't know if she was glad. Or sad. Maybe both. And maybe it hadn't even been the forest's voice—maybe it'd been her own...

Marnie stopped, placed her hands on her hips and arched her back a little bit. Her spine cracked into place and she groaned with relief. She rolled her shoulders and stood up straight to take a deep breath of the sweet air.

Her jeans fell to her ankles.

"Uh!" Marnie grunted, even though no one was there to hear her. She giggled. How embarrassing! Standing among the trees, with her middle-aged pantie-ass showing! She reached down to draw her jeans back up to her waist. Had the button popped off and the zipper fail—

Her waist...

The jeans fell from her nerveless fingers. The faded blue denim slumped back to the ground. Her eyes grew round as she stared at her front, her mouth dropping open.

Her belly fat was gone.

Pouchy and soft, her belly had been big enough to fold over, thick enough to grab with two hands. Nani? What! Nanda!

The elastic waistband of her underwear had enough tension to keep them up around her diminished middle but with no belly there to fill it out, the cotton material now hung loose and empty. She smacked her hands over the new flat plane again and again, as if she would find the answers in the motion.

Nothing to grab. No fleshly jiggle. What! Should she scream? Laugh? A sob burst out.

She scanned about her, but she couldn't see it. She crouched to draw up her jeans and she held them up with her fingers scrunched into fists at her sides. Marnie's eyes leapt and darted as she spun around and started backtracking along the path she'd taken. She fought the urge to cry out for her belly, as if she were calling a wayward dog...

She had lost her belly fat somewhere along the way, and hadn't even noticed. It couldn't have been so long ago, because wouldn't her jeans have fallen down sooner? It must be somewhere, nearby, in the forest, not back at the last gas station bathroom...

What's wrong with you! Another part of her brain demanded. It fell *off*! Don't go *looking* for it! Are you hurt? *No!* Are you wounded? *No!*

She hadn't realized she'd been gasping until she came to a stop. Sweat trickled from her hairline and the bead of moisture followed a downward wrinkle that funneled to her lips. The salt spread inside her mouth like a kiss.

She slid both thumbs past the waistband of her jeans and underwear and held the material out in front of her, like the photos of the before and after women who'd lost hundreds of pounds and were now on magazine covers.

Her belly was smooth. The most pleasantly smooth outward curve, but without the voluminous belly roll she'd carried with her the most of her entire life. There was no ragged torn skin, no blood. Just like the Japanese folk tale of the old man and his wen... the oni had plucked it off the old man's face and it had come away as easy as a clump of mochi. Without rent nerves, blood, injury. And how pleased the old man had been, with his new smooth face. How grateful to the ogres.

Marnie pivoted forty-five degrees. She stuck her forefingers in the two front belt loops to hold up her pants as she strode the shortest distance through the woods to reach the logging road. In her haste she did not even notice a large patch of golden chanterelles growing in the moss.

* * *

SHE DROVE BACK to Vancouver like she was being chased by demons. The highway along the coast swerved and curved as she raced the setting sun. She arrived at her home just as dusk bloomed indigo from the horizon. Marnie ran upstairs, shucked her clothes off in the middle of her bedroom floor, donned a shin-length nightshirt, and threw herself in bed.

Belatedly, her teeth chattered. She shivered and shook as darkness filled the room. She ought to take a bath, but the thought of staring down at her missing front made her teeth chatter even harder. She pulled the blankets over her head. Every rattle of the lids of the garbage in the back alley made her twitch like she'd be electrocuted. The slam of someone's door. A dog baying. The smack-clack as the lid of the garbage wheelie was dropped back down.

What was that noise! Had her belly come back? Could it find its way back home? Would it be mad?

"I never loved you!" Marnie cried out. Guilt spread inside of her like bad blood. She whispered, "I'm sorry."

When she grew too exhausted she fell into nightmares. Of bears eating vanilla pudding. Of someone locked in her bathroom, rattling the doorknob all night to be let out—she woke, heart so loud and fast she could hear her blood whooshing inside her ears. A metallic taste inside her mouth. Her palms pressed flat against her non-existent belly. She yanked her hands away.

No, Marnie thought. No, I don't want to fall back asleep. She wished she still smoked. A thick housecoat and a cigarette on the balcony would cure what ailed her. Along with a triple dirty gin martini.

But she'd given up smoking and she'd given up booze. And what did she have left, now, except movies and hamburgers?

You have sweet chestnuts and mushrooms in the fall, and berries in the summer, her heart reminded her.

Marnie rolled over and sat on the edge of the bed. She nudged her toes around until they found her slippers. The open gaps. She sluffed across the wooden floors in the dark. She didn't turn on the lights, just in case sleepiness might return to her. But it was probably a lost cause.

She stared at her charged cell phone on the kitchen table. She pressed the indented button and the small screen lit up. It was too late to call or text anyone. She and Cassandra remained friends, after the break up a year ago, but she had recently started seeing someone new. It wouldn't do to text her in the middle of the night... Besides—who could really give her advice in a situation like this?

Marnie found herself at her laptop and opening a new document. She started typing a letter to her dead mum.

Dear Mum,

Sorry I haven't written in a long time. I still really miss you... And I'm sorry I only write you when I have a problem. Next time I'll write when something good happens. Balance is important, you always said. And I believe that too.

Mum—something weird happened to me and I don't know what to do. I'm not hurt or anything, but it changed me. I can't say it was something I willfully actioned. But who knows? Maybe I did, subconsciously? I feel all mixed up and strange. Like I'm not myself.

What are you supposed to do when you lose part of your body?

Marnie's fingers stilled. Rested gently atop the keys. She never printed the letters she wrote to her mum. But writing them made her feel a little closer to her, and sometimes she could hear her mother's voice inside her head. Not her actual voice, but she could imagine what her mum would say and the echo of her voice as she remembered it would rise up inside her... And even the times when she didn't hear her mother's voice, the act of writing down what was troubling made things clearer. Letters to her mum made more sense to her than writing a journal.

Marnie closed the laptop and went back to bed. She read from an overdue library book she hadn't yet finished. It was a little boring, and exactly what she needed to help her fall asleep...

When she woke properly later the next morning, she moved from groggy unease to heart-pounding horrified recollection within three seconds. With a terrible hope, she'd rolled off her bed to stand up. Pressed both palms to her stomach.

Her belly was really gone. It wasn't all a dream. The extremes of emotions made her feel sick and woozy. Marnie didn't know what she thought her sister would do or say that could possibly help her make sense of what had happened. But Joan was the only family she had left. Marnie wanted to talk to someone who knew what it is to be a fat woman in this world. Marnie's friends from work were not fat.

"How could you!" Joan said.

"Wha—"

"We said we'd never get cosmetic surgery. We promised each other!" Joan's face was so red Marnie feared something inside her would pop.

"Let me expl—"

"How could you afford this! Did you get an all-inclusive at a clinic in Mexico?"

"What? I don't even kno—"

"Just shut up! Take off your pants and underwear. I want to see what you've done to yourself!"

"No," Marnie said. "I'm not putting on a show for you."

"I can't believe you'd do this to me. You know what? I actually can!"

Joan didn't slam the door shut—she left it open and the sound of her sobs were like punches to Marnie's gut. Down the hallway, the elevator tinged, followed by the low mechanical roar of its descent.

Marnie sank onto her soft couch. She wondered if she was supposed to chase after her sister. Marnie'd done nothing wrong! Anyway, what could she possibly say to her—that her belly fat fell off in the forest? Joan would think that Marnie was out of her mind, or else she was making fun of her. It was better that Joan thought Marnie'd gotten surgery done: Marnie hadn't even known such things were possible, for god's sake.

When had been the last time she'd seen Joan? Three months ago? No, not since Easter. God—over half a year...

They weren't close, were they.

Marnie took a deep breath and exhaled slowly. Rolled over to face the cushions of the couch. The scratchy weave of the synthetic fabric smelled a little like day-old socks. Marnie wished she could buy a new couch. She'd had this one for over thirteen years. It was a little disgusting. But who had money for a brand new couch? She rolled onto her back, arms straight at her sides.

She wondered if she should call in sick on Sunday night. Joanie hadn't handled the news well and Marnie didn't feel up to fielding questions from her co-workers at the warehouse. And there'd be plenty during lunch break. Thank god she didn't have children she'd have to explain to. She and her ex-husband had done at least one thing right after marrying straight out of high school.

Marnie sighed. What did it mean that none of her friends were fat? Not nothing, that's for sure, she thought.

And now Joanie thought she'd betrayed her, and that she'd gotten surgery done in Mexico... Marnie groaned. She should go out and buy some new pants. She didn't have any clothes that would fit properly for work.

Oh yah. She was going to call in sick...

Two tears slid down Marnie's cheeks. She should be feeling happy. What woman would feel sad that she'd lost her belly fat? For free! No cost, no exercise—it was a dream come true! It was a gift from the universe!

Why did she feel so sad?

Marnie dressed in a sweater and a pair of jeans, too big, cinching the waist with a piece of packaging twine through the belt loops, doubled against itself. She didn't have a proper belt, she hated them so much. Muttering, she gathered the things she needed: keys, jacket, water bottle. She grabbed her backpack and the strap caught against part of the chair. She gave the thing a decisive tug, it dislodged, and she ran out the door.

MARNIE WAS TIRED and hungry. She'd planned to stop at a Timmy's along the way, but she hadn't wanted to drive into the weird suburbs of Whistler, and when she reached Pemberton she learned, to her dismay, that they didn't even have one. So she stopped at the same gas station to buy a shitty cup of coffee and a packaged ham sandwich.

June wasn't there. The meat in the sandwich had been kinda grey in the middle so Marnie tossed it out... She kept on driving.

At long last she neared the turn-off for the logging road. A lone dog trotted along the shoulder, going in the opposite direction. Marnie did a double-take. Where had the dog come from? Oh—it was a coyote.

The coyote didn't even glance her way. It had serious business somewhere—

What had she been thinking? Her belly fat was probably long gone. Eaten up by a bear or pecked away by ravens. Nothing fell to the forest floor to be wasted. And it had been a good piece of fat. Delicious for someone, no doubt.

Marnie couldn't help but gag a little in her throat.

She'd stopped pressing the accelerator and her car had come to a complete stop in the middle of a flat stretch of road. Guiltily, she glanced up at her rearview mirror. But the road was empty, just a buckling ripple of air caused by the heat of the sun.

Marnie shook her head. How had she become so citified that she hadn't thought of this before she left home? What an embarrassment. She was so embarrassed with herself she wanted to scream.

"What the fuck!" she shouted.

Shouting did not make her feel any better.

Her foot started pushing down on the accelerator once again and the car surged forward. Why was she still driving? She should turn around, and get her fool city-ass back home. Wash her laundry and make sandwiches to freeze for the coming work week.

But her foot pressed harder and her hands steered, turning the tires up an unmarked gravel road that wound deeper into the coastal mountain range.

"Okay," she said, although she didn't exactly know why. "Okay, might as well take a look, we're all the way up here anyway." Maybe she'd find some chanterelles while she was at it.

When she finally pulled up to the good spot it was early afternoon. If the clouds rolled in she'd have very little daylight left... It was always hard to tell where the weather was coming from inside a forest. Marnie shuffled out of the car and stretched. The air was so sweet she felt like crying. A rapid tok-tok-tok-tok of a woodpecker. The sound, loud and deep. Pileated, she thought, and grabbed her backpack. The familiar jangle of the bear bell did not happen. Marnie turned the pack around. A short piece of string dangled from the strap.

"Che," Marnie exhaled. Now she'd have to whistle. She rummaged in the backpack and pulled out her folded knife, tucked it into the front pocket of her jeans. There were no more power bars. She sighed and took a drink from her water bottle. Slung the backpack on and stepped back into the forest to retrace the path she'd taken only the day before.

The only tune she could think of was the repetitive refrain from the *Andy Griffith Show*. Unhappily, she whistled it in an infinite loop of whiteness. The horrible sameness of the melody made her nervous. Like someone might come creeping up from behind while she distracted herself with her own inane whistling—

She spun around. The forest was quiet. Awash in a slant golden light. It was so beautiful her heart clenched with a kind of pain. Fuck it. She hadn't started using a bear bell until two years ago and she'd never seen a bear in these forests. Did bears even eat mushrooms? Because there were no berries in these woods. She wasn't going to whistle the ugly tune all day for no reason. She'd only started using the bell because it'd been a Secret Santa gift from work and she kinda thought it might be that adorable worker with a Yorkshire accent. Or Manchurian. No, Manchester. She didn't fucking know...

The far-off nasal craw of raven. The staccato chatter of a Douglas squirrel, warning her to keep away from their tree. Marnie settled into a steady pace, the back and forth sweeping gaze as she searched for her lost belly.

"Belly come back," she crooned to the melody of that 70s Player song, "Baby Come Back".

Something pale flashed in her periphery. She spun towards it. An extra quiver of a leaf still clinging to a low bush. A fallen log with a tumble of branches. There might be a small hollow under there... Did something rustle? Marnie's breath came shallow, fast. She crouched beside it and tilted her head sideways to see if—

It burst straight towards her face.

Marnie bellowed, toppled backwards in a flail of arms. The pale thing, rabbit-sized, leapt past her. Marnie turned her head as she fell, to get a real look, and as the details of what she thought she saw moved through her brain on the slowest of neurons, her face landed on the ground, a twig piercing the fleshiest part of her cheek. She screamed again.

The pale thing on the ground screamed.

Marnie scrambled to her feet and the twig that had been stuck in her cheek fell out. The puncture wound throbbed as hot blood began to drip, cool upon her skin.

Marnie stood, arms rigid at her sides, legs slightly spread.

Six feet in front of her stood a pale lumpin thing. It had two stumpy legs, and two stumpy arms, the roundness of a head. But it didn't have a face. Only two indents, where eyes could have been, and dimple of a mouth. On the dark moss tumble of forest floor it glowed as pale as a grub. The soft white texture and its shape made it look like a hanpen starfish...

All the tiny hairs on Marnie's spine shivered erect. What the holy hell—

"Belly?" Marnie croaked. "Bellyfat?"

The lumpin took a step backward.

"Bellyfat," Marnie cajoled, infusing warmth into her voice, "I came back for you."

What the FUCK! Marnie's brain shouted.

The lumpin jerked, as if electrocuted. It bolted across the forest floor. Running in great leaps, hopping over and under logs as carefree as the Gingerbread Man.

"Wait!" Marnie cried, as she crashed after it. "Come back!" Deadfall snapped beneath her hiking boots, as she thudded after her fleeing belly. Her cheek throbbed with every pounding step she took. How could her belly fat be faster than her?

"It makes no sense!" Marnie shouted.

Bellyfat ran even faster.

"Don't be scared!" Marnie panted. She had to stop. She couldn't breathe. It felt like her intestines were coming out of her gullet. She slumped over at the waist, hands atop her thighs, gasping and heaving. Almost gagging for air. Lord Jesus, she prayed. She felt like vomiting. Jesus, please help me.

Slowly her dying fish gulps returned to normal breath. She crouched onto her haunches. The moss was still damp from a night rain, but she plopped down on her butt, anyways. Cold wet seeped through her jeans and underwear. She dropped her head onto her raised knees. Her jeans smelled a little like ham sandwich. Her stomach growled, with both hunger and nausea.

She should just go home. She felt sick. Her belly fat had turned into a small person and had run away from her, so that was that. Marnie had done her due diligence. Or her duty. Whatever obligation one had with one's belly. She had *tried,* and that was all that mattered.

A sense of relief seeped from her chest and spread through her body. She took one long shuddering breath and exhaled slowly. She was allowed to be happy, now.

She raised her head, eyes bright.

Six feet in front of her stood Bellyfat. Bellyfat stared at her with indent eyes. Six feet behind Bellyfat stood an enormous adult black bear.

Marnie's eyes bulged. Run! her mind shrew screeched.

Her feet kicked weakly. No strength left in her legs. It was true. What they said. In Japan. Koshiga nukeru. Paralyzed with fear.

Behind you! Marnie silently mouthed the words at Bellyfat. With exaggerated lip movements. *There's a BEAR!*

Did Bellyfat even understand language, let alone lip read? Could it even *see*?! She didn't know! Shut up! The bear must be able to smell the oily richness. While the bear fed on the fat Marnie could crawl away...

The great beastie snuffled the air with their great snout. Their head weaved from side to side, their small brown eyes staring. At her.

There was intelligence there. Marnie could see it. Her heart clattered fast and thin. Her breath a whistling wheeze. She quickly dropped her gaze. You shouldn't stare at animals. Don't stare at the gorillas, the sign in the zoo had said. It's a sign of aggression. No, Bear. I'm not staring. I swear.

Not me, Marnie wished, fervently. I'm small. My flesh is bitter and tired. See! There's fat. Smell the delicious fat.

The great bear swung their quivering nostrils toward the pale lumpin on the ground. They opened their mouth, as if sucking in the flavor of the air. A long bead of saliva dangled from their jaws. Hoosh! Hoosh! They drew in huge draughts, then swatted at the moss with massive claws, a great clod of green and humus sailing through the air.

Bellyfat turned with slow motion gravitas, toward the bear.

Now, thought Marnie. Now I should run—No! Never run from a bear!

She remained seated. Sweat trickled from her hairline, down her cheek, to burn salty in the wound on her face. Oh yah, she thought, distantly. I hurt my face...

She watched Bellyfat tip back its head, back, way back, to take in the enormity of the black bear. The bear's jaw dropped open, into a long-snouted grin. A long pink tongue. Such teeth.

Bellyfat quivered.

Marnie was standing. She didn't remember doing it. She was on her feet. Her folded knife open. Gripped tight inside her hand, the sharp tip of the blade shivering with fear and adrenaline, pointed at the bear.

"Odd idea," Bear said. "Give me the pricking stick." Bear held out their paw.

It was true. The knife was not a good idea at all. Bear's paw was bigger than her head, and the claws massive—thick and deadly. Marnie's knife was no more useful against the bear than a Bic pen. "I'm sorry," Marnie said, feeling embarrassed that she'd pointed a knife at the bear. That she hadn't known they could talk. "May I keep my knife?" she asked in a small voice. "It was a gift from my father... He's dead now."

Bear exhaled, a snorting blast, before lowering their outstretched paw.

Gratefully, Marnie closed the blade and tucked the knife back into her front pocket.

Well, she thought. Well, well. A chunk of laughter burst from out of her. Marnie clamped her hand over her mouth. If she started laughing she didn't know where it would lead her.

Bellyfat looked from Marnie to the bear, back to Marnie again.

She cleared her throat. Pain crinkled, then beat a steady metronome inside her cheek. "I'm sorry to have left part of me in the forest."

Marnie gestured toward Bellyfat. "I've come back for them, and we will be on our way, now, if we may."

Courtesy seemed key, here. Who would try to bully or insult a bear? Make demands? Who could feel so entitled? Marnie bowed, a little. It made more sense than smiling. Baring teeth, for most other mammals, was not a sign of friendliness. Humans were weird. If she made it back to the city she would stop smiling. It was ridiculous. Well, maybe just smile a lot less. Definitely. Smiling was overrated. Especially for women.

A sob burst out of Marnie's diaphragm. Had she lost her mind? The bear spoke to her. Her belly fat was a lumpin animate. All she wanted was to pick mushrooms. Was this what the fortune from her fortune cookie meant when it said, "Unexpected events will bring excitement into your life"?

The bear sat down, on their bum. Like a person. Heavy furred legs in front of them. They lowered their forepaws atop their belly. Bear said, "How long will you hold your breath?"

Marnie gasped for air. Light burst around her, like sparklers. She closed her eyes and breathed in and out until her dizziness passed. She opened her eyes. The bear was still there, sitting on the ground, and now traitorous Bellyfat sat between the bear's legs, just like a small child.

"What. Are. You. Doing!" Marnie hissed through gritted teeth. "Get over here, Right Now!"

Bellyfat scooched backward until they were pressed against the bear's autumn-round tummy.

"I feel the awkwardness between us," Bear said.

If Marnie were to describe Bear's voice she'd say it sounded one octave higher than she would have expected. The pronunciation was completely recognizable, but the bear seemed to gulp at the close of each word, as if trying to stop food from falling out of their prehensile lips.

"Bellyfat wishes not to go back to you."

Marnie's eyes widened. "What?"

"Bellyfat knows you ran away. Abandoned." Bear raised their right front paw to scratch their outer thigh. The coarse sound of claws against fur. "Hard to forgive, yes?"

"I came back, didn't I?" Marnie said, indignant. She turned to Bellyfat. "I'm sorry—I didn't mean to leave you!" Heat and pain prickled in her cheeks. She was lying and she was pretty sure everyone knew it. "How do you even know?" she asked the bear. "Bellyfat can't speak!"

Bear blinked slowly. "Bellyfat spoke. A different wording than our utterance now. You don't understand this other language."

"Stop-stop bearsplaining my own body to me!" Marnie snapped.

"Gr! Gr! Gr! Gr!" The bear shook his head.

The saliva dried inside Marnie's mouth. Why was she arguing! For the principle? What principle? And now they were enraged. Were going to swat her out like a fly—

"Gr! Gr! Gr!" the bear smacked their paw on the ground, then clapped the coarse pads against their head.

Marnie's mouth fell open. The bear was laughing...

Bear swiped their paw across their eyes. Shook their head hard, dust flying from their fur. "You are a funny person," Bear said. "Funniness was in the air. I am going now. I need to eat more to prepare for Winter Dream. Bears want more fat. We love our fat and need our fat." Bear, still sitting, raised one paw, great coarse pads facing upward.

Bellyfat, who had been sitting snug against the bear, leapt up to land upon the bear's outstretched paw.

Resentment or jealousy pinched Marnie from inside. She had no idea why she was feeling this way. But it wasn't a good feeling and she didn't like it.

"I'm taking back what's mine," Marnie said.

Did the bear's eyebrows rise? Marnie wasn't sure. Because Bellyfat leapt from the bear's paw to land, plat, against Marnie's face. It stuck there, like a hanpen starfish. Plat! Plat! Plat! Plat! Bellyfat smacked her cheeks, a rapid alternating series of slaps, with both of their stumpy hanpen hands.

"Ugh!" Marnie shouted, her lips pressed against the firm moist of Bellyfat. "Get off me!" She tried to bat them off, but Bellyfat leapt away, to dash back to their new friend.

"Stay here, then! See if I care! Because you won't last long!" Marnie said. Bellyfat's one hand was sullied brownish red. From the mess on her cheek, Marnie realized. Even more delicious for the bear. An icing of human blood.

Marnie remembered to be scared.

Bear slowly shook their head. "You have strange ideas."

"Are you reading my mind?" Marnie whispered.

Bear shook their head again. "Your body says things, always. The changes in your scent. The muscles you clench. The sound of your heart. Your body is yelling because you do not listen. But that is you. Time for Bear to go, now." Bear looked down at Bellyfat. Bellyfat seemed to nod their little nubbin head.

Bear raised their massive paw and seemed to somehow tuck their claws right into their rounded middle. Then they gently pulled outward.

Marnie stared.

Like a seam parting, a kind of slit was exposed. But there was no blood, nor the flayed red of exposed flesh. Inside the thin gap Marnie could see something white…

Bear reached with their other paw, to hold out the flap of skin, several inches wider. It was almost like a pouch—

Bellyfat leapt up, high, then jumped, feet-first, into the slit of the bear's middle. Without a backward glance at Marnie, Bellyfat slid right in, disappeared. Bear pressed down at the crease, then ran their paw sideways, once, twice, like they were sealing Velcro.

Bear rose to their paws, stretched and yawned, then slowly swung their head to the east, nostrils waffling, snuffling up the air. The great beastie began ambling in that direction, with their slightly pigeon-toed, bow-legged stride.

"What!" Marnie yelled.

The bear continued walking away, old branches beneath the moss cracking beneath their weight. The snap, snap rang through the forest. An angry squirrel chittered harshly from a tree.

Belatedly, Marnie reached for her cell phone, jumbling through the pocket of her backpack. By the time she retrieved it and inputted her password the bear was a dark splodge between a stump and a cedar tree. She took a photo anyway.

The bear disappeared.

Marnie looked down at the screen of her cell phone. The bear's butt was too blurry to look like anything. A tear landed atop the screen.

She shook her head. Something gleamed, pale, a faint yellowish hue, in the moss, at the edge of her periphery. Not again…

As her eyes focused, the differentiation between moss, gaps, branches, fallen leaves, resolved. A chanterelle. Three, four, six fungi, more than a dozen, growing from the forest floor, forming a broad and loose circle.

"Oh," Marnie said. She knelt upon the moss. She began carefully picking some of them, the slightly peppery sweet apricot smell filling the air. She closed her eyes to breathe it in. "Thank you, chanterelles." She gathered half of what she could see, and left half for the forest. As she tied the fruit up in the red bandana she kept in her backpack she thought about what the bear had said.

She sank backward, onto her butt, and sat with the small bundle of wild mushrooms between her outstretched legs.

Bellyfat was gone now. Marnie took a deep breath. She turned her face toward the east, in the direction the bear had gone. She cupped a hand around her mouth. "I'm sorry!" she shouted. "I really mean it!" She truly felt sorry. She didn't know why she felt sorry, but she would start by not pretending she didn't. "Thank you!" she shouted.

The bear did not answer. From somewhere further in the forest came the slightly sad sound of the Varied Thrush's liquid vibrato.

She should get going. The sun would set soon, she had about half an hour of daylight left. Darkness bloomed especially fast inside a forest. But she didn't want to hurry back to the city. To her apartment, her job, the daily commute. Joan's disappointment. Her own. Because of how alone she felt…

Her cheek. It hurt.

Shhhhhhhhh.

A sweet fir breeze wafted over her face. *Shhhhhhhhh.*

Marnie closed her eyes. The coolness felt good against her swollen skin.

You're not alone…

That voice. The hairs along Marnie's spine shivered upright. She opened her eyes and they fell upon the bandana. With trembling fingers she picked at the knot and folded the corners flat.

The plump golden chanterelles smelled rich of humus and moss, the afterscent of sweet apricot twining in the air.

We are Forest, the voice swelled from the fruiting bodies. *We are everywhere. And we have always been a part of you. Eat of us. Be of us.*

A smile trembled across Marnie's lips. She chose the fattest fungus. Pale cream-yellow, meaty and dense. She bit into the flesh with tenderness. Love.

Know me.

HARVEST
Rebecca Roanhorse

NEVER FALL IN love with a deer woman. Deer women are wild and without reason. Their lips are soft as evensong, their skin dark as the mysteries of a moonless forest. A deer woman will make you do terrible things for a chance to dip your fingers inside her, to have her taste linger on your tongue. You will weep before it is over, the cries of one who has no relatives. But you will do whatever she asks.

"TANSI, TANSI," MY lover whispers my name. "Is it time to harvest the hearts?"

The horror of her question is always fresh, always a shock. I suppose in the daylight hours when she is not here, I am able to tell myself that it never happened. That her words are other than what I know them to be. As long as I don't look at what we keep in the old cooler on the fire escape, as long as I ignore her bloody breath.

The hand she rests against my cheek is still damp and smells faintly of rot. The air clots my nose with a coppery sweetness that has become familiar. Her eyes meet mine, vast and luminous. They say that if you gaze into someone's eyes, you can see their soul, but my lover has no soul. Her eyes are mirrors, showing me only myself, and I turn away from what I see. I reach for her instead, my hands compelled by something primal. If desire were a thing made physical, it would be the curve of my lover's neck, the slope of her shoulders. It would taste like the salt of her skin. It would sound like the susurrus of her breath. So, of course I say what I always say, every time she asks me to kill for her: "Yes."

"We only need a few more hearts now," she says. "Two? Three? I've lost count. Are you counting?"

"Three." Last week when she asked, it was five. The fifth we harvested on a Monday night in the empty parking lot of a deserted travel stop off I-95, a blonde-haired clerk whose steps were heavy with minimum wage and payday loan debt. Fourth was a grey-eyed mother of two, the backbone of her family. She fought hard, a strong heart, a worthy sacrifice, something to break the best of her people.

"They were monsters," my lover says to me. "And it does no good to have mercy on a monster. They will not have mercy on you." She tucks herself against my ribs and rests her head on my shoulder. The silver moonlight through the open window snags in her hair, the light of distant stars caresses her skin. She tilts her face up for a kiss. I lean in, eager, but she moves away, laughing. She rolls to her feet, drags at my hand. "Let's go!"

I go, stumbling out of bed, barefoot across peeling and cold plastic tiles, ignoring the residue of filth that sticks to my soles. I pull on my jeans, an old stained hoodie. Grab the black leather roll of chef knives from the console by the door. Hesitate at the feel of the leather in my hands, the blades of sharp steel unrevealed. And for a moment, I remember. A life before. Before I met my lover.

"It only has one knife right now," my fiancé Jeffery explains as I open the brightly wrapped box. It's a warm day in early September, the heat of summer still idling over upstate New York. He has obviously taken care in the wrapping of this gift, and my usually deft fingers fumble awkwardly with the green ribbon. When I finally crack open the box, I grin. The chef roll is the one I've always wanted, aged leather, smooth and supple with enough compartments to hold a whole catalogue of knives. Butcher and chop and paring.

"I could only afford one knife right now," he repeats, watching my face for disappointment. "But maybe after school, when you come back home. And we get married..." He pauses, waits for my reaction.

When I offer him nothing but silence, he goes on. "I know one is not enough, but it's a start, right?"

"One knife is a start," I agree. I don't mention the other thing. "Thank you."

We sit a little longer in this impossible place. A bench on a sprawling leafy campus like something out of a movie about bright college years, a wonderland of green sloping hills on the banks of the Hudson. It is more water, and more things that need water to grow, than I have ever seen in my entire life.

"When will you come home?" he asks.

Home. A tiny reservation town that I outgrew the day I won a local cooking contest, then a statewide competition, and then it was a Food Network culinary cook-off show for teen chefs. The red-haired celebrity chef who hosted it took an interest in my talent. Then an interest in other things. Enough that when I demanded more of his time, he found me a scholarship to a culinary school on the other side of the country, far away from his wife and child.

I unfold the leather bag. Draw the solitary butcher knife from its sheath and run my hands across the silver shine of the blade. I press the tip of the knife into the pad of my thumb until blood rises to the surface. I suck the redness from my skin, eyes closed.

"I thought you weren't doing that anymore," Jeffery says, alarm in his voice and eyes on the bloody thumb in my mouth.

"I'm not."

"I mean, it's okay if you are. I just think maybe you should see someone about it? Especially up here. I bet they have great doctors in a place like this." Jefferey babbles on some more about the superior health care available in the Mid-Hudson Valley, but I've already stopped listening. When he finally tapers off I give him a smile.

"I'm not trying to change you," he insists. "I already told you that."

The smile stays firmly in place. "Let me walk you to your car," I say. "It's a long drive back to New Mexico."

NEVER FALL IN love with a deer woman. Deer women are cunning and can see the past and the future all at once. Their eyes are deep and still as well water, their legs as long and slender as the high aspens. A deer woman will make you do terrible things for a chance to stroke the back of her knees, to hear her whisper your name. She will promise you home.

WE DID NOT meet in a chance encounter in a moonlit wood, in the way of fairytales. I did not chase her fleeing shadow through a dappled grove of ancient trees to the banks of an enchanted pool. I was not lured away, as is the way of hunters who have, on a solstice eve, somehow become the prey themselves.

I met my lover in a bar on a weekend trip to Manhattan, an impetuous late train from my upstate culinary school down to the city, a solo escape from a mind-numbing week spent on gastronomy etiquette. Spirit dulled by the proper way to sit at a table, the hand to use for the seafood fork, the ordering of stemware. I am lost in this world, drowning in a sea of their buttery sauces and unfamiliar histories, wishing for something known, something to remind me of home. I overhear a boy in class mention a food truck somewhere on the Lower East Side that serves oven bread and prune pastelitos. It feels like a sign.

New York City is big, noisy, a foreign place. But I am not afraid of it. It beckons, asking me to let go, to become someone else. I wander, looking fruitlessly for that truck, until I hear a deep drum beat, a high wailing through the open door of a corner bar.

She is there, wearing white. A dress that leaves her brown shoulders bare, a skirt that gambols lovingly around her long legs to brush the floor. Another Native woman? In New York City? What are the chances?

She dances the kind of dance that draws stares. The dance that reminds you of the whirl of the starry heavens, of places that exist far away from the concrete canyons. She is graceful and undisciplined all at once, an invitation to question one's life choices.

When she stops, she falls into the high-backed chair next to me at the bar, laughing and flushed. She ignores the others, men and women, who crowd around her offering to buy her a drink. She looks at me.

And I make the mistake of looking back.

We drink St. Germain. Her, neat, in a shot glass, because she says it's like a shot of summer straight to the vein. I take mine with gin and ice and lemon, and agree. We drink, and then we dance, until the night moves on without us until the bartender calls last call. And laughing, dizzy, reckless, we share a nectar-tinged kiss. I should have known then, but in the way of new lust, all I could know was the slip of her hips and the flirt of her long fingers. The flavor of white flowers staining her lips.

Now I understand, in the way of those doomed, that I was being seduced. But like all fools whose desires leave them dashed upon rocks or lost in a faerie's lair, knowledge comes too late for salvation.

I never find that food truck that tasted like home.

THE FIRST TIME she convinces me to kill for her, it is a hot June evening. The sun has already set, but the oppressive humidity refuses to allow the day to cool, so we idle, naked, in my bed, eating ice chips and huddling in front of the fan. The first year of school is done; instead of going back to New Mexico and Jeffery, I'm working an internship at a prestigious midtown restaurant. Long hours of backbreaking work for almost nothing. I sleep days and spend my nights in the fury of the kitchen or, on my rare nights off, in her arms. I am in love. I am naïve.

"Why do you only visit me at night?" I ask her. I trace the delicate lines of her back with a finger, brush her hair away from her face. I keep my voice light, teasing. "Maybe we should try to do something during the day."

She rolls over on her side. "Like what?"

"Go to Central Park. Catch a movie."

She groans and flops on her back.

"It's just a thought."

She waves a hand weakly in the air, clearing away my "just a thought." "Tell me about your people, Tansi."

"What do you mean?" We haven't spoken of our families, either of us. A strange thing for two Natives to do, but it seemed an understood condition of her attention. Until now.

"Your people back home in New Mexico," she repeats. "Your family."

"We don't talk. They wouldn't approve. If they knew about us—"

"My family is gone," she says, her face focused on the ceiling. She pulls a hair from her head, stretches it out above her. "They were murdered. A long time ago. But sometimes, it feels like only yesterday."

"I-I'm sorry," I stutter out, shocked at her confession.

She drops the strand of hair and rolls to face me, her dark eyes intent. "Tell me. What would you do if people murdered your family?"

"What do you mean?"

"What would you do? Justice? Revenge?"

"Justice, I guess." I'm still reeling, trying to find my way through the sudden thorns of this conversation. "Revenge sounds scary," I add airily, a poor attempt to laugh off her black mood.

"Whatever you call it, you would make it right, wouldn't you? If it was in your power, you would make it right?"

A trickle of fear now. Deep down I know that this is not a question lightly asked. That what I say now, it is an oath.

I should run. I should not answer. But I am frozen in the bright headlights.

"Yes."

Her nod is grim, satisfied. "Where are those knives, Tansi?"

"What?"

"The ones you always carry. Your chef knives."

"Here. Well, over there. By the door."

"Tansi," she says my name like an invocation. "I want to you do something for me."

I don't say anything, breath stuck in my throat.

"I want you to help me make it right."

MY HANDS UP to the elbow are covered in blood. My heart is thumping wildly in my chest, but perhaps not as wildly or desperately as it should be for what I have done. Shouldn't I be vomiting? Crying? Shouldn't I feel more than a desire for her blessing?

She smiles and my spirit soars, giddy. She leans forward to catch the drip of blood in her small hands, brings it to her mouth and drinks. Her eyes are bright, dancing flames of wildfire. Her long hair catches the light.

"Did you know the Aztecs could remove a beating heart in less than two minutes? But that took a team. Two men to hold the body still and prone, at just the right angle. Two men to hold the legs."

"I didn't. Know, I mean."

"But you and I, we only need each other." She laughs and twirls, her long white skirt flaring around her, blood soaking the hem. She licks her fingers clean.

"What do we do now?" I ask. At least my voice has the sense to shake, to sound too high with fear. "Will the police come? Will I go to jail?"

"We leave the body here in the forest," she says. "You'd be surprised what deer will eat."

"And this?" I hold up the heart, still warm and pulsing in my hand. Just another piece of meat. Not so different from preparing *coeur de boeuf*. At least, that's what I tell myself.

"We'll collect them, Tansi. For my family. For... justice."

I look at the dead white woman at my feet.

"Are you sure this is justice?"

She puts a finger to my lips, then her lips to mine. "I certainly feel better. Don't you?"

AFTER THAT I don't see my lover for days. I start to forget the screams, the smell, the horror. I go to the movies alone. I wander through Central Park. At night, I am thrown back into the insanity of the kitchen, taught to master fire and sharp steel and the incessant demands of perfectionists. After two weeks without her, I can almost believe it never happened. When the chef invites us all out for after-work drinks, I go. But I am lonely in the company of my co-workers, a foreigner unable to follow their words, their jokes all spoken in a language unfamiliar. I make excuses to leave early.

She is waiting for me when I get home. She steps out of her white dress and parts her legs. Runs trembling hands over her breasts.

"Please don't leave me, Tansi," she whispers, tears wetting her cheeks. "Please don't leave me."

I miss work the next day. And then the next. A terse voicemail from the restaurant manager, and terser message from the chef de cuisine. I delete them both. Finally, a concerned email from school about my internship status. I don't answer.

We don't leave my bed for a week.

"You're ruined, Tansi," she says, laughing. "Now all you have is me."

Her face dips down between my legs and I shudder. She is enough. She is my work. She is my home.

After, she asks. "Is it time to harvest the hearts?"

WE'RE IN A parking lot of a Quikmart. We have stopped to wash the blood from my hands, to clean my knives in the anonymous restrooms. The cooler in the back of the car is heavy and sated.

"Are we done?" I ask.

She nods. Somewhere in the distance, the sound of a police car streaks down the parkway. The summer has become one for the record books. The internet is splashed with the sensational story. Thirteen women missing between the City and upstate New York. All matching a description.

The streetlights flicker, casting shadows across her heart-shaped face. She sighs and runs a hand across my hair, tucks a strand behind my ear. I shudder down to the marrow of my bones. Even now, after all she has made me do for her, I want her.

"Let's go home now," I beg.

"And where is that, Tansi?"

"Wherever. Just... somewhere. We don't have to do this anymore, right?"

She leaves her hand but turns her head away from me, eyes toward the dark night, the myriad trails that vivisect the forest beyond the parking lot. The call of the wind through the thick trees that line the parkway.

"Home," she says, her voice breaking with sorrow. "I want my home back, too."

* * *

OUR LAST NIGHT together, while we're still in my little Brooklyn walkup and whatever comes next is still a sunrise and sunset away, she pulls something from her bag. A notebook, its velvet cover the deep green of secrets.

"I've been keeping a list," she says. "Of my family that were murdered."

She thrusts it towards me. The pages are full of tiny practiced handwriting. Name after name. Wessagusset. Pamunky. Massapequa. Pound Ridge. Susquehannock. Great Swamp. Occoneechee. I flip the page, and then another. Another. Skull Valley. Sand Creek. Wounded Knee.

The roar in my head is grief, wide and vast enough to drown whole new worlds. I know it is not mine, but hers. The book tumbles from my shaking hand. "I'm so sorry…"

"I felt them all when they died," she whispers, a hand to her heart, her eyes lined with tears. "Every one."

Her dark eyes find mine and she whispers the truth.

"Revenge."

I LUG THE full cooler across the National Mall, past the band playing the Star-Spangled, the screaming children with their Rainbow Rocket pops, the picnics and laughter and shouting masses waiting for sunset and the promised fireworks.

"What if this doesn't work?" I ask, nerves making my voice rattle. "What if doesn't bring your home back? What if it doesn't quiet the dead?"

I watch her ponder my question and for a moment, the night holds its breath. On its exhale she laughs, as free and enchanting as a rushing mountain stream.

"But, Tansi, what if it does?"

I PLACE THE last heart on the grass. Turn to where she lies sprawled in the middle of the circle. Some curious tourists are already starting to come closer, to see what ancient conjuration I am working with blood and muscle and grief on this most American of holidays. It is only a matter of time now.

I stretch out beside her. Gather her close to me, breathe in her scent for the last time.

"Are you sad?" she asks.

"No," I whisper, and it's true, but not. "Only that I will miss you," I say, picking words so inadequate they rise to the level of a lie. "Do I have to go?"

She draws a finger across my mouth and I taste the salt of my own tears.

I close my eyes and the children are gone, their melting popsicles only memories discarded on the lawn. The fireworks, reduced to suggestions of smoky trails in a blackening sky. The curious tourists, the monuments, the city. All vanished.

Time, rolled back to silence.

"Are they all gone?" I ask.

"Keep your eyes closed and they are gone."

"And your family?"

"They cannot come back, but their children are still here."

"Then we're home?"

When she doesn't answer, I open my eyes.

I am alone on the lawn. The crowd rushes back in, the noise, the children, the tourists, the smoke, the screams of horror, the sound of sirens.

LOVE A DEER woman. Deer women are wild and without reason. A deer woman will make you do terrible things for a chance to raise up nations, to lie down with a dream. You will weep before it is over, the tears of the blessed, the cries of one who has found lost relatives. And if they ever let you out of your cell, tell them that you will do it again.

KELSEY AND THE BURDENED BREATH
Darcie Little Badger

HAND STRETCHED TOWARD the bedroom ceiling, Kelsey climbed on her wooden footstool. "Here, Pal," she called. A shimmer—a tiny Fata Morgana, light bent through not-quite emptiness—flowed across the ceiling, down her arm, and around her shoulders. Pal's weight lessened hers; an alien gravity drew all last breaths from Earth.

"Good boy," she said. "It's work time."

She hopped down from the stool and used her bare foot to push it against her bed, a twin-sized, twenty-year-old mattress on the wooden floor. If repairs to the farm and the three-story white elephant of a house hadn't bled her of every cent she earned, Kelsey might have bought a proper bed, something with memory foam instead of metal springs. She didn't need a frame. Never had. But with every passing year, it became more difficult to sleep on a creaky, lumpy, tilted beast with steel bones and two hundred generations of dust mites woven through its skin.

Kelsey shut off her bedroom light and stepped into the hallway. As her pupils expanded, she navigated by floorboard creaks. Twenty footsteps to the staircase. Thirteen steps to the ground floor. Her father had constructed the house by hand; there were no coincidences. He built the number thirteen into the foundation thirteen different ways as a monument to his patience with the superstitions of the seventh-generation settlers who once employed him.

It had been a modest farm. Just a vegetable garden, one acre of corn, and thirteen bleating sheep. Enough for two new farmers, both retired from early-life careers, to manage. Now, all that remained was the last breath of the sheepdog Pal.

And, of course, the farmers' daughter.

After breakfast, a bowl of joyless shredded wheat and almond milk, Kelsey left the house; her car was parked across a grassy acre once used for grazing. "Nearly a full moon," she said, as if Pal could appreciate the view. When Pal was alive, he used to bound across the countryside, free, and then sprawl belly-up on the ground, panting. He couldn't do that anymore. He couldn't even see the sky.

Outside, Kelsey always carried Pal in a backpack to protect him from falling into the void. She secured the backpack in the trunk of her car before slipping into the driver's seat. It was a twenty minute drive to work with no traffic, one benefit of a very early morning. Because the hospital never closed, the best time for herding was that sweet spot between late night and early morning: 4:00 a.m. Despite the red-eye hour, a thirty-person crowd waited outside Maria Medical Center, filling the long rectangle of grass between the parking lot and street. Some sat on picnic blankets or collapsible lawn chairs. Others stood. All watched the marble, chimney-like chute jutting from the hospital dome. As Kelsey parked in front of the vigil keepers, she recognized several regulars who enjoyed witnessing last breaths rising, like smoke from a pyre, into the vestiges of starlight.

The new faces might be mourners, waiting to say goodbye. Last breaths rarely lingered near their cooling bodies; if they weren't captured immediately, they drifted away, indistinguishable from other shimmers trapped in the labyrinth of medical departments.

That's why hospitals were Kelsey's biggest clients. Hospitals and slaughterhouses.

She entered the clinic through a discrete side door. The security guy, Philip, smiled at Kelsey in recognition; he didn't even take a cursory glance at her badge. "I saw a couple on the second floor," he said. "One followed me around like a duckling chasing after its mama."

"Huh! Maybe they recognized you."

"How?" He crossed his arms and leaned against the wall. "Can they see? Maybe you don't need the dog. If I was a shimmer, I'd follow a beautiful woman."

"You will be a shimmer," Kelsey said. "Sooner or later."

"Christ." The flirty smirk dropped off his face, and she couldn't be more pleased. Philip's hints were tiresome, and he never gave her the chance—the courtesy, really—to reject him outright. It wasn't that Kelsey enjoyed telling people, "I'm not into you," but she had thirty years of practice under her belt and much preferred one direct, cathartic "no" to the awkwardness that had been happening twice a week at 4:00 a.m. for the past six months. It had been a mistake to confide that she wasn't married during a bout of friendly rapport with Philip. That's when his behavior switched from friendly to interested, and with every interaction Kelsey felt a little lonelier.

"It's the human condition," she said. "With that last exhale, you soar." Of course, that was only partially true. Fish released shimmers, too, and they sucked fluid life through their gills. Without giving Philip another thought, Kelsey unzipped her backpack, and Pal floated upward like a bubble in a lava lamp. Once his shimmery body hit the paneling, he zipped across the hallway ceiling and took the first left, so familiar with the hospital layout he anticipated Kelsey's directions.

Floor by floor, through sterile corridors and above sleeping patients, Pal ushered last breaths like he'd once herded sheep. He encouraged them into a huddle and up the stairs, where they gathered in the sixth-floor departure chamber, a hexagonal room with a white dome ceiling. Kelsey pressed a red button embedded in the wall, and the grate separating the marble chute from the dome slipped aside with a whir, converting the room into an inverted funnel.

"You're free," she said, peering at the nine last breaths that clung to the ceiling perimeter. "Just let go." Kelsey used a yard stick to guide Pal into his backpack. "Good boy," she said. Her bag shivered as he wagged a remembered tail. His work was done. After all, they weren't actually the breaths of sheep. Each one of those shimmers had carried a human through life, whatever that entailed, from the first gasp and scream to this. Kelsey needed the fall upward to be their choice.

One by one, the shimmers slid up the dome and through the chute until just one breath remained. The straggler clung to the concave ceiling so tightly their body was flat and wide like a quaking, gelatinous puddle. The poor thing seemed afraid to fall. In Kelsey's experience, many shimmers were reluctant, and she often wondered where that reluctance came from and why other shimmers—like her parents—left without hesitation. Some might fear the cosmic unknown or have unfinished business, she supposed. Others might be unwilling to let go.

"Hi there," Kelsey said. She checked her phone clock. "Six thirty. A beautiful time to fly. The sun has risen, and it's warm."

The shimmer sluggishly inched down the wall, fighting the pull of the sky.

"You can't stay here." She lowered her voice and continued, "I'm not supposed to ..."

Her phone rang, and for a panicked instant, Kelsey felt a rush of guilt, always her first reaction when the outside burst into private moments. She stared at the bright screen in wide-eyed confusion until the caller—unknown number—went to voicemail. It was barely past dawn. Who called so early? Even scammers had a better sense of timing.

"Sorry," she continued. "I'm not supposed to go until the room is empty." In the United States, it was illegal for shimmers to be contained by anyone but family or specific conservators, and the practice, even done legally, was generally considered tasteless. Sensibilities had changed since the Victorian era; back then, last breaths were often sealed in urns. There must be thousands of imprisoned shimmers still languishing in museums, catacombs, and tombs.

Kelsey sat against the closed door, her legs crossed at the ankles under her long, traditional camp skirt, homemade from yellow fabric with a pink flower print. "How about a story?"

It took forty minutes, but in the middle of an anecdote about her grandmother's tortilla-eating longhorns, the shimmer finally slid up the dome and through the chute. Maybe they missed their own grandmother.

As she left the departure room, Kelsey checked the voicemail. A deep voice rasped:

Good morning, Miss Bride. Jennie Smith—you clear her poultry farm—gave me your number. Sorry for the hour. I need help. Desperately. Can you banish burdened breaths? The one in my neighborhood has killed

A pause.

so many people.

He recited his name, Clint Abbott, and phone number.

Please call back. I'm acting on behalf of the Sunny Honeycomb Salt Pond Homeowner's Association.

Philip must have noticed something haunted in Kelsey's face, because he asked, "Everything all right?"

"It's a prospective client." She lowered the phone from her twice-pierced right ear. Kelsey wore a silver squash blossom through the lobe, but her cartilage piercing was half-closed from disuse.

"Is the city trying to poach you again?"

"Nah." She shook her head. "I don't know what this is."

Kelsey replayed the message as she crossed the parking lot, still shocked by the request. The repetition did not numb her dismay. Sure, her business card read: Kelsey Bride, Shimmer Finder and Guide. But that didn't make her a detective. She'd only searched for the burdened, murderous dead once, and that was a decade ago. They weren't exactly common. The act that made a last breath burdened was so terrible the word "murder" didn't do it justice.

She cradled Pal's backpack. "I'm sorry."

Kelsey returned Clint's call.

THE VICTIMS, ACCORDING to Clint:

Peter. Twenty-eight years old. Murdered six months ago during a recreational dive in the Honeycomb Sea Caves with several other scuba enthusiasts. His last words: "I'm stuck. All tangled up." Body never recovered.

Spencer. Forty-one years old. Murdered four months ago. A seasoned diver exploring the Honeycomb Sea Caves for the ninth time. Footage and audio were recorded by his GoPro camera. On Spencer's guide rope-assisted exit from the caves, he stopped moving forward. Audio includes: "Somebody got me." No abnormalities, including other divers or obstructions, were captured by the GoPro. However, visibility during Spencer's death was low, since he disturbed silt.

Kylie. Nineteen years old. Murdered two months ago. She had been swimming in the brackish pond over the sea caves. Nobody witnessed her drowning. Kylie's body was discovered by two divers inside the cave system.

The caves and pond were closed after Kylie's death.

Patricia. Sixty-one years old. Murdered this week. Crushed in her bed between 3:00 a.m and 9:00 a.m. Patricia was Clint Abbott's neighbor. Their community surrounded the brackish pond, which connected to the Atlantic Ocean through a narrow, marsh-straddled channel. On the night Patricia died, two outdoor cameras recorded evidence of burdened breath activity. Police investigation ongoing.

"Burdened breaths are rare," Kelsey said. She and Clint shared a booth in Sprinkle's Donut Diner, reviewing his notes. She ate a cinnamon bear claw and drank coffee with cream; he ate nothing but was finishing his third cup of oil-black coffee. They made an unusual pair: Clint, six-foot-three, stout and reddened by the Atlantic sun and Kelsey, four-foot-eleven, her round face a rich tan surrounded by a home-cut bob; her hair a mix of white and black strands which from afar resembled metallic silver. "They've never been observed in a controlled setting."

"What does that mean?" Clint asked. "Controlled?"

"A laboratory. All mice float." Kelsey glanced at Pal's bag. "Personally," she said, "I doubt that nonhuman breaths can become burdened. Well. Perhaps chimpanzees. They hunt monkeys for sport. Kinda messed up."

"Is it true that..." His jaw tightened, as if something innate resisted the question.

"Yes." Kelsey took a bite of her bear claw and immediately regretted it. "Dead that eat the dead get pushed against the Earth. In a curious way, it's like losing weight. The pull of that alien gravity weakens, and then it shoves the cannibal shimmers away. Crushes them against the land. That's why all the burdened breaths in historical records co-occur with disasters like coal mine accidents, earthquakes, and train derailments. Mass deaths trapping normal, buoyant last breaths in an enclosed space, providing the cannibal with ample time and opportunity. So my next question, Clint: has there been a recent catastrophe in town?"

"No," he said. "Not until Patricia and... and the rest, anyway. Can you help?"

"Maybe," she said. "You're staying with friends, right?"

"Yes," he said. "In Cape Cod. It's a commute, but it's less expensive than a hotel."

"Distance is good. Don't return home yet. In fact, avoid the pond. The murderer will kill again to maintain its reverse weight and stay tethered on Earth."

Who knew what waited *up there* for cannibals: a reckoning? Nothingness? Paradise? A larger, hungrier mouth?

"Have you handled one before?" he asked.

She nodded. "Once. About ten years ago. I travelled a lot back then. Life was fifty percent gardening and sheep-shearing at the farm, and fifty percent wandering. It was fun. Kind of perfect, actually. I had this '99 gold Monte Carlo, and when the urge struck, I bundled Pal into a fine silk bag and drove all the way to California. We made pit stops in every big city; when populations are high and buildings are like beehives, there's never a lack of work for people like me."

"You said you had a farm?"

"My parents did," she said. "Just a little one. They sold yarn and veggies at the farmer's market."

"A labor of love?"

"Yes," Kelsey said. "Exactly that." Heartache was always inside her, like the bile in her stomach, and now it swelled. All that remained of their love and labor were weeds around an empty house.

"And the encounter?" Clint asked. He seemed eager to change the subject.

"The job was at an abandoned high school in Houston," she said. "The kind for thousands of students. Imagine this massive brick building, seriously damaged by Hurricane Andrea, with broken windows and chained doors. It was fenced up for months before they started renovations. Apparently, the crew had only been working a couple hours when they found a pair of bodies in one of the classrooms. Two adults. The city contracted me to sweep the building and make sure their last breaths had escaped. The police had already checked and didn't find anything. But the glass kept breaking, and the renovation crew kept getting goosebumps. So they figured the police missed one or both breaths; in a building that size, it's understandable. I agreed. Figured it would be a quick and interesting job. Pal has keen ears, for lack of a better word. And the building was scary looking, but I had backup in the form of two police escorts. They gave me a face mask and a hard hat, too.

"Pal is faster than human breaths, but I still worried about his safety, you know? I asked the escorts, 'Are the shimmers dangerous?' I was worried they'd shove Pal out a broken window somehow and I'd lose him to the sky.

"This gruff police guy said, 'One of them is. Google it sometime.' So I did, right there in front of the brick building, with these storm clouds gathering overhead. I don't think the gruff guy expected me to own a phone that could Google stuff. Joke's on him. The first article that popped up characterized the deaths as a murder-suicide, which made me start shivering, like the realization ripped a hole in my jacket and let the chill of the city inside. I work with last breaths, but most... well, they go easy after a long life. Or they're chickens, pigs, and cows. Those poor animals don't go easy, but they aren't murderers.

"I didn't read beyond the title... didn't want to scroll down and see faces..."

Kelsey paused. The waitress, a brunette white woman wearing orange lipstick and black-framed glasses, was idling near their table, a carafe of coffee in one hand. "Can I top you up, Ma'am?" she asked. Kelsey glanced at her cup of coffee; it was only half empty.

"Maybe in ten minutes," she said. "Thanks."

Kelsey resumed her story, eager for the chance to talk. It was nice to reminisce about her life, even the dark parts. "Pal found them in a drama classroom, of all places. The far wall was set up like a mini-Broadway stage, red curtains and everything. I whipped those curtains aside and looked up. There they were. The two breaths. They went in circles. One chased, and the other ran—or maybe they were *both* chasing—embroiled in an unending game of tag." She bit her lip. "No. It ended.

"The two breaths must have started arguing, because a window in the classroom shattered. In swept the winter. I shouted, 'Hey! Hey!

You can escape now!' I should have known, though. I should have known they never wanted to escape. There were plenty of broken windows in that school.

"One of the breaths paused, like I'd startled it. And in that moment of stillness, the game ended. Two became one, and the one sank languidly, resembling this partially deflated helium balloon. Burdened. I remember thinking, 'I have to protect Pal.' So I threw my jacket over the burdened breath and pushed them through the broken window. A gust of wind blew them over the weedy strip of grass between the building and the basketball court. That's when I lost sight of them. They probably drifted over Houston a couple days before flying off. You know, Clint, I often wonder: had the cannibal been the wrathful victim or the violent murderer?"

"Does it matter?" he asked. "That's... terrible either way."

"Yes," Kelsey said. "For my own peace of mind, it does."

"Guess so."

She sighed. "I hate to talk business, but I'm going to need an advance," she said. "Unfortunately, home is three hours away, so I'm overnighting in a motel."

"Local one?" he asked.

"Uh huh. The one with a mermaid on the sign."

He smiled. "Good choice. I know the owner. Be sure to have their breakfast. Everything's local. You can order an omelet with wild mushrooms from the heath."

In addition to the advance, Clint gave Kelsey three files on a thumb drive before he left. The file names were MARTHA GIBBERT FRONT PORCH SECURITY, MARSH BIRD CAM, and PATRICIA LAWN PHOTOS. Kelsey used her tablet to view the pictures and videos. The waitress lingered nearby, sneaking glances at the screen with unconcealed interest.

MARTHA GIBBERT FRONT PORCH SECURITY: In a black and white video that was filmed between 2:34 a.m and 2:39 a.m, the porch door shakes. Moments later, its lower glass panel shatters. Inside the house, Martha's golden retriever barks. No further disturbances occur.

PATRICIA LAWN PHOTOS: Clint photographed Patricia's property after her body was discovered. Most of the thirty pictures show damage to the potted flowers and ornamental bushes outside her bedroom window. The plants are crushed, as if somebody had flattened them under a boulder. A photograph snapped through her open window shows her bedroom floor. A tube of lipstick has been flattened, its red, waxy stick pressed into the carpet like a spray of blood.

MARSH BIRD CAM: The green and black night-vision video, captured between 1:43 a.m and 1:47 a.m, shows a stretch of marsh outside the brackish pond. In the right-hand corner, grasses shake and bend, as if something unseen is rolling from the water to higher ground, crushing the vegetation beneath it.

As the waitress refilled Kelsey's mug, a tear slipped down her pale cheek, made gray by mascara and chalky foundation.

"Are you okay?" Kelsey asked.

"Sorry. Clint has such a loud voice. I heard... it's just... they used to eat here."

"Who?"

"All of them," she said.

"My condolences."

"What happens to a soul when it's eaten?" The question, whispered, seemed afraid to be heard. So Kelsey pretended that she hadn't.

After finishing her coffee, Kelsey drove to the coast and parked on Clint's driveway. He lived in a typical upper-middle-class New England home. It was painted pastel blue; every house along the street was some variety of pastel, no doubt coordinated by a strict homeowners' association. Kelsey wondered if the neighbors knew that Clint had hired her. Maybe it had been a collective decision. One discussed during an emergency homeowner's meeting. As she unloaded supplies from the trunk, a wind that smelled like the sea tousled her hair. She inhaled deeply and slipped into thigh-high wading boots.

"We're going on a walk, boy." Kelsey lifted Pal from the truck where he rode in his backpack, surrounded by pillows. Together, they hiked to the marsh; Kelsey located the two-foot-wide trail over the mud, grasses, and pickleweed. The plants were bent inland, their blades matted by sticky earth. "If you sense it, bark. Detect, boy. Detect." Last breaths sensed their fellows and communicated with them through a language that, although unheard by the living, raised goosebumps and broke glass.

The route became messy fast. Halfway to the pond, one misplaced step sent Kelsey's left foot calf-deep into the mud, which clutched her boot in a vacuum-tight grip; she leaned back with all her weight and twisted. The earth held fast.

"Shoot."

The hair on Kelsey's arms prickled. Was Pal barking? Perhaps her distress had upset him.

Or perhaps...

She slipped out of her trapped boot and hop-sprinted from the marsh. The mud seeped through her cotton sock, gritty and cold. A sharp edge poked her heel; no time to investigate, but she glimpsed feathers and cracked bones woven between grass blades, as if a plover had been crushed when the burdened breath rolled to land.

It must be fast.

She abandoned her second boot and sprinted.

Safe in the car, Pal's bag buckled to the passenger seat, Kelsey pressed her forehead against the steering wheel and waited for her heart to calm, her stomach to settle. She felt silly for visiting the marsh alone, like a real private investigator with the know-how and mettle to escape death. Now, she probably owed the wildlife center thirty bucks for the loaner boots.

At least the trip hadn't been fruitless. Clint said there was just one fresh path between the pond and neighborhood. Kelsey had not found evidence—such as grasses bent toward the water—that the burdened breath had retraced its figurative steps after killing Patricia.

It did not return to the sea caves.

Where was the murderer hiding?

Not in Patricia's house. The police scoured crime scenes for breaths, in case the victim or other dead witnesses remained.

Maybe the murderer had fled the neighborhood, a wanderer, traveling along the coast, drowning divers, feeding and leaving before people recognized its *modus operandi*.

That theory did not accommodate Patricia's suspicious death, however. Instead of moving when the pond closed, the burdened breath had lingered until desperation compelled it to murder a woman in her bed.

So it had a motive more complex than "eat and hide." But what? Why would it remain in quaint, unremarkable Sunny, with a population so small everyone knew everyone, except for the steady stream of tourists who were making a pit stop on the way to Cape Cod?

At a loss for answers and afraid to leave her car, Kelsey decided to drive around town. Pal was trained to search for other last breaths, and although that usually involved herding, he could detect noisy ones from inside his backpack.

She started in Clint's neighborhood. There were very few signs of life and no signs of afterlife. In the distance, a cloud of gulls flew in circles, occasionally swooping, their bodies bright against the graying sky; she thought of buzzards and endless games of chase and the Ouroboros consuming its own tail. She took a right, delving inland.

Most tourists passed through the town of Sunny, Maine in a day. They played a round at Mermaid Mini-Golf, viewed the nautical museum, and ate lobster for 3 p.m. dinner. Kelsey drove down Main Street twice, once going east and once going west, to check the storefronts on each side of the two-lane street. The candy shop advertised fresh fudge and seawater taffy. There were oil paintings of the sea in the art gallery window. She didn't notice any cracked glass, however. "Detect," Kelsey reiterated. "Detect, Pal!"

Nothing as they passed the nautical museum, which promised a wealth of REGIONAL MARITIME HISTORY and AUTHENTIC VICTORIAN TREASURES for just FIVE DOLLARS & FREE FOR CHILDREN, based on the sandwich board outside its door. The shop that sold beach supplies, postcards, and keychains had an orange "Closed" sign over its door. The coffee shop was also closed.

"Hear anything?" Kelsey asked.

Pal didn't make a peep.

"Well, then..." On the curb, a seagull nibbled salt from a french fry bag. It occurred to Kelsey that buzzards weren't the only feathered scavengers on earth. Gulls could eat meat, too.

She made a U-turn and returned to the street that passed the brackish pond. Kelsey continued along the coast, heading toward the swarm of gulls. Most of the birds were huddled near the roadside, although they scattered upward as her car approached. Kelsey parked and rolled down her window. From the awkward vantage point, she couldn't tell whether the dark smear on the pavement was an animal or garbage.

"Detect," she reminded Pal, slinging his bag over her shoulder. "We'll be fast." Outside, she could feel every grain of sand beneath her feet, a reminder that she wore mud-drenched, threadbare socks. It only took a moment for Kelsey to confirm that the shape used to be a racoon. The poor thing could be the casualty of a sports car. She hoped that was the case.

Kelsey called Clint.

"Did you find the bastard?" he asked.

"Not yet." She considered the street. "I did find evidence that it's still in town. Can I ask a favor?"

"What do you need?"

"Spread the word to watch out for fresh roadkill. It's probably too smart to hunker down near a meal, but any pattern we find may help pinpoint its location."

"He's consuming animal breaths?"

"Most likely. This burdened breath is an opportunist."

"I'll spread the word," Clint said. "What are your plans?"

"Widen my search." Her stomach rumbled. "After a late lunch."

After Kelsey ate lobster bisque in a café on Main Street, she took Pal on a walk, ostensibly to get a closer look at the storefront glass but actually to buy a bag of taffy. Along the way, she noticed the museum display window. Much like the sandwich board, it advertised:

REGIONAL MARITIME HISTORY!

OVER ONE HUNDRED DETAILED SHIP MODELS!

NEW! TREASURES FROM THE DAMNED *QUEEN MARY*!

"A *shipwreck*," Kelsey said. "That's a disaster. What do you think, Pal?"

"Were you talking to me?" An elder drifted behind them, her steps long and moonwalk-light. A yellow canvas balloon, easily large enough to cradle six human last breaths, was strapped to her back.

"Sorry, no. Just thinking out loud. I've never heard about the *Queen Mary*."

"Sad exhibit," the woman said. "All the *things* they left behind. Mary drowned six hundred people." A breeze snagged her balloon, and the woman nearly stumbled. "It used to be easier," she said, "when I weighed more, and they... and they were fewer."

"Who?"

"My family. I carry them."

"Me too."

"In that little backpack?"

"It's just my dog."

Her parents hadn't lingered. When the time came, they slipped out the eastward-facing window. Although Kelsey had not been there—in fact, she had been a thousand miles away, sleeping in a motel room with old timey circus posters on the wall—she knew they fell up together, as if holding hands.

Sometimes, the heartache in her chest demanded to know: why didn't they wait to say goodbye?

"Enjoy the exhibit," the woman said, waving as a gust of wind pulled her down the sidewalk.

It occurred to Kelsey that last breaths had little use for *things*. But family? Friends? Enemies? Those were eternally meaningful. Maybe the burdened breath was desperate to remain on Earth because somebody they loved *couldn't* leave.

Kelsey pushed her way into the museum—the door resisted her, dragging against a thick mat—and stepped into a small lobby; there was an unoccupied reception counter to her left and a laminated poster on the wall to her right. Navy blue text across the poster read:

Beyond this point, you will witness the following artifacts from the damned Queen Mary *on display in the Sunny Nautical Museum:*

Ornate pocket watch

Tobacco tins

Child's boots

Reading glasses

Jewelry and jewelry box

Multicolored vials

Paper money, playing cards, cutlery, keys, clothing, sealed urn,
suitcases and purses
A cherub's head
Binoculars, boarding passes, hand mirror, hats, toys, a toilet
Stained glass from the ballroom dome, a thousand pieces
splintered by the screams of six hundred last breaths.

After reading the poster, Kelsey was *certain* that she knew how to find the murderer. She strode into the dim exhibit room beyond the lobby. There, a young man in a tartan vest and a matching checkered bowtie guarded the cherub head, which had its own display case. A tag with the name "Billy" was pinned over his heart, but Kelsey would have guessed that the guy worked in the museum based on his professorial outfit alone.

"Hi there," she said.

"Hello. Did you pay for admission?"

"Nobody was at the front desk."

"Huh." He leaned to the right, making a show of checking the lobby for himself. "Mr. Kay must be on a break. You can buy a ticket on the way out. Unfortunately, I'm a guide, not a money-taker guy."

"Actually, that's great," Kelsey said. "Because I have questions. How long have the *Queen Mary* artifacts been here?"

"Six months," he said.

"Do you know where they came from?"

"The Iowa City Natural History Museum."

"Just a minute." She took her phone from her pant pocket, ignoring Billy's disapproving eye roll, and searched for "Iowa City accident" on her phone. Ten months ago, a child drowned in a drainage pipe. Thirteen and sixteen months ago, two unrelated people drove into the Iowa River, where they perished in their cars. And those were just the unusual deaths reported by a cursory internet research. "What's in the urn, Billy?" She pointed to the display case across the room; a three-foot-high crematorium urn shaped like a blooming lily dominated the collection. "Better yet: who's in the urn?"

"The urn? If I recall, imaging tech found ashes. They couldn't identify the person."

"Did they also screen for last breaths?" She recalled how a hundred years ago, it had been in vogue to carry the deceased with their ashes.

"Imaging tech *always* screens for breaths. It just has ashes."

"In that big thing?"

"Sometimes, a vessel is commissioned before the family knows whether the breath will linger."

"I think you should open it."

"The lid is soldered shut."

"Shimmer screens are unreliable. They just detect noisy last breaths. By the way, how often do you get goosebumps here?"

Billy crossed his arms and glanced at the display case. "I mean, in the evening, I guess I... but goosebumps aren't compelling enough of a reason to damage a relic. It's been five hundred meters under the sea."

"Have you heard about the murders in town?" she asked.

"Obviously," he said. "Are you implying that there's a shimmer in the urn, and it's... somehow... escaping? And killing people? That's impossible."

"No," Kelsey said. "I suspect that about one hundred years ago, a mysterious person—let's call him Frank—boarded the *Queen Mary* with that urn because he took it with him everywhere. He couldn't leave it behind; it carried the last breath of his beloved wife or child. And when the boat sank, Frank drowned—but instead of drifting up, he stayed with the urn. Frank dwelled down there, cannibalizing other stragglers and the breaths of crushed squid and fish. That was his existence, decades spent in the black and heavy water, until divers found the urn and stuck it in this exhibit, which forced Frank into the light. He won't let go of the person he loved.

"He'd rather be a monster."

Kelsey took a plain glass microscope slide from her pocket; during work, slides were her miner's canary. "Take this, Billy," she said. "Humor me." She crossed the room and knelt outside the Plexiglas display case with the cherub head, urn, and silverware. Kelsey shouted, "Who is he? Who follows you? Who carried you onto the *Queen Mary*? Who do you call at night?"

"Nothing happened," Billy said. He delicately held the slide between forefinger and thumb.

"Don't want to be found?" she asked. "It's too late. I found you, and I'll find your burdened breath. Tell him it's over! Say something, or you'll never be together again!"

The slide snapped in half.

LATER, AFTER SCRUBBING mud from under her toenails, Kelsey ate pizza in her motel room and watched Pal herd dust motes around the lumpy-paint ceiling. His shimmering body spun in wide and tight circles, clockwise, counterclockwise, bouncing wall-to-wall, dizzying. He never slowed. Boredom did not seem to survive death.

"Goodnight, Pal," she said.

She didn't need to spend the night in a motel with a mermaid on its sign—police had captured the burdened breath that afternoon, after the dreadful thing turned itself in for the sake of the shimmer in the urn—but when Kelsey thought about returning to the farmhouse, she was filled with a sense of dread. Like that husk of a home was actually *her* urn, and maybe that's the way her parents had felt when they escaped through an open window and fell into the sky.

For a few minutes longer, Kelsey continued watching Pal, her thoughts residing in memories of green fields and vast blue skies. Then, she walked across the room, unlocked the window, raised it high, and removed the protective screen.

Now, he had a choice.

Upon returning to bed, Kelsey tugged the cotton comforter up to her chin and closed her eyes, afraid she'd peek before sunrise. She wondered if Pal would be waiting for her in the morning. If so, she'd tuck him in the backpack, eat an omelet, leave Sunny, and sell the house her father built, sell it to somebody who loved the number thirteen. Somebody who'd cultivate the earth with the same care as her mother. That done, Kelsey would cram all her belongings in the back of her car, buckle Pal into the passenger's seat, and go west.

Or Kelsey might wake up to an empty room. She'd still buy an omelet, leave Sunny, sell the farmhouse, and go west. She'd just do it alone.

"It's all so mysterious, isn't it?" Kelsey asked the night.

AFTERWORD
Nisi Shawl

WE'VE BEEN SHINING a long time.

Decades back, as a recent graduate of the Clarion West Writers Workshop, I met with a committee to pick our next set of instructors. (Every year there are six different instructors for Clarion West's six-week intensive, all writers and editors of note in the speculative genre.) Since this was a special anniversary for the workshop, I proposed that we celebrate by choosing people of color for every slot.

We didn't. There were numerous objections to my idea, but the one that has stayed with me was the heartfelt complaint that by doing this we'd "use them all up." That is, if we filled our teaching roster with nonwhite instructors one year, we'd have none left to call on for following years—unless we kept inviting the same old crew back again and again.

"This is how we breed!" I fumed later to a sympathetic listener. Far from "using up" all available writers and editors of color, I thought that focusing on their existence would encourage others to ignite and burn and light the literary cosmos with hundred-hued flames. I thought we'd help even more potential writers of color reach critical mass and fire up their brain furnaces.

But there *were* fewer people of color writing speculative fiction twenty years ago. It was just conceivable that there would have been a (temporary) dearth of new nonwhite teaching candidates had my plan been accepted.

That was then. This is now—a time when the anthology you hold in your hands could easily have filled multiple volumes, when I never even got to issue a public call for stories because I received plenty merely by asking the writers of color I personally know.

This is not the first such anthology, as I note in the book's dedication, and these are not the first authors of color writing imaginative fiction, as many students of the genre's history are aware. For centuries we have been this brilliant.

Now, though, our numbers have grown. And we shine together.

Would you like more of what you've read here? Wider constellations, greater galaxies of original speculative fiction by people of color? Then seek us out. Spread the word. Wish on us, reach for us, and yes, let us gather together in the deep, dark nurseries of stars. Let us congregate. This is how new suns are born.

CONTRIBUTOR BIOGRAPHIES

Kathleen Alcalá is a Clarion West graduate and instructor, the award-winning author of six books, a recent Whitely Fellow, and a previous Hugo House Writer in Residence. Her latest book, *The Deepest Roots: Finding Food and Community on a Pacific Northwest Island*, explores relationships with geography, history, and ethnicity. Ursula K. Le Guin said of Alcalá's story collection *Mrs. Vargas and the Dead Naturalist*: "Not one tale is like another, yet all together they form a beautiful whole, a world where one would like to stay forever."

Steven Barnes was born in Los Angeles, California and attended Pepperdine University, majoring in Communication Arts. He has published over three million words of science fiction, fantasy, suspense, and mystery, comprising some 33 novels, as well as writing for film, stage, and television. He lives in Los Angeles with his son Jason and his wife, British Fantasy Award-winning author Tananarive Due.

Born in the Caribbean, **Tobias S. Buckell** is a *New York Times* Bestselling author. His novels and over seventy stories have been translated into 18 languages. He has been nominated for the Hugo, Nebula, and John W. Campbell awards for Best New Science Fiction Author. He currently lives in Ohio.

From *Roots*; to *Star Trek: The Next Generation*; to the Emmy-winning PBS series *Reading Rainbow*, **LeVar Burton** has captivated audiences worldwide with his authentic charm and his passion for storytelling, for over 40 years. As well as a beloved and acclaimed actor, he is an accomplished producer, director, and writer. LeVar's most recent triumph is his popular podcast LeVar Burton Reads, now in its second season. Through his company LeVar Burton Kids he is creating content that harnesses a child's unique curiosity, using stories as ways of exploring the world.

Indrapramit Das (aka Indra Das) is a writer from Kolkata, India. He is a Lambda Literary Award-winner for his debut novel, *The Devourers* (Penguin India / Del Rey), and has been a finalist for the Crawford, Tiptree and Shirley Jackson Awards. He is an Octavia E. Butler Scholar and a grateful graduate of Clarion West 2012. He has lived in India, the United States, and Canada, where he completed his MFA at the University of British Columbia.

Jaymee Goh is a writer, poet, critic, reviewer, and editor of science fiction and fantasy. She graduated from the Clarion Science Fiction and Fantasy Writers Workshop in 2016, and holds a PhD from the University of California, Riverside. She has been published in places like *Strange Horizons*, *Lightspeed Magazine*, and *Science Fiction Studies*. She coedited *The Sea is Ours: Tales of Steampunk Southeast Asia* (Rosarium Publishing), and edited *The WisCon Chronicles Vol. 11: Trials By Whiteness* (Aqueduct Press).

Hiromi Goto is an emigrant from Japan who gratefully resides on the Unceded Musqueam, Skwxwú7mesh, and Tsleil Waututh Territories. She's written four books for adults and three books for youth, and has won numerous prizes including the James Tiptree, Jr. Literary Award, the Sunburst Award, and the Carl Brandon Parallax Award. She has a graphic novel pending with First Second Books. Hiromi is currently at work trying to decolonize her relationship to the Land and to her writing.

Andrea Hairston is author of *Will Do Magic for Small Change*, finalist for the Mythopoeic Award, Lambda Award, and Tiptree Award, and a New York Times Editor's pick. Other novels include: *Redwood and Wildfire*, winner of the Tiptree Award, and *Mindscape*. She has also published essays, plays, and short fiction, and received grants from the NEA and the Rockefeller and Ford Foundations. Andrea is the L. Wolff Kahn 1931 Professor of Theatre and Africana Studies at Smith College.

Alex Jennings is a writer/teacher/performer living in New Orleans. He was born in Wiesbaden (Germany) and raised in Gaborone (Botswana), Tunis (Tunisia), Paramaribo (Surinam), and the United States. He constantly devours pop culture and writes mostly jokes on Twitter (@magicknegro). He also helps run and MCs a monthly literary readings series called Dogfish. He is an afternoon person.

Minsoo Kang is the author of the short story collection *Of Tales and Enigmas*, the history book *Sublime Dreams of Living Machines: The Automaton in the European Imagination*, and the translator of the Penguin Classic *The Story of Hong Gildong*. His stories have appeared in *Strange Horizons*, *The Magazine of Fantasy and Science Fiction*, *Fantastic Stories of the Imagination*, *Azalea*, *Lady Churchill's Rosebud Wristlet*, and two anthologies. He is an associate professor of history at the University of Missouri St. Louis.

Dr. Darcie Little Badger is a Lipan Apache geoscientist and writer. Her short fiction has appeared in multiple places, including *Love Beyond Body, Space, and Time*, *Robot Dinosaur Stories*, *Strange Horizons*, *The Dark*, *Lightspeed*, and *Cicada Magazine*. Darcie's debut comic, "Worst Bargain in Town," was published in *Moonshot: The Indigenous Comics Collection, Volume 2*. She lives with one dog named Rosie and all of Rosie's toys.

Karin Lowachee was born in South America, grew up in Canada, and worked in the Arctic. Her first novel, *Warchild*, won the 2001 Warner Aspect First Novel Contest. Both *Warchild* and her third novel, *Cagebird*, were finalists for the Philip K. Dick Award. *Cagebird* won the Prix Aurora Award for Best Long-Form Work in English. Her short stories have appeared in anthologies edited by Nalo Hopkinson, John

Joseph Adams, and Ann VanderMeer. She can be found on twitter at @karinlow.

Anil Menon's short fiction has appeared in a variety of magazines including *Albedo One*, *Interzone*, *LCRW*, and *Strange Horizons*. His stories have been translated into Chinese, Czech, French, German, Hebrew, and Romanian. His debut YA novel, *The Beast with Nine Billion Feet,* was shortlisted for the 2010 Vodafone-Crossword Award. Along with Vandana Singh he coedited *Breaking the Bow*, an anthology of speculative fiction inspired by the Ramayana. His most recent work, *Half of What I Say*, was shortlisted for the 2016 Hindu Literary Award.

Silvia Moreno-Garcia is the critically acclaimed author of *Signal to Noise*—winner of a Copper Cylinder Award, finalist for the British Fantasy, Locus, Sunburst, and Aurora awards—and *Certain Dark Things*, selected as one of NPR's best books of 2016. In 2016 she won a World Fantasy Award for her work as an editor.

Chinelo Onwualu is a Nigerian writer and editor living in Toronto, Canada. She is editor and cofounder of *Omenana*, a magazine of African speculative fiction, and a graduate of the 2014 Clarion West Writers Workshop, which she attended as the recipient of the Octavia E. Butler Scholarship. Her writing has appeared in *Uncanny*, *Strange Horizons*, and *The Kalahari Review*.

Rebecca Roanhorse is a Nebula and Hugo Award-winning speculative fiction writer and the recipient of the 2018 Campbell Award for Best New Writer. Her work has also been a finalist for the Sturgeon, Locus and World Fantasy awards. Her novel *Trail of Lightning* was selected as an Amazon, B&N, and NPR Best Book of 2018. She lives in Northern New Mexico with her husband, daughter, and pug. Find out more at https://rebeccaroanhorse.com/, and follow her on Twitter at @RoanhorseBex.

Nisi Shawl edited *Bloodchildren: Stories by the Octavia E. Butler*

Scholars; *WisCon Chronicles 5: Writing and Racial Identity*; and the special People of Color Take Over issue of *Fantastic Stories of the Imagination*. She co-edited the anthologies *Stories for Chip: A Tribute to Samuel R. Delany*; and *Strange Matings: Science Fiction, Feminism, African American Voices, and Octavia E. Butler*. She wrote the 2016 Nebula finalist and Tiptree Honor novel *Everfair*, and the 2008 Tiptree Award-winning collection *Filter House*. In 2005 she co-wrote *Writing the Other: A Practical Approach*, a standard text on inclusive representation in the imaginative genres. Shawl is a founder of the Carl Brandon Society and a Clarion West board member.

Alberto Yáñez lives in Portland, Oregon. His work has appeared in *Strange Horizons, Beneath Ceaseless Skies, Toasted Cake*, and *PodCastle*. He is a graduate of Clarion West, and was awarded a 2018 Oregon Literary Fellowship. Alberto went to Portland to become a registered nurse, and has since learned more about people, bodily fluids, and himself than anticipated. He draws on his Mexican and Jewish roots to inform "Burn the Ships." A native Californian, he misses easy sunshine, San Francisco, Chinese delivery, and other Mexicans.

E. Lily Yu received the John W. Campbell Award for Best New Writer in 2012 and the Artist Trust LaSalle Storyteller Award in 2017. Her stories have appeared in *McSweeney's, Boston Review, F&SF, Clarkesworld,* and *Terraform*, among others, as well as multiple best-of-the-year anthologies, and have been finalists for the Hugo, Nebula, Sturgeon, Locus, and World Fantasy awards.

FIND US ONLINE!

www.rebellionpublishing.com

/rebellionpub /rebellionpublishing /rebellionpub

SIGN UP TO OUR NEWSLETTER!

rebellionpublishing.com/sign-up

YOUR REVIEWS MATTER!

Enjoy this book? Got something to say?

Leave a review on Amazon, GoodReads or with your
favourite bookseller and let the world know!

THE
DJINN
FALLS
IN
LOVE

& other stories

Edited by
Mahvesh Murad & Jared Shurin

Including stories by Nnedi Okorafor • Neil Gaiman • Jamal Mahjoub • Kuzhali Manickavel
Sami Shah • Claire North • Kamila Shamsie • K.J. Parker • Sophia Al-Maria & many more

"Exquisite and audacious, and highly recommended" - *The New York Times*

THE DJINN FALLS IN LOVE AND OTHER STORIES

A fascinating collection of new and classic tales of the fearsome Djinn, from bestselling, award-winning and breakthrough international writers.

Imagine a world filled with fierce, fiery beings, hiding in our shadows, in our dreams, under our skins. Eavesdropping and exploring; savaging our bodies, saving our souls. They are monsters, saviours, victims, childhood friends. Some have called them genies: these are the Djinn.

And they are everywhere. On street corners, behind the wheel of a taxi, in the chorus, between the pages of books. Every language has a word for them. Every culture knows their traditions. Every religion, every history has them hiding in their dark places.

There is no part of the world that does not know them. They are the Djinn. They are among us.

With stories from **Neil Gaiman**, **Nnedi Okorafor**, **Amal El-Mohtar**, **Catherine Faris King**, **Claire North**, **E.J. Swift**, **Hermes** (trans. Robin Moger), **Jamal Mahjoub**, **James Smythe**, **J.Y. Yang**, **Kamila Shamsie**, **Kirsty Logan**, **K.J. Parker**, **Kuzhali Manickavel**, **Maria Dahvana Headley**, **Monica Byrne**, **Saad Hossain**, **Sami Shah**, **Sophia Al-Maria**, **Usman Malik** and **Helene Wecker**, and edited by **Mahvesh Murad** & **Jared Shurin**.

"Exquisite and audacious, and highly recommended"
The New York Times

 WWW.SOLARISBOOKS.COM

Edited by
DAVID THOMAS MOORE

NOT SO STORIES

With a foreword by **NIKESH SHUKLA**

Including stories by
**RAYMOND GATES · JEANNETTE NG · PAUL KRUEGER
CASSANDRA KHAW · TAURIQ MOOSA
ACHALA UPENDRAN** and many others
and illustrated by **WOODROW PHOENIX**

NOT SO STORIES

Rudyard Kipling's *Just So Stories* was one of the first true children's books in the English language, a timeless classic that continues to delight readers to this day. Beautiful, evocative and playful, the stories of How the Whale Got His Throat or How the First Letter Was Written paint a world of magic and wonder.

It's also deeply rooted in British colonialism. Kipling saw the Empire as a benign, civilising force, in a way that's troubling to modern readers. *Not So Stories* attempts to redress the balance, bringing together new and established writers of colour from around the world to take the Just So Stories back, to interrogate, challenge and celebrate their legacy.

Including stories by **Adiwijaya Iskandar, Joseph E. Cole, Raymond Gates, Stewart Hotston, Zina Hutton, Georgina Kamsika, Cassandra Khaw, Paul Krueger, Tauriq Moosa, Jeannette Ng, Ali Nouraei, Wayne Santos, Zedeck Siew** and **Achala Upendran,** with illustrations by **Woodrow Phoenix** and a foreword by **Nikesh Shukla.**

> "Moore, one of the most exciting editors in the field today, has nurtured a line-up of interesting and evocative talent for an extremely entertaining ride."
> *Starburst Magazine*

END of the ROAD

EDITED BY
Jonathan Oliver

An Anthology of
Original Short Stories

PHILIP REEVE
LAVIE TIDHAR
S.L. GREY
PAUL MELOY
ADAM NEVILL
IAN WHATES
JAY CASELBERG
HELEN MARSHALL
SOPHIA MCDOUGALL
ROCHITA LOENEN-RUIZ
BENJANUN SRIDUANGKAEW
VANDANA SINGH
ANIL MENON
RIO YOUERS
ZEN CHO

END OF THE ROAD

Each step leads you closer to your destination, but who, or what, can you expect to meet along the way?

Here are stories of misfits, spectral hitch-hikers, nightmare travel tales and the rogues, freaks and monsters to be found on the road. The critically acclaimed editor of *Magic*, *The End of The Line* and *House of Fear* has brought together the contemporary masters and mistresses of the weird from around the globe in an anthology of travel tales like no other. Strap on your seatbelt, or shoulder your backpack, and wait for that next ride... into darkness.

An incredible anthology of original short stories from an exciting list of writers including the best-selling **Philip Reeve**, the World Fantasy Award-winning **Lavie Tidhar** and the incredible talents of **S.L. Grey, Ian Whates, Jay Caselberg, Benjanun Sriduangkaew, Zen Cho, Sophia McDougall, Rochita Loenen-Ruiz, Anil Menon, Rio Youers, Vandana Singh, Paul Meloy, Adam Nevill** and **Helen Marshall**.

"Though this anthology is almost over, the road, and the road story, goes ever on. Would that we could go with it."
Tor.com

 WWW.SOLARISBOOKS.COM